WHITE SUN

The Author

John Newton was born in London and educated in Germany before serving in East Africa with the armed services and the Kenya Police.

After leaving the Kenya Police he stayed on as a businessman and travelled widely throughout Africa, Arabia and India. He speaks German and Swahili.

He broadcast extensively on Kenya and Uganda Radio, writing and producing his own programmes, and wrote of his travels in an English newspaper.

He lives in Bedfordshire with his wife and writes full time.

WHITE SUNRISE

John Newton

John

I hope you enjoy my work,

John Newton
Army Museum
27/1/05

Next Century Books
Leighton Buzzard

First published in the United Kingdom by Next Century Books

The Newton Group
Leighton Buzzard
LU7 3JN

A CIP catalogue Record for this title is available from the British Library

ISBN 0 9544011 0 7

To my wonderful wife Pam with all her patience and understanding

Apart from known historical figures all characters are my invention. Not one of them exists outside my imagination. So all responsibility for their frailties and foibles, their weaknesses and triumphs is mine. I accept it gladly for in the writing they became my friends.

Acknowledgements

I worked hard on this book. But so did others to whom I owe a debt of gratitude. John Hill, who helped me start; my sister-in-law Lesley Parfitt who spent so much time in historical research; Errol Trzebinski with her wonderful book THE KENYA PIONEERS (published by William Heinemann) which was the source of so much information and inspiration; my clever friends in the Bedford Writers Circle for their valuable comment; Brigitte Gant, with her detailed proofing of text and language and my wonderful wife, Pam, always there with support and encouragement and love. Thanks to you all.

Cover design: PMN

Cover Graphics: FutureFX, Leighton Buzzard

Prologue

Under Kilimanjaro

When I lay dying on that terrible dry plain under Kilimanjaro, I saw many images – my mother and father, my school friends and a glittering squadron of cavalry in bright uniforms cantering past, waving and calling compliments.

I waved back and cried out but they made no attempt to help me – a poor girl in distress.

In quiet times I saw a dark ridge and shadowed valley that I knew as a cool haven without fever or fear. If I could reach that dark ridge and slide into the shadowed valley, I would rest in peace free from pain and thirst. But I was confused and could find no path.

Then I saw Death come from the shadowed valley and called to him, 'Here I am. Take me.'

But he shook his head and said, 'Not yet, Madame.' And he left me on that awful plain…

Chapter One

Adam

British East Africa: February 1902

From below the horizon, sunlight tinted the Kilimanjaro snow-tips pink. Ten minutes would pass before sunrays could reach and warm the plain, still chill with cold night air.

Adam Early strode into camp through the pearl-grey dawn, hunting rifle slung over his shoulder. What a waste the last hour of searching for game had been: *Nothing. Absolutely nothing. Not a bloody thing to see or shoot...*

He handed his rifle to the gun bearer, threw his hat onto the camp table and slumped into a canvas chair, looking around at his little camp beginning to stir into the new day. He saw cook on hands and knees blowing at the overnight embers; a couple of servants tidying his small weather stained tent; bitter cooking fire wood-smoke drifting from the porters' lines a few hundred yards away.

A vision of the chief railway engineer in Mombasa rose in Adam's mind, frowning and strict – demanding a detailed plan with maps and recommendations.

Adam sighed in frustration: *What the hell can I write about?*

So far his daily journal gave little reason to extend the railway into this god-forsaken area alongside the huge German East African colony. He had nothing to report and nothing to show for twenty-one dry, dreary, beastly, boring wasted days in the bush: *What will the bloody man in Mombasa think if I write that...?*

During three weeks roaming the empty Tsavo bush-land he'd seen only a few Masai with cattle; some elephant; an occasional giraffe. Dry hot season winds blew from mid-morning to dusk each day, rasping the plain, driving most living things to shade and shelter: *Only I'm stupid enough to move in this heat....*

Exasperated – knowing he must write something – he called a servant to bring his book, maps and a pen. While eating breakfast and drinking a blessed cup of hot tea he checked his charts of the past few days. His instructions – to survey as close as possible to the German border without crossing – gave him great worry: *It's almost impossible to know where the border lies in this open bush. Anyway – if I do cross who the hell will know?*

Adam uncurled his most detailed map of the German East Africa colony and traced a forefinger across the creased paper: *Christ what a huge area. All the way from Kilimanjaro right down to the Rovuma River in the south and from the Indian Ocean to Lake Tanganyika in the west. What the hell will they do with it all?*

He chuckled and said out loud, 'And what are we British going to do with our damned Protectorate? Miles and miles of bloody Africa and a brand new railway just finished that runs from Mombasa to the Lake with no one to use it.'

He groaned at the stupidity of politicians and empire builders and settled to start a new entry in his journal, writing the date as 2nd February 1902. He scribbled an opening line and stopped, smiling. Without thinking he had written: *Today is my twenty third birthday and I am alone in the bush.*

He sat back, sipped at his tea and looked round: *I'm not truly alone. I'm with more than a hundred porters. What I really mean is – I'm probably the only European for a hundred miles in any direction....*

He pulled at the soft blond beard he always grew on safari: *As it's my birthday should I shave? Should I waste the water...? No. Why bother? It's not a special day. It's just another day on the plain....*

Still smiling he took up his pen to write but stopped as Musa, padding barefoot through the dust, came from the porters' lines, his shiny-black Sudanese face showing concern.

Speaking Swahili, Musa said, '*Bwana* Adam. We must close our camp and move forward.'

'Why? It's Sunday.'

'I have news. Yesterday I sent Sakayo out to see our best track. He found something that frightens him. A strange camp in the bush with no people. You must hear his story.'

Adam looked at Sakayo – a tall slim Nandi, an excellent tracker with good feel for terrain and game. Eyes rolling, thin face agitated Sakayo said, 'About an hour from here toward the mountain I found tracks of people. Many people. No cattle tracks so no Masai. I followed and found a *boma* with four European tents but could see no fires, no people, no cooking.'

'Did you enter the camp?'

'No, *Bwana*. With the sun gone and dark coming I was frightened there may be ghosts. I saw no people but heard strange noises. I saw European tents but no cooking. Why not? I know Europeans always eat at dusk. I said to myself – why no porters and cooks? They must all be dead and I am listening to their ghosts.'

'Why did you not tell me last night?'

Musa said, 'He told me, *Bwana*. But he returned in the dark after sunset and you had eaten. Sakayo's talk of ghosts would have worried our porters. I told him to sleep and say nothing while I thought.'

'Very well' said Adam. 'Close the camp. We'll move as soon as we're ready.'

Thank God. At last, something interesting may be happening....

From the column head Adam looked back to see a string of men unfold across the bush, shuffling forward at Musa's signal. Red dust billowed along the line, shafted by rays of newly risen sunlight. The plain, covered in thorn scrub and flat topped trees, took on colour and life as the sun climbed quickly. Insects, enlivened by sudden warmth, rose in a humming cloud round the column.

He stood aside to check the column – all in line and shepherded at intervals by his fifteen armed Wakamba *askaris* – small neat men, dressed in military style uniform with red fez and rifle. Adam knew them as trustworthy, honest and perfectly attuned to the boring task of watching, listening and guarding.

Following Sakayo's directions he led the safari southeast at steady pace, flowing over the rise and fall of land. By nine o'clock heat haze began to shimmer and Kilimanjaro started her daily retreat behind wisps of mist, soon to develop into great white clouds.

At the rim of a small ridge Sakayo halted and crouched in long grass. Adam crawled alongside to sit and study a shallow saucer-shaped valley. At centre on flat open ground stood the camp – four tents set in line behind a well constructed thorn-branch *boma* obviously home to a large safari but no people; no sign of life. Adam stood and said, 'Musa follow me with Sakayo and two Wakamba.'

Pushing through the thorn fence Adam saw an area showing signs of the movement of many people in scuffed dust and discarded sacks and boxes: 'The porters' lines,' he whispered to Musa. 'Where the hell have they all gone? We'll check the tents. You start one end, I'll start the other.'

Adam entered the left hand tent and looked round. On a small table, pen and paper, unmarked by writing, lay in lined-up military smartness that jarred with a rumpled safari cot and torn mosquito net dangling from a string.

Disturbed by the desolate silence Adam's nerves jolted when Musa shouted, '*Bwana* Adam. Come quick. There are three people. They are *Wa-Germani* and one is a woman. They are dying. Come quick.'

Adam hurried with Musa from tent to tent. One man and the

woman lay still, stinking with dried sweat and God knows what, not moving even when Adam touched and checked to find a pulse. The other groaned, gurgled and wailed as Adam approached. 'This one's Sakayo's ghost,' said Musa.

'Bloody hell.' said Adam, 'They're in a terrible state.'

All three seemed in the last extremity of thirst with swollen tongues, skin dry as compressed dust, cracked lips laced with stale blood, faces disfigured by insect bites, cheeks puffed with poison. Wherever Adam looked he saw agony – eyes slitted and almost disappeared behind ballooned red lids; ankles, wrists, necks and ears peppered with shiny bites running into hair line and over scalp.

The poor devils seemed already settled into death – so far gone Adam could not even guess their age or status. Only by hair and long khaki skirt did he recognise one as a woman.

Appalled, Adam said, 'Musa – stay here and see what you can do. Sakayo – run back to the safari. Send four water carriers and follow with the porters as soon as you can get them moving. Send the Wakamba out into the bush to find anything that will tell us what happened here.'

After twenty minutes the carriers arrived, moving fast and graceful through the bush, *dhebis* of water balanced on shoulders and heads.

Musa said, '*Bwana* Adam. You must let me look after these Wa-Germani for two days. I know this thirst sickness from the deserts in Sudan.'

In the woman's tent he poured water into a bowl. Adam raised her head.

'No, *Bwana* Adam,' said Musa. 'If she drinks she dies. This is what we do.' Leaning forward he pulled open the woman's clothes from neck to waist, baring her torso, dipped his fingers into the bowl and flicked water across her desiccated skin.

Adam watched in astonishment. The pearly droplets faded into her body leaving small round stains like raindrops in dust. Musa continued flicking water until the droplets sat on the woman's skin for half a minute before disappearing.

Musa covered the woman and Adam followed him to the other two tents, holding the bowl while Musa flicked water on the men until he said, 'We have done enough. Soon they will go to God or begin to recover.'

'What now?'

'We shall give them each a small drink and start with your European medicine for the illness and African medicine for the insect bites.'

4

In the woman's tent Adam eased his hands under her wasted body and lifted her to half sitting. Musa sprinkled water on to her flaking lips. She gasped and opened her mouth. Musa trickled water into her throat. She sucked, gurgled, coughed and spat, bringing up water and phlegm. Her body shuddered and she threw her head from side to side. Adam hung on, barely able to stop her from falling to the floor.

Musa waited before dribbling more water into her mouth. This time she gulped and swallowed, opening her mouth for more, straining her head towards the cup. Musa pulled back, whispering 'No, no, no, Memsahib. Later. In half an hour.'

He did the same for the two men, dribbling then refusing more, ignoring their silent pleas. The men fought harder than the woman but Adam managed to control their convulsions.

Adam's personal servants pitched sleeping and kitchen tents nearby. For the rest of Sunday Adam sat at his table making notes and watching Musa pass between the tents, tending his patients, looking the perfect nursing orderly in his white camp robe. Every hour Adam helped Musa to administer a few sips of water and managed to trickle a spoonful of quinine down each throat, smiling at the nicknames Musa gave each German – Moja, Mbili and Memsahib.

In the evening Musa returned from the porters' lines with a bucket of grey muddy mush that he smeared over all skin affected by insect bites, including the scalp. Within minutes, it dried to a hard white crust.

'Bloody hell, Musa, what is it?'

'Medicine, *Bwana* Adam, African medicine.'

'What do we do now?'

'We wait, *Bwana*. We just wait.'

On Monday morning Adam woke at dawn, his head whirling from a restless night – *Did I dream all that? Or did it happen?*

Shaky with sleep he leapt up and ran through the grey light to check and – by God – there they were. All three. Still and silent; still covered in that bloody white mud, still with Musa watching and waiting. So it *did* happen.

'Christ, Musa. Have you been here all night?'

'Leave me, *Bwana* Adam,' said Musa. 'Go to your work and leave me,' – so Adam dressed, inspected the porters' lines, then marched out with sextant and compass to survey the nearby foothills rising towards Mount Kilimanjaro.

Later he took Sakayo and a party of porters from hunting tribes to find meat. That first day he shot only a few guinea fowl.

Next morning Adam wounded a large kudu. The hunters raced to cut its throat whilst still alive and dragged it, thrashing and dying, to face Mecca, shiny bright blood spurting yards in the brisk early sun.

'Meat for our Muslim brothers,' they shouted, leaping and dancing round the dying animal. 'God is good. God is great.'

In a flurry of hands and string the hunters trussed the kudu by crossed ankles to a pole and trotted it back to camp, head swinging and flopping in the dust.

On arrival the blood soaked hunters acted out their kill with great theatre to a thrilled audience of porters in a vibrant tableau of movement, colour and excitement. Swirling dust, swirling crowd, shouts and shrieks of high laughter, flashing teeth, rolling eyes.

The hunters leapt and crouched, happily overacting their way through the story in a scene of harsh energy. Sunrays filtered through raised red dust. Fluttering robes and sparkling teeth in bright black faces added further thrill.

Adam, unable to remain aloof, became part of the play. In his mind the hunt came alive – the shot and chase, the gurgle of pumping blood. His imagination smelt again the mingling of dust and blood – and tasted the coming feast. Entangled in the swirling, shuffling crowd; acrid red dust covering his face and blocking his nose Adam – caught up in the mood – danced with them.

When the play and dancing finished the porters swarmed round, shaking Adam's hand, shouting compliments and thanks for allowing them the meat. The strong smell of blood, sweat and wood-smoke affected and overwhelmed Adam. He remained thrilled and excited for hours after.

On Tuesday afternoon Adam sat in the shade checking his survey – he calculated the camp as four miles from the German border – when Musa called, '*Bwana* Adam, come and see.'

Adam hurried to the woman's tent to find Musa washing white residue from her body. 'Good God.' said Adam. 'It worked.'

He saw that most insect bites across her chest and shoulders had subsided from poisonous red lumps to angry skin weals, already healing. Her eyes and cheeks had regained shape and Adam leaned close, stirred by her newly cleaned fragrance and emerging feature; ill and drawn but definitely the face of a young woman: *Bloody hell. She's not bad looking....*

6

'How are the others?' he asked.

'The same, *Bwana* Adam. And they are all starting to sweat. This means they will survive and tell us what happened.'

At sunrise on Wednesday morning Adam saw three Masai approach with a herd of scrawny humped cattle. Leaning on spears, legs crossed at ankle, the Masai stood staring at the *boma*. Adam needed news of the area so approached them with Sakayo and two Wakamba.

The Masai waited in confident arrogance, unafraid and unsurprised at the presence of a European with armed guards. Tall, slim and angular; hair sculpted into shape with a mixture of red dust and cattle dung, they wore dusty red blankets knotted at one shoulder.

They nodded at Adam's greeting and looked down long Nilotic noses at the Wakamba, lips curled in contempt. The Kamba gripped their heavy rifles and glared back. Adam saw generations of tribal hatred spark between them.

Speaking Masai the Kamba corporal asked for news of the area.

'No game. All hiding. Waiting for rain. Some lion nearby – lazy or tired for they are not hunting.'

The Masai asked for maize meal *posho* and in an afterthought mentioned finding human remains nearby – 'Bones and clothes. European.'

'European? Are you sure?' asked Adam.

'We are sure. We know from the teeth and clothes and the feet have boots.'

'Can you show me?'

'Pay us three blankets and we will take you.'

Led by the Masai, Adam and a tracking party found human bones scattered over a small valley several miles from the camp. Picked and licked clean by hyena, jackal and vulture the bones gleamed white and shiny in the sun.

'They have been here only a few days,' said Sakayo. 'It must be the fourth M'Germani.'

Horrified at the carnage Adam saw where scavengers fought and ripped over the body and clothes. Ribs and arm bones lay about in the dirt. A leather belt gnawed by sharp teeth lay abandoned. Discarded fingers, chewed and twisted, littered the trampled dust.

Sakayo located the skull behind a rock, picked white and eyeless – hanks of fair hair still held fast to sections of scalp. Adam found splintered shoulders and hips strewn in the grass and a putrefied left foot still in its leather boot. It stank – a foul reek, harsh and horrible. *God, what an end for the poor bastard....*

Forcing himself to make a list of everything gathered, Adam packed the bones and skull into a jute sack. He buried the foot and boot – a sad task but moving the boot released a stench of rotting meat. He shuddered at the alternative – too disgusting to strip and clean the foot of flesh. Inhuman. Impossible..

To honour the burial spot Adam fashioned a rough cross from thorn branches, lay the jute sack alongside and gathered his trackers to pray. Christian Kamba stood with heads bowed, eyes closed. Muslim porters stood quiet and attentive. The Masai leaned on their spears, baffled and amused at the short ceremony.

At midday Adam led the death party back into camp, two porters carrying the bones on a small canvas hammock.

Musa appeared, hurried forward, saying, '*Bwana* Adam you must come. *Bwana* Mbili has woken and is making trouble.'

Adam and Musa entered the tent to a volley of noise. *Bwana* Mbili lay in his cot, arms waving, bellowing in German, his face red with effort.

He glared at Adam, eyes popping with anger and surprise. '*Was ist passiert?*' he shouted.

'I am Adam Early. Do you speak English?'

'*Englisch*? *Englisch*? You are an *Engländer*?'

Bwana Mbili glared – obviously taking in Adam's khaki drill jacket, army style puttees and heavy boots – 'You are a soldier?' he shouted. 'What are you doing in German territory? Am I your prisoner of war?'

'No,' said Adam. 'We found you dying in your tents. We cared for you.'

The German shook his head, shouted, 'Dying? Dying. I am not dying. If you are *English* what make you in German territory and why am I your prisoner?'

Adam said, 'Please calm down. Please listen. You are not my prisoner. You are my patient. You are ill. This is British territory. You crossed the border.'

'*Britisch* territory?' The German slumped back onto his pillow. '*Britisch* territory? *Mein Gott.*'

He closed his eyes, waved a hand and turned in his cot, muttering, 'I shall think.' Within seconds he fell asleep.

Musa said, 'He has been like this for some hours. He wakes and shouts then sleeps. He is foolish with illness but he speaks good Swahili.'

'How are the others?' asked Adam.

8

'*Bwana* Moja is improving. Come help me give him water and you'll see. He is young and will be strong again quickly. The Memsahib still sleeps. She may take longer.'

Bwana Moja – a tall slim young man; fair of hair, long of face, sipped in small controlled gulps – not the greedy slurping of a man near death from thirst. Adam spoke to him in English and Swahili with no response.

Switching to Arabic, Adam asked Musa, 'Do you think he may be deaf?'

'I don't think so *Bwana* Adam. I think he will not speak until he is sure who we are and where he is.'

In the cool, soft light of sundown, Adam sat smoking his pipe and scratching at a mosquito bite on an elbow when, from her cot the Memsahib spoke.

Startled, Adam looked directly into her tent. Despite her ravaged face, clear grey eyes looked straight at him.

Her voice creaked and failed. She swallowed and tried again. In a harsh whisper she managed, '*Was ist passiert?*'

Adam ran to her bedside.

'Thank God you're awake. Do you speak English?'

'*Ja*. Yes. Some. Who are you?'

He leaned forward to hear properly and catch her unfamiliar accent.

'My name is Adam Early. We found you in distress.'

'Adam?' she said. 'Your name is Adam?'

Her faced screwed and creased into what he took for a smile.

'Adam...*Ach, mein Gott* how I wish I had an apple.' she croaked. 'Here I am in the wilderness and you are Adam. I should give you an apple. My name is Eva.'

Chapter Two

Eva

The Englishman brought a cup and dribbled water onto Eva's lips. She spluttered and sucked, trying to gulp the liquid in. Desiccated; starved and confused she lay looking round, licking at the wonderful moisture.

'Am I still in Africa? What place is this?'

'You're in a tent.'

She squinted and blinked; forcing her eyes to focus on the Englishman – *a young man, thank God.*

She managed to make out fair hair, straggly blond beard, khaki safari tunic…and trousers with puttees and heavy boots.

Another soldier. Another bloody soldier….

She closed her eyes in exhausted frustration, trying to ignore discomfort and pain from what felt like a million insect bites. Her whole body – so desperately dry – ached and itched. Her head, throat and limbs cringed in agony until she drifted back to blessed oblivion for God knows how long but after uncounted hours she opened her eyes to crisp sunlight and cool air – *So I'm still alive and it must be morning….*

A tall broad-faced African, dressed in white servant's robe, came and smiled down at her. She managed a few hoarse words in German. He replied in Swahili then in slow English which she managed to understand. With gentle deference he offered water, holding her head as she sipped, wiping her chin when she dribbled, frustrated at her inability to control her slack lower lip.

He tidied and tucked in her bed sheet and left with a smile. She again slipped away – into and out of sleep – sometimes dozing, with the click and buzz of Africa sounding all round, others descending into a healing state of deep unconscious. The African came and went. She sensed his presence through the heat of day.

When next she came fully awake, a fire flickered in velvet dark outside her tent. Remembrance rushed over her. She moved and groaned. The Englishman appeared at her side.

'How do you feel?' he asked. 'How are you?'

Concentrating hard to remember English she said, 'I feel bad. How are the others?'

'Like you, getting better. You may soon be able to travel. Are you able to tell me what happened here?'

'Can I sit?'

He slipped his arms round her and pulled her against his chest to lift. Did she imagine life flowing from his body to hers as he eased her upright? – guiding her legs off the bed; supporting her to a sitting position. She lay her head on his shoulder in relief and pleasure at his touch and her feeling of returning strength. The African came and stood, watching.

She said, 'All our porters ran away. Our safari leader Weiss argued and swore at his porters most of the time. He is a rough rude man and after a terrible argument with the headman over missing food all our servants and porters deserted us.,

'How long ago did this happen?'

Eva paused to gather strength then said, 'I don't know when... Since then I've lost time...they ...disappeared one night...with all our things...all our food and all our water.'

With further effort she managed a shrug and whispered, 'We woke one morning and they'd gone. How long since you came here?'

'Four days. We found you Sunday. Today is Thursday. Musa has been caring for you since then.'

She asked the African 'Did you throw water at me?'

He nodded.

She said, 'I thought I dreamt...such a wonderful feeling. It was like having life thrown at me.'

She hung her throbbing head at the effort of remembering. 'And you took me to the latrine. You washed me and dressed me in this robe?'

The African nodded gravely.

'You also?' she asked the Englishman.

'Yes. We had to. Do you mind?'

She struggled with the translation and the notion of these two men handling her so intimately.

'Do you mind?' asked the Englishman again.

She frowned, sorting out phrases in her head, then said, 'Sir. I am eternally grateful to you both. You have saved me. For the moment this is my hospital and you are my nurses. Did you do the same for the others?'

'For the other two. Yes.'

'Why two? Why two? There should be three.'

'Oh, Madam,' said the Englishman. 'I have bad news. But first we'll move your bed outside for some fresh air.'

Propped on pillows and sipping water she sat looking out across the fire at the camp and dark bush beyond, sniffing the sharp night air of Africa while the Englishman told her of the past four days.

'...so two survived and one died,' he said. 'The two have not yet told me their names, but you called one Weiss.'

'He's the older man,' she said. 'Our safari leader. He's a coarse fool. The younger is my cousin Paul. The third is my fiancé Manfred....the third *was* my fiancé, Manfred. He went off to find help.'

The Englishman patted her shoulder and said, 'I am sorry for your loss, Madam.'

She shrugged, not bothering to hide her indifference.

'I see you find it hard to take in.' he said. 'The shock of such news added to everything else is probably too much.'

'Probably,' said Eva, closing her eyes: *And thank God that idiot Manfred is gone for good. I'm rid of him....*

At sunrise next day the African wrapped Eva in her blanket and carried her to sit in the early morning air with Paul and Weiss. Propped in a camp chair she felt able to sip at a breakfast cup of light soup and tea. Paul sat with eyes closed, not moving, even when the African tried to feed him. She ignored Weiss and his stupid hissing complaints. The damned man had caused too much trouble for her to be polite. And who cares if this Englishman is a soldier? Who cares if he's in our territory? We're lucky he turned up or we'd all be dead, you idiot.

Weiss shut up when the Englishman strode in from the porters' lines, dumped himself into a chair and stretched his legs, saying, 'Good to have company for breakfast. I found it damned lonely out here on my own. How do you feel?'

'Better,' said Eva and glared at Weiss until he grunted, 'Better also.' Paul stayed silent, eyes closed.

The Englishman said, 'My men are building hammocks to carry you. I've checked our position and we're not far from Moshi so I plan to take you there. We'll start tomorrow at sunrise. By Monday you'll be safely back with your own people.'

Eva slept till noon, drank soup then slept again until sunset when she jerked awake in fright at the touch of fingers trailing across her brow. The Englishman's bright blue eyes stared at her from only centimetres. He snatched his hand away and sat up, saying, 'God, you made me jump.'

Eva squeaked, 'What are you doing? Why so close?'

'Sorry. I'm checking what state you're in.'

'I feel better. I already told you.'

'Yes, but your cousin's come down with fever and may not be able to travel tomorrow. Musa's watching over him and I'm looking at you and the other fellow.'

'Paul is ill?'

'You're all *ill*. But he's worse.'

'Weiss,' she said. '*Herr* Weiss. How is he?'

The Englishman made a face.

'Recovering well but he's damned difficult. Not at all friendly. Takes his soup and turns away without a word. Won't speak to us.'

Embarrassed at her reaction – *after all this Englishman is only doing his best to help us* – Eva said, 'I need fresh air. Please help me up. Can we sit outside together, just you and me?'

'Good idea,' said the Englishman. 'We'll have dinner by the fire. Hang on a moment.' He scrabbled about and found a hat and veil – *How does he know where they are?* – saying, 'You need air but not mosquitoes.' He wrapped her in blankets and carried her to a chair by the campfire. Eva allowed her head to drop on his chest, enjoying the ripple of his strong young muscles: *Mein Gott. I must be getting better....*

He fed her soup from a bowl and laughed when she whispered, 'I am like a baby again.'

Her strength and voice renewed by the hot soup she felt well enough to ask a question; perhaps even hold a conversation. In slow English, concentrating on pronunciation and accent she said, 'What do you do in our German territory?'

The Englishman smiled and said, 'No. *You* are in British territory.'

'But *Herr* Weiss says you are in our German colony and out of British East Africa. Are you sure you are in British land and not German?'

'Absolutely sure.' said the Englishman. 'I'm a surveyor. I know exactly where I am. We're four miles inside British East Africa. Your safari crossed the border. Not that it matters. Why should it matter?'

'You are a *surveyor*.' said Eva. 'Weiss thinks you are a soldier looking into our land to see what we are doing.'

The Englishman said, 'Why should I do that? I'm surveying for the Uganda Railway to see where we may site trading posts and perhaps run a branch line towards Kilimanjaro and Taveta. I am a surveyor and bridge engineer, not a soldier.'

Eva laughed – shocked at the painful gurgle that came out.

She put a hand over her mouth and whispered. '*Oh mein Gott.* How funny. We thought you a *soldier* because you wear khaki and heavy boots and some of your men wear uniform and carry rifles.'

He chuckled. 'Simple misunderstanding. They're Railway police guarding my safari.'

'Do not laugh,' she said, touching his arm. 'Weiss thinks you are a spy.'

'Me a spy? Bloody ridiculous.'

'Oh please. Be serious.' She clicked her tongue, annoyed at her inability to make him understand and said, 'My English is not good but I must try to tell you.'

'Please do.'

He folded his arms and settled back, head cocked to one side.

'Do you take what I say as serious?'

He nodded. She did not believe him but ploughed on – 'Weiss used to be a soldier. My cousin Paul *is* a soldier and so is – *was* – my fiancé Manfred. Our Kaiser has turned Germany into a military camp. These stupid Prussians support him in every way, wherever they are. And they always watch out for spies.'

'Even here in Africa? Surely not.'

'These *dumme* soldiers see danger and spies *everywhere*. Please believe me and do not speak of being a surveyor. You will be in danger.'

'In danger. Come now. I'm an Englishman in English territory. How can I be in danger?'

'*Please* listen to me.' Feeling too weak even to grit her teeth or argue, tears of absolute frustration sprang from her eyes. 'You *must* listen. You will in a few days be in *Moschi.*'

'What on earth are you talking about?'

Surprised at herself – *Mein Gott, I'm crying.* – she hissed, 'Please. For me. Tell them something different. Tell them you are on a hunting safari. Do not say you work for your railway, and *never* say you are a surveyor or engineer.'

'You're asking me to lie?'

She nodded, sobbing.

Perhaps because she wept, the Englishman leaned forward and patted her arm, saying, 'Very well. But without tusks or trophies that'll *really* look like a lie. So I'll be a civil servant making an animal count and census of people for the District records. Will that help? Can you stop crying now?'

Eva nodded again, embarrassed at this un-Prussian snivelling. But

14

it worked. He'd agreed, thank God. With a blanket corner she wiped her eyes and said, 'Yes, it will help.'

'Very well. I think it is rather silly, but if that's what you want; that's what I'll say.'

'Yes.' she said, 'That's what I want.'

'It seems an odd game to play.' said the Englishman, 'But if it makes you happy… Here – let me carry you back to bed.'

With pleasure…. She nestled against his chest again, savouring the feel and smell of a healthy young man again.

In the crisp pre-dawn Eva woke feeling stronger. The African came and carried her to a chair by the fire where Weiss already sat, wrapped in blankets. She whispered her news and Weiss hissed, 'A civil servant? Is that *all*? We were rescued by a damned civil *servant*.'

Just before sunrise the Englishman joined them for breakfast and said, 'I've checked your friend. He's still ill but able to travel so we'll be on the march within an hour.'

Sipping soup and tea, Eva closed her eyes and listened to the dawn chorus mingling with the clang and clatter of general packing as the safari prepared to move.

The sounds vied in her ears with a sudden upsurge of humming, buzzing and clicking. With sunlight flooding the plain, several million birds, flies, insects and small creatures began to wake; move; test the day – shouting their noisy way into the new morning, making ready to hunt, chase and eat each other.

Squinting at the sudden brightness and stirred by an abrupt feeling of excitement and change – *Oh how wonderful it all is. My life will never again be the same* – she heard a lion cough nearby and saw every man in the camp pause. Heads swivelled; ears cocked.

The Englishman said, 'Hah! That's the first lion since we left Voi. I'll send Sakayo to see where it is and what it's doing.'

Half an hour later the tracker returned to say, '*Bwana* Adam. The lion are hunting. The game has returned.'

As the safari broke camp and headed south east, Eva saw that the plain seemed full – scattered flocks of various deer, zebra and wildebeest browsed at yellow grass; in the distance a herd of tall giraffe nuzzled treetops for breakfast. She laughed in delight at this miracle of Africa. The game – invisible yesterday – today reappeared from nowhere. Magic. Absolute magic.

The Englishman and his tracker led the safari across rolling grassland towards rising bald hills spilling off the lower slopes of Kilimanjaro.

Rocking along in her rear facing chair hammock carried by four porters, Eva looked back down the column. Rising wind and sun fluttered and flashed through colourful robes. Beams of early sunlight sparkled off pots, pans and water *dhebis*. Bright morning colours of Africa at sunrise reflected through clouds of dust raised by shuffling feet.

She saw a small group of Masai – *probably those who found Manfred* – leaning on their spears under thorn trees, watching the safari uncurl across the plain. *What do they think, standing there so still? What did they think when they saw Manfred chewed to pieces and scattered all over the ground? What on earth do they think of us now? They're from the Stone Age and we're from the future....*

She waved but the Masai made no movement nor recognition that this is part of the new century passing across their land. She tried again and Weiss, from his hammock nearby snarled, 'Leave them. They have no interest in you.'

Eva twisted in her chair and glared but Weiss turned away to watch the Englishman. In the other hammock Paul lolled along, eyes half closed, still seeming weak and ill but Eva knew him better: *My clever cousin...your military brain is ticking – calculating, checking. How does the Englishman organise his column? How many guns to defend how many men? You'll have it all in a report as soon as you're able, you typical damned Prussian....*

She laughed out loud and in her head sang a silent ditty, *'Here we all are. Four jolly Germans. On our way back. Three in lovely hammock chairs. The fourth in a sack....'*

As the column settled into stride between brilliant white mountain to the west and brilliant gold sun to the east, her mood changed and she almost wept at a barely remembered dream of death. But she had won. She avoided that dreadful valley and really *really* won.

Her spirits lifted and a feeling of life renewed swept through her body at the magnificence of this African morning. Until moments before sunrise the plain lay grey and silent. Then in seconds a glory of sound and colour sprang alive into the new day.

How can such a beautiful country kill so many people? Now it looks as though God has blessed this place. Most of the time it seems as though the Devil reigns. He nearly got me.

'He certainly got you' she said out loud, talking directly to the sack following behind on its stretcher. 'Goodbye, Manfred. I am glad to see you go, though I wish you could have gone otherwise. We'll bury you in *Moschi* and never see you again, thank heaven.'

Chapter Three

Moshi

Heading for the cool highlands around Kilimanjaro Adam pushed his safari across dusty yellow grassland under blazing sun and on the third day marched his men into a range of low green hills.

The mountain loomed and bright fresh water came easily from many streams skipping down scarred slopes, straight from the blinding white snow-cap.

Sakayo roamed ahead seeking the best route through a pattern of tree lined rivers and sharp ridges into an area of small villages among the foothills.

Stopping near a scattering of huts surrounded by gardens of Indian corn, vegetables and groves of leafy banana trees Adam told Musa, 'We'll camp here. Go and barter for food with half a dozen blankets.'

Musa returned with several goats, big bunches of bananas and the first vegetables Adam had seen in weeks.

'How much?' he asked.

'Four blankets, *Bwana* Adam.'

'Good. Are the Wa-Germani strong enough to sit up and eat with me?'

'I think so.'

'In that case, carry them out and arrange dinner by the fire at seven.'

At dusk Adam checked the porters' lines then joined the Germans at a table by the campfire. They sat huddled in blankets, obviously waiting for him to speak. He studied their ravaged faces – *Christ, they look awful* – and forced a cheerful smile.

'Allow me to introduce myself properly,' he said leaning forward to shake hands and swap names. Thank God they responded, tongues twisting over strange vowels in this first attempt at proper conversation.

Barefoot servants brought dinner of delicious roast goat, vegetables, and a strangely appetising banana soup.

Adam laughed at the Germans' interest in his background. 'I was born in Bombay. When my father transferred from India to help build the Uganda Railway we moved to Mombasa and that's where I grew up.'

Weiss nodded and said, 'I now understand how you learned to talk such good Swahili and to navigate in the bush. These are necessary things. And I see you have special navigation equipment. You must tell me more.'

Eva's eye caught Adam's in warning so he said, 'But you also have experience in the bush. Are you a hunter?'

Weiss shook his head. 'I am a planter in Chagga district. I am in Africa many years, for my Kaiser. Now we have pacified these people we are trying to teach them new crops – coffee and sisal and things they have never experienced.'

Paul said. 'I am a soldier and came to Africa to experience a different world. What I see and what happened is very different from my expectations. I am a soldier since very young and used to difficulties – but these colonies and these people are a surprise to me.'

Eva laughed and said, 'Anything that doesn't give or take orders surprises you thick headed Prussians. All you do at home is shoot boar and play at being soldiers.'

Paul shook his head and mumbled, 'Take no notice of my cousin, *Herr* Early. She is always a mutiny.'

Adam smiled. 'Chatting like this makes me realise how much I miss European company. I think we'll dine together again – if you are all strong enough.'

'Yes please,' said Eva.

'*Ja*,' said Weiss.

Paul nodded and said, 'A good idea.'

On the seventh day of marching Adam led his safari down from the forest into an area of mature coffee plantations – neat lines of bushes sitting across sunlit slopes.

'How wonderful to see order again,' said Eva to Adam walking alongside her chair hammock. 'See what we Germans have made here?'

Further down the mountain they passed from fertile land to semi desert covered by ranks of sisal, marching across rock and scrub.

Adam said, 'My God. You even manage to grow a crop in the desert.'

Reaching the outskirts of Moshi, Adam halted the column alongside a small stream and said, 'Musa. Set up camp here. I'll go into the town with our Germans and a few men.'

'I'll show you the way,' said Weiss and from his hammock, guided Adam along neat streets and well-built brick houses to a town square – 'The District Commissioner's office,' he said. 'Wait here. They'll see us and come out.'

A group of men in khaki drill ran from the building shouting in German. Weiss struggled from his hammock and saluted. The men gathered round and listened as Weiss gabbled an explanation.

Eva called Adam and said, 'Please help me out of this chair.'

Adam took her hand and as she struggled to her feet she whispered, 'Trust none of these men, they are all soldiers and will suspect you.'

'Of what?'

Before she could reply a small man with hard, cunning eyes, detached from the group and shook Adam's hand. Speaking perfect English he said, 'I am the District Commissioner and must thank you for saving our people. Please wait here with the remains of our poor dead friend while we take the living to hospital.'

Weiss and Paul waved as they went. Eva said, 'Will I see you again?'

'I doubt it. I'll be leaving first thing tomorrow.'

Clambering back into her chair, Eva whispered, 'Remember – be careful. These men will be watching you.'

The group of Germans turned and stared at Adam. He stared back with equal force until they turned and hurried back into the Commissioner's office.

A few minutes later Adam and the Commissioner escorted Manfred's bones to a small church nearby and stood in silent tribute for two minutes.

Shortly after Adam's return to camp, a German officer approached and, speaking English, said, 'I am Major Kreuz. Our District Commissioner requests the pleasure of your company for dinner. I shall call for you at sundown.'

In the early evening Adam sat with Kreuz and a heavy bearded man on the Commissioner's veranda, drinking imported German beer and enjoying the cool air.

The District Commissioner said, 'You must forgive my ignorance but I am new to Africa. And find much that puzzles me.'

'In what way?'

'For instance, I wonder why an English gentleman walks through such an inhospitable part of Africa – and alongside our border – without apparent reason.'

Adam laughed. 'You make me sound sinister. I'm an innocent civil servant making a census of animals and people. Quite legal and well inside our territory.'

Kreuz said, 'You impressed *Herrn* Weiss with the discipline of your caravan.'

All three men stared at Adam. He shrugged and said, 'We pay our porters well. No work means no money. Very simple and very effective.'

The Commissioner laughed and said, 'As you say – simple and effective. Let us now relax and enjoy ourselves. I hear you plan to leave tomorrow. Please stay one day longer and attend the funeral of poor von Heinseck tomorrow afternoon. After all – you brought him this far and should stay to say a proper farewell. In addition our Governor, the *Graf* von Goetzen is making a special safari to meet you at noon and thank you.'

The evening passed in dinner and small talk – although the bearded man took no part until the Commissioner said, 'We Germans are new to colonies and have much to learn from you English.'

Kreuz smiled and agreed. 'Look at how many colonies your English kings and queens have collected over the past few centuries. Other than this beautiful East African colony all we've managed to grab for our Kaiser in the last few years is two fever hell holes and a long stretch of useless sand in West and South-West Africa.'

The Commissioner said, 'God knows how we are expected to make a profit for Germany. At least your railway to Uganda is built and complete all the way to the Lake while we still struggle with our poor little line barely half finished. How does your British government plan to make money from British East Africa?'

Adam said, 'I suppose we'll need to bring in settlers. I reckon we have only two or three hundred Europeans in our whole territory although a few new people have arrived – some missionaries, a few hunters and half a dozen army officers with orders to raise and train a local battalion of African troops.'

All three Germans leaned forward, even heavy-beard showing interest. 'African troops?' said the Commissioner. 'How many? How will they be armed?'

Alarmed at this turn in the conversation, Adam said, 'God, I don't know. Just a couple of infantry companies to form a small defence force.'

'To defend against whom?'

'Against trouble with the tribes – and to help the police. Nothing complicated.'

Kreuz said, 'This is very interesting. Our Governor asked us to say he is happy to have chance of contact with a British official.'

'For God's sake – I'm not an official. Just a simple civil servant.'

Kreuz studied Adam with a knowing smile. The Commissioner

chuckled and heavy-beard grunted. Puzzled by this polite scepticism Adam shrugged and drank no more wine for the rest of the evening – *Better keep a clear head around these damned people....*

Escorting Adam back to his camp through the darkened town, Kreuz said, 'You should understand we Germans think it important to talk to the English and avoid competition between our colonies. We must remain calm in Africa, whatever happens in Europe.'

'Of course,' said Adam.

'Good,' said Kreuz. 'We are clear between us.'

'Yes,' said Adam wondering what the hell the man was talking about.

'I shall come for you about eleven thirty tomorrow morning. Our Governor will see you at twelve.'

To meet the Governor Adam shaved off his safari beard and dressed in crisp starched khaki. Kreuz arrived wearing a perfect white uniform, leading four well turned out *askaris* and snapped a brisk salute saying, 'Please tell me your military rank so I may introduce you properly.'

Adam laughed. 'I told you last night I have no rank. I'm only a civil servant.'

Kreuz frowned and said, 'Very well. If you insist. I shall introduce you simply as *Herr* Early. Please march with me.'

'Good God. Is this a guard of honour?'

'Of course. Please come. We'll be late.'

Amused at the fuss, Adam fell into step alongside Kreuz and glanced back at the four *askaris* thumping along behind, heels hitting the dust in precise time.

To Adam's relief, the *Graf* – a slim elegant man in whites and gold braid – had a charming manner and made easy small talk about weather and crops and the difficulty of bringing modern farming and civilisation to Africa.

Adam relaxed – *Not as bad as I thought* – when over coffee on the veranda, polite conversation turned into political message when the Governor's face became serious and his voice dropped an octave. In studied diplomatic tones he said, 'Our two countries are for many years in disagreement here in Africa. But that time is past, thank God. On instructions from Berlin I tell you we desire continued peace and co-operation in this area of Africa. Please pass this genuine message to your High Commissioner and ask him to respond in kind.'

Adam said, 'But I'm–.'

Kreuz raised a hand and said, 'Having brought white civilisation to these poor Native people we Europeans must not spoil it by disagreeing in front of them in either political or military matters. And we must certainly not go to war here, regardless of any situation that may arise in Europe.'

Stiff with embarrassment Adam looked at Kreuz, hoping for a gleam of encouragement – *What the hell does he expect me to say?*

Kreuz smiled and raised an eyebrow.

Frowning to imply deep thought Adam struggled to cobble together some phrase or response that sounded sensible.

After what seemed an age the Governor nodded and said, 'Of course I realise you cannot reply here and now. You must obviously wait and refer to your government. But I ask for some despatches and advice from your High Commissioner in due course. Can you please arrange it?'

Relieved at this lead, Adam matched the Governor's serious tone and said, 'I shall pass on your comments.'

The Governor stood and shook hands. 'Now we must part. Unfortunately I must leave Moshi and am unable to attend poor von Heinseck's funeral. So I must say goodbye. Major Kreuz will escort you back to your camp now and to the church later. Again I thank you for saving our people.'

At the camp Adam sat and chatted with Kreuz while Musa brought tea.

Kreuz removed his heavy sun helmet; ran fingers through thick brown hair and said, 'I am interested in the rifle your men carry. May I take a few shots?'

Adam set up a target and Kreuz banged off four magazines in quick succession, working the bolt with expert ease.

'This is the rifle you use against the Boers? No wonder they cannot win. In the hands of a good platoon it could be as effective as a machine gun.'

Before leaving he fixed Adam with intelligent brown eyes and said, 'Please don't think we are stupid. We realise you are not a high government official but you are the only Englishman available to us right now. Our Governor signalled Berlin when he heard of your arrival and received a telegram from Berlin authorising the message he gave you. We are anxious for a response.'

Adam said, 'I'll pass the message to my High Commissioner in a few weeks when I reach Mombasa.'

'Thank you. I'll return here at four so we may attend the funeral together.'

At a simple service the pastor droned rolling German phrases while Manfred's coffin lowered into red dusty earth. 'It's packed with stone to make up for what's missing,' whispered Kreuz.

Adam shivered in the late afternoon breeze blowing from the Kilimanjaro snow-cap, remembering Manfred's chewed bones scattered round the valley. About twenty people attended the service, including Weiss, Paul and Eva, sitting in invalid chairs and wrapped in blankets.

After the funeral Adam shook hands with Weiss and Paul before their nurses wheeled them away. Eva stayed for a moment and asked, 'When do you return to your own country?'

'I leave at dawn tomorrow.'

She said, 'Come to my hospital at sundown, I must speak with you.'

Adam entered a small hospital room as bare as a monastery cell. Eva smiled from a bundle of blankets and pillows. Behind the fading scars and stains of insect bites Adam could see the emergence of a handsome young woman. 'You're beginning to look better,' he said.

She laughed – 'Rouge and powder. But even with my hair clean and brushed I still look awful. When next we meet you won't recognise me. I'll be finished with these damned mosquito marks and look right once more. You'll wonder who I am.'

'We may never meet again.' said Adam. 'You'll return to Germany while I stay here in Africa.'

She said, 'It is important that I keep contact with the man who saved my life. Can we write? You can tell me stories of Africa and I can tell you news of Europe. It will also help my English. Where do you live?'

'On Mombasa Island. Soon I'm moving to the new big engineering campsite at an area called Nairobi near the Kikuyu highlands. If I have your address in Germany I'll write when I'm settled.'

She pulled a piece of paper from beneath the blanket and said, 'My address in Berlin.'

In passing the note their fingers brushed. Her eyes widened a fraction and she said, 'I'm sorry I have no proper way to thank you for saving me.'

A shiver passed down his spine but before he could speak she grabbed his hand and said, 'I told you to be careful of the men you met here but today you showed Kreuz your guns and he will now write a report to Berlin.'

'A report? Why?'

'Because he is…not a spy…but a man who looks after security and secrets.'

'An intelligence officer.'

'Yes. That's what he is. And he must report on you because all these men think you are a spy.'

'Why on earth should they think that?'

'Because they are stupid. What is there to spy on in this empty country? But Weiss told them you were in our territory with special navigating equipment. So they are suspicious that you were spying on our border.'

'Oh for God's sake, what nonsense.'

'Yes, but they are difficult men. So military. So far from home. Surrounded by all these Natives, and trying to do what they think their Kaiser wants.'

'I'm leaving at dawn tomorrow so I'll have no more to do with them.'

'Good. And good luck. I shall write from Berlin the minute I arrive home. Please let me kiss you goodbye.'

Her grey eyes shone into his as he leaned forward and allowed her soft lips to brush his cheek.

At dawn Adam led his safari out of Moshi to the east, happy to be leaving the town and these damned puzzling Germans. By noon on the third day he crossed into British territory and worried by the weather, pushed on across the plain, heading for the railway halt at Voi, where Adam planned to take a passing train to Mombasa.

With dry season ending, each day showed heavier cloud build up and the day he marched into Voi, a gigantic storm crashed from the sky. Raindrops fell so hard they bounced a foot back into the air, pulverising into fine mist.

A wood burning locomotive hauling eight small wagons and guard van wheezed into Voi Station at just gone midnight. Adam's men crowded round to see him off, pushing, chattering, giggling and calling to each other and to Adam, ignoring the rain beating down and soaking them all.

In a few chaotic minutes Adam gave Musa last instructions – 'Bring the safari to Mombasa as fast as possible so we can pay them off.' – said farewell to Sakayo, saluted the Wakamba, shook hands with most of his porters and clambered into the rear cabin with an Indian guard.

The cheerful crowd swirled, surged, shouted and waved as the train hissed out into driving dark rain. Wrapped in a railway blanket on the hard top bunk, Adam slept all the way to Mombasa, arriving at sunrise.

Alerted by a telegraph message from Voi, Adam's father waited on Kilindini station with rickshaws and bearers.

'You look awful,' he said. 'And what on earth have you been up to? The German government have invited you to Tanga. They're sending a ship.'

Chapter Four

Visit To Tanga

A few days after returning to Mombasa, Adam received summons to meet Sir Charles Eliot at his office near the old port.

Nervous at what to expect, Adam walked into the High Commissioner's office; wondering why on earth the Germans wanted him to visit Tanga.

A tall plump young man with smooth blond skin, smooth swept-back blond hair and smooth practised manner hurried forward saying, 'Good to meet you. I'm Hocklyffe-Evans, Political Secretary in this fair castle. I've been through your written report. My, what an adventure you had. Dear old Commissioner's waiting with bated breath to hear more. So am I. Do come on through and enthral us.'

He ushered Adam into a large oak-panelled room with large windows looking out over the sights and smells of the old harbour.

Eliot – a neat stocky man with intense eyes – rose from behind his desk, shook hands and said, 'Please sit down. I've read your report in detail but need more. Tell me everything – absolutely everything – in your own words from start to finish.'

'There's not much more to say Sir, but…'

Adam spoke for half an hour; filling gaps in his report; feeling more confident as he went on; sensing Eliot's enormous intellect grasping and holding every tiny detail.

When Adam finished Eliot sat in silence, head bowed. Hocklyffe-Evans turned to stare through the window at a dhow moored in the old harbour. Puzzled, Adam said, 'I think that's all, Sir. The main point is that *Graf* von Goetzen wants a reply as soon as possible.'

Eliot nodded and said, 'The reply is ready. You are to take it to him.'

'Me? Why me? I'm not qualified. I'm an engineer not a diplomat. I won't know what to do or say.'

'Nonsense. You obviously did and said the right things in Moshi. The Germans have asked for you and have arranged a three day official visit. I agree with them that we must avoid economic and military competition in Africa. I'm sending you to explain our position. Hocklyffe-Evans will travel with you so go now and sort it out. We can then telegraph Tanga and tell them to send their ship.'

Hocklyffe-Evans stood and ushered Adam from the room, chatting all the while, 'I'm new out from England. Arrived while you were off on your great adventure. Wonderful stuff. Fascinating story. Don't worry about the trip to Tanga. I'll be there to steer you through the diplomatic nonsense.'

Three weeks later Adam stood on deck, enjoying the breeze, as the German liner SS 'Safari' rode the afternoon tide out to sea.

'What a bloody awful ship,' said Hocklyffe-Evans. 'Have you ever seen anything so dirty and slipshod. If their navy is the same standard it'll be easier to beat the buggers when we eventually fight them.'

'Do you think we will?'

'Of course. The Huns have been squaring up to the rest of Europe for years.'

Over a greasy dinner Adam listened to Hocklyffe-Evans explain his posting to Mombasa. 'With my name a lot is expected. I mean would *you* want to be called The Honourable Ewan Hocklyffe-Evans? What a bloody mouthful. Worse still – my father's Lord Taunton. He's one of those clever devils good at everything. So are all my brothers. Do you have brothers?'

'No. I'm an only child.'

'Christ, you're lucky. No bloody competition. My clever-cock family all waltzed through Eton and Oxford while I scraped it by a whisker. But I *like* being family dunce. No responsibility. *That's* what drew me to the civil service. No responsibility and no decisions. And with three older brothers all in great health I'll never have the title hanging round my neck. So I sat the Colonial exams and before you could say abracadabra I'm on a boat for Mombasa and dear old Sir Charles.'

'And now you're on a boat with me.'

'Exactly. Sailing down Africa to God knows what and where, mainly because Charlie is so busy he hasn't seen through me yet.'

Adam said, 'You'd better tell me what I'm supposed to do in Tanga? Exactly why are we going?'

'Easy, old chap. To make sure we European powers keep to our own slices of Africa without arguing. Provided we're good neighbours – no fighting each other in front of the natives – the Hun can keep their bit and we'll keep ours. Being good Christians we'll probably push the blacks into reservations and make them work for all the European settlers Eliot plans to bring in. In no time at all we'll have the place all sewn up – just like America.'

'Why the hell am I involved?'

'Same reason as me – you're young and fit and available.'

'Christ, Hocklyffe-Evans – surely there's more to it than that?'

'Oh no, my dear fellow. Britain always sends young men to do the dirty work. So you and I are off on what may be a bout of diplomatic skulduggery. Should be quite a lot of fun.'

'It won't be fun for me. I'm not a bloody diplomat. I won't know what to do.'

'Listen, old boy. Diplomacy is just a matter of high grade idiocy. The trick is to show interest and say nothing, just nod occasionally and smile. The nod is important. Nothing too brisk. Just a slow intellectual nod to show you're awake and listening. A well judged nod every so often keeps diplomats burbling for hours. The more they burble the more they are likely to give away.'

'Give away what?'

'Anything. We're on the lookout all the time.'

'But for *what*?'

'Anything, old chap. Anything that may be of interest his Majesty's Government. Ears open. Mouth shut. Nod and listen.'

'Bloody hell,' said Adam.

'And don't worry about diplomatic talks. Eliot wrote out several speeches and crib sheets to cover every occasion. We just select the right piece of paper and read it. Our friends the Hun know the game. They'll have crib sheets to match ours. They're called discussion documents.'

'Can I see them?'

'Tomorrow, old chap. We'll have plenty of time. Just remember in all this – I'm the conductor and you're part of the orchestra. Just follow my lead and we'll have no problems. By the way, call me H.E. Everyone does. Even the natives have got hold of it and call me *Bwana Aichee*.'

Next day Adam sat with H.E. under awnings on the first class deck, studying and discussing Eliot's notes, ignored by the German passengers. The ship sailed on a wide loop – avoiding coral and rock shoals along the coast – before slipping between Pemba Island and the mainland to catch the afternoon tide into Tanga as heat of day waned.

'Good looking harbour,' said H.E., standing at the rail with Adam. 'Room for several big warships in here.'

Adam's attention strayed to the dockside. 'I think we have an official welcoming party,' he said.

'Good God, yes. That bunch of fellows in white.'

Adam shaded his eyes for a second look and saw in the group a slim elegant young woman in long cotton dress with gloves and parasol, waving and smiling.

'My God, I think that's Eva. What's she doing here?'

H.E. leaned out for a look.

'Aha. Your bird from the bush? What a beauty. I wouldn't mind having *her* in my hand.'

'Bloody hell, H.E.. Be careful. You'll fall over the rail.'

H.E. said, 'Come on. Let's get off this bucket and start work. You're the important one. You go first.'

The welcoming party shuffled into line on the dockside and an officer stepped forward.

Adam paused – nervous – at the head of the gangplank. Over his shoulder he said, 'That's Kreuz – the major I told you about. God, they've brought everyone down here to meet us.'

H.E. poked him in the back. 'Get going. Looks like he's our introducer-in-chief. Be ready with the diplomatic burble.'

Kreuz saluted and said, 'Mr Early and Mr Hocklyffe-Evans. Welcome to Tanga. Allow me to introduce you.'

Adam moved along the line of crisp white uniforms, shaking hands and mumbling a greeting. Eva gripped his fingers and held on, laughing, 'Do you recognise me? Do I look better than the last time we spoke?'

'You certainly do,' said Adam. 'And I *did* recognise you. But only just.'

'And what about me?' asked the tall young officer standing next to Eva. 'Paul von Ansbach. I hope you remember me.'

'You look so different,' said Adam. 'I'm happy to see you recovered.'

Kreuz touched Adam's elbow and said, 'We must move to meet our Governor at his official residence for a formal greeting and short ceremony.'

Eva released Adam's hand and said, 'We shall speak later. I promise.'

Kreuz escorted Adam to a line of a waiting rickshaws. The whole welcoming party sorted itself out into some sort of seniority and clambered in. Adam looked back at Eva.

'Don't worry,' said Kreuz. 'She's coming to the ceremony. And to the dinner tonight. And to every other function. She asked to be included and we could not refuse.'

From the last rickshaw in line, Eva dipped her head and smiled from under lowered eyelids.

Kreuz called an order and the rickshaw men hauled the whole party up a steep cliff road at barely walking pace.

After the welcoming ceremony Kreuz took Adam and H.E. to a bungalow on the cliff, saying, 'This house is yours while you stay with us. The servants will care for you in every way. I return at eight to take you to dinner with the Governor – a formal affair so please be properly dressed and ready.'

As soon as Kreuz left, H.E. called Adam onto the veranda and said, 'Look at this view. The whole bloody harbour laid out like a map. We must make the most of it. Get your pad and draw the bloody place.'

'You want me to make a sketch?'

'You're a surveyor. Start surveying. Draw like mad. Sketch everything. Get the harbour entrance with as much scale and distance as you can. We'll need it later if we fight these buggers.'

Caught up in H.E.'s urgency, Adam ran to find his pad. Drawing fast he sketched and scribbled; flicking from page to page; forming a continuous plan to include cliffs and hills and a large island opposite the town that curved round towards a mainland point and formed the harbour entrance.

H.E. said, 'Don't forget that railway line coming up from the jetty and going off into the bush.'

Adam said, 'Stop looking over my shoulder. You're putting me off.'

'Just making sure you get everything in.'

'Leave me alone.'

H.E. moved round and perched on the veranda wall. He said, 'Your little lady friend told me that tomorrow the Huns are taking us on a beach picnic. Bring your pad and make drawings of the people with harbour views behind. That'll give us different sight of the place. While you're doing that I'll go swimming and check how deep the water is.'

'That's devious.'

'No. It's spying. That's what we're *really* here for. By the way – what did your little bird from the bush say after the grand *Graf* handed over your medal?'

'Nothing.'

'Come off it. I saw her nibbling at your ear.'

'All she said was... 'I'll see you this evening at the Governor's dinner.''

'I'll bet she will, you lucky dog.'

Dressed in formal whites and black cummerbund, Adam strolled with Kreuz and H.E. through soft tropical darkness towards the

Governor's residence, thinking of Eva.

By God, she'd looked proud when the *Graf* pinned the medal on. *Almost as if she belongs to me. Perhaps in a sense she does. After all, if I'd not come along that day in the bush, she'd still be there. Just a pile of dry bones.*

Looking towards the brightly lit veranda he picked Eva out in the crowd of guests and remembered the promise in her whispered words that afternoon – '*I cannot speak with you now among so many people. We will have time to meet and talk later. I owe you much. I will see you this evening at the dinner.*'

He sighed in anticipation and turned his mind to the evening's planned meeting with the Governor – 'Read your notes and check your little speech,' H.E. said while they sat drinking brandy and waiting for Kreuz. 'Be ready to pipe up when I give the signal.'

'Let me get it right,' said Adam. 'We walk to the Residence, have a quick drink with a crowd of German guests, meet the Governor for our official discussion, then go into dinner.'

'Right. A quick bit of protocol then goodbye *Graf* and on with the drunken brawl. Should be a lively evening.'

'How do you know?'

'Kreuz told me.'

'Did Eliot know about the medal the *Graf* gave me this afternoon?'

'Probably.'

'So that's how my speech matched the occasion.'

H.E. laughed and said, 'You must hand it to the clever little bugger. I'll bet he and the grand *Graf* fixed up this whole thing between 'em.'

'How?'

'By telegram, old boy. The rapier of modern diplomacy. It banishes embarrassment and removes all doubt on who will say what. No errors – no problems. That's how it works.'

'This whole visit is all arranged?'

'Down to the last word on the crib sheets.'

'Good God.'

'Don't complain. It's brought you close to the lovely Eva again.'

After ten minutes of drinks and introductions – including an almost intimate brushing of hands with Eva – Adam joined H.E., Kreuz and the Governor in a study and, prompted by H.E., read his short speech.

The Governor delivered his own short speech with almost identical wording then produced four glasses and wine for a toast – 'To peace and progress in Africa.'

Adam stood and sipped with the others, trying to read their blank faces for some reaction to what he thought an important occasion.

After a brief silence the Governor said, 'Our business concluded we should now rejoin my guests.'

Filing from the room, Adam tugged H.E.'s sleeve and whispered, 'Is that all?'

'Until we need to fight the buggers in a year or so.'

'But didn't we just agree not to fight?'

H.E. winked and murmured, 'We only talked. We didn't sign.'

After about an hour of polite eating and chatting Adam heard a sigh of relief go round the room when the Governor stood, raised his glass in a final toast and left the thirty men and five women to start their party. The men loosened ties, removed jackets and cummerbunds and settled to heavy drinking – German beer; German wine; German schnapps.

Adam tried to make his way to Eva but, waylaid by Kreuz, sat drinking schnapps and trying to talk over the noise of slurred voices and bursts of patriotic songs.

'God, this stuff is strong,' he said to Kreuz.

'This is how we Germans enjoy ourselves,' shouted Kreuz, throwing an arm round Adam's shoulder. 'You can see we are happy people and do not want trouble fighting you and your king.'

Adam nodded and felt the room sway.

'Keep still, old chap,' he mumbled to his head and straightened up to recover. Across the table he saw H.E. leaning close to a pretty woman; whispering in her ear. She laughed; dipping her head on to H.E's shoulder and patting his hand.

Adam blinked through a haze of alcohol – *Good God. That's Eva. What's she doing making up to that bastard H.E.?*

He rose and weaved out onto a veranda to stand in warm darkness sniffing the fragrant air.

With a rustle of silk Eva appeared beside him.

'These German men drink so much, but also the women,' she said, giggling. 'We learn this early in life. It makes up for much.'

She leaned against Adam, her breasts brushing his chest. He shivered at the unexpected soft touch and looked down in delight.

The starving, desiccated young woman from the bush – now well rounded, uncorseted and rubbing against him – looked deep and bold into his eyes in the velvet dark. *Bloody hell.*

'Your *Herr* Hocklyffe-Evans is a naughty man,' she whispered. 'But I owe him nothing. It is you I must repay.'

'Madam,' he slurred 'you are very kind, but you owe *me* nothing.'

'I do, I do,' she murmured, 'But now I cannot repay you. Later before you leave we shall meet and talk. Then I shall find a way.'

She squeezed his hand and drifted off into the dark, leaving him tensed and quivering.

For several minutes he perched on the veranda wall to recover then went back inside to find H.E. leering over another of the women.

Adam said, 'Time to go,' and dragged H.E. away, found their rickshaw and returned to the care of two watchful African servants at the bungalow.

H.E. sat in an armchair drinking brandy and grumbling, 'Why did you bring me home? I was almost in that girl's drawers. Did the lovely Eva find you by the way? When you went outside, she shot off like a bullet. Did you get your hand onto anything interesting?'

'Shut up and go to bed.'

'No. I want another drink. Did you get hold of her? Did you? Should be easy. She's got her eye on you old boy.'

'Bugger off,' said Adam and weaved from the room to collapse on his bed.

Next morning Adam woke with a terrible headache and went out to find H.E. laying in a long chair on the veranda. 'You look awful,' Adam said.

'You look pretty bad yourself, old chap. Sit down. Drink some tea and please don't speak for an hour or so. I need to recover before that bloody picnic. They're coming to collect us at noon and it's already ten.'

Adam nodded and sat without moving, easing his hangover with tea and a large straw hat to keep out the light.

'Headache?' asked H.E..

'Only round the eyes.'

'You're lucky. I ache everywhere.'

At noon Adam squeezed into a tiny rickshaw alongside H.E. and hung on as it bumped down a rough cliff track to a small bay set with tables and awnings under palm trees. White sand and clear blue sea sparkled in the afternoon sun. African servants in white robes stood waiting in a marquee full of food and drink.

'Oh God,' said H.E.. 'Another bash.'

To Adam's relief the party turned out to be a decorous affair with no apparent memory of anything said or done the night before. About fifty guests sat on the sand or at tables, sipping wine and eating a dainty picnic. Adam and H.E. circulated, talking to anyone with enough English.

Adam caught sight of Eva sitting under an awning with several women. She waved and called him over – 'These ladies want to meet my English rescuer and his friend,' she said, smiling.

Adam looked deep into her eyes hoping for some signal but she gave no hint of their encounter last night. She shook hands and chatted for a few minutes before Kreuz came and ushered Adam – 'To meet an interesting friend. You may remember him from *Moschi*. You'll be pleased to meet him also, *Herr* Hocklyffe-Evans.'

He pointed to a heavy bearded man and said, 'I must introduce Captain Tom von Prince. A captain in our army but he is English, you know.'

'Scottish,' said von Prince. 'My father was Scottish.'

Adam shook hands. 'We met in Moshi but you didn't speak.'

Von Prince smiled but his eyes remained hard. 'Nothing to say.'

'Let me understand,' said H.E.. 'You're a German soldier with a British passport.'

Von Prince nodded. 'My father married into the German nation so I am born German, I think German and I serve the Kaiser. The piece of paper showing citizenship is nothing.'

'Interesting,' murmured H.E., his wide blue eyes showing polite puzzlement.

Adam relaxed and allowed H.E. to carry a conversation that ranged over land, crops and African labour to settle finally on military matters when von Prince said, 'It seems you have won your South African war.'

H.E.'s eyes became wary. 'Not yet. Negotiations are still going on in Pretoria.'

Von Prince leaned forward and said, 'And you won in such a brilliant way. When faced with a new form of warfare by the Boers your generals rewrote the rules.'

Kreuz nodded and said 'How original to isolate the fighting men then concentrate all their families into special camps. A very clever move from which we have learned.'

'Really?' said H.E..

'Ah yes. With this action you destroyed the enemy will to continue and forced them into peace talks. I think the Boers have no choice but to accept your terms and surrender. Do you agree?'

H.E. stood and stretched. 'Don't know, old chap. Military's not my province. I only work in an office. About time I went for a swim. Where do I change?'

Kreuz smiled and said, 'Behind any tree large enough.'

H.E. drifted off and joined a group of men splashing at the water edge. Minutes later Adam watched him playing and shouting like a schoolboy, goading his new friends into a noisy diving game that took them deep and far out into the bay; awarding points for farthest, fastest, deepest.

Eva's group of German ladies seemed fascinated; shading their eyes to watch H.E's large pink shoulders and strong legs plunging through crystal clear sea and swimming under water as far as possible.

Adam moved to sit near the ladies and make a passable sketch of the scene. It survived as a water colour – a delicate picture of fluttering long dresses; dappled shade; broad hats and pretty women on a sunlit colonial beach. Many years later it hung in place of honour as a picture of Eva's young womanhood, her memory of the day as warm and golden as the sun filtering through trees and sparkling across the hillside and harbour entrance.

As Adam shaded finishing lines of the outer harbour entrance and signal tower, von Prince looked over his shoulder.

'Do you sketch only in pencil? Are you interested in architecture or portraits.'

'I make rough pencil drawings and turn the best of them into water colours.' lied Adam. 'It's easier than carrying paints everywhere.'

'Can you sketch me with some of my men and send me a picture?'

'Let me arrange you into a proper group.' said Adam.

This second picture also survived to hang on the wall of a hunting lodge in East Prussia. It shows a small group of German officers at ease on the beach. Behind them, clearly seen, are the inner harbour, main jetty, railway sheds and dockside.

The painted figures, faces shaded under hats and helmets, give a dreamy Impressionist feel to the scene. Only one figure is distinct and recognisable. At water edge, shoulders heaving from black bathing suit, blond hair agleam, H.E., frozen in some schoolboy prank, would look back at Kreuz half a century later, defying the years. Kreuz would sigh and turn away, remembering long dead comrades.

The picnic ended at sundown and back in the bungalow H.E. checked through Adam's sketches, saying, 'This is all good stuff. These from the beach show wonderful detail. The navy will be really pleased – especially when I tell 'em the water shoals deep only a few yards out.'

'That damned man von Prince thinks I paint water colours.'

'Yes I heard. How does it feel to be portrait artist to the German aristocracy?'

'It's not funny. They've asked for copies. What do I do?'

'Don't worry, old chap. We'll get someone to daub a few pictures from your sketches and send 'em here. They'll never know the difference.'

'I'll be glad when it's over.'

'Never mind. Only the farewell dinner tonight and we'll be home and dry. This'll be a last chance to get your hands on the lovely Eva, so make the most of it. And by the way – watch that bugger von Prince. He told me they knew you liked to draw as they'd seen you sketching from the bungalow. Cheeky sods must have a telescope on us. Can't trust anyone can you?'

During the dinner Adam felt frustrated at having no contact with Eva other than exchanged smiles down the long table. But when, at the end, Adam moved down the line, shaking hands and saying farewell, she whispered, 'I'll come to your bungalow later to say goodbye.'

Half an hour later Paul appeared at the bungalow door, bowed saying, '*Herr* Early. Fräulein Eva is here to speak with you. She waits outside. *Herr* Hocklyffe-Evans, shall I join you for a drink?'

Ignoring H.E.'s leer Adam slipped past Paul onto the veranda.

'Shall we walk?' said Eva, linking her arm into his. 'We have never done anything so normal since first we met.'

She led him from the house in silence, heading through fragrant white moonlight to a fringe of palms overlooking the shimmer of sea.

Eva said, 'Perhaps I am a silly girl but I feel it is here romantic.'

Pushing Adam against a tree she leaned against him, brushing her breasts across his chest, rolling her hips in an exciting circular motion; standing on tip toe to reach up and kiss him with soft moist lips.

He crouched to fit his body exactly to hers and felt her shiver as excitement flitted through their embrace.

Leaning back to look up she ran her hands over his chest and shoulders and whispered, 'I must know you better. I want to be your friend. You promised to write to me. Please promise again and perhaps visit me in Berlin. I can repay you properly there, not here in the open.'

Adam ran his hands down to the swell of her buttocks, thrilled at the feel of damp silky skin through the thin dress.

She sighed and whispered, 'Will you come to see me? Please say yes.'

'Yes. I will. I will, I will.'

'When?'

'Soon. Later this year. No next year.'

'Promise me.'

'I promise.'

She stepped back.

He grabbed at her. 'Don't go. Not yet.'

'I must. Paul will worry. But we are not now saying goodbye. We are saying only...you have a word...is it... Farewell? Not a real goodbye?'

'Yes. Farewell. I'll see you in Berlin within a year.'

'You promise?'

'I promise.'

'Good. Now we must go back to the house or they will think the worst.'

She smoothed her hair and dress and with a handkerchief wiped her brow and lips. 'Are you ready to return?' she asked, running fingertips between their hips.

He stiffened at her touch.

'Mein Gott.' she said. 'We must walk back slowly.'

Next day on the deck of a small coaster, belching black smoke as it heaved into blue waves off Pemba, H.E. sipped a drink and said 'I reckon you did well with the lovely Eva, old boy. Last night was your grand farewell I think. You haven't stopped sweating yet. Pity you won't see her again. What a filly.'

Adam smiled and remembered the note she slipped him last night before leaving. It took him a moment to decipher the strange spiky script: *See you in Berlin for full and proper payment of my debt.*

Chapter Five

Birth of a City

Walking through drizzling rain near the station Adam heard his name called and turned to see the huge figure of H.E. hurrying forward with outstretched hand, calling, 'Stop, damn you. I need a friendly face in this god-forsaken place.'

Laughing in pleasure at sight of that large pink face and blond tumbled hair jammed under a broad brimmed hat, Adam said, 'So they've allowed you out of Mombasa.'

'My dear Early. How wonderful to see you. I'm here to help set up local government in this damned sea of mud. I'm living at the Club. It's a bit of a shanty but if you can stand roast goat come and have dinner right now. I'm dying for some intelligent company after the shysters and rogues I deal with here.'

'Doing what?'

'I'll tell you over the goat. Come on.'

Settled with drinks in a quiet corner at the Club H.E. said, 'In three weeks I open a land office. My job is to divide this whole area – including the town – into plots and sell 'em to the general public.'

'But this is only a railway siding. Surely a proper town is planned elsewhere.'

'It's a risk. The town *may* go elsewhere but I don't think so. Everything we need is here. Rivers and forest. Wood and water. Fire and steam. I think the town will build up and stay here. Anyway the surrounding area will develop into farms and plantations so we still have opportunities even if the town moves.'

'What are you suggesting?'

'Well, old boy. There's a big plan for European settlement and I want to be part of it – buy my own land and that sort of thing. But being bloody-well in charge of land distribution I'm not allowed. So in a few weeks when I start to parcel out land sections around Nairobi, and up on the highlands I'll put you in for the best bits to mark and buy for both of us in your name – I can't be seen as being involved.'

'So we'll be like all the other shysters and rogues you mentioned.'

'I suppose so. But who cares? We'll be rich. And it'll be a new life for us both.'

'I must admit I'm bored. I enjoyed helping build the railway but now it's finished all I do is draw and supervise completion of new culverts.

H.E. laughed and said, 'Time to change, old chap.'

'Let me think about it.'

'Good idea. We're about to be interrupted by this fellow I met on the train last week. We'll go into more detail later. Come to my office day after tomorrow at six in the evening.'

Adam looked up to see a small brisk figure marching across the room to shake hands, saying 'Richard Thinman. Lieutenant, Kings African Rifles. Pleasure to meet you.'

'Join us for dinner,' said HE, winking at Adam.

Thinman glared at Adam and said, 'Are you here to talk about land?'

'Not as far as I know.'

'What do you do?'

'Railway engineer. I'm helping complete this stretch of line.'

'You have my admiration, Sir. Damn railway's a modern miracle. Brings plenty of opportunity to this wonderful new country.'

HE said, 'Quite right. Grasp the opportunity. Buy land in this town. You'll make a fortune.'

During the next two days Adam found himself looking at Nairobi with new eyes and increasing excitement, calculating money against morals. For the first time he noticed a new virile group of men around the new town – a tough confident bunch – independent adventurers, ready to build, deal or hunt in order to make a fortune.

'How the hell didn't I see them before?' he asked.

'Had your head buried in railway culverts, old chap,' said H.E., spreading a sheaf of papers across his desk. 'These fellows are vultures piling in to scavenge a slice of your nice new country. The difference is that you and I have the advantage. Look. Land maps. You have about three weeks to get out to survey and mark the areas I've marked in red.'

'Is this legal?'

'Not quite. But others are already sniffing round, so there's no reason why you shouldn't sniff too. Only with these maps you'll have the advantage of knowing where to look – around Nairobi, and up on the highlands. So you won't be wasting time.'

Adam frowned; disturbed by a conflict between greed and conscience. He weighed one against the other then – in a rush of relief – said, 'Damn it. No harm in looking. I'll take a few weeks leave and scout around.'

Engaging a dozen porters Adam set off northeast through a brilliant clear morning. After ten miles he halted at the top of a lightly wooded rise, calculating his position as being on the northern edge of an area ringed in red pencil by H.E..

Adam looked through the trees across a rolling vista of red fertile land opening out towards the beautiful white peak of Mount Kenya and felt strange kinship with this place: *Looks great for cattle, even better for crops. I could certainly settle here....*

'Musa. This seems about right. Set up camp and tell Sakayo to scout the area for signs of life.'

He began his survey immediately, continuing until late afternoon when Sakayo returned and said, 'No people here, *Bwana* Adam. No villages, no cattle, no crops. We are alone.'

At sundown Adam sat in the peace of evening, watching Mount Kenya fade to a shimmer of silver under early starlight; his mind dreaming and planning – *I'll build a house facing the mountain and bring water from the river. Cattle pens over there, crops out on the open land...my God, what a place....*

For a week Adam checked and surveyed west into an area marked on the map as Muthaiga and north towards the Kiambu forest; setting posts to mark out five thousand acres of what seemed to be fertile and well-watered land. He spent a further day completing notes and marking the land office map before marching twenty five miles further to camp by a waterfall where the Chania and Thika rivers meet.

From here he surveyed north and northwest over a magnificent area of ridges, woodland and rich red earth; watered by streams and rivulets from the highlands around Mount Kenya. Apart from a few elderly Kikuyu tending smallholdings or cattle the whole area seemed empty of people.

After seven more days trekking and surveying Adam stuffed his safari box with notebooks and drawings and marched back to Nairobi to find half the town burnt down.

'Plague m'dear man.' said H.E. 'We had bubonic plague in the bazaars. Bloody rats everywhere. Only solution was to burn the place. So we did. Hope it works.'

Adam spent several hours showing H.E. his drawings and survey notes and asked, 'How much money will this cost?'

'About two rupees an acre upcountry. That's about a shilling. Doesn't sound much but you'll need money over five years to develop the land or lose it without compensation.

'So we'll need about three hundred pounds for each five thousand acres. I marked about twenty thousand acres. That's about a thousand pounds but how much will we need for development?'

'The same. Two rupees an acre over three to five years.'

'When must we be ready?'

'Soon, old chap. If we put up six thousand pounds we'll go for as much farmland as possible – up to a hundred thousand acres – plus some plots in Nairobi. Can you rustle up three thousand?'

'I'll try.'

'Then get on with it. In a few days the news will be out and every prospector in the Protectorate will be hunting cash. Make sure you beat the buggers to it.'

Adam borrowed five thousand pounds from the Bank of India, newly opened in Nairobi. 'Three thousand immediately to buy the land and two thousand available later for development,' he told H.E. in triumph.

'Bloody well *done*,' said H.E., his eyes gleaming. 'My three thousand gives us a total of eight, so we'll get our hundred thousand acres of farm land.'

'Is that definite?'

'Already agreed, old chap. Eliot feels he owes you something for your work in Moshi and Tanga. And between you and me he's agreed you'll have first pick of the land in Nairobi when it comes available.'

'Is that fair?'

'Who cares? It's settled. Eliot's given my office permission to complete titles for all the land you surveyed, and anything else you like up to a hundred thousand acres.'

'Including the area by Muthaiga?

'It's yours.'

'Bloody hell. And we can take more at Chania and as much as possible down in the Rift Valley.'

'Exactly. And *now*, m'dear man, what are we going to do with it all?'

'Cattle. We start with cattle and see what happens.'

Next day Adam spoke with Musa.

'Cattle, *Bwana* Adam? No trouble. I know a Somali who is good with cattle and meat. I'll bring him to see you.'

'Do you know him well? Can I trust him?'

'Yes. I saved his life in a slaver's band so he calls me brother.'

'Slavers? You were a slaver?'

Musa's eyes hooded and sweat broke out on his face.

41

'No Sir. Not really. I was escaping from the troubles in Uganda and met the slavers by Mount Elgon.'

'You were in the Uganda mutiny?'

Musa's eyes hooded again.

'Yes Sir. I was with the Sudanese soldiers at Busoga.'

'The soldiers who killed their white officers?'

'Yes. We wanted to return to Sudan. It seemed the only way.'

Adam shook his head in disbelief. 'You were in the mutiny? Good God.'

'It was before I met your father, Sir and entered his service.'

'But you joined the slavers?'

'Yes, Sir.'

'For how long?'

'About six weeks, Sir.'

'Six weeks. Did you go on any raids? Did you capture slaves?'

'*Bwana* Adam. It was a hard time. Most of our men at Busoga died when Captain Lugard came with big guns. I escaped and walked for two weeks before meeting the Arab slavers. If they did not take me in I would have died. The Arabs saw me as a brother Muslim. We were helping the ungodly tribes by taking them to serve the true believers.'

'Did you believe this?'

'No, Sir. But I pretended to. Otherwise the slavers would have chained and sold me also.'

'How did you get away?'

'One night my Somali friend and I slipped away into the dark. I came to the coast and found your father. God was good to me.'

'But you don't believe in God'

'I do when He gets something right.' said Musa. 'He led me to your father and now I have you.'

Musa brought a plump young Somali to Adam's house. 'I am Abdi Elmi, Sir,' he said, speaking Swahili. 'Musa tells me you need a man for cattle and meat. I know that business well.'

'How well?'

'I can buy and run cattle, supervise herders, set up a slaughterhouse, sell the meat. You can trust me to do all this, Sir.'

'Where do you live now? If I need you when can you start?'

Abdi Elmi turned to Musa. Speaking Arabic he said, 'Can I trust this man brother?'

In perfect Arabic, Adam said, 'If you have a question ask me.'

'Sir. You speak the true language. Many pardons, Sir; may God take my tongue.'

'Are you a rogue or an honest man?' asked Adam.

'Honest, Sir. I am honest. I owe my life to this man, my brother Musa whom God placed in the path of my enemies. God must have saved me for you, Sir. You will have me for the rest of my life as God intended.'

'So be it,' said Adam and shook hands.

A few weeks later H.E. called Adam to the Land Office to sign and collect his title deeds and asked, 'Have you thought of a name for your estate? We need it for the deeds. Your new neighbour, Sandbach-Baker has called his place Homestead Farm.'

Adam laughed and said, 'Mzito. I'll call mine Mzito.'

'What does that mean?'

'Honestly, H.E. You really must learn the language. *Mzito* is Swahili for 'heavy'. Like my bank debt.'

'Write the name on that line and sign. On these other deeds we'll call the rest of our land Chania, since it's along the Chania River. What are your plans? '

'I'll send Abdi Elmi north to buy cattle and bring them to Mzito. Musa will build pens and a slaughterhouse. In three or four months we'll see our first income. Then we'll decide how to use the land at Chania.'

At Mzito, Abdi tucked Adam's money into his waistband and shook hands. 'I'll be back in two months, *Bwana* Adam. You will be happy with the cattle I bring.'

Adam watched him march off at the head of a mixed crew of Masai and Somalis, unsure if he'd ever see any of them again.

Musa must have sensed his unease because he said, 'Don't worry, *Bwana* Adam. He is my brother. You go back to your railway work in Nairobi and leave me here to build a place to kill our cattle.'

Adam said, 'No. I have a better idea,' and returned to H.E. and said, 'I need land in Nairobi.'

'Why?'

'If we kill at Mzito the meat will spoil before it reaches town. We should hold the herds at Mzito and bring down a few at a time for slaughter.'

'Not easy m'dear man. The bloody Railway still own all land in Nairobi and refuse to release it. I'll speak with Eliot and see if he can force them to let you have some on the edge of town.'

In early December H.E. offered Adam a large plot at Ngara, across the river from the old Indian Bazaar.

'A good clean area since we burnt the bazaar down.' said H.E..
'Free of plague. Plenty of water. Close to town. We struggled to get it
for you, but argued with those Railway buggers that if they want meat
for their workers they'll have to co-operate.'

Adam raised more money to pay for the land and a small stockade.
A few weeks later Abdi Elmi arrived with the first cattle. His Somali
butchers insisted on Muslim slaughter – each throat individually cut,
bleeding the animal to death. The killing stockade earth became
soaked with blood and turned to soupy amber mud, covered in flies.

The Africans, as always, coined a perfect description for the place
– *Mahali Ya Damu*; the Place of Blood – and called it Damu for short.

Adam laughed and entered the name on his title deeds. 'God, what
an awful place,' said H.E. when he came to visit, shuddering at the
stench and the cone of vultures circling above and landing to fight and
scavenge over piles of discarded heads, hooves and offal.

'It's even worse at night when hyena and jackal creep in to clear
what's left,' said Adam. 'And thank God for the work they do. Without
them we'd need fifty more men just cleaning up.

By start of the rains in April 1903 Adam felt overwork and
exhaustion draining his mind and energy and said to H.E., 'Every day
and every weekend I finish work with the Railway then start all over
again on the cattle and meat business. It's killing me.'

'Come now, old chap. You're young and fit. You can keep it up.'

'It's easy for you to say that with an office full of clerks doing all
your work. End of the day you just go home, have dinner, get drunk
and go to bed with one of your women.

'True. But I learn a lot from the women.'

'Swahili?'

'Oh yes, I learn that too. But look at the help I give you in other
ways.

'Such as?'

'Such as early warning of good news. For instance – yesterday
Government and Railway agreed that this town is to be permanent. So
after long gestation and labour pains the city of Nairobi is finally about
to be born and the dear old Railway – God bless 'em – is releasing land
in the town centre. I want you to apply tomorrow and get us some good
plots.'

'Why? Don't we have enough land? Don't I have enough work?'

'Bloody hell man – we'll make a fortune. We're getting rid of this rag tag and bobtail collection of wood and tin to build a proper town with a proper centre – roads; telegraph poles; street lights; a couple of churches and some mosques – all that sort of thing. We'll plant trees and parks and…just think…it'll be like Europe in Africa. What a place to live.'

'When does it happen?'

'Plans already well advanced, old chap. Indian traders will take land up by the new Bazaar and along the river and we're giving Europeans commercial plots in the centre and residential plots on higher ground to the west.'

'What about land for Africans?'

'We're putting them in locations to the east of town. Out of the way but in easy reach as labour. Brilliant arrangement, don't you think?'

'Sounds like it.'

'So come in tomorrow and choose some plots. We'll get them into your name quickly and start building.'

Adam applied for several commercial parcels around the town and two residential plots among trees on high land to the west – 'Perfect for a couple of houses,' he said to H.E. after making a survey – 'One each. Shady in the day, cool at night and with lovely views out over the plain.'

'Heaven,' said H.E. 'Absolute heaven. When will you build?'

'Not yet. I'm too bloody busy. We need money so I'll put something up on the town plots first.'

In September Adam built several wooden houses for rent in the town centre and three small shops near the Bazaar, which he let, to Indian traders – one a butcher selling meat from Damu.

Adam continued ceaseless work until November, each day surveying and supervising for the Railway; each night calculating and planning for Mzito and Damu.

One evening he said to H.E., 'I need some leave. I'm killing myself.'

'What about your job on the railway?'

'I'll resign.'

'What about Mzito and Damu?'

'Our meat contracts with the army and railway are all settled. Musa and Abdi can keep things running while I'm away.'

'Where will you go?'

'Europe.'

'England?'

'No. Germany.'

'Hah. Your bird from the bush. The divine Eva. Sly dog. You never told me.'

'We've been writing every month,' said Adam. 'She's invited me to meet her family. So I plan to go in May when it's warmer in Europe.'

'She's got you.' said H.E. 'I knew she'd win. She had her eye on you from the start.'

'Nonsense.' said Adam. 'I'm going to meet her family. They want to thank me for saving her.'

'We'll see m'dear man,' said H.E. with a leer in his bright blue eyes. 'I say she's got you. We'll see soon enough.'

Chapter Six

Visit To Berlin

Skipping from foot to foot with impatience, Eva waited with Paul in the crowded *Zoogarten* railway station, one hand raised to protect her wide-brimmed hat from gusts of wind swirling through the great dome.

She felt bright and alive in her soft blue dress buttoned high at the throat, long skirt rustling at her ankles and the hat – topped by a bright crown of flowers matching her mood and the shining spring day. Passing men looked in admiration, some tipping their brims with murmured suggestions. She ignored them as she searched along the train for Adam, holding Paul's sleeve to balance on tiptoe.

'There he is,' she cried. 'There – by the fourth carriage. Go and fetch him Paul. Hurry.'

She saw Adam's sun-tanned face light up in recognition. An unexpected charge of pleasure surged through her body. *Why am I so excited at seeing him? He's only another man.*

The thought swept away in a flurry of jumbled words and greetings and the shock of his touch as she shook hands. Unwilling to let go, she clung to Adam's arm while Paul made a sharp bow and said, 'Welcome to Berlin *Herr* Early,' then she hurried him from the station, chattering all the while.

Baggage safely stowed she climbed into the horse-drawn carriage and sat, still holding his arm and chattering in excitement – 'We stay a few days in our town house then into the country we move later. My English. Is it better?'

She laughed, delighted that Adam so obviously stunned by her welcome, her closeness and her interest in him could only reply, 'Yes.'

'Say more. Say more. Tell me about your journey. Say what you think of Berlin.'

Paul said, 'You haven't given the poor man time to breathe yet – how can he speak?'

Adam laughed. 'Let me arrive first.' he said. 'You tell me where I am in Berlin and where I'm going.'

Happy to have Adam's full attention she calmed down and pointed out places of interest, intrigued by his wonder at the crowded streets and massive buildings.

The carriage drove out of the city past rivers, canals and lakes into the woods of Grunewald to a big brown house set back among trees.

'It's a dark old place,' said Eva, 'But we've always lived here. Our servant will bring your luggage. I'll leave you for an hour to unpack then take you to meet my family and some friends for dinner.'

Overwhelmed by Eva's welcome and unable to settle, Adam wandered round his large gloomy room, depressed by the heavy wooden furniture and a dank dark green copse of heavy fir trees outside the window – such a change from the clear light and air of Africa.

He unpacked and splashed water over his face and by the time Eva returned felt better.

'Come and meet my father,' she said. 'He can be a strange man – sometimes quite rude – but please take no notice.'

Taking his hand she led him down stairs through a long hall hung with antlers and hunting trophies and into a big sitting room, releasing her grip as she pulled him through the door. Her palm left a hint of perspiration on his fingers and he realised – *By God, she's frightened.*

He followed as she tiptoed forward to where her father stood with Paul and in a small voice said, 'Father – this is *Herr* Early from Africa.'

Adam looked up into von Lettow-Ansbach's lizard stare, determined not to be intimidated by the man's tall elegance; the hooked nose and high forehead; the shiny black hair oiled flat; the icy eyes made fierce by a steel-rimmed monocle gripped between left eyebrow and cheekbone.

Eva stepped back, head dipped, nervous at how her father would react. But to her relief he offered his hand, and, speaking German, said, 'You saved my daughter's life. Thank you.'

Paul translated and Adam said, 'Please don't mention it.'

Oh God. What does he mean? Eva looked at Paul who seemed equally confused but translated as best he could.

Puzzlement crossed von Lettow-Ansbach's face. 'What did he say?'

'It doesn't matter, Father,' said Eva. 'It is an English expression.'

Her father frowned and said, 'Let us go in for dinner.'

During the evening her father made it clear that he did not approve of Adam and saw no reason to acknowledge his presence further. Eva felt grateful to her mother and the half dozen guests who helped her through the ordeal by keeping up lively conversation; fascinated by tales of Africa.

Her father sat frowning, obviously annoyed at not being the centre of attention. Eva ignored him and kept the stories and talk going until

48

near midnight when von Lettow-Ansbach abruptly stood, bowed to the room and left.

Eva leaned towards Adam and whispered, 'Thank God. Now we can relax. I told you he's strange. I hope you are not offended.'

'Not at all.'

'Paul and I will see you to your room. Tomorrow we show you Berlin. Next day we go with the whole family to our hunting lodge in the country. This you will like.'

At his bedroom door she leaned close, allowing him to savour the touch of her fingers and the scent of her body; making sure he realised that – but for Paul – she'd linger for a kiss.

Next day, on a whirlwind tour of Berlin, Eva sat close to Adam in the horse-drawn carriage. In the swaying vehicle she made sure her thigh and bosom touched and teased the whole journey; fingers fluttering on his arm as she drew attention to some interesting detail.

Her eyes sparkled when he handed her in and out of the carriage. Her cheeks flushed as she stumbled against him on steps in museums and art galleries or an uneven path in the park; working hard to turn herself from pretty young lady into desirable, *available* young woman.

At one point she winked at Paul – he'd seen it all before. Planned like a military operation, it rarely failed.

'Wait till Kristina sees this,' he whispered as they separated to dress for dinner. 'She'll be furious you got him first.'

Eva thought hard on how to introduce Kristina her younger sister and competitor since childhood. First for dolls, then dresses, then boys, and, eventually, for men – especially after Father explained their duty to the family on Eva's seventeenth birthday.

'You must find and marry sons with rich fathers. You must find land and fortune for our family. You two girls must plan to be beautiful wives to rich men.'

'Yes Father.'

A quick obedient bob and out of the room giggling.

'*What* did he *mean*?' shrieked Kristina; face down on the bed hilariously out of control, drumming her feet on the mattress. 'What *are* we supposed to do? Sell ourselves in the market?' She rolled on to her back; waved her legs in the air, showing her knickers and shouted, 'I think I'm going to wet myself.'

'Be sensible,' gulped Eva. 'You'll get us into trouble.'

They clung together; weeping with mirth.

Now – four years later – Eva knew *exactly* what their father meant. He put her and Kristina up for sale; presenting and showing them off at balls; dinners; parties; picnics; theatre and opera and all but advertising his daughters on hoardings as eligible and from a good military family.

Now – she hoped – such humiliation would come to an end.

But first she would need to mention Kristina.

Next morning Eva found Adam in the study writing and asked, 'What are you doing.'

'Writing letters home.'

'Come. It's a beautiful day. We must walk in the woods.'

Wearing a high necked white blouse, straw boater, dark blue skirt from which peeped button boots, she knew she looked winsome and young.

'Alone? Is that right?'

'Yes. Come. We will walk.'

She took his arm and led him through the trees, smiling and chattering; strolling through dappled shade towards blue water.

'The Havel.' she said. 'Berlin has much water. This is the most beautiful. Do you miss Africa?'

'I think of it all the time.'

'I also.'

'I thought you were happy to leave.'

'At first, yes. But now I dream and remember light and space and the beautiful warm sky. Germany seems so dark and cold and crowded. I would like to come back to Africa.'

She peeked up for his reaction but his mind seemed elsewhere.

He said, 'I am not sure how long you want me to stay here. You've not told me.'

'Do you want to leave?'

'No. But I need to know how long I am expected to stay.'

'Very well. Tomorrow we go to our hunting lodge in the north. There you will see others of our family and friends. And you will meet my sister.'

'Your sister? You've never mentioned a sister.'

'She's younger than me and very pretty. You will like her – but not too much I hope.'

She squeezed his arm and felt a tightening of his forearm as he hugged her hand against his body.

She said, 'This year our mid-summer party is arranged early for you. We will stay at the lodge for a week. After that you will be free to go if you wish. But why must you talk of leaving?'

'Business in England.'

'Business? For your Government?'

'No. I told you in my letters that I left the Railway. Now I have land and cattle. I suppose you'd call it an estate.'

'Is it a big estate?'

He laughed – 'Enormous.'

Eva squeezed his arm again and leaned against him as they walked.

'An estate,' she whispered. 'An enormous estate....'

That evening she said to her father, 'He owns an enormous estate in Africa with many cattle.'

Her father raised his eyebrows.

Adam gave two letters to a servant to post.

To his father: *The Germans are great engineers and the railways here are magnificent. You would be so interested to see their new ideas. They built the fastest engine in the world. It pulls at 83 miles an hour so they have developed first class track to carry it. I'm enclosing some drawings and notes I took as I travelled. If they build such a railway in their East African territory, it would transform their Colony....*

To H.E.: *The Germans have stable political and economic systems. Their Kaiser is powerful and well respected. Here in Berlin I saw Government buildings that are surely designed to rule a much larger area than Germany. I'll tell you more on my return. Meantime I've enclosed a few notes that might interest you about the military here with a few drawings to whet your appetite. Good equipment, as you can see. Well armed, well organised, and certainly dangerous....*

Major Kreuz sat at his desk in the Army Ministry studying Adam's letters and sighed.

'Perhaps you're right. Maybe he *is* a spy. But this detail is only the sort of thing any intelligent tourist with special interests might write. We can hardly arrest him on this evidence, especially as the letters are going to Africa, not London.'

'When do we see him?' asked von Prince.

'In a few days at von Lettow-Ansbach's hunting lodge.'

'So – no arrest or interrogation for the time being but we'll talk with him at the hunting lodge, then decide. What will you do with the letters?'

'Copy them and send them on their way.'

At the hunting lodge Eva arranged with Adam that he went shooting with the men every morning and walked in the woods with her every afternoon – 'Our only chance to be alone,' she said. 'The house is too full with my stuffy relatives.'

During their walks she held his hand, brushing against him as they wandered, trying to gauge his reaction.

On the third afternoon, strolling back through tree-dappled sunlight she tickled his fingers and said, 'This evening I want to make our mid-summer party a special occasion.'

Dressed and about to leave his room for the party Adam answered a knock – hoping it might be Eva – to see a servant who said, '*Graf* von Lettow-Ansbach wishes to speak with you *Herr* Early.'

Adam followed the servant: *What does the old buffer want? He's shown no interest in me so far....*

The servant led Adam to the main room where Von Lettow-Ansbach stood alone; ramrod straight, stern.

Adam's heart sank and he looked round for an interpreter but to his surprise von Lettow-Ansbach spoke in slow English. 'You are...a soldier, *Herr* Early?'

'No, Sir.'

'Some of my...friends...think you are a soldier.'

'No, Sir.'

'Have you ever been a soldier?'

'No, Sir.'

'My daughter tells me...you...own land.'

'Yes, Sir.'

'Much land?'

'About forty thousand hectares sir.'

'Forty thousand *hectares*?'

'Yes, Sir.'

'*Herr* Early. Please sit.'

Von Lettow-Ansbach moved to a large chair opposite and stared at Adam.

'Are you...sure? Forty *thousand* hectares?'

'Yes, Sir.. Absolutely, Sir.'

'Mein Gott.' said von Lettow-Ansbach.

'There's a lot of land in Africa, Sir.'

'Is this an English...joke?'

'No, Sir.'

'What...do you...make with...this land?'

'Mainly cattle, sir. But I plan crops – maize and perhaps coffee if it will grow.'

Von Lettow-Ansbach nodded and said, 'Thank you, *Herr* Early. You are...interesting. Thank you.'

Adam said, 'So you speak English, Sir.'

'No.' said von Lettow-Ansbach and stood up in obvious dismissal.

Adam rose, mystified.

'Thank you, Sir.'

'Yes.' said von Lettow-Ansbach.

Adam wandered out and went to join the party.

Fifty guests, boisterous from beer and wine, mingled on the lawn in bright summer-evening light. Adam circulated with Paul, meeting a succession of names and faces. Ten minutes of heel clicks from the men; delicate hand shakes and enquiring looks from the women then – a familiar face.

'Good evening, *Herr* Early. We meet again.'

'My God. Kreuz. What are you doing here? And von Prince. How nice to see you both. What a surprise. And dressed like gentlemen not soldiers.'

'We also need a break from Africa,' said Kreuz, smiling. 'We avoid the rainy season there, and meet lovely ladies in the party season here. Ah...talking of lovely ladies...'

Adam heard the party babble falter and die. All heads turned towards the house as Eva stepped out on to the lawn, looking lovely in a flowered green dress, cut low. Beside her walked an impossibly beautiful young woman. So beautiful she seemed to shine.

'Kristina...,' whispered Kreuz.

'Good heavens...,' murmured von Prince.

Quite stunned, Adam looked at Kristina gliding through the crowd, exuding beauty in the way some people exude character or intelligence.

Christ. What a sight....

Clear skin of such quality, it could have been applied by Rembrandt. Violet eyes and the figure of a goddess. Burnished brown hair glowing bronze and gold in the evening sun.

Adam found it almost impossible to drag his eyes away. Then with an effort he looked round and saw every woman on the lawn staring in obvious hate and envy; every man in desire.

Kristina acknowledged the attention with a brilliant smile and the moment of malice and lust passed. Party hubbub renewed and Kristina

– surrounded by a group of guests – disappeared.

Eva came through the crowd and said, 'Adam. You saw my sister Kristina? I will introduce you later. Now I must speak with my father's guests. I shall sit with you at dinner.'

Kreuz took Adam by the arm and strolled with him to a quiet corner.

'*Adam*?' he murmured, eyebrows raised. 'She calls you Adam? You have become a close friend of the family? And so soon.'

'We walk in the woods most afternoons. It's impossible to remain formal.'

'Of course. Naturally. What do you think of our wonderful Germany?'

'A very modern country.'

'Your journey. It was good? You have studied our culture? I am interested in your comments – but later – we are being called to dinner.'

The evening turned in to an eating and drinking marathon – heavy food and strong wine – course after course and bottle after bottle. The dining room – at first so sophisticated with its summer flower decorations – became a noisy German drinking hall wreathed in cigar smoke.

Adam, sitting between Eva and Paul, lost touch with reality and – awash with alcohol – slipped into a state of gentle euphoria improved by the feel of Eva's fingers tingling along his thigh.

When at midnight a small orchestra began to play under the trees Eva pulled him out into the warm darkness to mould their bodies and sway in a cloud of wine and perfume.

He whispered, 'Am I in heaven?'

She kissed his ear and sighed, 'For only a few minutes. I must find Kristina and make sure she is not causing trouble. I shall come to you later. I promise.'

She led him back to the house and disappeared in the crowd. He stood, unsure what to do next when von Prince appeared and said, 'Join me in the library for a dram. It's quiet and I have some good Scotch whisky.'

'God, no. I've already had far too much to drink.'

'Come now, man. You can take one more. Kreuz is in there waiting for us.'

In the library von Prince poured whisky and said, 'How long will you remain in Germany?'

'About a week. Maybe two.'

'Have you seen much of our country?'

'Not yet.'

Kreuz said, 'That beautiful picture you sent me – thank you so much. It makes a happy reminder of our meeting in Tanga. Have you completed any drawings of trains or installations in Germany? If so I would like to see them.'

Feeling sudden anger, Adam said, 'Why the hell are you asking such a strange question? Are you interrogating me?'

Von Prince grunted and said, '*Herr* Early. We find your position strange. As an English official you turn up in Moshi then in Tanga. Now you are in the centre of Germany no longer an official but making friends with a noble German family with links to our military and government. We find this odd and wonder how you made it all happen?'

In silence both men stared at him.

Grappling with the alcohol whirling in his head Adam stared back, trying to make sense of this strange conversation. 'You're talking nonsense,' he said. 'You *know* I'm here by chance.'

'That is what *you* say.' said von Prince. 'Others may put different explanations on why you are here and what you hope to achieve. I think-.'

Eva burst through the door calling, 'There you are Adam. Kristina. I've found him. Come. Come. He's here. Come and meet him.'

Von Prince rose and left as Kristina danced into the room. In slow English she said '*Herr* Early. I hear much of you from my sister.'

Adam stood to take her hand and felt himself nearly fall into the deep violet eyes staring wide and innocent at him. As their fingers touched an electric tingle passed through his whole body. Startled, he bowed and said, 'Wonderful to meet you.'

'I hear much from Eva. I have no time to speak with you now but can we meet again? I will practise English with you perhaps?'

She enveloped him in diamond bright smile and something deep in her eyes changed abruptly from innocence to...what? A tug of warning passed through Adam. The shift altered her whole face. Red lips turned scarlet. Smile became calculated. Perfect skin became part of a siren's disguise – her voice transforming into an enticing and dangerous song.

From the corner of his eye Adam saw Eva watching closely and shook his head to clear the moment.

'That will be nice.' he said. 'Perhaps you can walk in the woods with Eva and me one day.'

Kristina laughed; slipped fingers loose and danced back through the door; graceful and light as a bird. Eva waved and followed.

Kreuz sighed and shook his head.

'Ah Kristina,' he said. 'What a naughty girl. She is...you have an English word...tease...am I right?'

'Yes. Tease. Is she always like that?'

'Always. She is only eighteen. All the young officers want her. Many are handsome. Some are rich. But so far no one rich *and* handsome has captured her. By the way. Do not be too upset by von Prince. He distrusts all Englishmen. I must tell you as a friend to beware of the man. Both he and Weiss think that you are a British secret agent.'

'Ridiculous.' said Adam.

'Quite.' said Kreuz.

Through lizard eyes von Lettow-Ansbach watched Eva and her Englishman sitting in a corner, heads close, whispering. He frowned: *Should I let this continue? Should I stop it? Does he have money? He must have. He must be rich. Forty thousand hectares. Mein Gott....*

Adam stumbled to his bed, head ringing from political intrigue, wine, violet eyes, red lips and murmured promises.

Between dark and dawn, Eva came. Quiet as a whisper she slipped through the door, slipped out of her gown, slipped into his bed and began their love affair in earnest.

Chapter Seven

Berlin Triangle

Kristina woke troubled by a dream. Naked in bed, eyes closed against bright early sunlight she ran her hands across her perfect body from shoulder to thigh – a habit she enjoyed every morning.

She checked breasts, thighs and buttocks. Firm. Interesting. She stroked and pulled at the silken mat covering her lower stomach. Smooth. Soft.

She lay quiet; fingertips fluttering; but stopped before pleasure diverted her from the fading dream; trying to remember – *What was it? Something to do with Eva and her new man...?*

But the dream vanished so she allowed herself another caress – *Why is she so caught up with the Englishman? What does he do? Perhaps I should have a closer look at him....*

Intrigued by this thought – and her own delicate touch – she fondled the caress into a velvet ripple of contentment that helped her drift off to sleep again.

At Sunday breakfast Eva introduced Adam to two young officers, saying, 'I told them you are from Africa so they want to meet you. This is my cousin Captain von Lettow-Vorbeck. He is a Marine-soldier. And his friend Lieutenant Abel of our German Army.'

Adam shook hands with von Lettow-Vorbeck a solemn round faced man with one eye bandaged.

Abel, young and blond, greeted Adam with brisk enthusiasm and speaking English, said, 'You are from Africa? How wonderful. I go there soon. To *Moschi*. You have been there I understand.'

Before Adam could speak Abel continued, 'My colleague von Lettow-Vorbeck is just returned from West Africa. His wounded eye is from battle with the natives.'

Adam said, 'I hope you recover soon.'

At that moment Kristina swept into the room in a flurry of lace and sparkling eyes, ignoring everyone but Adam who felt himself reel under the force of her brilliant smile.

Enveloped in her charm Adam smiled back and from the corner of his eye saw Eva frown.

In the hour before lunch Eva sat at her window watching Adam stroll on the lawn with Kristina, annoyed at the way he dipped his head, laughing at one of her stupid extravagant stories.

Kristina tapped Adam's arm and stretched her lovely face towards him, violet eyes sparking in the sun.

Eva clenched her teeth: *The witch knows I'm here. She's doing this on purpose. I found him first and she's jealous. If she takes him into the trees I'll be out after them. She won't get her hands on this one....*

Later, Eva said to Adam, 'You are here for only three more days so tonight we shall go for dinner in Berlin. I am sick of all these people and want us to be alone.'

'Alone? Will your father mind?'

'I told him we're meeting friends so he is quite happy.'

She took him to eat in the garden of a small restaurant famous for the discreet inability of owner and staff to remember any face or name. Sitting at her usual inconspicuous table, veiled by hanging roses, Eva sat thigh to thigh with Adam, drinking wine and holding hands.

Near midnight she took him to stroll in warm twilight through crowds along the Kurfürstendamm. Strangely stimulated by an array of brightly dressed prostitutes lining the street she hugged Adam's arm.

'Some of them are so beautiful. Look how well dressed that one is. And what a wonderful figure. Why do they do it?' She shivered; surprised by the pleasure of sudden arousal.

'Money?'

'No they must *like* it. They make much money, but they must enjoy it also. Think of all the different men they meet – all the *exciting* things they do and see. Kristina said once she would like to try it. I am not sure she joked.'

'She knows about this? Ridiculous. She's so young.'

Eva squeezed his arm and laughed.

'You are in Africa sheltered from the evils of Europe. In these big cities we young ladies see and hear and learn so many naughty things. One of the handsome high-born officers you met last week at the hunting lodge often comes here. He picks up one or two of these girls; takes them home and performs with them in front of his wife. Sometimes she must join in.'

'Who told you? His wife?'

'No. He did.'

'My God. Is this true?'

'Ask Kristina. He told her also.'

'How did the subject come up?'

'I cannot remember. But it is true. He told us both.'

Eva decided to share some of her secrets and plans with Kristina. 'I'm sleeping with him but don't tell anyone,' she said.

Kristina shivered with excitement. 'Is he rich?' she asked.

'Of course. But it's all in Africa.'

'How do you know?'

'He told me. And he told father.'

'When does he leave?'

'Wednesday. The day after Midsummer Night.'

'You'll have him for the Carnival – or you'll have him *after* the Carnival.'

Eva giggled.

'Will you miss him?'

'Yes.'

'What will you do?

'Go to Africa and marry him'

'*No*. Really?'

'Yes. I've decided.'

'Does he know?'

'Not yet. But he will before he leaves.'

This news made Kristina determined to gain Adam's interest – *Why let my sister win?*

For three days Kristina placed Adam under subtle and brazen siege. At every chance she touched him; brushed against him as they passed; asked him to fasten a necklace and edged firm buttocks back to test reaction. She dropped her hat and leaned forward to show almost full sight of her perfect breasts as he moved to help.

Like all men exposed to her game she watched him become…fascinated.

Soon. Soon I'll have him….

But Eva knew the game. After all, she had played it so many times on Kristina.

So she said to Adam, 'Be careful of Kristina – she is a bad girl.' Always when we were small – anything I had she wanted. Now I think she wants you. Kristina wants all men who show interest in me. She is using you in a game.'

'Nonsense. She's just a young girl with high spirits.'

'Your naughty Mr Hocklyffe-Evans would know the game and understand what she is playing.'

Of course Adam agreed and tried to ignore Kristina but – *Oh God how difficult.*

With her startling beauty and determination she attacked his senses at every turn.

I'll be glad to leave in a few days. Get to England and some sanity. Meantime – make the most of it. Sleep with one and lust after the other. Impossible not to....

When Kristina sensed the game slipping away she felt cheated and took cunning revenge.

Von Lettow-Ansbach asked to see Adam again – as before, wintry faced, speaking his careful English.

'*Herr* Early...you leave in two days.'

'Yes, Sir. Thank you for your hospitality.'

'My... daughters. Both show in you interest because... you are... different to... the young men...they mostly see.'

'Yes, Sir.'

'Eva is your...special friend...because...her life...you saved.'

'Thank you, Sir.'

'*Herr* Early. I must...give you gratitude...formally...for... saving my daughter.'

Von Lettow-Ansbach bowed; shook Adam's hand and for a few seconds stood in awkward silence.

'*Herr* Early. With English it is difficult for me to express. You do...not speak...German?'

'No, Sir.'

'French?'

'No, Sir.

'Only English?'

'No, Sir.. I speak Arabic, Urdu and Swahili.'

'Arabic? *Urdu*? *Swahili*? Mein Gott. These... are not languages. These... are... heathen things. Barbaric. They are not... *educated* things.'

Von Ansbach's features frosted further, his lips an icy twist.

'And now *Herr* Early. I must ask...I must...*insist*...that you leave here and do not...contact my daughters again. Not Kristina. Not Eva. Not...ever.'

'Goodness gracious, Sir. Why not?'

Von Lettow-Ansbach bowed his head, lips moving; apparently checking his English grammar and what to say next. Apparently

satisfied, he nodded and said, 'They have duty here. They cannot...
be... diverted. That is all.'

'What on earth was he talking about?' Adam asked Eva.
'Kristina. She has done this. She is awful. She told him a secret. I
will kill her one day.'
'What secret?'
'I'll tell you before you leave. I promise.'

Adam sat holding hands with Eva in the first of two carriages
trailing across Berlin to the railway station and tried to feel regret at
leaving. After all, Eva seemed everything a young man could hope for
as a holiday companion and he'd miss her.
But the others?
He looked at Paul, sitting opposite in the carriage – pleasant but
sombre – and thought of Kristina, Kreuz and Abel following in a
second carriage, accompanied by a servant – 'To protect those two
poor men from Kristina,' Eva had observed.
No interest in seeing any of them again....
But Eva? Adam sighed, confused by his pleasure at having no more
to do with these people and his increasing desire to – somehow – hang
on to Eva.
He looked at her melancholy face and wondered whether to speak
but decided not to and they continued to travel in silence. She leaned
against him, fingers linked and he took comfort from a tear in her eye
– *So she'll miss me too....*
At the station Adam stood with his new friends and his new lover
in a nervous group alongside the train, wishing they'd go home and
leave him with Eva. Paul wandered off with the servant to supervise
loading of Adam's trunks. Eva stood close, her face pale, shifting from
foot to foot. Kreuz broke the mood.
'*Fräulein* Eva. Why do you not make a private farewell on the train?
Herr Early. I bid you farewell, not goodbye. I am sure we shall meet
again in Africa.'
He shook Adam's hand and whispered, 'I'll be glad to get back. I
fear a war here in Europe. Our Kaiser is determined to make the most
of this latest Russian problem.'
Abel bowed and shook hands. 'In *Moschi* perhaps? We meet in
Moschi?'
Kristina stepped forward, offered Adam her hand. The tingle of her
touch shivered through him.

She said, 'I look forward to our next meeting.'

Her eyes opened wide, for a moment innocent and appealing. Then she lowered her lashes and smiled right into his soul and transformed into a devil of lust; tiny pink tongue-tip peeking from crimson lips; lewd eyes; sinuous touch tracing patterns across his palm. Entranced he swayed forward then back and away from this witch.

He managed to mumble, 'Wonderful to have met you. Perhaps we *will* meet again. Who knows.'

She bobbed a mocking curtsey and grinned.

'What a stupid game she plays,' said Eva as Adam helped her climb into the train. 'Ignore her.'

In the compartment she threw her arms round him.

'I shall miss you,' she said in a tragic whisper and started to weep. 'Will you miss me?'

Adam hugged her. 'Please don't cry. What will the others think?'

'Will you write?'

'Of course. As soon as I get to England.'

'And from Africa?'

'Of course.'

'But for how long before you forget me?'

A whistle. Through the window Adam saw a guard waving his light. The engine hissed and eased forward, taking up strain. Their carriage shuddered.

'Quick you must get off. We're going in a moment. Oh damn. I haven't said goodbye to Paul'

'Forget Paul,' she wailed. 'Say you will remember me.'

'Always,' he cried over increasing noise from train and station. 'Always, always, always.'

Train doors slammed.

'You must go. You must go,' he said, pulling from her embrace.

'Not until you kiss me properly.'

She fell forward into his arms; wet face and firm body full against him. He felt lost and overwhelmed as they kissed hard and fierce, heads rolling, tongues and bodies writhing.

She broke off and hissed.

'I am coming to Africa to marry you. Soon. I will come soon. You will have me? Yes?'

A split second pause.

'Yes.'

Triumph surged across her face.

'So. We are engaged. But it is our secret. Tell no-one until I say.

62

Give me one last kiss.'

'You were to tell me a secret. Was this it? Did Kristina know?'

'Yes. I'll tell you in Africa. Write from England.'

The train pulled out. Adam stood by the window waving to the small group. Paul bowed goodbye. Kreuz and Abel saluted. Eva at the front, dabbing at her tears and smiling, waved her handkerchief.

Kristina at the back caught Adam's eye and blew a kiss that said…
The Game Is Not Yet Over.

Chapter Eight

Birth of a Colony

Adam arrived in England excited but surprised at his unexpected engagement and pleased to find that he missed Eva – her image filling his mind and imagination.

His train journey to London passed through quiet countryside, seemingly untroubled by growing turbulence in Europe. During two days shopping in Regent Street and Mayfair, Adam found London relaxed and so...*civilian*...after the aggressive atmosphere of Berlin with all its uniforms, spiked helmets and talk of war.

Adam travelled to the West Country where H.E.'s father and three brothers met him at the station. From the same mould as H.E. – tall smooth men; confident and easygoing – dressed in country tweeds they seemed to Adam as typical of England as Kreuz and von Lettow-Ansbach seemed typical of the Kaiser's Germany.

'How was it among the Hun?' asked Lord Taunton over brandy and cigars after dinner on Adam's first evening at The Hall. 'An odd lot I always think. Are they getting ready to fight anyone? Could you glean if it will be us or the Russians?'

'Difficult to say, Sir. Plenty of sabre-rattling but not in a particular direction. I met mostly soldiers or military families and....'

Lord Taunton sat draped across an armchair; mild blue eyes half closed, listening with polite interest for ten minutes before asking, 'Can you tell me what the Hun *really* thinks of Britain and the British?'

'My friend Major Kreuz felt it strange that our navy dominates the world but we complain when Germany wishes to dominate only Europe.'

Lord Taunton chuckled and said, 'The bugger's probably right. Let's hope they go for the Russians and leave us out of it but if they come west I suppose we'll have to give 'em a hiding and save France.'

Adam smiled to hide his scepticism: *How on earth can these people hope to fight Germany? The Hun will eat them alive. Swallow them in a week.*

He said, 'Then let's hope they go east not west.'

During five days in Somerset, Adam bought and paid for a dozen cattle of different types from Lord Taunton who said, 'This lot should crossbreed well with native animals until you find a good strain. Mix 'em up a bit to discover best combinations for milk or meat and resistance to disease. Rely on your Somali chap. He'll know how to go about it. My experience in India was always to trust a good local if you have one. By the way, a letter arrived for you this morning from my black sheep son in Africa.'

H.E. wrote: *Eliot resigned over some spat with the Foreign Office and is replaced by Donald Stewart. A bit of a boozer, but he seems all right.*

Hurry back. Things are happening quickly here and we need to be involved. Remember the Norfolk Hotel? Started building just before you left? It's become an absolute hotbed of politics full of settlers buying up land and planning to turn this into a white man's country.

That's why you must be back soon. Plenty of good chances going but I can do nothing without you – if I'm nabbed dealing in land there'd be an awful stink.

Be a good chap and bring me some marmalade from London. Simple things are devilish expensive and difficult to get here.

Adam returned to London and saw his cattle loaded on to a cargo ship before travelling by train to Marseilles and boarding a French passenger liner bound for Mombasa where his father waited at dockside.

'Glad to have you back. Your mother will be pleased to see you. How was Germany? How was England? Your cattle arrive on a ship next week. Hocklyffe-Evans asked me to give you this note.'

H.E. wrote: *Waste no time in Mombasa. Come up to Nairobi quickly. We are in trouble....*

Two days later H.E. met Adam at the station and said 'Thank God you're back. We're running out of money'

'How?'

'Everyone buys but no one pays. Your Indian clerk keeps a beautiful set of books with every damned chit filed neat as a pin so we know who owes what. I can't get involved so you must chase money fast. The bank's making threats. We'll be broke in no time if you don't act. I've arranged a meeting for you straight after we've had breakfast.'

Adam met his new bank manager; a surprisingly young man with an open friendly face. He said, 'I'm John Martins. I've been rushed across from Bombay to replace old Smithson and sort a few problems out – such as no money coming in to cover your big loan.'

Adam said, 'But business is good.'

Martins said, 'Absolutely. Your Somali is doing well supplying cattle and meat; your Indian is good with the books, but neither knows how to collect. The damned Europeans here ignore an Indian asking for money, and ignore a Somali completely. Get to your office. Check the chits and invoices. Get out and round up the cash.'

Adam went to work. He had never chased money before but learned fast. First he tackled the Railway.

'Just pay,' he demanded, leaning across the chief accountant's desk. 'You've had the meat so bloody-well pay up.'

'The Railway's in trouble, old boy. Now building is complete there's no more cash from London. We have to earn for ourselves. Until more white settlers arrive and start using the bloody line it's going to be a struggle. We're losing money like mad. We have to make the Railway pay but heaven only knows how.' .

'None of this is my fault.'

' Nor mine but tell you what. I'll authorise half now, and pay the rest over six months or so....'

'Not a bad deal.' said John Martins. 'Better than most. I hear the Railway's looking for wood to run their engines. Why not offer to supply? Sell some of your farmland and buy a tract of forest. It'll be cheaper than the land you sell so use the profit to set up as a wood cutter. Should be easy.'

'Typical impractical banker,' grumbled H.E. 'Never have their feet on the ground.'

Sitting on the Norfolk Hotel veranda, surrounded by early evening noise and smells Adam looked round and said, 'Every bloody European in Nairobi must be here, boozing and arguing politics or tapping each other for money.'

'You're right,' said H.E.. 'Every single damned one.'

Adam said, 'They're all looking to build something and they'll need materials to get started. I'm going to sell our Nairobi plots. We should get a good price. I'll clear them and use the cash to buy forest and set up to cut wood.'

'Are you sure?' said H.E. 'Shouldn't we hold on to the plots? They'll be worth a fortune later.'

'If I don't do something we'll go bust. It's not practical to hold on. And I have a buyer to take our fifty thousand acres in the Rift Valley, too.'

66

'Who?'

'Delamere. He wants to extend his Rift Valley estate and we need the money.'

'Oh very well. You're probably right and I may have some forest for you. Lots of trees. Come to the office tomorrow. I'll see what we can sort out. You'll be a wood cutter in no time.'

Adam managed to drag a large overdue meat payment from the Army and sold the shops and Rift Valley land to Delamere for cash.

'You're doing well.' said Martins. 'How much do you need for the forest land?'

'I'm renting not buying. Long lease at one hundred and fifty a year.'

'Good. Use your cash to buy equipment.'

'That's my plan.'

H.E. gave Adam title to a large area of virgin forest high on the Kinangop escarpment eighty miles from Nairobi. 'Difficult to reach up there, old chap, but there's nothing nearer and it's bloody cheap. Look – you'll be selling wood to the Railway. Get them to transport it for you. Cut it. Lay it along the line and let the buggers pick it up. They'll have to agree or their toy trains won't run. You see.'

Abdi Elmi introduced Adam to a young Sikh. Tall, tough and turbaned, with beautiful smile shining through his curled beard.

'I am Anwar Singh, Sir. You need a wood cutting man. I am wood cutting engineer, Sir. I can serve you well.'

Adam climbed the Kinangop with Anwar and twenty Africans, halting on a wide rolling shoulder of grassland facing a mass of grey-green trees crowded together as far as he could see left and right along the escarpment. Thick undergrowth made a barrier through which it seemed nothing could pass.

Adam's heart sank: *What the hell have I taken on?*

He checked his map and said, 'This is the place,'

Two thousand feet below the Rift Valley shimmered in late morning heat. Clear cool air rolled down the mountain, drying his sweat.

Adam said, 'Anwar. Go up and have a look. Tell me what you think.'

'I need no further look, Sahib. I can see that here we have a fortune. From this place we will be rich.'

'Really?' Adam's spirits rose.

'Sir, this wood is good. Straight trees for roofing and planks and soft wood for building houses. You have a good place, Sahib. This week I bring the machinery up *from* the valley and next month I pull logs down *to* the valley. I will do it all for you. You see. I can serve you well.'

At sundown Adam sat in his camp chair looking down at the startling view and, consumed by excitement, wrote to Eva: *I feel as though I am sitting on a great step. The escarpment is so steep below, I think if I fell I would drop straight into Lake Naivasha. We hope to start cutting within fourteen days with a new steam saw. My wood contract with the Railway starts next month. I miss you. We should be together and I want you to see what I am building in this new country. When will you come?*

Eva replied: *Next year. I shall tell my father at Christmas and will be with you by June.*

A few days later von Lettow-Ansbach called Eva to his study.

'I have a fine young officer for you to meet. You will welcome him tomorrow.'

'I have no interest Father.'

'You will show interest. Since you lost Manfred von Heinseck I have been planning your next introduction. This offer is from a good family. They like you.'

'I have no interest Father.'

'You will do as I say.'

Eva bobbed a curtsey and went to bed, where she stayed for two weeks. Kristina brought medicine and food. Eva ate the food, and threw the medicine away.

In fury von Lettow-Ansbach offered Kristina to the fine young officer. He liked Kristina but his parents did not. No marriage contract transpired.

'He was useless anyway,' Kristina complained to Eva. 'I couldn't get him out of his trousers.'

Delamere came to Adam's table at the Norfolk and said, 'I hear you're cutting wood on Kinangop? Can you supply me two thousand fence posts for Njoro? I need them quickly.'

Adam signed a contract next morning.

Others heard of his wood cutting business and gave orders for posts, planks and logs.

'Can you cope with it all?' asked H.E.

'I'll try.'

'Just as well, 'cos we have new settlers arriving on every ship. You'll have a wonderful market when they all start building farms and houses.'

'I'll need more machinery up on the Kinangop.'

'Don't wait. Buy it now. Get it installed or you'll never be able to keep up.'

'You're sure we're not going too fast?'

'No such thing as too fast. Everyone here's trying to grab their piece before everyone else. We're ahead of the buggers so just keep bloody-well going and stay in front.'

On Christmas Eve Adam met Thinman at Nairobi station.

'Good of you and H.E. to ask me for the festive season,' said Thinman, 'But you look exhausted.'

'Too much damned work,' said Adam.

'You'll kill yourself. You must put your feet up and rest over the holiday.'

'Fat chance with H.E. around.'

At one point over Christmas and New Year Adam wondered if he could survive the continual drunken parties at the Norfolk and the Nairobi Club.

On New Year's Eve the three men staggered into H.E.'s house some time after midnight and sat smoking cigars.

H.E. groaned and rubbed his face. 'Oh God. Nineteen-Four was hard but I think Nineteen-Five will be worse. What can we do to make it better?'

Before Adam could stop his tongue it said, 'I'm going to get married.'

He clenched his teeth in anger – *Bloody alcohol.*

'Married?' mumbled H.E. *'Married'?* To your German I'll bet. What on earth for?'

'Why shouldn't he?' snapped Thinman. 'Tell me why he shouldn't?'

'Because she's a bloody Hun that's why.'

Having committed himself, Adam decided to blunder on and mumbled, 'She's coming in June. You'll be best man.'

'Will I, by God? Will I? I knew you were up to something. I knew you were getting letters. *And* I knew you were writing back. I've seen you scribbling away.'

H.E. rolled his large blond head from side to side in a slow wise wag and said, 'I suppose you've found *one* way of making Nineteen-Five better. I'll tell you another. It's a secret. Not a word to anyone. The secret is...that this Protectorate is being transferred from Foreign Office to Colonial Office.'

'What difference will that make?' asked Adam.

'Think man. It's bloody obvious. As a Protectorate we're....*foreign*...here in East Africa. Under the Colonial Office this *Protectorate* could become a *Colony*.'

'I see no practical difference.' said Thinman.

'Oh for God's sake wake up. In a Protectorate we're *visitors*. We're only *protecting* the bloody place. As a Colony we *own* it. Lock stock and barrel. All the land. All the lakes. Every-bloody-thing. Think of the opportunities.'

'And the dangers,' said Thinman. 'How can a few thousand white men keep several hundred thousand natives under control?'

'That's what you buggers are for,' said H.E. 'That's why we have an army.'

In February Adam met H.E. in his office and said, 'This wood cutting idea is not so good. It needs a lot more capital than I planned. The wood is difficult to get at. Anwar's doing his best, but I'll need help if I'm to continue.'

'What do you want?'

'More markets. I need to export.'

'But this country is building fast.'

'Not fast enough for me to continue and survive. I'll have to give up.'

'You can't. Things are hard for the High Commissioner just now. He's trying to bring in more white settlers to convince London we can turn this place into a viable Colony.. He needs industry and building materials to show we're serious. *And* we need logs to keep the trains running. You can't just give up.'

'I shall unless you help.'

'How?'

'I can't continue without export. I'll find markets but need land at the Coast – about 200 acres with deep water frontage – to use as a wharf. Without that I'll have to give up.'

H.E. looked uneasy. 'I can't be involved in this one. Too risky.'

'Then I'll do it alone.'

'It'll be expensive. How much can you pay?'

'Nothing. I want it free to help me invest properly up at Anwar's.'

'Hang on a minute old chap. Taking land without paying is a new idea. You're being a bit hard aren't you?'

'No. If you can't agree I'll stop cutting and bring Anwar off the mountain.'

'That's a bloody strong line.'

'I must be tough and selfish like everyone else here. I stand to lose everything. If the wood cutting goes under so do Mzito and Damu. So you'll lose as well.'

'I'll speak to the High Commissioner.'

A week later Adam received a message from H.E: *You win. Come and see me. Stewart's granting you two hundred and fifty acres at the Coast. You bloody pirate.*

In Berlin Eva stood with her father in his study.

'You cannot leave Berlin.' he said.

'I am going, Father.'

'I forbid you.'

'Father. I am twenty three years old. You cannot forbid me.'

'I am arranging your marriage into a rich Prussian family. They have money and land.'

'I also have money Father. Enough to get to Africa where I will have a rich husband and plenty of land. Forty thousand hectares.'

'The Englishman. The damned Englishman. You will not go. You will do as I say.'

' I'm engaged. It is too late for you to tell me what to do.'

He shouted 'I'll cut you off with nothing.'

'You fool.' Eva shouted back 'You absolute fool. You have nothing to cut me off from. You and your stupid father lost all this family had.'

'Go then you wretched hussy. Abandon your family. Run to your foreigner. Forget your country. Leave your Kaiser. Desert us all.'

'With pleasure.' said Eva. 'With great pleasure. I *hate* it here.'

'Did you say all that?' asked Kristina. 'Did you really?'

Eva wrote to Adam: *I sail from Marseilles in May. What a great adventure. It will be wonderful. Kristina is coming with me as companion on the voyage and to be my bridesmaid....*

Chapter Nine

Arriving

Nairobi: 1905

'I am here expected to live?' Eva asked, aghast.

Adam looked at his wife staring in anger at the small mud house.

'What's wrong with it?'

'This is the Mzito Estate you told me about?' she asked, incredulous. 'I cannot live in such a place. *Es ist ein Loch.* A hovel. In Prussia the lowest peasant would not put *animals* in such a bad home.'

She pointed at a small shack a few yards away. Inside two Africans crouched by a small charcoal stove, fanning at glowing coals with a couple of wide banana leaves.

'What's that?'

'The kitchen.'

'The kitchen? The *kitchen. Himmel.* And that?'

'The lavatory.'

'But it is fifty meters from the house. I am to walk fifty metres across Africa to shit?'

'Darling. Don't talk like that.'

'It is true. You expect me to leave this hole I will live in to go to that hole and shit? At night? In Africa?'

'You've been in Africa before. You know what it's like.'

She ducked under the low door. Staring hard at the brushed mud floor and rough wooden furniture she moved through the two rooms.

'This is where I am to sleep?' she asked. 'This is a bed?' She pointed at the large home made frame balanced on eight thick cut logs.

'Darling this *is* Africa.'

'So was Mombasa but there we slept in a real house. In Moshi we Germans had real houses. What have I come to here? A railway camp for a town. A hut for a home. Why could we not stay in Mombasa? You have land there.'

'All our work is here, that's why.'

'I thought you had a big estate. I expected a big house. I thought you were rich. You did not tell me the truth about this place.'

Eva stormed outside into the sun, turned and glared at him. Straight back, frozen face. An angry Prussian. 'Why have you told me lies?'

'We do have a big estate. This is only part of it. In Africa all estates are big. This house is just a start. We build from what we have. If you don't like this you'll have to live in a tent. Now for God's sake settle down.'

Her shoulders slumped in despair.

'What have you brought me to? *Mein Gott*. Perhaps Berlin was not so bad after all.'

Standing at Kilindini dockside in late May Adam knew he would never forget the flutter and sparkle of that moment when Eva and Kristina stepped ashore. Sun and wind caught their mood – two brightly beautiful young women, brimful with youth and excitement. A fresh warm breeze whipped their long dresses into colourful banners. Their wide brimmed hats flapped and twisted like bird wings. Tense and happy Adam embraced Eva.

'Darling,' said Eva, kissing him on the cheek but brushing her body against his in a move full of promise.

'My parents,' introduced Adam. 'And you know my friend H.E.'

Kristina curtsied at each introduction. H.E. bowed and smiled. To Eva he said 'How lovely to meet you again,' to Kristina, 'Adam never mentioned you.'

For seconds Kristina seemed transfixed, deep violet eyes wide and startled, her small hand lost in H.E.'s. Adam smiled and later laughed when H.E. said, 'She hung on like a leech, by God. I couldn't get free. Is she always like that?'

'I thought you'd *never* let go,' hissed Eva in German as they travelled by rickshaw through Mombasa. 'You really are terrible. You must behave here. You must promise.'

'But he's so beautiful,' said Kristina. 'I've never seen anyone so tall and blond and beautiful. I just fell in love with him. So it *does* happen at first sight.'

'Promise you'll behave.'

'I'll try.'

'If you spoil my wedding, I'll kill you.'

Two days later, wearing a beautiful white gown, Eva married at Mombasa Cathedral. She felt so alive and beautiful and knew she dominated the gathering as a bride should. Almost the whole European population of Mombasa attended – six women and forty men – the ladies colourful and pretty in their best gowns. Eva felt relieved that Kristina, dressed in pale blue, managed to look virginal and did not try to dominate the ceremony..

Drawn from her wedding in a carriage decorated with white and pink frangipani, Eva gripped her husband's strong young hand and whispered, 'Nothing is more perfect than this day.'

At her reception Eva laughed without jealousy when the men – young, bronzed and virile – crowded round Kristina, the only unmarried woman present. 'They're so wonderful.' Kristina whispered to Eva. 'Not like our poor pale Prussians. Only that man Thinman. *He's* like a Prussian.'

At her honeymoon cottage. – flower covered thatch glowing among palm trees by a beach of brilliant white sand – she embraced Adam and whispered, 'I did not think any day could ever be so wonderful.'

Eva had slept with a number of men in and around Berlin – either on her father's instructions or out of curiosity – but she found her honeymoon a different encounter. Fascinated by this new experience and the man she had taken for husband, she felt sure that love – whatever that is – would come and grow.

For seven days she wandered the deserted shore with Adam; floated naked in green-blue sea as warm and smooth as milk, happy to do whatever he wanted as they stroked, touched, nuzzled and explored each other all day and night.

Low tide left a shallow lagoon of crystal clear pools to splash through, collecting shells and coloured weed. Musa and the servants gathered fresh fish and fruit to be eaten at languorous breakfast or long slow lunch into the heat of afternoon. Dinner at dusk – a slow dreamy affair served at a table set on white sand away from the trees and mosquitoes, under a white crescent moon above silver sea. Then to bed, for a night of love.

'I could stay here forever,' she whispered one morning, waking in soft dawn light. Wrapped only in a shawl she watched the sun rise from the sea, 'Our own Garden of Eden.'

At first Kristina felt dissatisfied when Eva left for honeymoon. All the bronzed young men disappeared back to wherever they came from and left her with Adam's boring parents in their boring house.

Then H.E. turned up – 'Sorry I couldn't come earlier. Affairs of state y'know. Now I have a couple of days off let me show you some of the island.'

On their first rickshaw ride she started her seduction game, swaying against him; pretending alarm and grabbing at his arm or thigh when a wheel dipped through a pothole. She giggled at his jokes, and gave full attention to his every word – and when out with him dressed to show herself at best advantage.

From the first she realised H.E. understood the game and played it back in his own way – his casual blue eyes sweeping across her pretty display with only mild interest and a lazy smile.

She worked hard to snare him and once – when walking on the beach – she slipped and fell against him; holding on and connecting hard with her hips, laughing up into his eyes.

He pressed back briefly, then without effort lifted her clear of the ground and swung her round to regain balance.

'How light you are,' he said.

'How strong *you* are,' she giggled, cringing at the sound of a schoolgirl with a crush.

For two days he played his side of the game well but in the end his resistance weakened – as she knew it would – *Takes a strong man to win against me....*

She said, 'We shall go swimming together.'

'Alone? Without a chaperone? How naughty.'

On Bamburi Beach she selected a tree in sparse undergrowth so he could peek at her changing. Before pulling on her bathing suit she managed to lose her shift to a sharp breeze.

Turning to grasp at the fluttering material she stepped from behind the tree to give him full view of her beautiful body gleaming in the sun. Long hair flying, she stooped to half-cover her modesty and – almost in her bathing suit – danced across white sand into the sea, turning to watch him follow, huge shoulders heaving, blond hair flying. *Oh how lovely he is. I'll have him here in the water....*

No. The damned man still resisted.

She stood close to him, chest deep; breasts swaying in the warm waves. Excited by the movement she threw her arms across his shoulder, clamped her hips against his thigh and slithered round crotch to crotch to give him a real feel of what she could do. Gentle currents moved them in a slow dance. His hands lingered across her buttocks, holding her hard against him, then, to her disappointment he lifted her away and said 'Let's swim.'

He splashed off across the blue water, laughed and looked back. Pouting, she paddled after him, annoyed at losing this round and decided to change tactics, almost ignoring him for the rest of the day.

At dinner she observed him studying her in the candle glow and – feeling victory may be near – allowed him a few flashes from her violet eyes: *Tonight perhaps....*

Normally Kristina sat chatting after dinner but tonight she said, 'Such a tiring day in the sun,' and went early, down the corridor to her room.

Knowing that H.E. always stayed up alone for a last cigar, she waited until sure the others had retired then opened her bedroom door, set the lamp to a soft glow and draped herself in display across the bed – sheet tossed aside as though too warm in the sultry night.

Arranging her nightgown to show a swell of buttocks, she threw out an arm to emphasise her breasts and lay with legs just enough apart to be interesting, fingertips fanned along an inner thigh. Spreading her long hair across the pillow she turned her head towards the door, closed her eyes and breathed through soft wet lips.

She heard him pause at her door...heard him enter...sensed him standing...felt him gazing down at her charms. She did not move: *Look you bastard. Just look and see what you're missing. When you're ready – come and get it....*

She heard a puff of breath and the click of her door latch as he blew out the light and left. *The bastard. He's gone. He's abandoned me.*

In furious frustration she beat her pillow into shape and lay fuming for an hour before drifting off to sleep

Just before dawn she heard him return. Through half open eyes she saw him standing just inside the door, blond hair tousled, *kikoi* folded round his hips, his shape showing through the thin material.

At last. He's ready. I have him....

To keep up the game, she stirred and turned away from him; stretched; moved her legs; rolled back and opened her eyes to greet... an empty room.

Mein Gott, the bastard's gone. What the hell can I do to get him into bed and on top of me?

During that day Kristina ignored H.E. but went into dinner wearing a light low cut dress, skin glowing, burnished hair brushed long down her back, prepared for a final fling at winning. H.E.'s table talk remained as smooth and urbane as always, but – *at last* – she saw his eyes continually slide over her body and his sexual tension rise. Delighted at his obvious surrender, she began to plan her winning moves for tonight: *Tonight. I'll win tonight....*

After the others left for bed Kristina and H.E. sat up longer than usual, not speaking. H.E. finished a second cigar, drained his glass and raised an eyebrow. Kristina sipped the last of her wine, smiled and nodded.

With true grace she lifted herself from the sofa and walked with H.E. down the corridor. At her door he stopped, took her hand, looked deep into her glowing violet eyes and said...'Goodnight.'

With a mocking smile he turned and went to his room.

Shocked and angry she flounced into her room and stood before her lovely image in the mirror. *What's wrong with the man? He's not natural.*

She glared at herself and decided – *Action. Now for action. Like a soldier. A Prussian. The final assault.*

She stripped naked and slipped into a filmy white nightgown then tiptoed down the corridor and in through his unlatched door.

He lay back on his bed, *kikoi* thrown casually across his middle and watched with a lazy smile – *Good God – the bastard's waiting for me....*

She tiptoed to the bedside, bare feet whispering on the floor, making sure that soft lamplight shone through the gossamer gown to give full display of her lovely young curves.

She leaned over the light and her breasts tipped forward: dainty; enticing.

He smiled.

Her whiff of soft breath blew out the flame.

She threw herself upon him.

They wrestled and sweated the whole night.

No words.

No love.

Just lust.

Eva returned from honeymoon, relaxed and happy to settle with Adam into a large room overlooking the dhow harbour. Later she sat on the veranda with Kristina, head to head, whisper to whisper. True sisters.

Kristina said 'That man H.E. is so wonderful. But very strange. I got him to bed once but since then he shows no interest in me. I don't know why. I don't know what to do.'

'Kristina. You promised to be good while you were here. Do you want to ruin everything for me? Why are you so attracted to him?'

' I never before met such a man, so difficult to understand. I find him fascinating. From the moment I saw him.'

'Perhaps you love him.'

'Impossible. I never love any man. I never will.'

'How do you know?'

'What does either of us know about love? Do you love Adam?'

'Almost.'

Adam returned white and angry from the District Office with a sheaf of land maps. Taking H.E. aside he said 'You've cheated me.'

'How?'

'Look at these plans. This is not land on the Island. It's on the north coast.'

'What's wrong with that?'

'I wanted land on the Island. I've been cheated.'

'Not by me, old boy. I asked for what you wanted. Two hundred acres you asked for. Look at these plans – you've been given almost three hundred. Deep water frontage. At Mombasa. That's what you asked for and that's what you have. Completely free. You're not paying one rupee. Why should you complain?'

Adam took a boat across to the north shore with Eva, Thinman and his father to check his plot of land.

While Thinman and Eva strolled through the bush chatting, Adam and his father surveyed and marked the area in growing satisfaction – especially when Adam found a small freshwater spring trickling from the plot towards the sea.

Adam double-checked his survey and said, 'Thank God this water rises inside my boundary. Say nothing to H.E. or anyone else. This makes the land much more valuable. We'll get the plot properly registered before we let anyone know. Not a word.'

Thinman returned with Eva and said, 'This is a good flat plot. And look the water depth on your frontage. This'll make an excellent wharf when you need it.'

Eva hugged Adam and said, 'Darling. This is lovely. We can build a house here?'

'Why not? Good idea. We'll think about it.'

With H.E.'s help Adam managed to get the land registered within five days.

'You seem more satisfied with your piece of land now,' said H.E.

'I have to make the best of a bad job,' Adam replied.

'Talking of a bad job – how much longer is the lovely Kristina with us?'

'She's leaving next week. Thinman's taking her down to the German border. Her father arranged for her to meet Abel, that officer I told you about from Berlin. He'll escort her to Dar-Es-Salaam and a ship home.'

'Thank God for that.'

'Why are you so bloody offhand and rude to the poor girl?'

'Not married, old boy. I like my doxies married. No responsibility, you see. I hate responsibility. *And* Madam Kristina's a bit of a tiger – or perhaps a leech. She's made several grabs at me. Interesting story. I'll tell you later when we have time.'

'I don't want to hear.'

'Oh you'll enjoy the tale. We'll swap stories when I see you in Nairobi in a couple of weeks. Did I mention I'm off tomorrow morning?'

At the station next day H.E. shook hands with Adam, pecked Kristina on the cheek, hugged Eva more warmly than he should and waved as the train puffed and shuddered out.

Just after dawn three days later Thinman marched into the bush with a small line of porters, two tents, and Sakayo. Kristina, trotting along beside Thinman, looked back and blew kisses with a bright smile.

'Seems pleased to go,' said Adam.

Eva said, 'She lost interest in us when H.E. went. Now she needs new places and new men to interest her. Darling...when do we go to Nairobi and our estate?'

'Next week.'

Riding through Nairobi in a rickshaw Eva looked round in shock.

'This is a town?' she asked. 'There's nothing here.'

'It's new,' said Adam. '

She winced as the rickshaw rattled through rain filled potholes, jarring her spine.

'This is a dirt track not a road,' said Eva. 'Are those trees dead?'

'They've only been planted a short time. We're trying to smarten the place up. The road is new. Everything's new. Only really started two years ago from a railway camp. Before that no one expected it to be a town.'

'It still looks like a railway camp,' said Eva. 'I see no proper buildings, just these few wooden places on legs. How can this be a town?'

'To us it's a town. It will be beautiful in a few years. We're staying a few nights at the new Norfolk Hotel. That'll give you some idea of what the future is.'

The Norfolk pleased her. 'Built from stone,' she said. 'Just like Europe. When do we go to our estate?'

'Next week.'

'Good. I'm dying to see it and get settled in.'

Eva stood with Adam on the hill overlooking Nairobi.

'This is where we'll build our town house,' he said. 'See out over the plain. Lovely isn't it?'

She laughed. 'But darling. What is a town house when we have no town?'

She held his hand, looking down the slope at Nairobi. Adam pointed out the railway station, the Norfolk Hotel, a few scattered wooden buildings, the lines of dirt roads threading through empty grassland.

She said, 'It's spread out, but really all so small with nothing here. In Berlin when you spoke of Nairobi I expected more.'

Adam hugged her and said, 'It'll be more. It will *all* be more and *we* shall build it.'

'We will, we will,' she cried and overcome with excitement she spread her arms and danced in the sun; skipping through the trees; hair and skirt flying.

'But darling,' she cried, whirling and laughing. 'This is a lovely spot for a lovely house. I don't care about your silly little town. When do we start to build? Can it be soon? Can it be soon?'

Caught up in her mood he laughed and joined in her dance, holding hands and spinning with her.

'When we have the money,' he shouted at the sky. 'When we have the money.'

Lost in her thrill of the moment she didn't hear.

Eva's mood of excitement lasted all week. She loved everything. The people, the place, and, most of all, Adam. When, at last, they left for Mzito, walking out of Nairobi at sunrise, she continued to bubble.

Their small safari wound through the bush, following a well worn track north. Eva strode along in front with Adam. A strong young woman, marching with her man.

After three hours Adam said 'We've arrived.'

'Where?'

'Mzito. We just crossed our boundary.'

'I saw nothing.'

She looked round.

'Oh we have no fences or markers yet.'

They climbed up through trees and over the rise. Adam pointed.

'Our house,' he said.

Eva looked.

'Where?'

'There. See those cattle. Just beyond.'

'I see no house.'

'Of course you do darling. Look. There.'

'That is our house? You are making fun? It's a doll's house made of grass and dirt. You make fun of me. Really darling. Where is our house?'

'Eva. That's it. That's our house.'

'It can't be. You are joking with me.'

'Come and look.'

She followed him past the cattle, her face white and strained. Stunned, she stared in anger at the small mud hut. In shock her heart fluttered.

Her mind reverted to German: *Mein Gott. He's not joking. He says the truth. He's not playing with me. It is true.*

'I am here expected to live?' she asked, staring in anguish at what seemed to be an outhouse for storage of rubbish.

Oh God. What have I come to? Kristina. Father. What have I done...

Chapter Ten

Mzito

Unsure how to deal with Eva in this mood of angry despair, Adam went about estate business through the afternoon, touring and inspecting the cattle stockade, grazing area and herders' huts. Eva trailed along, nodding when he pointed out or explained some matter of interest. He could see her taking it all in but could not tell what she made of it.

At sundown Adam sat with Eva outside the house drinking beer and watching the snows of Mount Kenya change colour from white, to pink to purple then back to white as the moon rose.

'Beautiful, isn't it,' he said.

Eva shrugged and sighed but later, over dinner, her mood seemed to improve when she smiled and said, 'These Africans are more efficient than I thought.'

In the small living room, lit by oil lamps, she sat opposite Adam on a rough wooden chair at the rough wooden table. Servants brought food at a trot across grass from the kitchen while Musa stood by the door supervising and keeping things moving the serving and clearing of four courses.

Eva said, 'And this food is very good. Imagine it is cooked only on that small charcoal burner'

Adam leaned across and took her hand, relieved at the change: *Thank God she's back with me.*

Eva said, 'That soup was good. What is it made from?'

'I don't know,' said Adam. 'I never know what I'm going to have. Cook decides with Musa, same as every other meal. I just eat what they bring.'

'You leave it to the servants to decide what you will eat?'

'Yes. It seems simpler than worrying myself. Musa sorts it all out and makes it work. It's always like that.'

'This cheese. Where does it come from?'

'Sandbach-Baker's place, next door. His wife Queenie makes it. Nice couple. You'll meet them once we're settled in. She'll be company when I'm away. Queenie makes good butter and cheese from a dairy herd she's started. Quite clever.'

'I will start to do some work,' said Eva. 'I shall think of something.'

An hour later she lay beside Adam in the big bed.

'This is more comfortable than it looks.' she said. 'Who made it?'

'Anwar. He found special wood for the frame and spent hours

cutting and measuring the legs. He carried it down from the mountain with porters and brought it the rest of the way by train. Musa and a couple of men wove the base straps from dried cowhide then spent two days scraping and levelling the floor so the bed didn't tilt.'

Eva bounced up and down. ' And the mattress is so soft.'

Adam laughed. 'A little Greek in Nairobi made it and stuffed it with dried grass then couldn't find needles anywhere so sewed it with sharpened bicycle spokes. Very clever. Next time I see him I'll say you like it.'

'It is better than my bed in Berlin. And made in such a way. How funny.'

'You can tell Musa in the morning and the Greek when you meet him.'

'I shall thank them all for working so hard to make sure I sleep well. Now come over here and I will thank you...'

Adam took Eva everywhere with him in the next few weeks – 'So you start learning about the estate,' – and watched her mood swing almost daily from happy interest to dull annoyance. He found it difficult to understand why some days she seemed bright and excited and other days woke in silent gloom. Then she remained listless and sullen until – for no apparent reason – an abrupt switch brought her back to life.

But he could see her beginning to settle and take part in his daily life. She tramped with him round the estate and began to take interest in running the house and kitchen. Walked to and from Nairobi several times. Helped check and count cattle in from the North and out to Damu.

One morning after a count he frowned and said, 'Abdi didn't collect enough this time.'

'They seem many to me.'

'Not enough to fill our contracts. We need more. We'll be in trouble soon.'

'What trouble?'

'Money trouble.'

'Before I came I thought you were rich.'

'No one here is rich.'

'How did you buy all the land?'

She sat and listened as he told her everything, including H.E.'s involvement.

'How much do we owe the bank?' she asked and whistled at his reply. 'Will we ever repay?'

'I don't know. Not at this rate of cattle buying.'

He expected the bad news to cast her back into black moods and felt surprised at how happy and cheerful she became.

'Why?' he asked. 'Aren't you worried?'

'About money? No. Our family never had money. But here I can work and help you do something about it. In Berlin my father did not allow me to work. He kept me as an ornament. Here I can be a normal person. I shall build us a proper house. Your man Anwar from the sawmill can help me.'

Over the next two months Eva put all her energy into planning her house. While Adam travelled upcountry she stayed at Mzito. She planned and drew and paced and studied and measured and calculated for days before choosing a grove of trees on a rise, looking north towards the Kenya mountain. When Adam returned, she said, 'Darling, please survey this plot for my house.'

Dissatisfied, she said, 'Survey again,' and moved the plot two hundred yards and asked for a third survey.

Finally satisfied, she kissed him and said, 'This I accept. Here will my house be.'

Anwar came down from the mountain twice and sat with Eva all day and most of the night then returned to the sawmill and exchanged long letters and documents by messenger and post. Anwar wrote in elegant beautifully crafted copperplate. Eva replied in angular sharp edged German script, as distinctive as her accent.

By early October Eva hugged Adam in triumph and said, 'Soon my house will be started to build.'

He smiled and kissed her, saying, 'Perhaps you'll have it ready for when I return in two weeks.'

Eva waved him goodbye and, depressed at the prospect of two weeks alone in this damned wilderness, went to bed early.

She woke next morning at dawn from a dream of Berlin with her hometown so clear in her mind that for a moment she could not focus. She blinked to clear her eyes and brain. Reality flooded back and with a trough of depression.

Of course. I'm in Africa. I'm still in bloody Africa....

Her eyes roamed round the primitive room made worse by the grey dead pre-dawn light. She almost wept in despair. *Windows?* Square holes in the mud walls. *Curtains?* Hemp sacking tacked to the wall through which curious cattle sometimes pushed their heads. Mosquitoes, insects and occasional birds entered at will.

Oh God. How did I come to be in a place like this?

Movement on the ceiling caught her eye. *Ceiling?* The inside ragged grass of a badly made thatched roof across which a lizard crept.

She lay back, watching the lizard hunt following its slow movement over the thatch, each foot lifting and hovering as the lizard – small, white and muscular – reached position near a large yellow butterfly.

Her heart went out for the lizard and butterfly: *How beautiful they both are. What a pity one must die.*

From twice its own length the lizard uncurled and whipped its tongue as fast as an arrow. The butterfly with no time to move – not even quiver – crunched into the lizard's gullet and disappeared.

Eva shivered: *Thank God I'm not a butterfly. Or perhaps I am. If so I must change into a lizard or I'll die. I survived Africa once. But only because of Adam. Now I'm here for a lifetime I must change and become stronger and discover how to live and survive in this country for myself.*

She rose; wrapped herself in a shawl and went out on to the grass, breathing the cold air of morning. Fresh and crisp it flushed through her body, cleaning her lungs and clearing her mind.

Holding her head high she sniffed at the morning: *Air like wine. Air like wine. An old phrase I've heard so often but this morning I know what it means. This is air like wine. This they don't have in Berlin. This is real air like wine.*

Holding her shawl tight Eva wandered into her grove of trees. *Here is where I shall live. In my wooden house under my African thatch.*

She opened her lungs and breathed again – a huge inhaling of her new air; her new life.

An inner eye opened in her soul and Eva saw her new Africa in pure fresh sunlight shafting through the trees and into her heart.

She leaned against a tree savouring the perfumes of Africa – trees; flowers; dung; wood smoke – and fell deeply; instantly; irrevocably in love with the place.

Mein Gott. I really love it here. Have I loved it all the time and not noticed? Or has it seduced me?

With new eyes she looked around at her wondrous new morn and almost wept.

Musa appeared from the labour lines.

'Breakfast Memsahib?'

'Yes. Out here. Among the trees.'

Impassive, Musa brought a camp table and chair.

Completely in love with her newborn world, Eva sat and marvelled at the beauty of an English breakfast. Bacon and eggs. *What perfume.* Tea. *What flavour.* Toast and marmalade. *How crisp and sweet. Why have we Germans never discovered it?*

She sighed in ecstasy.

I shall build my house veranda here and relive this moment every morning of my African life. Breakfast at dawn. Outside. Watching Africa reappear. Rediscovered each day. My own personal miracle.

Chapter Eleven

Eva's House

Eva, sitting with her damaged foot up on a log watching five Sikhs beating heavy wood piles into the ground, turned and waved when H.E. turned up with a small safari. He strode over the rise, huge shoulders heaving, long blond hair straying in damp lumps from under a heavy sun helmet.

He bent to kiss Eva. She made a face and pushed him away. 'How horrible. Your face is all sweaty.'

'Course it is,' he grumbled. 'I'm not designed for this bloody safari business.'

As his servants pitched camp and raised a tent he sat drinking tea with Eva and talking at high speed, 'Darling Eva. You look lovelier than ever. Marriage suits you. What's wrong with your foot?'

'I fell and broke my ankle.'

'How?'

'Went for a walk and slipped on a stone in the river. Some Kikuyu saved me. They used to live in this area so I've let them build a village in the valley.'

'Kikuyu? *Saved* you? Heavens. What luck. But do you want them nearby. They're terrible robbers. Likely to steal anything you leave lying around – including cattle.'

Eva laughed. 'Musa said the same but I didn't understand him and thought he said 'Rowbas', so that's what I named their village. A good name, don't you think?'

'Where's your husband? Out on the estate? Send someone to fetch him. What are those Sikhs doing? Building a house? How clever of you. Better than this old mud hut. Can you do one for me on the Nairobi plot? I'm sick of Government quarters.'

That evening, over dinner, Adam said, 'It's good to see you but why have you stopped here when you should be halfway to Nyeri by now?'

'Partly official business, partly unofficial business. First the official stuff. I'm instructing you to go north with a Government warrant and full rights of passage to make a rough survey and report on routes between here and Abyssinia.'

'What on earth for?'

'To give you an excuse to get up there and buy as many cows as you can. A new outbreak of damned cattle fever is so bad that we're planning to close Nairobi to all stock from that area. Movement through affected areas is to be banned and anyone who disobeys arrested – native or European. Only cattle from inside the closed area will be allowed into Nairobi. I've made sure that Mzito is just inside the quarantine boundary.'

'When does the ban start?'

'In two weeks. But we're not telling anyone yet to stop a rush of cattle coming in. So get on with it and bring down enough cows to last several months. If you manage we'll be rich. If you don't we'll be bust. Simple choice.'

'It'll take me at least four weeks to go north, buy cattle, get back, *and* survey.'

'True. So if you're driving cattle back through the quarantine area, for God's sake don't get caught.'

'Why can't I just show my warrant?'

'If you do we'll all be in jail, not just you. I haven't mentioned the warrant and survey to the Commissioner. I'll tell him when you get back – provided you're not in prison.'

Later in bed Eva whispered, 'Why should H.E. talk of prison? Is what you are doing wrong?'

'Not wrong. Just illegal.'

During Adam's absence Eva's broken ankle improved then healed. She began to take control of day to day estate work, learning as she went along and at the same time supervising the building of her house.

The Sikhs built with speed and expertise. They had first arrived on three ox-wagons loaded with a bewildering assortment of wood and planks.

'We are from Anwar, Madam,' beamed grey beard. 'I am Inderjeet – Anwar's uncle. He sends good wishes.'

For two days Inderjeet and his men plotted, checked, measured and prepared, before hammering a pattern of heavy wooden piles into place – 'To take the floorboards, Madam,' said Inderjeet. When he suspended heavy flat-planed logs to link the piles Eva could see – with growing excitement – the ground plan of her house, just as on the drawings she and Anwar had scrawled those months before.

Eva's neighbour Queenie Sandbach-Baker came to stay for two days.

'Darling. What a wonderful house this will be. What is that long section?'

'A long corridor to the long drop – the lavatory. I want it well away from my bedroom.'

Queenie laughed in delight.

'No more stumbling through darkest Africa in the dark. No more being chased by hyena. How lovely. What a wonderful idea. Can I have one when you do my house?'

Another few days of setting, hammering and sawing brought more excitement for Eva watching the walls go up.

Receiving a message that Anwar had sent more wood for the house, Eva travelled with three ox-carts to Nairobi, accompanied by Musa and three of her Sikhs. She planned to stay three days checking Damu – although she hated the place – and buying a large tin bath and water tank. Delamere turned up on her second evening. He sat, drank and chatted for ten minutes then handed her a bag of money.

'For some fence posts I bought from your husband,' he said. 'Tell him I'll need more when he gets back from the north.'

'How do you know Adam is in the north?'

'Bush telegraph .'

'Does everyone know where he is?'

'Yes. Where he is and what he's doing.'

'People in the Government too?'

'Yes.'

'Will he get into trouble?'

'Only if he's caught.'

'Will the Government try and catch him?'

'No. They need beef here as much as anyone. Unless he drives his herd through a police post no one will see a thing.'

'*Mein Gott*,' Eva said.

'Exactly. Now get that money down to the bank first thing tomorrow. Martins will be pleased to see you.'

Next morning Eva sat in shade by the railway station watching the Sikhs and Musa load wood from Anwar's on to ox-carts when a short handsome European dressed in khaki trousers, jacket and large brimmed sun hat marched forward waving a short stock-whip.

'Move this bloody stuff out of my way,' he shouted. 'Come on you lot. Now. Move it away. I have stuff to load. You're blocking me.'

The Sikhs, unsure, stopped work. Musa ignored the man and continued.

'You there. *Nigger!* Stop I said. Stop and move this damned stuff out of my way.'

Musa took no notice. Lifting the end of a large plank he motioned a young Sikh to help. The Sikh began to lift but stopped when the man jumped forward waving his whip.

89

'Stop I said. Bloody well stop now or I'll bash you one with this.'

Musa continued to lift, heaving the plank on to the ox-cart.

The man raised his whip and struck Musa across the back shouting in Swahili, 'I told you to stop, you bloody baboon.'

Musa stood immobile as the whip slashed across his shoulders again and rose for a third blow.

But Eva jumped up to snatch the whip from the man's hand and bring it down hard on the back of his neck. He roared in pain and surprise and turned, fist raised.

Eva stepped back and tossed the whip over his head.

It rattled down into the wood-piled ox-cart and disappeared.

'Good God. *Madam*. What on earth did you do that for?' cried the man. 'Where the hell did you come from? Why did you hit me?'

'You were hitting my servant,' shouted Eva. 'Why should you do that?'

'Hah. That accent. I know you. You're Early's wife. You're the bloody German.'

'I may be a bloody German but you have no right to beat my servant.'

'Listen, Madam. I am Stewartby. I'm an Englishman. If I want to discipline a damned African in *British* East Africa I shall do so without interference from a foreigner. Please go. Sit down and leave me to it.'

Eva stepped between Stewartby and Musa.

'To hit him you must first hit me.' she said.

'*Damn* you, Madam. You have no bloody right to interfere. I shall speak to your husband when he returns. And I expect my whip back when you find it. Good day to you.'

He marched off into the station, stiff and important, small aggressive puffs of dust flying up from his heels.

The Sikhs giggled. Musa said nothing. He nodded at Eva and lifted the end of a plank.

An hour later the three ox-carts passed out of Nairobi in procession. Eva perched on the first cart under her coloured parasol, hat brim dipping as she nodded to passing Europeans.

In the desert beyond Mount Kenya, Adam completed his task and set off home with a herd of several hundred cattle. In an area below the mountain, while striking camp at dawn, his herd came under attack by a Somali bandit gang armed with bows and arrows and long spears.

'None of my clan, Sir.' said Abdi Elmi. 'These are bad people.'

Just after sunrise a few of the gang cut out a group of cows and drove them into the bush. Abdi's Somali chased off in pursuit, whooping and calling.

Abdi shouted after them but his men raced away, yelling in excitement, opening the herd to a main thrust from fifty raiders who swept in among the cattle from a concealed gully, waving weapons and shooting arrows.

'Sir,' called Abdi. 'We are alone. Give me a gun. We must shoot at them.'

Abdi, with Adam, his two gun bearers and three servants formed a circle. Adam, Abdi and one of the bearers shot off a few rounds, aiming high to frighten.

The raiders stopped; swung away from the cattle and charged, skipping through thorn bush and over rocks and logs.

Abdi brought up his gun and shot a tribesman.

The raiders paused then howled and charged again.

Adam bent his head taking aim on a tall Somali, robes fluttering in the sunlight, face distorted in a long tribal scream.

Adam fired and killed his first man.

Within three minutes he killed four more.

Adam returned at sunrise five days later. Eva fell upon him, hugging and kissing and talking all at the same time – 'Darling. I've missed you so much and have lots to tell. I want to show you my house and my garden and my bathroom. We have hot water. Will you bathe with me?'

He said, 'The cattle are still a day away. I came ahead because I wanted to get back to you. My heavens, you look lovely. What's this? The house. It's finished. Why are you sitting out here in the cold. Why not have breakfast inside? A bath? A *bath*? In the house? We have a bath? I will. Yes. If you come in with me. Is the water hot? It is? Good God. What a woman.'

Eva said, 'I have some news. While you were away I had a letter from Kristina. She wants to come for a holiday with us. I shall ask her to bring a lavatory.'

'A *lavatory*? What on earth are you talking about?'

'When she comes she can bring a lavatory from Berlin. A proper one in porcelain. It will be more comfortable than those terrible planks we sit on now.'

'When is she coming?'

'Next month. It says so in this letter.'

Adam felt an electric charge of memory – violet eyes...soft

hands...softer skin...glowing hair....

'Is it a good idea? After Berlin she'll find it primitive here.'

'Darling. She loved Africa. Besides I need company. You're away so much with your business and stuffy meetings in town. We'll go to Mombasa to meet her. I can see how the Creek House is getting on.'

Chapter Twelve

Kristina

Berlin: 1907

Kristina woke and looked round. A strange room.

Beside her in bed a long lump under the cover: *Who is he?*

A second look: My God a second lump. *Three of us? I wish I could remember last night.*

She sighed and started her early morning check – breasts, thighs, buttocks – stroking, touching, exploring with delicate fingertips. All sound and firm as always. Every morning the same. Thank God for beauty.

Happy with herself she turned her attention to the room. From the vantage point of her pillow she saw a rich man's bed chamber. Expensive furniture, beautiful tapestries, lovely pictures. A room full of colour – and money.

What did I do last night?

She concentrated. Flashes of memory forced through. She remembered Count Steiner – *That damned fool politician from the Finance Ministry.*

Pulling back the cover she peeped. *Yes. It's Steiner. Very rich. Very influential.* 'Spend time with him.' her father had instructed. 'Treat him well – extra well – and he'll give me what I want.'

She thought hard, trying to remember the previous evening. Detail eluded her: *What happened? I must drink less. And no more of that white powder. It does odd things to me.*

Her companion stirred and smiled – a tousled middle-aged face.

'Kristina...,' he sighed.

He kicked out, waking the third partner.

'Darling,' he said, 'Fetch the rope....'

A naked woman rolled grumpily out of bed to fetch a silken cord.

As they tied her to the bedposts Kristina remembered: *It's his wife. Good God – his wife. My father's turned me into a whore. I'll have to go – run away. Eva...will you have me....*

Unable to resist she relaxed into their caresses as familiar waves of welcome pleasure swept through her body....

Kristina's father said, 'You have a letter from your sister.'

'From Eva?'

Von Lettow-Ansbach nodded, refusing to speak his daughter's

name.

'When you have read it please give it to your mother. Such news interests her. By the way – Count Steiner and his wife invite you to spend a holiday with them. The Countess finds you a pleasant companion. The Count has agreed with my financial proposals. I shall tell them you accept.'

A flick of his hand dismissed her.

Kristina read Eva's letter in delight: *Thank God. She'll have me. I'll book passage today. Mother will give me the money. She wants me out of Berlin. What on earth does Eva mean by a lavatory? I'm changing my whole life and she wants me to bring a lavatory?*

As the only unattached woman on board, Kristina found passage to Africa exhilarating. She would never see these French people again so lack of chaperone caused her no worry. She danced with whom she wished, slept with whomever took her fancy, ignoring the French wives as they ignored her.

Her voyage from Marseilles to Mombasa turned into a non-stop party. When she stepped ashore at Kilindini into Eva's excited embrace, most men on board hung over the side, waving and whistling.

'Who are those men?' asked Eva, laughing.

'Just friends,' said Kristina. 'Where's H.E.? Not here to welcome me?'

'You'll have to do with Adam and me,' said Eva. 'Now stop speaking German. Here you must practise English.'

Kristina hugged Adam, unsurprised at his enthusiastic response.

'Lovely to see you again. You've not changed,' he said, looking into her violet eyes. 'How long will you stay?'

She gave him full benefit of her smile and ignored the question – *It's up to Eva to tell him I'm here for ever....*

'When will I see H.E.?' she asked.

'In a couple of days. He's coming down on Government business.'

Eva took Kristina to Creek House, now half built.

'How beautiful. Will you live here?'

'For holidays. When the jetty is finished we will use it to export wood and coffee. And sail a boat. You will love Africa. It was made for you and me.'

For two days the sisters talked without cease, Eva wanting to know all about Berlin, Kristina all about Nairobi and H.E..

'Why do you ask so much about him?' asked Eva.

'Because he is such a beautiful man.'

'Kristina, darling. Men are not beautiful. They are handsome. Women are beautiful.'

'No. He is beautiful. Lovely skin and hair, and such blue eyes. And he's not a soldier. Nothing like the men we endured in Berlin.'

'Don't mention that here.' warned Eva.

'Of course not. I wrote to H.E. several times but he never replied. Perhaps my letters didn't arrive. Do you know if they did?'

H.E. arrived in Mombasa three days later. Kristina, consumed by excitement, met him with Adam and Eva at the station, and felt cast into misery when he hardly acknowledged her beyond a polite handshake.

'Why is H.E. like that to me?' she complained. 'Am I not worth more?'

'I think he's worried,' said Eva. 'Adam says H.E. is depressed by so much work and so much to think about here at the Coast. When he can relax it will be better.'

Kristina could not understand H.E.'s depression and sought chances to help improve his humour. But H.E. kept out of her way by staying at Government House so she had no chance to trail her beauty before him as she had done two years ago.

'What can I do?' she wailed to Eva in a moment of weakness.

'When we are all back in Nairobi he'll have more time,' said Eva. 'You'll see.'

Kristina loved the train journey to Nairobi, ignoring the dust filtering through every crack and seam of the wooden carriages. And she loved Mzito, deciding to settle in and forget H.E.: *To hell with him. There'll be plenty of other men here.*

Eva introduced Kristina to Queenie and her husband. His eyes widened when he saw Kristina. By the time she made her first visit to the Norfolk a few weeks later, Sandbach-Baker had passed the news round and the hotel filled with men eager to see this new gem.

During one visit to town Kristina saw H.E. walking in Station Road. She grabbed Eva's arm – 'Quick. Call him over.' She gave him her most brilliant smile but – beyond a nod – he ignored her and said, 'Eva. When is your husband back? I need to speak with him urgently.'

A few days later Adam took Eva and Kristina to stay a night at the Norfolk. At dinner time he said, 'I've asked H.E. to join us. We'll wait out here on the veranda.'

Sipping wine in the golden lamplight, Kristina knew she looked lovely, her mane of deep gold hair and tanned skin glowing in the warm dusk. She kept her bold eyes lowered, glancing up occasionally to accept and enjoy the lust and longing of every man in the place.

H.E.'s lazy blue eyes took on a glint as he arrived. He squeezed into a seat beside Kristina and – after a moment's pause – leaned across and kissed her cheek.

Pride surged through Kristina: *This time he must take notice. Here he can feel the competition. It's just like in Berlin. Any man will react and try to win. This may bring him to me.*

'The Government needs your husband for a few weeks, Eva,' said H.E.. 'We have an important visitor, a politician. Bloody man arrives soon in Mombasa on a Navy ship. Amazing. It's a private visit but he gets the Navy to bring him.'

'What's his name?' asked Adam.

'Churchill.'

'Never heard of him. Why do you need me?'

'He telegraphed ahead from Aden. Asked for you by name. You must guide him through our territory to Uganda. From there he goes on to Sudan. We'll make sure he shoots a few animals, meets a group of settlers, and generally gets through safely. By all accounts he's a wild one, but with influence.'

'How does he know of me?'

'He's number two in the Colonial Office. Powerful man from a powerful family. He can find out whatever he likes. Anyone with use of a Royal Navy cruiser to bring him and his friends on a jaunt to Mombasa will have no difficulty getting any information he needs.'

'Why me?'

'Don't know. It could be your German connection. You can never tell with politicians. He'll have a reason. But enough of work. Let's relax and eat out here on the veranda. It's such a bloody hot evening.'

From an alcove a small band started to play. The few men with women began to dance, waltzing slowly, watched intently by groups of noisy unattached males, perched and packed into every chair and corner. Envy thickened the warm evening air.

Insects buzzed and rattled round the lamps. The small prison opposite clattered and clanged to sounds of shutting down for the night. A train squealed and stopped a hundred yards up-line.

'Coming down from the Lake,' said Adam. 'Shouldn't halt there.

Someone knows the driver. Perhaps it's Ainsworth getting off at his house. They'd stop for him.'

The train started again, rattling past in a shower of sparks, the noise drowning the music for a few seconds.

Kristina sat close to H.E., leaning against him and feeling the heat of his huge body transfer through her thin dress. Oh how she enjoyed the moment and the atmosphere: *So different from Berlin. So exciting. Such fun...*

A small energetic figure marched in from the dark and skipped on to the veranda, bold dark eyes narrowed at sudden light. Dust-covered torn safari suit, dark unshaven face, large black moustache in need of attention. Slim, muscular, radiating confidence, he looked round.

Kristina, startled, caught his eye.

He stopped. Clicked his heels. Bowed. Swept off his sun helmet with delicate grace. Long strands of damp black hair fell across his ears.

Speaking fast in a thick accent he said: 'Madam. You are the most beautiful woman I have ever seen.'

He turned and strode on through the crowd, into the hotel.

Kristina laughed.

'Who on earth is that?' asked Adam.

'He must be Polish,' said Eva. 'Perhaps an educated man from Warsaw. I've heard them speak like that in Berlin.'

'A mid-European madman.' grunted H.E.. 'Ignore him.'

'You know him?'

'Yes. As I said. Mid-European and mad. Ignore him.'

An hour later the man returned, moving with dancer's grace through the drinking throng. Dressed in neat dark trousers, crisp white shirt, purple cummerbund, gleaming dancing pumps, he posed before Kristina, arms held wide, teeth gleaming in a bright smile.

She laughed. 'My God, you look different,' she said.

Showered, perfumed – moustache waxed into perfect points, black hair oiled and set, shaven face shining – he looked the immaculate, elegant European-city gentleman.

He bowed.

'Madam. I introduce myself. I am Kinskii. Spelt with three i's please. One in the middle and two at the end. No y. Otto Kinskii. Count Otto Kinskii.'

'You are Polish?'

'No, Madam.'

'Russian?'

'No, Madam.'

'Hungarian?'

'Yes, Madam. But *Austro*-Hungarian. I am a hussar of the Empire. Bodyguard to the Emperor.'

Kristina, speaking German, asked, 'What do you do here?'

'We must speak English Madam. We are with the English. I hunt. I hunt animals. I show rich tourists how to hunt animals. Please wait. I will be only a moment.'

He danced away into the crowd.

'How bloody rude,' said H.E., red with annoyance. 'What makes the little devil think he can push in on us?'

'Hungarians are like that,' said Eva, laughing. 'They make their own rules.'

'He is a Count,' said Kristina. 'A Count in Hungary expects everyone to do as he wishes.'

'If he's a Count I'm a one eyed whale,' said H.E..

Adam translated for Kristina who laughed and said, 'But you are an English Lord. You always expect *us* all to do what *you* want.'

'Nonsense. Anyway I am not a Lord. My father's the Lord. I am only an Honourable and with three older brothers I'll never be anything else.'

'So I will not marry you,' said Kristina. 'I want to be a Lady or a Countess. I do not want to be only an Honourable.'

'M'dear lady. I've no intention of marrying you or anyone else.'

Kinskii reappeared beside Kristina as though by magic. He carried glasses and wine.

'If you will not marry this lady, Sir, perhaps I will. Until that is decided, please drink wine with me. But first I shall take the lady for a dance.'

He whisked Kristina to her feet and off into a skipping polka, hair flying, eyes shining with excitement.

'I won't put up with this rude bloody nonsense,' said H.E.. 'I'm going home.'

He stood and stamped out into the dark.

'I think he's jealous,' said Eva. 'What shall we do?'

'Nothing,' said Adam. 'He's not interested in Kristina. She seems happy dancing with that strange man. None of it's our business. We'll have a few more glasses of wine and go to bed. Leave them to it.'

Adam watched Kristina whirl by several times. Flushed, excited, she waved once, but mostly she listened to Kinskii talking non-stop into her ear, missing neither step nor breath, as he raced her round the dance floor in hectic circles.

Adam felt a tug at his heart: *Jealousy? Am I jealous? Was H.E.?*

Kristina went to her room and waited. Just after midnight Kinskii came, slipping through the unlocked door, silent as a shadow.

'Tell me more of hussars in the Emperor's court.' she whispered.

'I shall show you the best riding tricks of the Empire.' he whispered back.

Oh he rode well. And – to Kristina's delight – the lesson lasted all night.

Chapter Thirteen

Travels With A Great Man

In humid October morning sunlight, Adam stood at Kilindini and watched the Great Man come ashore.

A Royal Navy warship nosed into harbour on the dawn tide. Trim, menacing and well handled, the sight of this powerful expression of Britain's place in the world filled Adam with pride and excitement.

But H.E. snorted and grumbled, 'The good ship 'Venus'. What a bloody awful name for a man o' war.'

The welcoming party shuffled into line as Winston Churchill scrambled on to the jetty from a smart Navy cutter.

Adam expected a Great Man to be imposing and felt disappointment at this small lumpy Great Man in baggy khaki trousers, long brown jacket buttoned in tight wrinkles across his stomach. In the damp heat Churchill's mottled pink face shone wet beneath a solid military pith helmet.

'What a desperate sight,' murmured H.E..

'Shut up,' whispered, Adam fighting back a giggle, 'You'll get us into trouble.'

Adam spent two hectic days with Churchill in Mombasa, following him on a busy round of inspections and meetings. The Minister moved at speed from place to place, studying new wharves and bridges, checking the harbour in detail – depth of water, number of berths planned, tides, water movement, and weather pattern. All the time dictating notes to Marsh, his secretary, or in deep discussion with his uncle, Colonel Wilson.

An evening reception arranged at Government House allowed Churchill to meet European residents, greeting every one with a ferocious stare. Deep. Direct. Eye to eye.

Churchill held Eva's hand for a fraction longer than Adam thought necessary as he studied her face, obviously committing it to memory.

'What a strange man,' Eva whispered to Adam.

During the evening Churchill said little, ate little, drank nothing; giving full attention to traders and senior railway engineers telling him of their difficulties. Not enough banks to develop credit for expansion, problems obtaining workmen from India: 'Impossible to use Native labour, Sir. They've never *had* to work you see. Not in an *organised* way like us.'

Adam noticed Marsh taking occasional notes at a nod from Churchill.

H.E. whispered, 'Some of this'll be part of a speech in Parliament. Look at how the little bugger's listening to your father's story.'

Adam edged closer to where the Minister stood, head thrust forward, listening in total concentration to Adam's father tell the story of his part in the Railway survey ten years before.

Churchill nodded and growled, 'My God, what wonderful tale of British endeavour. A hard and complex nine month trek across plain and mountain, applying modern mathematics to land never before seen by Europeans. I salute you, Sir. I salute you and all your companions, both white and black. With this wonderful modern railway you help bring civilisation and peace and plenty to the darkest of Africa. History will thank you for it.'

Adam watched Marsh scribbling quietly in his corner, setting down every word The Great Man said.

Next morning at dawn Adam and Eva assembled by the station with a group of other Europeans, several Indians and a few dozen Africans.

Churchill bustled over, his fierce politician's eyes selecting Eva.

'Mrs Early. We did not speak properly last night. I apologise. Rude of me.'

With a jerky bow, he said 'I understand you to be from Germany. How wonderful you saw fit to go some way towards uniting our two peoples by marrying an Englishman. I admire your great people and history. When next you communicate with your family please pay my respects to your father, Count von Lettow-Ansbach.'

He bowed again, murmuring, 'Charmed, madam – charmed,' and walked briskly away.

'How did he know my father?' asked Eva, astonished.

'Probably doesn't. He's just showing off,' said H.E..

But in a private moment H.E. said to Adam, 'The man's a brilliant politician. That little act is probably in the hope that your wife writes to her father who'll let the German Government know he's here. It'll stir 'em up and show England takes the East African Protectorate seriously.'

In damp heat of sunrise the train prepared for departure. Leaving Musa to load the luggage, Adam walked a few yards away from the crowd with Eva for a private farewell.

Eva hugged him, her head on his shoulder. 'Be careful of that man Churchill,' she whispered. 'He's too clever for us.'

Adam chuckled and said, 'I'm only the head servant in camp. Beyond that I'll keep out of his way.'

Eva said, 'You must go now. I can hear Churchill calling.'

Adam stooped for a final kiss and trailed his fingers along her arm before moving forward along the train, glancing back for a final view of his wife.

He arrived at the engine and fought back a laugh at the sight of Churchill perched high a garden seat tied firmly to the cow catcher, his stiff wing collar and formal blue coat at odds with his heavy pith helmet and solid boots. The Great Man sat waving his arms and calling instructions to Hayes-Sadler and Marsh clambering up to join him.

'Come on, Sir James. Hurry, Eddie. Here. Let me help you. Ah. Mr Early. I want you to take a picture with this camera. Can you work the thing? You can? Excellent. We'll just get my uncle up and Mr Currie in position by the engine then you can make our picture. Pray be careful. Hold the apparatus steady. Good. Stand there, Currie. On the sleeper so the camera can see you. Excellent. We're ready. Be still and look at the lens everyone. Right. Now. Got it Mr Early? Capital. Well done. Now Mr Early, please give Currie the camera and change places so we can do it again with you in the picture.'

Adam took Currie's position on the large wooden sleeper.

Many years later after Churchill became a world famous statesman, Adam would look at his copy and smile. The Great Man sits completely at ease and in command, staring at the camera, hands folded, jacket tight and wrinkled across his stomach. He seems not at all out of place on a wooden bench attached by a piece of frayed rope on the front of a great metal engine in Africa.

On the trackside stands Adam, face hidden in the dark shadow of his hat. A slim young man in khaki jacket, jodhpurs and long boots. Diffident. Slightly awkward in the presence of these important men.

'Good,' said Churchill again. 'We're ready. Mr Early. Pray take charge of the camera and make a picture whenever I tell you. You are appointed as my official photographer. Thank you. I'm quite ready to go now. Tell the driver.'

Whilst travelling on the train Adam had few duties as Churchill spent most of his time with Marsh, dictating, discussing, checking documents, dictating again. He worked without pause in fierce and absolute concentration, appearing unaffected by the discomfort of heat and constant dust.

Only when the train halted did Churchill look up, leave Marsh, and show interest in his surroundings, hopping off to rush back down the line and study the effect of hot sun on metal rails and bridges or hurry into the bush to look at whatever caught his attention. He showed particular interest in the position of the railway and the border with German East Africa, asking Adam to draw maps that he studied and discussed with Colonel Wilson.

Two days after leaving Mombasa the driver uncoupled Churchill's special carriages in a siding at Simba Station and steamed off towards Nairobi, leaving the party to spread out in the comfort of a camp set up nearby.

After dinner, Churchill retired to his tent where Adam saw him bent over a table, writing in deep concentration; his pen racing across the page.

'Your evening off?' Adam asked Marsh, as they strolled together in cool night air with a last cigar before bed.

'Only because my master needs to make some private money out of this trip,' said Marsh. 'When he dictates to me it's British Government business. When he writes alone he's trying to earn his keep.'

'But surely he's rich? From a wealthy family?'

'A wealthy *family* yes. But his cousin holds both Dukedom and inheritance. My master's father died a few years ago leaving a pile of debt and no money. Mr Churchill couldn't afford to stay in the army and went to the South African war as a journalist. Being captured by the Boers then escaping in dramatic fashion turned out to be a stroke of luck. That little adventure made him famous. Since then, as well as spending time in Parliament, he writes for a living.'

'Is he any good?'

'Oh yes. He's completed a couple of books that sold well. On this trip he's writing articles for Strand Magazine to cover expenses – and dictating memoranda by the hundred for Whitehall, to justify this visit. What a man.'

'Does he always work so hard?'

'Always. He's driven by the memory of his father, Lord Randolph – brilliant man. So sad an end.'

'What happened?'

'He died of...an...illness. A brilliant man...so sad.'

'Churchill's mother is American?'

'Yes. A beautiful clever woman. Remarried you know. To a man not much older than my master. Very disappointing. Before that she did have a...very close friend nearer her own age. An Austrian nobleman. But by the time Lord Randolph died the nobleman was betrothed to a rich princess in his own country. Great pity. Quite tragic.'

'Mr Churchill seems young to be so high in Government.'

'He's brilliant. Cleverest man I've ever met. Frightens me to death.'

'Why?'

'Brain as big as the universe. Trouble is in controlling it and him. Chases whatever enthusiasm catches his attention. It'll be the death of him one day if he's not careful.'

Next morning Adam saw Marsh's prophecy almost come true when, before dawn he led the party into the bush seeking a lion for Churchill to shoot.

For an hour, in rising sun, The Great Man stalked deer, shooting two. A third, wounded, led him round the shoulder of a hill towards a rhinoceros grazing in the cool morning air a few hundred yards away.

Churchill grunted, 'Hurrah,' and set off at fast pace through yellow grass towards the animal. Adam and Marsh, with Musa and a gun-bearer, followed close behind. The rest of the party spread left and right to form a sweep line.

Churchill closed with his target and aimed, firing one shot that hit the beast with a loud *slap*. The animal stumbled and turned. Catching scent of his attackers he dropped his head and charged towards the right firing line.

The whole line began to shoot. The rhinoceros, confused, swung across the front from right to left about fifty yards distant, so heavy and strong that bullets whacking into his hide took no effect.

Moving at a fast trot he suddenly swerved and charged straight at Churchill.

That night Adam sent a letter to Eva in Mombasa with the guard of a passing train. He wrote: *An amazing thing happened. Churchill showed no fear. He neither flinched nor stopped firing. The rhino showed such determination it refused to fall. No one could make a killing shot. Churchill stood blasting away like the rest of us but with the rhino almost on him ran out of bullets. Churchill just stood and watched this huge beast thundering down, intent on flattening him. Nothing else he could do.*

Then Musa jumped forward, snatched my gun and in a second had the beast down with an incredible shot that hit the rhino plumb in his left eye. Bang! Straight into the brain. I've never seen luck like it. The animal fell and slid through the dust stone dead, almost at Churchill's feet.

You know what the man did? Patted the rhino as though it were an old friend, reloaded, then raced off after a couple of others nearby. Odd thing is that over dinner that evening he expressed sympathy with the rhino. He said we made unprovoked assault with murderous intent upon peaceful animals. Not a word of thanks or gratitude to Musa for saving him. Not even a comment on the lucky shot. After we tidied up the rhino and laid it out properly, he asked me to take his picture – stood by it with his gun as though he'd downed it himself. No hint of what really happened. Now he's retired to his tent to write. We're preparing to hitch on to the morning train to Nairobi....

After a formal arrival at Nairobi – guard of honour in full drill at the station – Adam found himself caught up in several days of dinners and meetings between Churchill and the settlers.

'Let us rule ourselves,' Delamere and the others argued from the floor of rowdy meetings. 'Give us self-government.'

Churchill made several speeches in his flat lisping voice, impressing everyone with his skill and grasp of detail, but leaving most who heard him uneasy at lack of concrete promises.

'Didn't actually say a damned thing,' complained Stewartby to Adam over a peevish drink. 'Talked a load of rot and guaranteed us nothing. You're his friend. You have a go at him. Tell him what we want. Get him to understand.'

Churchill insisted on visiting Kikuyuland in a motor car he had brought from England, and carried up to Nairobi on the train. On rough bush tracks it gave endless trouble, boiling over; falling in potholes; sticking in mud.

'He's so proud of the damn thing but it doesn't work in London either,' said Marsh to Adam. 'Probably confirms to the Natives that we Europeans are all mad. Brought it against all advice.'

After a meeting with Kikuyu chiefs at Fort Hall Churchill insisted on travelling to the government post at Embu on Mount Kenya. Wilson set off on ponies while Churchill bounced along in his car. The party arrived in Embu just before dark to the astonishment of two young Europeans in charge at the post, an army officer and a civilian District Officer.

Recovering from surprise at receiving visitors – let alone a Government Minister from London – the two men set up an excellent dinner and gave over their beds to Churchill and Wilson, insisting on moving out to sleep in tents set up in the compound. Over brandy round the campfire after dinner, Churchill asked about trade routes to Abyssinia.

'Simple,' said the army officer. 'Straight through here, down on to the desert, up to Abyssinia with goods from England then back with ponies, cattle and other things needed to build this country. Easy as wink if you allow us the guns to protect ourselves from Somali in the desert. Early will tell you. He's done it. Passed here a while ago on a trading expedition – and looked after himself very well. Didn't you Early.'

'Passed through here?' asked Mayne, the District Officer. 'When? I don't remember you passing through here.'

'I had to hurry,' said Adam. 'Went by without stopping.' He frowned at the army officer. 'How do you know I'd been up here trading?'

'I heard of you...a friend of Thinman. Am I right?'

'Yes.'

The officer looked at Mayne who nodded and said, 'Ah yes...I remember. Now I remember. About a year ago. Yes.'

In camp the evening before returning to Nairobi, Churchill invited Adam in to his tent and said, 'Please sit down, Mr Early. Coffee? No? Are you sure? I have a matter to discuss. Please be comfortable.'

He paused, looked across the calm grey-green bush, seeming deep in thought.

'Tomorrow we part. I am uncommonly grateful for your efforts on my behalf during our journey together. I have one more thing to ask of you. I find you an intelligent young man.'

Turning full force of his personality on to Adam he smiled – a puckering of plump cheeks – while his fierce eyes looked cold and direct into Adam's.

'Our lives and experience are different and I want us to keep in touch by exchange of occasional letters. You will inform me of happenings here in Africa and I will warn you of changes in London which may affect your life or livelihood. No one but you, Marsh and I know of this arrangement. Pray keep it that way. Thank you. That is all.'

'It's the way of politics my dear fellow,' said Marsh. 'You are now part of the club. Welcome. One thing he'll want from you is information relating to the Germans here in Africa. Easy enough with your connections.'

'I can't do that,' protested Adam. 'You're asking me to let my wife and her family down.'

'Not really, old boy. Just general information. It's not spying if that's what you think. Not really. Anyway, my master doesn't believe the Germans will ever go to war. He thinks they're bluffing and puffing up their military might for show. Says it's all a charade so their Kaiser can play soldiers. He's probably right. Usually is.'

Adam walked through the trees to Mzito just after dawn. Musa hurried on down to Rowbas to see his new Kikuyu wife. Eva, sitting on her veranda eating breakfast, stood and ran down the steps to meet him, her nightgown and robe flying behind her.

He swept her into a hug. She hugged him back.

'Oh darling,' she cried, 'I've missed you so much. I have things to tell you. Important things. I'm planning to build H.E. a house on his Nairobi Hill plot. I'm planning one for Kristina too, on our plot. We need to build or the Government will take it back. But more important....'

She paused.

'...Kristina is going to marry Kinskii, and I'm having a baby.'

Chapter Fourteen

Kinskii

Mzito Estate: 1908

On a hot afternoon in January Eva looked up to see Count Otto Kinskii galloping gracefully through the trees, sweeping down on Mzito in fine style.

With a delicate sway of shoulders he slid his brown Somali pony to a halt, leapt to the ground, skipped on to the veranda, embraced Eva, shook hands with Adam, dropped into a chair, accepted a drink and said, 'My wife, the Countess, follows by coach.'

Wearing a loose white shirt with khaki jodhpurs, he looked fit and relaxed. His oiled black hair, exquisite moustache – waxed and set – gleamed in unison with perfectly polished riding boots,.

'Hah. There she is,' he cried pointing. Coming over the rise, a small donkey cart attended by two African servants bore Kristina towards Mzito.

In one fluid motion, he rose to his feet, leapt off the veranda, on to the horse and galloped to meet his wife.

Eva watched his slim muscular body move in perfect harmony with the pony and clapped her hands. 'Oh darling,' she cried. 'I can see what Kristina sees in him.'

'My God he rides well,' said Adam.

Last time Adam saw Kinskii at the wedding four weeks earlier he looked neat and handsome in ruffled silk shirt, tight black trousers, gleaming riding boots, standing beside Kristina in the District Commissioner's office.

'We cannot marry in your protestant church,' Adam heard Kinskii tell Kristina. 'My family – all true Catholics – would never accept it as a true union. We'll hold a proper cathedral marriage in Austria when we return.'

After the wedding Kristina and Kinskii led a procession back to the Norfolk where he carried her gallantly over the threshold to cheers and loud encouragement. For several hours the party went on and expanded as more guests arrived from up-country to join in. Adam kept a close eye on Kinskii moving courteously through the throng, introducing Kristina as, 'My wife, the Countess.'

Adam asked H.E., 'What do you know about this man?'

'Not much. Why?'

'I need to safeguard my sister-in-law.'

'My dear fellow, *we* need to be safeguarded from her.'

'For God's sake be serious. What do you know about him?'

'Very little. But what do we know about anyone who turns up in Nairobi these days? Like most in this room he just appeared, applied for licence as a hunter and guide then set off about his business.'

'Where did he come from?'

'Ask him. He'll have a story same as the others. There's not many like you and I with a simple reason for being here.'

At midnight Kinskii leapt on to a table, thanked all for coming to celebrate his wedding, threw his glass into the large stone hearth and disappeared with Kristina.

The party continued till dawn then transferred to Mzito, trailing out to the estate, arriving by noon to find Adam and Eva already there with Kristina and Kinskii.

Delamere arrived late with Stewartby. The few women present sat in shade, watching and listening to the men drinking and boasting. Several with horses cleared a small arena and started a cavalry contest, picking small rings off the ground with long sticks, handled as lances.

Into the arena rode Kinskii astride his shining brown Somali pony. Moving at full gallop he leaned out of his saddle and ran along the line of rings, collecting every single one with a loud click.

He raised his filled lance in triumph to Kristina, rattled the rings, swung his horse into a graceful arc, raced back down the line and replaced each ring as neatly as though it had never been moved.

The watching crowd cheered and clapped as Kinskii dismounted with a flourish and bowed to his wife with a flashing smile.

'Brilliant riding, Sir. Brilliant,' shouted Delamere. 'Show us more.'

Kinskii remounted and for several minutes galloped to and fro. His black hair flew, his muscular body twisted and turned as he threw himself and the horse through a series of complex manoeuvres.

He leapt from the saddle at full speed, one hand on the pommel; swung himself over the horse's back from left to right and back with a skipping heave. He slipped sideways from the saddle, one leg hooked to a stirrup; leaned under the horse's belly to collect the line of rings by hand.

Finally, at full gallop he rolled off the saddle in a somersault to land breathless and triumphant, arms held high, head back, to cheers and applause.

From the crowd Stewartby called, 'Seen it all before in the circus. Bloody man's a performing gypsy.'

Silence fell.

Kinskii's face whitened in anger.

'A gypsy? A performing gypsy? You insult me at my wedding? Come forward to discuss the matter. Come close and call me gypsy again.'

'You bloody idiot, Stewartby,' said Delamere. 'Why can't you keep your mouth shut.'

Stewartby's handsome face, red with anger and whisky, twisted in disdain.

'I'll fight him if he wants. I'll fight the bloody fraud. Let me at him.'

Delamere and H.E. moved into the group surrounding Stewartby, grabbed his arms and shuffled him away to the far side of the house where they loaded him on to a donkey cart and sent him off towards Nairobi with his African servants.

The wedding party continued. Kinskii returned to good humour, drinking and chatting with Delamere and Adam.

'In Austria and Hungary everyone rides well,' Kinskii said. 'I have an uncle, or maybe a cousin – we are a large family – who won your English race, The Derby, some years ago. He did it for a wager. Some stupid Lords thought it impossible for a foreigner to win such a race. But my cousin – or my uncle – showed them how. He made much money on the bet and found his way to friendship with one of the great English families as a result.'

Later H.E. said to Adam, 'This is the trouble with Kinskii. Turns up here and says he is a Count, but one is not sure. Why should a well born mid-European nobleman come to a place like this? So one wonders. Then he comes out with a story like that. And it's true. I checked up. A Count Kinsky – Austrian political attaché in London – won The Derby in 1883 on a horse called Zoedene and became well known in London society – and a special friend to your friend Winston's mother. Almost caused a scandal. I wrote to my father and asked. He confirmed it all.'

To Eva's delight Kinskii took complete control of Kristina.

'I've never seen her like this with a man,' she told Adam. 'Perhaps she loves this one. At least she must respect him. In Kristina this is not normal.'

Two days after the wedding party Kinskii told Eva , 'Kristina and I leave for safari tomorrow. I have some hunters to take out. Kristina shall come with me and help look after them.'

Eva stood on the veranda at dawn and watched Kinskii and Kristina march off towards Nairobi. Kristina strode along beside her husband without a backward glance.

Four weeks later after a successful safari they returned with Kinskii in expansive mood.

'My clients paid me well,' he told Adam. 'We have a great future here. More and more rich men will want to come and shoot the animals. They will make us rich, too.'

'But are we not already rich, darling? Our estates in Austria and Hungary?' asked Kristina.

'Of course. But they are there and we are here. We must also be rich here.'

Adam said, 'Why did you come to Africa?'

'Adventure, my dear friend.'

'Not enough adventure as a Hussar?'

'No one to fight. I found little adventure strutting about in fancy uniform or keeping Serb peasants under control. I became bored. We were the Emperor's young lions, but dressing up for parades in Vienna did not suit *this* young lion, so I left.'

'What about your family estates?'

'They are well cared for. I am not needed for a few years yet.'

'Where are the estates?'

'Scattered round Austria and Hungary. When I inherit I shall return. With Kristina and our children. She will be a proper Countess with big houses and many servants.'

'I find it hard to understand why a man with such riches at home prefers the hardship of Africa to the comfort of Europe.'

'Why? Comfort is for old men. Comfort will come later. For now I need excitement and love. Africa supplies excitement – Kristina the love.'

He laughed. 'Come my friend. Let us not be so serious. I shall ask my lovely sister-in-law to show me her new coffee plants. How is it going, my dear Eva? Which shall we see first? Baby or berries?'

Adam felt uneasy after this conversation but made no mention to Eva. Kinskii had such a pleasant manner that small contradictory points seemed of no consequence. Kinskii rode well, shot well, and seemed entranced with his new wife. And to Adam's relief Kristina no longer turned her disturbing violet eyes on him in warm enquiry. And her handshake was simply a handshake, no longer a subtle invitation. Kinskii now took all her attention.

'Seems to have tamed her,' commented H.E.. 'Not a bad thing I suppose.'

In July, while Adam rested from collecting cattle in desert north of Mount Kenya, a runner trotted into camp with news from Eva of the birth of his first son.

Eva wrote: *My Kikuyu women helped with delivery. It was all very African but went well. We have a lovely son. Strong and healthy. Come home to meet him.*

Adam immediately set out for home with his personal servants and Sakayo, leaving Abdi to bring the cattle. In four days hard walking he reached Mzito. His son, christened Thomas Adam at a small ceremony in Mzito, gurgled happily. Adam's parents came from Mombasa. Kristina and Kinskii managed to arrive just as the service started.

Eva looked round the group and whispered to Adam, 'Thank God we're building a family here. We no longer have one in Germany. Kristina told father she married an Austrian so she's not allowed to return home either. He thinks we're both failures. We married beneath our rank. To a Prussian officer an English gentleman or an Austrian Count mean nothing.'

Chapter Fifteen

Two Wives Talking

Eva and Kristina sat drinking tea in Kristina's new house. Eva watched her son playing among the trees with his African nurse.

Eva sipped her tea and asked, 'Where is Kinskii now?'

'On safari with a group of rich Americans.'

'Why did you not go?'

'I'm bored with safari. Those stupid men are interested only in shooting animals. They never think or talk of anything else. It's more fun here in Nairobi. This is such a lovely house you built me. And near to H.E.'s house, too.'

Eva listened to her son's piping voice as he shouted to his *ayah*, in Swahili. Not yet two and already giving orders. She still felt unsure at leaving her son with an African woman most of the day: *But what can I do? Adam is always away buying cattle, or up at Anwar's. All my time is taken up running the farm alone. It's very hard. And very boring. Oh God, I'd like some excitement now and then.*

She sighed and looked again at her son scampering through the trees and grass, chased by his *ayah*. Beyond them she could see H.E.'s house.

So close. Too close. I built Kristina's house too close to H.E.'s. I don't trust my sister. She'll try to get into bed with H.E..

Kristina took a cake and said, 'Do you notice how things change? We sit here just like Berlin housewives, sipping tea, eating cake, chatting. Whatever next? Soon it'll be even more like Berlin. We'll be taking lovers and whispering secrets.'

'Kristina. Promise me you are being faithful to Kinskii while he's away.'

'Of course. I promise. He'd kill me otherwise. When Kinskii is here I concentrate only on him. When he is away in the bush with those stupid rich Americans and English lords he can't expect me to live like a nun. I can't just sit here and do nothing. I go to the Norfolk with friends to have a drink and a dance. No more.'

'Are you sure?'

'Yes. Honestly. It would be easier if Nairobi had more European women. With so few of us we must be extra careful not to cause scandal. Like you and Queenie. You always bring her into town with you. Why? So when you speak to men at the Norfolk, you are together.

Two women. No scandal.'

'Are you always careful?'

Kristina smiled brightly; violet eyes shining.

'Mostly.'

She laughed and said, 'Big sister. Stop worrying about me. I'm always good and always careful. I promise.'

Eva stood and said, 'We must go.'

She called Thomas. He waved and trotted to his *ayah*.

Kristina stretched and said, 'Ach. It's so good to speak German again. I wish you came in from the farm more often. Kinskii will never let me speak German – even when we are alone. Can you come again soon? We can go dancing at the Norfolk.'

'No. I have the farm to look after. Today I came only because of trouble at Damu. Cattle keep disappearing between Mzito and the killing place but I cannot see how.'

Kristina laughed again.

'Have we changed so much from Berlin that we are now two angels? Life is so different here. Many beautiful men, but none for us. I wonder if it would have been like this had we married in Berlin? Has Africa changed us?'

'I hope so,' said Eva, praying that she meant it, especially with the new baby coming.

Chapter Sixteen

Christy

Nairobi Races: February 1913

Sitting in a canvas chair at the Race Day picnic Eva sipped her wine and sighed, wishing that Adam, Delamere and Stewartby would shut up.

'What *are* they arguing about?' she whispered to H.E..

'Local politics, m'dear. Most boring subject in the world unless you're involved. Ignore them. Go and sit with Kristina. Watch what's going on around you in the paddock. Not many places in the world you'll see so many crazy eccentrics in one place. As good as a stage comedy. Watch and listen. You'll enjoy every minute.'

Eva smiled.

'You're right,' she said and moved across to sit by her sister and Kinskii.

'Anything interesting?' she asked.

'Everything,' said Kristina. 'They're all mad.'

Eva laughed, suddenly excited by the crowded paddock and its swarm of colour and noise.

'I always enjoy Race Day,' she cried.

'I can tell,' said Kristina.

Eva shivered. Every time she came to the races she felt an almost erotic surge at seeing the vitality, energy and colour of this new country meeting in a gossiping frenzy of competition, politics and scandal. Everyone gathered for the occasion, some travelling for days to reach the parched grassy plain just east of Nairobi.

They ate, drank; argued.

They swapped news, prices, crop and cattle information.

They bought and sold.

Haggled and gambled.

Eva loved to watch the coarse and the suave, the handsome and the ugly, the rich and the struggling all joining together for Race Day, surrounded and pampered by hordes of servants.

She loved to watch them flirting and skirting with each other.

Oh those healthy young men – fresh from the isolation of their farms or bush camps – spent much of Race Day casting hot eyes over other men's wives, prettily poised on cane chairs, sipping from delicate tea cups, nibbling at picnic lunch.

Eva knew that many of the women, equally isolated – their

husbands preferring bush hunting to domestic life – responded with warmth.

She shivered again and turned away to check on her children when a deep cheerful voice boomed out.

'Good God – its Willy Woggers. What on earth are you doing here?'

She saw Adam's face drain of colour.

'Christ. It's Jesus.' he said.

Two men approached. One she knew as Finch-Hatton – a well-built young man wearing an odd blue bowler hat, pushed back from his forehead.

The other – a young army officer dressed in crisp uniform whites smiled and saluted. Eva felt her heart stop at the sight of him.

It actually stopped.

A shaft of pure instant love jolted through her body.

Stunned, she looked at the most beautiful man she had ever seen.

White-blond hair. Glowing golden skin. Bright blue eyes, merry and light. Straight back. Superb muscles that swept from his neck, rippled under his tunic, across his shoulders to form sculptured arms. His broad chest heaved as he laughed and spoke again in a deep musical voice, 'Willy Woggers. Never thought I'd see *you* again.'

Eva exchanged a glance with Kristina: *Does she see the effect of this man on me? Is it the same for her? No. Impossible.*

Adam jumped from his chair, staring at the man in obvious shock and said, 'Christ. It's Jesus Christ. Tim Christy. Of all people. Is this the Second Coming? What the hell are you doing here?'

'Indian Army old boy. Captain. Posted here to help you against the horrible Hun when we start to fight 'em. You'll never win without me. Do you know my friend Finch-Hatton? You do. Not surprised. Everyone does. And who are these two beauties may I ask? Never thought I'd see Willy Woggers with such lovely ladies. Have you cornered a market?'

In German Eva asked Adam 'Why are you using these silly names?'

'We were at school together. That's how we used to speak to each other.'

'What language is that?' asked Christy.

'German you ignorant devil,' said Adam and made a round of introductions. 'This is Tim Christy. We went to the same school.'

'Your wife?' said Christy. 'And sister-in-law. A Countess? My heavens you've moved up in the world. And a *Count*. My dear Sir, how good to meet you. Austrian? My word. An Austrian Count. Certainly we'll stop for some lunch, won't we Finch-Hatton?'

He laughed. A deep rich gurgle. The most beautiful sound Eva had ever heard.

She almost gasped at his touch when he bowed to offer a warm firm handshake. Her heart fluttered again as he smiled – perfect white teeth in golden tanned face.

'Pardon my little joke about the horrible Hun, Mrs Early. And you too, Countess.'

Eva watched with jealous pain as Kristina turned her violet eyes on him at full strength. He moved on to greet Kinskii and H.E. and acknowledge the two children. 'Yours Early? I see the likeness. They have your features. Exactly. Both from the same mould. Lovely children...lovely.'

Eva – thrilled by this man – watched his beautiful smile light on each of her friends and family. Her eyes roamed over his perfect frame. The music of his deep voice enveloped her. Years later, she told Kristina, 'Cupid doesn't use arrows. He shot me with a thunderbolt when I first saw Christy.'

Adam did not realise Christy's affect on Eva and moved away to rejoin the political disagreement between Delamere and Stewartby. Their argument continued until Stewartby broke away and stormed off to watch the first race.

Adam returned to sit with H.E.. 'Where are Eva and Kristina?' he asked.

'Off with your friend Christy to see Kinskii race.'

'He's never been my friend. He was a senior at my school. He was an absolute shit – hated by everyone.'

H.E. smiled, only half listening. Adam saw his lazy eyes following Beatrice, Stewartby's wife, making her way delicately through the crowd, her soft green dress rippling in the breeze. A small round woman – round, not plump – with wispy blond hair, vague blue eyes, delicate peach skin untouched by sun or heat.

'Lovely isn't she?' H.E. murmured. 'She never tans, never perspires.'

'How do you know? What are you up to?'

H.E. sighed. 'Just look. What a stunner. A lady in waiting. Those beautiful eyes, just waiting to be startled. That lovely skin, just waiting to be stroked. And what about those beautiful bosoms. Are they not exquisite, encased in quivering cotton? Just waiting to be...'

'Bloody hell, H.E. You haven't got her into bed, have you?'

H.E. turned his smooth gaze on to Adam with a slow droop of one eyelid.

'Not yet old boy....'

'Oh Christ. Be careful. Stewartby'll kill you.'

'My dear fellow. The man's a bloody little popinjay – a bag of wind. Thinks he's important. He's about as important as my arse. And just as dangerous.'

From the racetrack Adam heard a rolling shout of excitement.

'Kinskii's probably won again,' said H.E..

'Do you still think he's a phoney?'

'Kinskii? Not sure. Difficult to tell. He masks it well. Much easier to see through your friend Christy. Something missing there. It may be brains, it may be morals, but someone like me can see straight through the likes of him. One bad hat can always recognise another. I'll wager he feels the same about me.'

'Why say that? You've only just met him.'

'Don't know. Premonition perhaps. Or because I make it a rule never to trust anyone called Tim. Talk of the devil – here he comes with your wife.'

Adam saw Eva returning through the crowd walking close beside Christy. Crossing a rough patch she stumbled. Christy threw out an arm and caught her. As she straightened she brushed her breast in a delicate roll against his hand and smiled up into his eyes.

Tanga. Bloody hell. That's what she did with me at Tanga. Memories of a warm moonlit evening and the soft press of her body flooded into Adam's mind. Blood rushed to his face as he jumped to his feet.

H.E. laughed and said, 'Go and rescue your damsel m'dear man. Be quick before the dragon gets her.'

A week later Adam and Eva travelled by train into the Rift Valley to stay at Delamere's farm. At the races Delamere had invited Adam, saying, 'Bring your wife. She'll be company for Florence. And bring your two trackers, Musa and Sakayo. I plan to hunt lion and they'll be a great help.'

Arriving at Delamere's farm Adam felt surprise at seeing Kinskii waiting to greet them.

Kinskii said, 'I've been in the north hunting. Delamere sent a runner calling me here to help clear lion from his land. Stewartby is here with Beatrice and several others are coming, too. Delamere plans to go after the lion with dogs and horses. An interesting idea and worth a try. How is my wife, the Countess? Is she caring for your lovely children while we're all away? Good. That will keep her busy until I return home.'

At sunset Adam and Stewartby sat with Delamere on the veranda discussing politics. At one point Delamere marched up and down waving his arms, 'We must make this bloody place work,' he shouted. 'We settlers must cooperate to build a business and political base and make the British Government realise this is a white man's country – our country.'

Florence appeared on the veranda, walking slowly, leaning on Eva's arm.

'What noise,' she said. 'Why are you shouting?'

Adam looked at Eva and wondered at her flushed face: *Is she unwell*

Florence said, 'We've come for a sundowner. Where are the others?'

Delamere helped his wife into a chair and said, 'Beatrice is resting. Kinskii is attending the horses for tomorrow, Mayne and Rainey are checking the dogs and...ah...here's Captain Christy now.'

A pony cantered across the plain. Christy waved as he rode easily through rough grass towards the house.

Christy. Anger ran like fire through Adam's veins: *Bloody hell. What's he doing here?*

While dressing for dinner Eva paused in brushing her hair and asked, 'Why do you not like Captain Christy?'

'He's an awful fellow.'

'No. He's charming. Everyone finds him so.'

'Nonsense. He's a shit. Stay away from him.'

At dinner Eva forced herself between Delamere and Kinskii to claim a chair opposite Christy, giving him full benefit of a brilliant smile and shivering at the signal his thrilling blue eyes sent back.

Beatrice sat between Paul Rainey, a tall young American, and the District Commissioner, Mayne, who shook hands with Adam, saying, 'We've met before. At Embu. I was District Officer when you came with Churchill. He's done uncommonly well for himself, hasn't he?'

Eva's fascination with Christy grew during dinner and she had difficulty keeping her eyes off him. Soft lamplight spun his white-blond hair into a gossamer halo, glowed golden on his handsome face and turned his merry blue eyes into exciting pools of danger, desire and attraction.

She felt...entranced...bewitched by the force of his charm and the way his beautiful eyes sought and held hers time and again.

Excitement stirred through her whole body: *He's a devil. A saint and devil. That's what I see. He's both. He's both.*

When Delamere tapped a glass and called, 'Right. Here's our plan for tomorrow.' Eva reluctantly dragged her attention from Christy and turned to listen.

Delamere said, 'I'm losing sheep and cattle to a pride of damned lion. My Masai can't seem to clear 'em so we're trying a new idea. Rainey here has a pack of dogs to hunt the cursed things down. We'll follow on horseback and shoot whatever we find. It'll be good sport, and may save a few of my animals. Tell 'em, Rainey.'

The young American said, 'My farm near Naivasha is small but using dogs I've almost cleared the place of lion. I'm anxious to try on a bigger spread like this. Tomorrow we go out before dawn with the dogs and see what we set running.'

Eva looked round and caught Christy's eye. He raised an eyebrow at her, corners of his mouth turned down.

'Do you mean we're going out in the dark to frighten lion into running?' he asked.

'Yes,' said Delamere. 'Good idea isn't it?'

'What if they run toward us?' asked Christy.

'We shoot the buggers.'

Christy looked doubtful.

'Sounds dangerous to me.'

Kinskii said, 'My dear Sir. Many things on this plain give greater danger than lion. Mosquitoes for instance – so small you pay them no heed. But each year they kill far more people than lion, buffalo or rhino – even if calculated all together.'

Christy shrugged but appeared unconvinced.

Eva raised a hand and said. 'I'd like to come too.'

'Good God no,' said Delamere. 'Much too dangerous.'

'But Count Kinskii just said the opposite.'

Delamere looked at Adam. 'What do you think, Early?'

'No reason why not,' said Adam. 'My wife has experienced far worse in the bush than being chased by lion.'

'I'll help keep an eye on her,' said Christy smiling towards Eva.

'In that case Beatrice and I will come as well,' said Florence. 'Why should you men have all the fun? I'm sure you can keep an eye on me too, Captain Christy.'

'With great pleasure, ma'am,' said Christy.

Next morning at four o'clock Eva, Beatrice and Florence, well wrapped against the pre-dawn chill, bumped along in an old mule cart under black velvet sky, pin-cushioned with a million stars. The men led on ponies, outlined against the starlit horizon in ghostly procession.

Eva leaned out to peer at the line of shadows, trying to tell one from the other. Her heart jumped when Christy's cheerful voice whispered in her ear, 'How the hell will we see any lion in this?'

'Where did you come from?' she asked.

'I've been catching up but that crowd of damned Masai following got in my way. Can't see the buggers in the dark.'

He laughed and Eva laughed with him, surprised at the girlish giggle that came out. Adam must have heard because he pulled his pony round to ride alongside the cart.

Christy clicked his horse forward and joined the lead group. Adam stayed with Eva until they arrived at the first stakeout.

In the hour before sunrise, Eva watched from the mule cart in growing excitement as grey light replaced the stars and gave good sight through grass and thorn trees. The dogs started several lion from kills or nearby bush. The horsemen chased hard, blasting away at lion racing from the baying dog pack to blend into bush and gully and disappear.

Eva thrilled at the speed and cunning of these great animals, clapping her hands at their grace and guile.

Despite all effort the hunt shot no lion.

'They're not doing very well,' Eva said to Florence, who responded with a weary smile and a shrug at the folly of men.

Shortly before sunrise, Delamere called everyone round the cart, and said, 'It's not bloody-well working. We'll stop now for a quick breakfast and think again. Speak up if you have any ideas.'

Kinskii said, 'I think we cannot shoot straight from horseback. Why do we not dismount to shoot? This is how we trained as hussars. Our horses carry us to battle. Once there we fight on foot, except in a following charge.'

'Good idea. Early, when we've finished breakfast, get your man Musa to arrange a line of beaters half a mile ahead. We'll raise lion with the dogs and when they're trapped we'll form a stop-line on horseback and walk our horses forward while the beaters flush them at us. All agreed? Good. You agree too, Christy? Are you well man? You look pale. Are you having trouble with your horse? You've had trouble keeping up.'

'I'm fine, Sir. But my horse seems reluctant to go.'

'Would you care to change with me?' asked Kinskii with a courteous smile. 'I am sure you will find my pony more willing.'

'Kind of you, but no. Can't let the damned animal get the better of me. Anyway, it may spoil your enjoyment of the morning.'

'I doubt it,' said Kinskii, still smiling, his eyes fixed firmly on Christy.

'Change horses if you like, Christy,' said Delamere, spluttering through a mouthful of sausage and bacon. 'See if it makes a jot of bloody difference.'

All six men stared at Christy and in the seconds of silence that followed, Eva saw a flush pass over his face.

Christy said, 'No. I'll keep this nag, thanks.' A couple of the men chuckled and exchanged glances. Eva felt anger, realising they were being rude in some subtle English fashion. She determined to ask Adam later what on earth they found funny.

After breakfast, Eva climbed back on the cart to watch the Masai lead the hunt into an area of grass and thorn trees. Oh, they made a thrilling sight loping through the long grass in their lion mane plumage and red blankets, spears held high.

The mule cart soon dropped behind, held up by rough ground and thick bush, leaving the three women and their two servants dragging along in clouds of grey volcanic dust. Eva endured the creaking, crashing and rolling for ten minutes before saying, 'This is terrible. I want to see the hunt. I'll walk ahead.'

She jumped down and hurried forward.

'Be careful,' called Florence.

Eva waved, and strode on. After a few hundred paces she met Musa returning through head-high grass, hunting rifle over his shoulder.

'Why are you walking, Memsahib?' he asked. 'Where is the cart?'

'Back there. It's too slow. I want to see what's happening. Why are you not with the others?'

'My work is finished so I came back to guard you. The lion are moving and Sakayo is tracking them with the Masai. I will take you to see but stay near me all the time.'

Shading his eyes against the rising sun, Adam stood up in his stirrups to see better. In a flurry of excitement, the dogs started up three lion and chased them into an area of long grass. Rainey cantered forward, called off the dogs and sent a message for the beaters to sweep the lion into his trap. He returned at a trot and arranged the horsemen into skirmish line.

Delamere called out his orders – 'Now we have the buggers. Move at slow pace toward the beaters. Stay mounted till we sight the lion. Dismount to shoot if they come towards us. Follow on horseback at best speed if they go away. We'll see if that works.'

Adam, in the centre between Stewartby and Rainey, watched Kinskii trot out to the right saying with a smile, 'As a hussar I must be right of the line.'

Christy took up position between Kinskii and Stewartby. Delamere and Mayne covered the left. At a signal from Kinskii the line of horsemen walked forward. From the corner of his eye Adam saw that almost immediately Christy dropped back. Kinskii waved an arm, urging him forward but within seconds Christy lagged yards behind.

Ahead, the Masai shuffled towards the horses, waving spears and yodelling. In the tall yellow grass Adam could only see their heads. At times they disappeared completely in the sea of waving fronds.

Adam, rifle held ready, concentrated hard, guiding his horse with pressure from his knees. Along the line he saw the same tension in every face as Kinskii turned in his saddle and again signalled Christy into line. At that moment Adam saw a huge lioness break from thick grass to their right and race for the gap Christy had opened between Kinskii and Stewartby.

Christy dragged at his reins – left then right. His horse fought back – reared high and fierce, eyes rolling, teeth grinding at the cruel bit, mouth foaming white spittle.

Christy seemed unable to control the horse as it plunged into a turn and galloped back into the trees and bush.

Confused, the lioness swerved into a determined charge at Stewartby.

Kinskii kicked his horse forward and turned to shield Stewartby.

Blocked, the lioness gathered all her force and strength into a furious leap at Kinskii.

A graceful, deadly, beautiful sight.

Kinskii managed one shot but missed and disappeared under his horse's neck as full weight of the lioness hammered into its flank. The screaming horse crashed sideways.

Stewartby's pony skipped away, leaving Adam full view of the incident.

With sleek graceful movement, Kinskii cleared his saddle a split second before the lioness struck. He released his right foot; stood briefly on the left stirrup; grabbed the mane and dived forward over the horse's shoulder, swinging under its neck to reappear kneeling on the other side. Somehow he had taken his rifle with him and loosed off a second shot that skidded off the lioness as she raked and split the horse's belly with her long hind claws.

Howling in anger and pain the lioness twisted and rushed for the thick bush and trees into which Christy disappeared moments before. The whole line of horseman, released from fear of hitting Kinskii, fired after her in a crashing volley of bullets. All missed. The lioness, blending into yellow grass, was gone.

One more shot cracked and rattled through the morning, as Kinskii despatched his horse. Adam jumped from his horse and ran with the others to gather round Kinskii who stood looking at the dead animal; pale entrails spilling pinkly silver on to the red dust.

'Bloody hell. I owe you my life, Sir,' said Stewartby. 'The damn thing would have got me had you not intervened. Never seen riding like it, Sir. Never. You're a brave man, Kinskii. A brave man.'

'The sort of thing one learns in a circus,' said Kinskii, smiling and dusting himself down. He retrieved his hat, smoothed his moustache. 'We must follow the lioness. She's gone towards Christy and the ladies. No doubt they are safe, but we should make sure.'

'If that bloody man had held line there'd be no danger,' snapped Stewartby. 'What's wrong with the fellow? I've ridden that horse. Always docile as a lamb – was as docile as a lamb....'

Adam said, 'Kinskii's right. We must get back. The lioness may be wounded. We should check on the ladies.'

'They'll be safe on the cart,' said Delamere.

'We should check on Christy then.'

Kinskii laughed. 'I feel he will also be quite safe,' he said. 'You go ahead. I shall follow with Sakayo and the Masai.'

Eva, walking with Musa, heard the shooting and stopped. Seconds later her heart shuddered at the sight of Christy cantering from the trees ahead. Oh how handsome he looked riding through the fresh new sunlight. What a beautiful man. And what a wonderful horseman. See how he controlled his mount. Such skill.

She stood on tiptoe and waved, heart thumping, blood racing. *Oh God. I haven't been like this since I was fifteen....*

Christy broke from the trees and saw movement ahead. *Bloody hell. It's the German woman. What's the stupid minx doing out here....*

He waved and flashed his best smile.

'What happened?' she called, 'Did you shoot any lion?'

He curved his horse into a graceful turn, slid to a halt beside her and jumped from the saddle, delighted at her shining eyes and enthusiastic welcome – *So I didn't mistake last night. The damn woman really does fancy me....*

'We saw several,' he said, wiping sweat from his brow with a sweep of a hand. 'One came close. I'm not sure if we shot it. The others are following up. My horse gave trouble so I came back to see how you and the ladies are. Why are you on foot? Where's the cart?'

As he spoke the mule cart appeared, making painful progress through the trees.

Eva said, 'Musa and I are going ahead to see what's happened. The cart's too slow and Beatrice must stay with Florence. Why don't you leave your horse here and come with us.'

The cart creaked to a halt nearby. Christy threw a gallant bow at Florence and ran an eye over Beatrice: *Not quite so peaches and cream at this time of morning, but still edible....*

'What are you up to?' called Florence from deep in her swaddle of blankets.

'Taking Mrs Early up to see the excitement,' Christy shouted back, slipping his rifle from its holster. 'I'll leave my horse here, if you don't mind.'

With a manly wave he called, 'Off we go then,' and led Eva towards the trees, tossing his reins to Musa and – *Bloody hell* – the damned man passed them over to one of Florence's servants and followed.

'Does he have to come, too?' Christy whispered into Eva's ear. 'I'd prefer us to be alone.'

To his delight she arched an eyebrow and whispered back, 'Another time, perhaps.'

Her foot caught and she stumbled, brushing him with her breasts – so soft, so sweet.

'Steady, m'dear.' He threw out a strong arm to help and she leaned against him for a few delicious seconds.

At that moment Delamere and the horsemen cantered from the bush two hundred yards away, waving and shouting. The lead horseman raised an arm and dragged his horse to a slithering halt, pointing. The others pulled around him in a cloud of red dust and fell silent.

'Why have they stopped?' asked Eva.

Christy knew instantly why. Fright snatched at his heart but before he could say, 'We must go back,' a wounded lioness, her belly spraying blood, dashed from a thicket, raced across their front and went to ground in an area of long grass thirty yards ahead.

Eva clutched Christy's arm, fingers digging into his flesh. He tried to pull away but she hung on. In a tight high voice full of panic, she said, 'Aren't they going to come and help us?'

Christy stood stiff and still, unable to move or speak, wishing the bloody woman would let go.

He heard Musa hiss in Swahili, 'Their horses will frighten the lion towards us, Memsahib. They cannot move. This *Bwana* and me must kill the lion. I'm not sure he knows how.'

Of course I don't know how, you stupid bastard.

The bloody African switched to English and said, 'We must kill the lion, Sir. You go forward and shoot. Go slow and quiet. I will follow with a second gun.'

Christy felt his spine turn to jelly but forced his muscles to move. Lifting his rifle he stepped half a pace away from Eva. Overcome with dread he lowered the rifle and froze. *If I don't threaten the bloody thing perhaps it'll give up and bugger off....*

From behind, he heard Eva whisper, 'Don't worry about me. I'll be safe here. Go forward and shoot.'

Christy's mind screamed, *Go forward? Shut up, you brainless bitch. I need to think....*

The hidden lioness snarled – a harsh grunt that rasped through the quiet morning and jerked Christy into motion. He turned a pleading face towards Musa.

The African stared back. No sympathy or help in those knowing brown eyes. *Oh God. What do I do...?*

Musa pointed with his chin and flicked his head, motioning Christy towards the lioness. With no other choice Christy knew he had to move. Forcing his quaking legs into motion, he took the lead, creeping from tree to tree; stopping to look long and hard before moving on.

Seeing that the final fifteen yards of approach would take him over open ground, Christy crouched behind a last tree trunk feeling he would die of fear. He waited an age before edging a few yards out.

The lioness moved.

In a blur of liquid amber she swept from the bush and charged straight at Eva.

'Shoot, Sir,' shouted Musa.

Christy stood rigid.

Could not move.

Could not look at the lioness gathering her fierce muscles into a great leap.

From the corner of his eye he saw Musa swing and with one shot hit the lioness.

Straight through the left eye.

The lioness – knocked sideways – rolled and tumbled through a cloud of red dust to fall stone dead in a tangled heap, three yards short of Eva.

Two more shots rang out

Crack! Crack!

The lioness jerked as two heavy bullets from Christy's gun thumped into her head and chest.

'Got it by God.' he shouted. 'Got the damned thing....'

Chapter Seventeen

A Dangerous Affair

Eva sat on the veranda with Florence watching the men drinking and reliving the morning's excitement.

Christy sat, feet stretched, drink in hand. A picture of young, handsome confidence. Enjoying his own bravery.

'Got the damn thing in two. Brought it down with a head shot. Then banged one in the heart to make sure. Musa? Oh yes. He hit it too. Just after I'd bowled it over. Lucky shot in the eye as it tumbled. Well now. What a to do. Must write and tell the chaps back in India.'

Eva heard Stewartby snort and several men snigger but none spoke – probably due to a sharp look from Delamere.

'A dangerous affair, Mrs Early,' said Florence. ' You're shivering. Are you still affected by the awful event?'

'Not really,' said Eva. 'It happened so fast. I'm unhurt thanks to Captain Christy. I feel lucky that he came back to check on us. I'm sorry he's leaving this afternoon.'

She felt relieved to get away from everyone after lunch when the ladies retired to rest but stood half hidden by her window to watch Christy's departure.

From behind her curtain Eva watched him swing into the saddle and canter off.

The men gathered to see him go. Turning in the saddle he waved gallantly, with a broad confident smile, white-blond hair ruffling in the breeze.

She peeped her head out, sure his farewell was for her: *What a handsome rider he is. How expert....*

The men returned to their seats and drinks and she ducked back behind her curtain. She heard Rainey laugh and say, 'Hope he doesn't meet any more lion.'

'Bloody man's a danger,' said Mayne.

'Bloody man's a coward,' grunted Stewartby.

'Hang on,' said Delamere. 'You can't say that about an officer and a gentleman. Especially when he saved Mrs Early.'

'I can,' said Stewartby. 'He abandoned us, and damn near did for Mrs Early. You saw what happened as well as the rest of us. Bloody man stood and did nothing till almost too late.'

'I saw him wait till he had a clear shot, then fire,' said Delamere. 'Hit the animal twice. That's good enough for me. What do you think,

Early? You know Christy best.'

Eva listened, head close to the open window.

Adam said, 'At school he always avoided the dangerous or damaging. Seems he hasn't changed.'

Stewartby laughed.

'As I said. A bloody coward.'

Returning by train to Nairobi, Adam and Eva spoke little until she said, 'I heard you all insulting Captain Christy. Why did you not support him against Stewartby and Mayne?'

'What is there to support?' asked Adam. 'The man's still a coward and liar. Hasn't changed since school.'

'No,' said Eva. 'Captain Christy saved me. He killed the lion with two shots. Musa hit it as well, but Captain Christy saved me. He shot it through the eye.'

'No. Musa hit it in the eye. Same shot he used to kill Churchill's rhino six years ago. Straight into the brain.'

'Nonsense. Musa was lucky then. You said so when you came home.'

Adam said, 'I know better now.'

She shook her head. 'You dislike Christy and want everyone else to dislike him. That is very bad.'

'What I think bad is his way with you,' said Adam. 'He paid you far too much attention.'

'No more than the other men.'

'I didn't like it. The man's a menace. There'll not be a second chance. We won't be seeing him again.'

'We will,' she said. 'I've invited him to Mzito with the others next month for my Sandbach-Baker farewell party. He accepted. We cannot now cancel the invitation. I won't allow it...'

On her return to Mzito Eva scribbled a note to Christy thanking him for saving her and inviting him to the party : *I told my husband I asked you when we met at Soysambu. If we had managed a few moments alone, I would have done so. Please come or he will know I used a little lie. Bring some friends so you do not arrive alone.*

She sent the letter by runner to army headquarters, but received no reply.

Kristina came to stay for several days with Eva at Mzito, while Kinskii went on a hunting safari with rich clients.

'Where is Adam?' Kristina asked.

'Gone to Anwar's then north over the mountains. New land may be available soon on Laikipia Plateau and he wants to look at it.'

'More land? Why more land? Can you afford it?'

'No. But he must look to see if he can run cattle there. We need more cattle to keep going until my coffee is ready for sale. Let me tell you of my adventure at Soysambu.'

'Kinskii told me but you tell me again.'

When Eva finished, Kristina said, 'So Christy saved you?'

'Yes. I must repay him.'

'How?'

'I'll find a way.'

'Darling, be careful.'

Eva sighed, wondering if she'd ever be alone with Christy again.

Kristina must have read Eva's mind because she said, 'If you need a place to thank Captain Christy properly, you can use my house while Kinskii is away. It would be very discreet.'

Eva said, 'I can't. I would let my husband down.'

Kristina smiled, her violet eyes glowing.

'Let me know if I can help,' she said.

Eva invited everyone she knew to her party for Queenie and Freddie Sandbach-Baker, with an open invitation for their friends. Arriving guests pitched tent wherever it suited, surrounding the house with a small camp, fluttering in the breeze, shining in the sun.

By mid-morning Saturday fifty guests – ten women, forty men – crowded the veranda and garden. Eva, tense and unsure if Christy would come, studied each arriving group.

'Why are you so nervous?' asked Kristina. 'It's only a party. For heaven's sake be calm.'

To Eva's delight, Christy rode in at lunchtime with three army officers. Busy with Musa and her cooks by the kitchen she resisted an impulse to run across and greet him. He waved and smiled, indicating he would see her later with a flick of his fingers.

By late afternoon whole sheep and haunches of beef turned over pits of hot charcoal. At sundown, servants carved and served great chunks of meat with bread, soup and potatoes.

After dark, beer and whisky flowed. The men stood or sat in groups around large log fires set among the trees, arguing and getting drunk, faces glowing red.

In the crowd, Eva managed a private word with Christy.

'Tomorrow we'll have time to talk,' she whispered. 'Tonight I am busy.'

He nodded and tickled her hand. For a brief moment she held his fingers, looking deep into his eyes. A message passed...

Sunday morning dawned clear and crisp. African servants cleared away all trace of the party before sunrise and carried breakfast to the tents. By ten some guests began to depart. At lunchtime only twenty remained, scattered on chairs and hammocks, across grass and veranda, eating cold meat and drinking wine.

Adam and H.E. sat at one end of the veranda with Delamere, Stewartby, Kinskii and several settlers when an argument started.

'Trouble is we have no support from you bloody government people,' Delamere shouted at H.E. 'And there's no point just walking off when we want to talk to you about it.'

H.E., retreating down the steps, smiled and said, 'My dear fellow, you know very well I can't involve myself in such discussion.'

H.E. joined Eva, Kristina and Beatrice, sitting in shade under the trees. He eased his large frame into a cane chair and said, 'These settlers are terrible. More than three of them together, and it's a political meeting. My God this is a funny country. Every European is a politician.'

'Not me,' said Christy appearing through the trees. 'May I join you? I promise not to argue. Especially politics.'

Beatrice shifted her chair towards H.E. and made space. 'What are they complaining about now?' she asked in her little voice.

'The Masai move,' said H.E.. 'The Government plans to transfer the northern Masai down off the Laikipia Plateau and free more land for white settlers. We'll reunite the tribe in a big reserve on the Mara plain. Been planning it for years. The Masai are not stupid. They know Laikipia is good cattle land. Last year they took us to court. Who would have thought it? Bloody people may still live in the Stone Age but they're sharp enough to hire lawyers and take an injunction against the Government to stop the move. Meantime a lot of the Masai are trickling down and joining the southern tribe anyway. Delamere and his cronies want us to push the rest into following so they can get their hands on the Plateau. But the Government can't act – or even discuss it – because of the court case.'

'It's all too much for me,' said Beatrice,

'Me too,' said Christy. 'Mrs Early. I've seen nothing of your estate. Why don't we all go for a walk? You can show us round.'

131

Unsure what to say, Eva looked at Kristina. Beatrice looked at H.E., who said 'It would certainly clear the cobwebs from last night.'

Kristina smiled at Eva and said, 'You four go. I'm too tired. Take the children, Eva. It will give them exercise.'

Eva hesitated for a second then said, 'Good idea.'

Kristina watched the little group set off towards the cattle pens. Thomas, now five, trotted ahead on sturdy legs. Three year old Alexandra toddled along with her *ayah*. Eva seemed to be walking as close as possible to Christy, her arm brushing against him every couple of paces. Kristina smiled, her violet eyes glowing with malice: *Is this the start of Eva's new game?*

At the cattle pens Eva pointed out her own small herd.

'Beautiful animals,' said Christy, 'What are they? And why the hump?'

'Boran from the northern desert,' said Eva. 'They store water in their back, like camels. Adam brought some down for me specially a few years ago and I've bred more.'

At her coffee plantation she stopped to speak with a group of Kikuyu women working between rows of bushes.

'When will your coffee be ready to pick?' asked H.E..

'Later this year,' said Eva.

She led the way down into Rowbas village. Thomas shouted in excitement and ran to join a group of African children, playing among the huts. Alexandra trotted after him, followed by the *ayah*. Thomas began to arrange a game involving every child in sight, his sharp high voice piping out orders in a mixture of Kikuyu and Swahili.

'We can leave Thomas and Alexandra here to play,' said Eva. 'Let's go down by the river. I'll show you where these Kikuyu rescued me.'

'I've heard that story several times,' said H.E.. 'I have something interesting to show Beatrice back in the coffee bushes. See you in fifteen minutes or so.'

He winked at Christy, took Beatrice by the arm and led her away.

'I think they want to be alone,' said Eva.

'So do we,' said Christy, taking her hand.

Eva's heart thumped and she pulled away, saying, 'Come on. Let's go down to the river.'

Christy stood with Eva on a slope above the river, listening to her story. Bending forward to hear her voice above the water noise he felt silken lips brush his lobe: *Perfect....*

Clambering down the damp bank he offered a steadying hand. At river edge her soft fingers clung moments longer than necessary, teasing his palm. Despite mid-day sun, the valley air felt cool and damp. As Eva released his hand he felt her shiver.

'Cold?' he asked.

'No. Just remembering.'

'Remembering what?'

She shivered again, laughed and took hold of his sleeve. 'Help me balance. I'll show you how I fell into the water.'

With her free hand she lifted skirt hem to knees, pulled him into the shallows, skipped on to a round stone and danced upstream, hopping from rock to rock, dragging him along, splashing and laughing until she found a moss covered boulder and cried, 'It was about here.'

She wobbled, slipped carefully sideways and fell into his arms.

'Pity you weren't here to catch me last time,' she whispered, lips brushing his earlobe again.

He stood in shallow rushing water, holding her tight, then, in a sweeping movement lifted her on to the bank.

'Oh dear. I'm all wet,' she cried. 'I must dry my shoes. Look away.'

He half turned, smiling and watching over his shoulder as she sat on the grass and lifted her legs, showing a flash of white thigh. She whipped off her heavy shoes and stockings and half dropping her skirt, rolled backwards, saying, 'You can look now. Take these and put them over there to dry.'

He placed her shoes on a patch of warm bare earth and draped the stockings – half damp from the stream, half warm from her body – over a bush and bent to untie his own bootlaces

She lay back on her elbows, head tilted; smiling at him; skirt rolled above her knees.

'I must dry my legs also,' she said. 'Do you mind?'

'Of course not.'

He set his boots and socks alongside hers, and stood looking down.

'What now?' he asked.

She patted the grass.

'Sit and dry with me,' she said.

He knew he had won.

Two paces. He strode two paces to join her. Two paces that he knew would take them into a different world.

She lay back as he settled beside her. Did not resist as he measured his body against hers. Closed her eyes to his first kiss. Ran her hands down his back. Pulled his haunches hard against her. Sighed. Returned his kiss with soft lips; eager urgency; increasing passion.

For a second he paused.

Did he sense danger? Did a cloud cover the sun?

He had done this so many times with other men's wives – lightly and with little care – but this time the dark moment passing through his soul with that first sweet kiss touched him deeply.

For a second. For a brief second...he held himself back.

Then thought: *Sod it.*

And rolled over to apply himself to the task of pleasing her....

Chapter Eighteen

An Open Secret

'We must be careful,' Eva said, strolling with Christy back up the slope towards the coffee plantation. She clung to his hand. Stroked the muscles of his arm. Stood on tiptoe to kiss his cheek. 'We must be very careful.'

'Of course.' he said.

'He would kill you if he knew.'

'Your husband?'

'Who else.'

'He doesn't have it in him.'

'He does.'

Christy laughed.

'Old Willy Woggers couldn't kill anyone.'

'He already has,' said Eva, 'In a Somali bandit ambush in the north.'

'Good God! How many?'

'Three, four, five...I'm not sure.'

'He really shot that many? Honestly? Did *he* tell you?'

'No. Abdi told me. They were together in the fight. And I've heard from others. This is a small country. News and scandal travel fast.'

'Especially scandal,' said Christy. 'Talking of which...'

He pointed towards H.E. and Beatrice emerging from coffee trees nearby deep in conversation, Beatrice patting her soft blond hair into place. Her perfect peach skin glowed.

'Cat's had the cream,' murmured Christy.

As he spoke, Adam rode over the hill, cantering fast on his pony.

With a gasp of panic Eva contrived to stumble, making it appear that Christy reached out to catch her before she fell.

'Where the hell have you been?' shouted Adam, face white and angry.

'Down at the river showing our friends where I fell and nearly drowned.'

'Eva, you were very lucky,' said Beatrice in her soft voice, as she and H.E. joined the tense group. 'It looked so dangerous.'

'How the hell do you know?' snapped Adam. 'You were in the damned coffee with H.E..'

'Hold on, old chap,' said H.E.. 'We stayed together until just now. Beatrice saw a deer among the bushes and we went to look. Eva and

135

Christy waited for us.'

Adam ignored him and glared at Eva. 'Your guests are leaving. You should be at the house. You've been gone ages. *Ayah* brought the children back half an hour ago. Bloody well hurry. I'll see you there.'

He wheeled his horse and cantered off.

'Dear me,' said H.E.. 'What an angry Adam. We'd better get back. Interesting little story you told us at the river Eva – tell us again as we walk back so we know more detail.'

An hour later Christy and his three soldier chums cantered off towards Nairobi. At top of the rise Christy swung his horse in a graceful turn and halted to look back at Eva and Kristina, two small figures on the veranda.

Posed against the sky he removed his hat and held it high.

'Two fine fillies,' said one officer. 'Which one's yours?'

'Blow them a kiss, you devil,' said another.

Christy laughed. 'I'm in enough trouble with her husband. I'll avoid more for the moment, thank you.'

'We saw you sneak off to the woods, you cad. Did you manage a gallop?'

'More of a canter I'd say, old boy. But I certainly got a foot in the stirrup. She's almost broken in. A longer ride'll follow.'

He brought his hat down and slapped the horse into a fast run, shouting, 'Come on fellows – slowest to the Norfolk buys the beer.'

With the last guest gone, Eva sat in dead silence on the veranda ignoring Adam. She went through her usual evening routine – watched sunset, saw the children to bed but without speaking a word to Adam. She continued to ignore him during dinner, keeping her gaze down, concentrating on her plate. Drinking coffee and leafing through a book afterwards she jumped when Adam suddenly snapped, 'I'll not have it. I'll not have that man Christy upsetting our life. He'll never come here again.'

'What if I invite him?' asked Eva in a cold sharp voice. 'I find him interesting company.'

'That's damned obvious. You made a fool of yourself, and of me.'

'What nonsense. We went for a walk with H.E. and Beatrice.'

'When I rode over the hill they were nowhere near and you were holding Christy's hand.'

'I tripped and grabbed at Captain Christy. He held me for a second or I would have been down.'

'You expect me to believe that? What I saw was different.'

Eva shouted, 'What if I *do* make some friends of my own. You are never here. You're always away with your damned woodcutting sawmills and in the north collecting damned cows. You never spend time here with me. I do all the work on this damned farm, not you. You leave me here alone to do everything.'

'That bloody man Christy caused me misery at school in England,' Adam stormed back. 'Now he's going to do the same here. I'll kill the man before he ruins my life. I'll see him dead.'

Exhausted and shocked by this turn in the argument Eva fell silent. She glared at her husband, refusing to speak first. He sat staring at his drink.

Finally he said, 'I think you are fascinated by Christy.'

She frowned and whispered, 'Yes. I do find him fascinating.... Yes. He *does* fascinate me.'

Adam stood and stared down at her. 'Did anything happen between you?'

'No.'

'Are you sure?'

'Yes.'

'Will it?'

A further deep silence then...she sighed and tried to speak. Unable to express herself she fell into further silence, head bowed, a hand covering her mouth.

'Will it?' he asked again.

'I don't know. I can't tell.'

'If it does I'll shoot him. And perhaps you too.'

She shrugged.

'Then we'll all be dead. Christy and me shot. You hanged.'

Eva marched off to bed and slept surprisingly well although fearful and worried. Adam slept in another room and to her surprise joined her next morning for breakfast at sunrise in a better mood.

'Are we friends again?' she asked.

He frowned and said, 'I suppose so. There's no point in keeping an argument going. I said what I needed to say. You did the same. Now we must continue to live together and make the best of it. These things blow over.'

A few days later Adam went north to buy more cattle.

'I'll be gone a week,' he said but two days later sent a runner with a note: *Sorry. I must go farther north towards Somalia. I'll be away about three weeks.*

Eva showed the note to Kristina and said, 'He's still angry with me and this is his way of trying to win the argument – by leaving me for weeks at a time. He's punishing me.'

Kristina laughed and said, 'That makes you freer than before. You are lucky. Make the most of it. Use my house. Come down and enjoy yourself while your husband's away. Get your own revenge.'

Eva said, 'I can't. I'm too busy here on the farm.'

For ten days Eva worked hard, walking and riding around the estate supervising the coffee plantation, cattle pens, and building work on a small school she planned at Rowbas. Alone each day and night her obsession for Christy returned. His strong body, warm arms, blue eyes, filled her imagination. *Why not? My husband leaves me alone. Why should I not enjoy my memory of a wonderful afternoon? Why not more? I must meet him again....*

She sent a runner to Kristina with a message: *I am coming to town. I've written to Christy and told him to meet me at your house.*

She packed her children into the pony trap and set out for Nairobi. Leaving the children and their *ayah* at the Norfolk she drove her trap up the hill to Kristina's house and said, 'I've arranged to meet Christy here tonight. I must see him.'

Whilst travelling in the north Adam also had Christy on his mind and found himself brooding over Eva's whispered near-confession, hearing her again and again: *Yes – he does fascinate me –* and after eight days, decided to go home.

He sent Abdi north to buy more cattle and, with a couple of servants, set off back towards Nairobi, diverting across Laikipia Plateau to check several land parcels before crossing the Kinangop to Anwar's. This added several days to his journey and brought him into Nairobi during the early evening. Needing to discuss buying some of the land on Laikipia he took a rickshaw straight up to H.E.'s house, arriving at dusk.

Alone in Kristina's house in the warm evening twilight, Eva – dressed in a simple white gown – waited to welcome her lover.

Unsure whether she felt nervous or excited, she moved around checking final arrangements – the table set with a supper of cold meat and salad, wine and beer cooling in the icebox, oil lamps set low to spread soft pleasant light.

Eva caught sight of her reflection in a mirror and paused. Satisfied at the way her hair flowed loose across her tanned shoulders and wispy white dress, she checked and touched at her eyes and lips until happy with the portrait of a beautiful woman smiling back from the glass.

Before departing to join Eva's children at the Norfolk, Kristina sent her servants back to their quarters, saying, 'I'll see you in the morning at the Norfolk. Make sure you arrive in time for breakfast with Thomas and Alexandra. Have a lovely time...'

As darkness fell Eva heard faint voices. She checked out the window and saw movement at H.E.'s house through the trees two hundred yards away: *A guest for dinner? Or someone arrived to drink and talk politics....*

Eva drew back to close the curtain and in a surge of excitement saw Christy riding slowly towards her through the dusk. She hurried and opened the door a few inches. Waiting in calm excitement she heard him tiptoe on to the veranda. Heart beating she stepped back into the shadowed room and opened her arms wide to accept his embrace...

Just as H.E.'s servant opened the door, Adam heard a horse walking among the trees. Squinting through deepening dusk he saw a rider disappear behind Kristina's house. The figure looked familiar – *Bloody hell. Is that Christy? What's he doing sneaking up on Kristina?*

Intrigued, Adam stepped off H.E.'s veranda and peered across just in time to see Kristina, dressed in white, step back from her window. The man slipped round the house on to the veranda and inside before Adam could be sure – *I bloody well hope it's Christy. A fling with Kristina should take his bloody mind off Eva....*

Adam found H.E. in the dining room, sprawled across two chairs, glass in hand, bottle nearby.

'Are you drunk?' he asked.

'Not yet... Expect to be soon. Join me?'

'Why drink this early?' asked Adam.

'Why not? Stay for dinner. Stay and get drunk.'

'I'll certainly have dinner. Did you hear a horse just now? I'm sure I saw Christy in the trees.'

'Oh God. He's not coming for dinner too is he?'

'No. I think he went into Kristina's house. Is Kinskii at home?'

'No. He's off hunting with a party of fat Americans. Not expected back for days yet. So Christy's set for a ride with your sister-in law, hey? He'd better be careful. I'm not sure Kinskii would take the thought kindly.'

'I may be wrong but I think it was Christy. Anyway – none of our business.'

'Fun to know about it though,' said H.E. with a coarse laugh. 'Good luck to the poor fish. Have a drink.'

Adam saw that H.E. was in no mood to talk business so relaxed and stayed for dinner then sat drinking with H.E. until after midnight.

Next morning Adam woke before dawn, found H.E.'s head cook, drank hot tea from a big mug and set out for Mzito on one of H.E.'s ponies a few minutes before sunrise. His head hurt from too much alcohol the night before. Annoyed that he had drunk so much and allowed H.E. to avoid discussing land, he rode halfway to Mzito before remembering the man he saw sneaking in to see Kristina.

Damn. I should have checked if the bugger stayed till this morning. I never even thought to look at the house....

Eva woke, as always, before dawn. Her lover lay on his back, fast asleep, white-blond hair tousled. She crept from the bed, wrapped herself in a shawl and eased out on to the veranda. Breakfast could wait but not her need to see sunrise.

She settled in a cane chair, breathing the crisp cool air: *How beautiful this is. How lovely the world. So peaceful, so....*

Her world stopped. Her whole body clenched in shock.

Mein Gott! Adam. What's he doing here? He's seen me. He knows....

Unable to move she sat rigid, shoulders hunched and stiff.

Through grey dawn light, she watched her husband mount a pony and ride away towards Nairobi without looking back, thank God.

Shaking with fright she hurried into the house and woke Christy. 'You must go. I've just seen my husband. He could come in here and find us....'

Without a word Christy jumped from the bed, threw on his clothes, snatched a kiss and left, leading his horse away into the woods behind Kristina's house, well hidden from H.E.'s windows.

Overcome by fear, Eva ran about, dragging on a khaki shirt and long skirt and hiding herself in a black Somali shawl with a big hat pulled down over her face. She crept out the back door, harnessed her pony to the trap and started out for the Norfolk and almost fainted when she heard her name ring out through the trees.

H.E. waved from his veranda and called out, 'Need a cup of tea or a brandy or anything?'

Eva's heart sank. She hauled the trap round and guided it across to

H.E.'s house.

He gave her a big wink and said, 'Heard your pony on the stones and saw you from my window. '

She looked at his leering face and tried to speak but he raised a hand and said, 'Don't worry. I'll not say a word. We all have our little secrets and yours is safe with me.'

Eva arrived at the Norfolk before her children woke. Kristina listened in wide-eyed concern, and secret laughter, to Eva's hushed and urgent story. 'If there's any trouble we'll think of something,' she said. 'Don't worry.'

Half an hour later, as Eva and Kristina sat at breakfast with the children, Beatrice appeared hurrying across the dining room. 'Eva, I'm so glad to see you,' she said. 'I want you to build me a house here in Nairobi. I need a small place, on the hill. I have some land near the house you built for Kristina.'

'H.E. has a house close by,' said Kristina, smiling.

'Does he?' said Beatrice, patting at her soft hair and blushing.

When Beatrice left Kristina laughed and whispered, 'God, you're lucky, Eva. Beatrice just gave you a reason for staying in Nairobi last night. *And* a reason for coming down to town whenever you want.'

Eva prepared her story on the way back to Mzito.

Showing great surprise at seeing Adam she hugged him and cried, 'Darling, how lovely to see you home early. I didn't expect you for another week. What happened? Wait till I settle the children and I'll tell you some interesting news. Where have I been? Nairobi, darling. The children and I stayed at the Norfolk. I took cattle to Damu, went to the bank; did some shopping then spent the evening with Beatrice planning a new house she's asked me to build. I had a lovely couple of days. So much better than staying here alone all the time you are away....'

She surrounded Adam with excited chatter – smoothed away his annoyance at her absence – listened with interest to his news from the north...and of his visit to H.E.'s.

'Oh darling,' she said. 'If only you had known I was at the Norfolk. You could have come into town and joined me. What a pity.'

After lunch she sat with Adam on the veranda drinking coffee when – with a sharp look – he said, 'You're chattering an awful lot and seem nervous. Do you have some secret I should know?'

Eva felt her face freeze and knew she must have turned white.

'Why do you ask? What have you heard?'

'I've *heard* nothing. But I *saw* Christy creeping into Kristina's house last night. I know Kinskii's away upcountry so it looks as though Kristina is up to something.'

Eva felt the blood flow back into her face. Thinking fast, she said, 'So you know. Kristina hopes to keep it secret. Promise you'll say nothing to Kinskii.'

'Not a word. He'd kill the bugger.'

After this fright Eva wondered whether to continue her affair with Christy. 'But I find him so fascinating,' she whispered to Kristina.

'Then enjoy yourself,' urged Kristina, violet eyes glowing with excitement. 'Use my house whenever Kinskii is away. No one will ever know.'

But Kristina lied, hugging to herself the knowledge that news of the meetings trickled like water along the conduit of house servants and rickshaw drivers then spilled down the hill to lap quietly round the Norfolk bar and dining room. In quiet delight she waited for the soft swirl of rumour to break surface as full-blown scandal.

Adam's continual absences allowed Eva freedom to visit Nairobi at will. Anwar came down from the mountain and helped design Beatrice's house. A few weeks later a gang of jolly Sikhs arrived to start construction. Eva brought the children down from Mzito to spend days at a time supervising and checking, slowing progress wherever possible.

Caught up in her warm private world of illicit love Eva began to take risks. More obsessed with Christy each day, she arranged apparently accidental meetings whenever visiting Nairobi – always in the presence of others: Kristina, Queenie, Christy's brother officers – anyone at all to give reality to 'chance' encounters.

One evening she sat with Kristina and Christy on the Norfolk veranda when H.E. arrived. 'Four is better than three,' he said, 'I'll join you. Let me buy you a drink.'

Before he could sit down Kinskii appeared, skipping on to the veranda from the darkness.

'What are you doing here?' asked Kristina in surprise.

Kinskii ignored her. Bowing to Christy he said, 'I wish to speak with you, Sir. Please come with me.'

Without a word Christy stood and followed Kinskii into the shadows.

'Where the hell did he come from?' hissed Kristina. 'He's supposed

142

to be upcountry with his Americans.'

H.E. chuckled. 'Is he now? Well it looks as if he's back.'

Moments later Eva heard a horse canter away. Kinskii rejoined them and said, 'Captain Christy remembered duties at his barracks and felt he should leave. I think he will not return this evening.'

Kinskii ordered wine and toasted his wife then smiled at Eva and said, 'I hope your evening is not spoiled by Captain Christy's urgent need to leave.'

For several weeks after the incident with Kinskii, Christy made no contact. Tormented by his silence Eva wrote several anxious notes, taking risks by using her African maid to deliver them. Finally Christy replied with a short unsigned note: *Sorry you've had trouble getting hold of me. They posted me to the desert. I'm back in Nairobi for a few days. Send a note by return to tell me when we can meet at K's and I'll tell you what happened....*

Kristina refused to help Eva. 'Christy had to tell Kinskii it is you he's seeing, not me. Kinskii's furious you used our house. I must stay out of it. Find somewhere else if you want to see Christy again....'

In desperation Eva arranged a meeting in Beatrice's half built house during the heat of afternoon while the Sikhs rested.

When Christy arrived and hurried into the almost completed room Eva jumped into his arms. She embraced and kissed him hard then pulled him to sit on a rough wooden bench, holding hands. She played nervously with his fingers, tense with a mixture of fear and passion. 'Darling, I've missed you,' she said.

'And I've missed you but – as you said at the beginning, we must be careful,' said Christy. 'That silly bugger Kinskii challenged me to a duel. What the hell does he think this is – some mid European opera house? Darling – you'll be annoyed, but I had to tell him it's you, not Kristina. I told him the truth because he wanted to fight me there and then. I'd have killed the silly little devil. Then everyone would know our secret and I'd be hanged for murder. My Colonel heard of the argument – God knows how – and sent me straight to a guard post in the desert between the railway and Taveta. Nothing I can do. We'll just have to bear it. I return to the desert tomorrow. Not sure when I'll be back in Nairobi.'

Eva looked into his eyes and saw nothing but clear blue honesty.

Christy stood and said, 'Darling' – again the open honest gaze – 'I'm a soldier. I have no choice.'

She leaned forward, threw her arms around his waist and sobbed,

'Nor do I have choice. I must see you.'

He stepped back, pulling away from her grasp. 'No. I must go now. It's dangerous for me to stay. I'll write....'

She remained seated; head turned away – felt his lips brush her cheek and knew he would taste her tears.

In early September H.E. sent a note asking Adam to call at his Government office.

'This is an official meeting, old boy,' said H.E.. 'I have a sealed letter for you from the Government in London. You are to open and read it out loud in my presence.'

Churchill wrote: *I must call upon your services again. I wish you to join a Government delegation and take part in meetings with the German authorities in East Africa as my personal observer. Pray report any opinions or findings directly to me as before....*

'You certainly do have some important friends, m'dear man,' said H.E.. 'The First Sea Lord seems to like you. But don't worry. I'm sworn to secrecy so no one else will know.'

'Will know what?'

'That you're his personal spy.'

'What bloody nonsense.'

H.E. laughed and said, 'We've been instructed to add you into the discussions as guide and interpreter – same subject you and I dealt with at Tanga in '02. If the stupid politicians want a war in Europe, we must avoid fighting here. No help to anyone if we Europeans kill each other in front of the Natives. Logical for you to be included, since you completed the original mission. For secrecy we're meeting in the bush as though it's a hunting safari. We're including Count and Countess Kinskii, and your wife – for the languages, you understand. It'll be like a jolly family party...Oh...Your friend Christy will be along too. Thought I'd better let you know....'

144

Chapter Nineteen

A Moment Of Murder

September 1913

Christy marched at the head of his small safari, across a grassy plain near the German border.

His orders – to take a platoon of *askari* to meet, guide and accompany a party of five Germans from Longido to a map reference in Namanga district – seemed vague. But Christy's tracker knew the area well and led them towards a crop of rocky hills.

Shortly before noon Christy climbed a ridge and sighted his destination half a mile away – a surprisingly large group of tents set up in a clearing among thorn trees. He saw a number of people emerge and stand looking down the slope. Some waved. Christy waved back: *Women? Are two of them women?*

He stopped, removed his hat, fumbled for his field-glasses and focused on a group of ten Europeans. A few he did not know but: *Good God! What the hell are they doing here? Hocklyffe-Evans, Kinskii, and – bloody hell – Early. And the women? Christ. The two Germans. Eva and her bloody sister Kristina. Hells teeth, what am I in for....?*

He thrust the field-glasses into their pack, threw his hat back on his head and said, with a charming smile, 'Well *Herr* Kreuz, we seem to have a welcoming committee. You must be very important....'

Eva watched the small safari advance through yellow grass and thorn trees. One of the leaders removed his hat. She saw a flash of white-blond hair and her heart jumped: *No. It can't be. What's he doing with the Germans? Why is he here?*

Taking a deep breath to try and control her thumping pulse she borrowed a small telescope and focused on the officer leading his men forward across the valley. *Yes. It's Christy. Mein Gott. What shall I do when he gets here...?*

In panic she passed the telescope to Kristina, received a raised eyebrow in return and looked at her husband to see him standing quiet and unsurprised with H.E..

He knew, the devil. Adam knew Christy would be here. He didn't tell me. Why didn't he tell me?...Why should he?...He knows nothing....

Kristina chuckled and passed the telescope back.

'What now?' she whispered in German, violet eyes glowing.

While Kreuz made formal introductions along the line Christy stood to attention with his file of askaris and considered his situation: *A mixed bunch, these Huns. Kreuz and Abel are obviously soldiers. The other two...what the hell are they? Politicals, I'll bet. Out of place in the bush. Must be from Berlin....*

He heard Hocklyffe-Evans welcome the Germans and say, 'I trust we have fruitful discussions, and enjoy our hunting also. Today we rest. Tomorrow we talk. Next day we hunt. Then more talk. I hope this programme suits you'

Christy relaxed: *So that's it – several days of chatter. It's political. They'll all be in the big tent. That'll give me free time. Perhaps I'll be able to get at Early's wife again – or her sister. Both fair game in a place like this....*

Unable to turn his head, he swivelled his eyes just enough to see Eva, standing at the end of the line, next to her sister. Both dressed in long khaki skirts and jackets, hair pushed up under wide brimmed hats. He saw Kristina watching the ceremony and... *My little bird's watching me....*

He caught Eva's eye and managed a slow wink. She smiled – a brief twitch of those lovely lips – and lowered her eyes.

Christy grinned scenting fun ahead.

An hour before the Germans arrived H.E. called his group together in the big tent and explained, 'You're all sworn to secrecy. We have arranged to discuss security matters with the German East African authorities. I lead for our Government. My two colleagues from London have a watching and recording brief. Mr Early is our local observer. Count and Countess Kinskii, plus Madame Early are interpreters. We must look after our German guests and be aware of the importance this meeting holds for us all. Our futures may depend on success here.'

Polite conversation flowed in English and German. Adam followed both languages with ease whilst keeping an eye on Christy and Eva. Apart from an occasional glance he saw nothing pass between them so he concentrated on an intriguing comment from Kreuz to H.E..

'But my dear Sir,' said Kreuz, speaking English, 'You must realise that since you took Zanzibar into your Empire this year our German East Africa is surrounded by you British on three of our borders and your Belgian allies on the fourth.'

And H.E.'s reply, 'But *you* must understand our worry at the recent

146

raising of a further two hundred thousand troops by your Kaiser. Why has he done this? Is Germany planning war in Europe? If so, what are your intentions here? It's a fair question that needs clear response.'

Adam leaned forward to catch Kreuz's answer, 'But in Europe we must match the French and Russians who arm themselves for what? Adventures in the west, perhaps? And the Balkans? How dangerous are the Balkans after last year's war between Serbia and Bulgaria? Let me ask Count Kinskii. He knows the area well.'

Kinskii said, 'Who can tell? The whole area is a mess of changing loyalties and intrigue. God alone knows what will happen and who may become involved in more death and destruction if the current stalemate flares up again.'

Bored with politics Adam checked again on Christy, now deep in whispered conversation with Abel and ignoring Eva. The two soldiers, no doubt discussing military matters and camp security, seemed quite friendly.

Adam relaxed: *Perhaps Eva's reaction was just surprise at seeing Christy? Maybe I should have warned her he'd be here.*

Christy quickly made friends with Abel and immediately felt kindred spirit when the German whispered, 'Can you help me speak with Countess Kristina alone? We became…friends when she passed through Moschi in 1905. I am anxious to renew acquaintance.'

'You slept with her?'

'Several times. She is wonderful. Have you tried her yet?'

'No, but she's on my list.'

'Can you assist me?'

Christy chuckled and whispered back, 'Only if you help me find time alone with Madame Early. We should be able to arrange it. Early and Kinskii will spend plenty of time in the big tent negotiating. If you and I keep contact I'm sure we'll find a chance to get our hands on the women….'

Next morning the conference started at ten. At ten thirty Eva restarted her affair with Christy, slipping away to the bush to talk; touch and revive her passion. She made it back into camp ten minutes before lunch and spent the afternoon in the conference, trying hard to listen and translate when needed, but her mind strayed constantly to Christy.

As soon as dusk fell she abandoned caution, found an excuse to leave Adam in their tent and met Christy again for a few minutes, embracing in the warm dark, among nearby trees. 'This is crazy,' whispered Christy, as excited as she. Eva, unable to speak, strained against him in desperate desire. At dinner in the big tent, she could not take her eyes off him, her mind whirling: *I must be with him. I cannot be without him....*

Adam's anger grew at Eva's obvious fascination with Christy: *She's humiliating me in front of all these people. What's wrong with the bloody woman?*

Next day at dawn Adam and Kinskii led two separate shooting parties into the bush. Adam took Eva in his group and sent Christy with Kinskii.

Adam waited for a refreshment break and strolled away from the group with Eva. Once alone in the bush he asked, 'Is something going on between you and Christy?'

She walked a few paces in silence, then whispered, 'Yes'

'Are you deceiving me?'

'Yes.'

'How?'

'I meet him in secret.'

'Why?'

'Because I cannot help it. He fascinates me.'

'Is he your lover?'

'We talk.'

'Is that all?'

She turned and he saw defiance flood into her eyes.

In a stronger voice she said, 'Sometimes we kiss. It's harmless.'

He said, 'I don't believe you.'

She tipped her head sideways, raised her eyebrows and twisted her lips into a tight little smile that said, *'Who cares?'*

Taken aback, he said, 'Are you going to leave me?'

'Perhaps. I don't know.'

Adam thrust his head forward and snarled, 'At least I know now what you're up to.'

She shrugged and said, 'You had to find out some time.'

Over the next hour Adam's fury grew. Returning to camp he found Christy and said, 'I've spoken to my wife. I know what's going on between you two.'

'Do you, old boy?' said Christy. 'Tell me then. What did she say?'

'You're having an affair.'

'She told you that? How stupid. No, my dear fellow. We flirt a little. That's all. Just a bit of harmless fun. Anything else is her imagination. Speak to her again. She's pulling your leg, old chap.'

Eva whispered her news to Kristina who said, 'Why did you tell him? There'll be awful trouble.'

'I don't care,' said Eva. 'I want him to know. I must be with Christy.'

Christy told Abel who said '*Mein Gott*. What will you do now?'

'Nothing, old chap. These silly women take everything too seriously. It'll blow over. I'll deny everything and tell her to shut up. I'll be back in the bush in another few days, and not see her again for months. It'll all be forgotten. How are you getting on with the other one?'

'Not well,' said Abel. '*Fräulein* Kristina treated me *very* kindly a few years ago when we in Moschi. Now she's married she's frightened of her husband. She'd like to play again, but won't. So my chance has gone. Good luck to you, my friend, but be careful.'

Christy laughed. 'Nothing to be careful about. I knew her husband in school. A wet sod. Very wet indeed.'

At a meeting with H.E. and Kreuz in the large tent Adam's attention wandered to the sight of Christy and Abel leaving camp. Through the open tent door he watched the two men stroll side by side round a rock outcrop a few yards outside the camp boundary.

Less than a minute later Eva and Kristina strolled from the camp. Adam watched them disappear round the rock outcrop in the same direction as the two soldiers.

Adam forced his concentration back to Kreuz, who said, 'Before we start our main meetings I must state that our Kaiser is a peace-loving monarch but must follow his peoples' need for defence and security. However, our political masters in Berlin insist that whatever happens in Europe we Germans avoid conflict with you British here and in our West African colonies. We are told that this political decision does not have full support in Berlin. A new military commander arrives in January and may have different ideas – or different orders.'

'What orders?' ask H.E..

Kreuz spread his hand and said, 'Who knows? But our political masters in Berlin require us to control a soldier's naturally aggressive

149

nature and we meet here to form political agreement with you British before he arrives. It is important nothing stands in the way.'

Adam's eye caught movement in the trees – Abel and Kristina strolling back to camp alone: *No sign of Christy and Eva. Where the hell are they?*

He half heard Kreuz saying, '…You are in some way related to our new commander, *Herr* Early, as he is cousin to your wife. His name is von Lettow-Vorbeck. I think you met him in Berlin. *Herr* Early, are you ill? You have become quite pale. Is it surprise at hearing this news?'

Adam dragged his attention back, fury mounting throughout his body.

'No…no. I'm not ill….I'm perfectly well….please continue.'

With a polite smile Kreuz said to H.E., 'That is all. I have no more to say until tomorrow in official session.'

Adam left H.E. and Kreuz sipping their beer and discussing methods of taxing the African population and from his tent collected a light hunting rifle and cartridges. Walking out of camp he passed Kinskii who said, 'What are you after? Shall I come too?'

Adam hurried past saying, 'No. I want to practice tracking and stalking. Sakayo showed me a few tricks. Best done alone.'

He rounded the crop of rock, and found clear marks of four people meeting then splitting. One set of tracks turned back to camp. The other led away to an area of trees and long grass on rolling ridges further along the hillside.

Adam, moving swiftly, followed neat imprints of heavy boots and small walking shoes side by side in the dust. A pre-sundown breeze rustled through the grass. Adam shivered, feeling tense and cold in the warm air.

Hearing a faint sound carried in the quiet evening air – *A woman laughing?*- he stopped to clip bullets into his rifle magazine and study the hillside: *They must be along the ridge. This is a natural path. They're bound to return this way….*

He moved across the hill, angling away into the cover of a group of trees where he settled to wait – the patient sniper at ease in the calm of the hunt.

Ten minutes passed on the silent hillside. Only wind shifting through grass and branches made soft sound.

The lovers strolled into view, arms entwined, heads close, whispering and walking; relaxed and alone in their secret world.

150

They stopped – outlined against the horizon facing each other.

Eva took Christy's hands and leaned back. She looked up into his face, laughing. He smiled down into her eyes.

Adam slid his rifle bolt into place, enjoying the deadly efficient ease of a bullet gliding into the breech.

He took aim.

Close aim on the side of Christy's head, just behind the temple.

Then he tracked right, placing the sight bead directly on Eva's left eye: *That's Musa's spot. Straight through into the brain.*

He shifted aim back to Christy – just above the ear.

Right again. Plumb on Eva's eye – a millimetre below the beautifully curved brow.

Him first? Or her?

Which one will I give the brief moment of knowing what happened?

A gust of wind rustled the yellow fronds of grass and whisked Eva's hat from her head.

She ducked, laughed, ran out of view down the slope, pulling Christy by the hand in a chase after her hat.

The moment of murder passed.

Adam lowered his rifle.

The time will come....

H.E., sitting alone, sipped an early brandy, and watched the charade, as Eva and Christy wandered back into camp, chatting; pointing out items of interest to each other. They separated with a friendly nod, Eva going to her tent, Christy disappearing towards the *askari* lines at a brisk soldierly walk.

Five minutes later Adam stalked round the hillside, thrust aside the tent flap with his rifle barrel and ducked inside. H.E. heard sharp voices raised – Adam shouting, Eva yelling.

Calling a servant H.E. said, 'Bring *Bwana* Christy. Tell him to hurry.'

Christy came and made for an empty chair. H.E. said, 'Don't sit down. You're leaving. Take half your men and go for a sweep patrol across the plain towards Longido. Go now. Return at dawn the day after tomorrow to escort the Germans back to their border.'

Christy said, 'It'll be dark soon. I'll wait till morning.'

H.E. said, 'Go now. Immediately. Without delay. Your order is to check the return route to Longido.'

Christy said, 'Yes, Sir.'

Fifteen minutes later H.E. watched Christy stride down the hillside in front of his platoon. He did not look back.

Faced with Adam's shouted proof during an argument in their tent, Eva denied everything. 'You dislike me having friends of my own.' she shouted back.

Eva did not appear for dinner that night. Adam made no comment on her absence – not that he felt it necessary. He knew that everyone heard the row and was relieved that no one mentioned Christy's departure.

When walking with Kinskii in the cool dark after dinner, Adam said, 'I suppose you know why Christy is banished.'

Kinskii chuckled and said, 'Challenge the man to a duel. I did when I heard he was chasing my Countess. He almost died of fright at the idea. He'll never face you. By the way, did you shoot anything this afternoon?'

'Nearly,' said Adam.

Chapter Twenty

An Invitation To Mombasa

On her return from Namanga Eva collected the children from Beatrice and settled back into Mzito trying to ignore the frigid atmosphere. Eva could see no reason for Adam's anger at something beyond her control.

She said to Kristina, 'Why should I feel guilt or conscience? I can't help liking Christy. Why shouldn't I? After all he saved my life. I'm bound to be grateful. A Berlin husband would understand.'

Kristina laughed. 'Oh yes. A Berlin husband would make the most of it. He'd simply go off and find a lover of his own.'

'Exactly,' said Eva. 'In Berlin a couple would be amicable and enjoy themselves for a few years before settling together in middle age. Why can't it be the same in Africa?'

Seeking relief from his cold mood Eva went several times to Nairobi and stopped overnight with Beatrice. Together they hatched a plan.

One evening at the end of the month Eva said to Adam, 'I need a holiday and Beatrice suggests I go with her to Mombasa for a month or so. My coffee is picked and drying so there's nothing to hold me here.'

Her husband shrugged but said nothing.

Eva said, 'You don't mind then. We'll stay at the Creek House. The children love it there. They can see your parents and have a pleasant holiday away from here. So can I.'

Beatrice, Eva and the children left in early October, accompanied by several servants, and a pile of baggage. Stewartby joined Adam at the station in a stiff and formal farewell.

Eva managed to remain solemn until the train left. Once out of the station she burst out giggling and shouted, 'What a pair of old frosty-boots. Thank God we're rid of them for a while.'

Beatrice kicked up her legs and cried, 'We're free. We're free. Everything worked out. Oh what a time we'll have.'

As soon as the train left both men hurried to the Norfolk for a drink.

'Thank God for a bit of peace and quiet,' said Stewartby. 'I love my wife, of course, but I'm glad to see the back of her for a few weeks. Beatrice seemed so determined to go to Mombasa. Don't know where she got the idea. Lucky your wife wanted a holiday too. Company for each other.'

Adam went to see H.E. in his office.

'Sorry, Sir,' said his Indian clerk. 'Not here. Gone to Mombasa for leave. Back in a month....'

For the next five weeks alone at Mzito Adam worked hard and the events of September began to fade in his mind except for deep anger at Christy. He found that any time of day or night he could recall the moment of calm hatred when his rifle sight settled on that white-blond head: *Damn the breeze. I'd have got him there and then but for a gust of wind.*

He did not retain the same angry pictures of Eva. He began, without conscious effort, to remember how she was before Christy. His dislike for her began to fade. She wrote several letters from Mombasa to which he did not reply until early November when she wrote: *I plan to stay here until January. If my coffee crop is ready, please send it to Mombasa. Prices are good here, and I can sell the lot. Better still if you bring it. You should be with your children at Christmas. Please come. We all miss you.*

Kristina is coming down to meet our cousin Colonel von Lettow-Vorbeck. He is posted to Dar-es-Salaam as military commander to the German forces in East Africa. His ship calls into Mombasa during early January. We plan to see him. Kristina will tell you more. Go and see her. You can bring the coffee and travel together by train.

A week later Kristina stood alone in the usual pre-departure chaos of Nairobi station when she saw H.E. forcing his way towards her through the swirling crowd. Waving and laughing she called, 'Thank God you're so big and strong. Who else could rescue me from this mob.'

'I don't think you'd ever need rescuing from *anything* m'dear,' growled H.E., sweeping off his hat and bending to kiss her cheek. 'Where's your husband?'

'Looking for Adam. He's somewhere with Musa loading Eva's coffee. Fifty sacks. Not bad. She'll be pleased.'

'But will she be pleased to see her husband?'

'I hope so. He's certainly looking forward to seeing her.'

'How do you know?'

'Adam told me. Eva wrote him a letter saying she missed him.'

H.E. raised an eyebrow but said nothing.

Kristina asked, 'Did you see Eva when you were in Mombasa?'

Placing the tip of a finger to his lips H.E. hissed, 'Shush. You know I did. No questions. We are no longer alone.'

Kinskii and Adam burst from the crowd, laughing.

'God what a scrum,' said Adam. 'Glad you've come to see us off H.E.. Something I wanted to ask – did you see Eva while you were at the Coast?'

'A couple of times...Yes...A couple of times,' H.E. replied, frowning as though trying to remember. 'Of course I was busy with my master, our dear Governor, Sir Henry. Busy that is trying to get him to work. Damn man prefers fishing. If we're not careful he'll move Government back to Mombasa so he can dangle his damned hook at fish all day and night. The man's a bloody menace.'

'When did you see my sister?' asked Kristina, her violet eyes widely innocent, as in her mind she read again an excited letter from Eva written shortly after her arrival in Mombasa.

'Oh, just a couple of times when we went for a picnic on the beach.'

'With the children?'

'No...no. When I went to the Creek house the children were with their grand-parents in Mombasa town. Beatrice was on holiday at the Creek House with Eva, you know. So Eva and I went to the beach with Beatrice.'

'How lucky for you all to meet and be company for each other,' said Kinskii with a courteous smile, his eyes fixed firm and hard on Kristina.

'Yes....True...Coincidence we were all there at the same time,' said H.E., grinning. 'Great fun too. Jolly games on the beach and that sort of thing y'know.'

Kristina, ignoring her husband's glare, smiled up at H.E., remembering their own jolly game on the beach years ago.

Her mind continued to race through Eva's letter: *Captain Christy is in Mombasa for a short while on army duty. H.E. brought him to the Creek House and we all went for a picnic at Bamburi beach. We had a wonderful day. I enjoyed it so much and Christy promised to come again.*

Kristina fought back a giggle: *I'll bet he came again. And again, and again. A lot of coming can happen in a month. I'll drag all the news from my naughty sister when I see her – including how many times Christy came....*

In the chaos of Mombasa station Adam spotted Eva and the

children standing in a group with his parents among the swirling crowd. Eva met him with a bright smile, a long hug, and a kiss full of promise.

She whispered, 'Darling, I'm so happy to see you. Have you missed me?'

The party squeezed into four rickshaws and rode through hot narrow streets. At his parent's house, Eva said, 'Kristina and the children are staying here. You and I will be alone at the Creek House for a few days rest. Then your parents will bring the children across for Christmas.'

At the Creek House, Adam felt overwhelmed by the attention Eva gave him; chattering, laughing, holding hands; concentrating her whole being on making him welcome.

Musa served dinner on the veranda. Mombasa town looked like fairyland across the creek, lights shining through the smooth warm night and glinting bright points off the water.

Before bed they wandered along the creek shore through groves of fragrant palm trees shimmering in the white light of a new moon. Eva nestled against Adam and sighed, 'I do love evenings...so romantic.'

Adam did not question the change in his wife. The cold angry woman of recent months had become a loving wife, anxious to please, eager to make amends. He wanted to support her obvious need to reconcile and forget the pain they had caused each other.

So he missed the slight hesitation of her reply when she said, 'H.E.? Oh yes...he came here a couple of times for a picnic. The children like him and they enjoyed it. Of course, he really came to see Beatrice. They're quite friendly, you know....'

That first night, Eva settled beside him in bed, threw off her gown and made love to him as though for the first time. During the next two days and nights she took him to bed at every opportunity, using all her skill and wiles to pleasure and exhaust him. Carried away by this new enthusiasm, Adam joined in, happy that their difficult times seemed over. 'We are in love again,' Eva assured and reassured him. He seemed to believe her.

On Christmas Eve Kristina crossed the creek with Adam's parents and the children. Adam and Eva stood hand-in-hand on the new jetty, waiting in welcome.

Kristina smiled. *Aha. A real pair of love-birds again. It looks as though my clever sister has done it. She's glued things back together....*

Dying to know how, Kristina waited until a chance came to ask when the children, full of excitement, ran ahead to the house with Adam. Kristina and Eva followed, leaving Adam's parents on the jetty supervising the servants unloading presents and food.

Speaking German, Kristina asked, 'Is all now well between you and Adam?'

Eva nodded.

'What about Christy?' asked Kristina.

'It's over. Finished. It must finish. It is no more. I cannot see him again.'

Eva spoke fast, her face white. Kristina – delighted to see tears start in Eva's eyes – asked, 'What happened? Tell me what happened.'

'I can't. I can't tell. There's nothing to tell. I want him away. It's over. Finished. No more. Don't ask again.'

Kristina said, 'Is he still in Mombasa?'

'Yes. But I cannot see him again. I've promised.'

'Who did you promise?'

'Myself.'

January 1914

During the second week of the New Year Eva received a telegram from von Lettow-Vorbeck in Aden: WE ARRIVE MOMBASA ON 13TH JANUARY YOUR COUSIN PAUL IS WITH ME AS AIDE STOP WE SHALL COME ASHORE FOR A FEW HOURS STOP LOOK FORWARD TO MEETING YOU FOR DINNER END

Adam arranged dinner at the Mombasa Club and afterwards everyone sat round the table, chatting. A full moon rose, and transformed the sea into shivering silver. Eva, sitting next to von Lettow-Vorbeck, pointed out the Creek House across the harbour, shining ghostly white among pale moonlit palm trees. She said, 'A pity you have no time to see it. I love the place at night. It is so beautiful, so romantic.'

Von Lettow-Vorbeck said, 'We must be back on board by midnight. The ship sails at one. I think we should go. Paul and I will make our own way back to Kilindini.'

'No!' said Eva. 'My husband will take you. It would be bad if you became lost in the narrow alleys and missed the boat. Kristina and I will wait here until he returns. It will only be an hour or so. Then he can take us back to the Creek House.'

All stood to make formal farewells. Von Lettow-Vorbeck said,

'*Herr* Early, may we walk some of the way? It is a lovely evening, and I would like to see more of this interesting town.'

During the conversation, Kristina noticed that Eva became restless and flushed and asked, 'Do you feel unwell?'

'I need some air. I think I'll walk a few minutes to Fort Jesus.'

'I'll come with you.'

'No. I prefer to walk alone. Just for ten minutes fresh air. I'll be back soon.'

Kristina sat alone for thirty minutes before deciding to find Eva. She crossed the square to Fort Jesus, expecting to meet Eva on her way back. The massive red-stone walls, made pale by moonlight, towered above.

Kristina passed through an ancient portcullis into a gate-house tunnel and up a curving sharp stone-paved slope to the first courtyard. She shivered at the feel of this cruel dark and empty place. No moonlight reached over the tall walls to ease the sense of death and destruction or lighten the hot damp air.

She stood for a moment, listening: *Eva must be here somewhere. Perhaps up on the battlement....*

Holding her long skirt high to avoid snagging on the uneven stone Kristina climbed a flight of rough stone steps set awkwardly into the wall. Halfway up she met a cooling current of air. Turning her face in the blessed breeze, she caught a sound. A sigh? A soft cry? A moan?

At the top she stepped out into bright moonlight on to a wide flat roof lined with ancient black cannon sitting huge and heavy along the sea-facing rampart. Guns and battlements cast sharp black shadows across paving stones shining white in the moon-rays.

Confused and apprehensive in this ghostly place, Kristina stood for a moment, calming her nerves.

Again came the sound – a sad, shuddering sigh carried on the breeze. Kristina crept towards deep soft shadows in the southwest corner, straining to see.

'Eva,' she whispered. 'Eva – is that you?'

Stepping into the shadow, Kristina's eyes adjusted.

Her sister lay curved over the smooth round barrel of a cannon, head thrown back, arms flung wide and – *Oh God* – on top of her lay a man.

He lifted his head. At that moment the moon, moving higher, cast a silver beam across white-blond hair.

'Eva,' gasped Kristina, in shock and delight. 'Eva...*Darling*! What *are* you doing...?'

158

Chapter Twenty-One

Death Of A Young Lion

Otto Kinskii stood tense and still in a small forest glade, his rifle raised and aimed at a huge black-coated bull buffalo that appeared without warning from thick forest opposite.

Kinskii, with Sakayo and their employer, the rich American newspaper tycoon, had left camp for an evening reconnaissance of the lower mountain slopes. After thirty minutes of struggle through trees and heavy undergrowth they pushed into the clearing. A portcullis of clinging bramble closed behind, leaving no quick escape.

The buffalo, twenty feet distant, glared at Kinskii, raising its head and fearsome spread of horns, small wicked eyes sparking with anger. Kinskii could smell acrid sweat, rising as steam from its thick black coat. He hissed, 'Keep still. Keep absolutely still.'

'The hell I will,' snarled his employer, and stepped forward two paces, 'This is what I'm here for.'

He loosed off three shots in quick succession. Poorly aimed, they whacked into the buffalo at shoulder level. The animal staggered and coughed a spray of blood into the calm forest air. A fourth bullet hit the base of a horn and flew off, whining and skipping through the trees.

'Got the bastard,' shouted the tycoon.

The buffalo snorted in rage, lowered its head to cough more blood and hammered angry hooves at the ground, raising a cloud of grey dust.

Kinskii keeping his aim tight and firm shouted back, 'For God's sake move now. Get behind a tree.'

'The hell I will. I want to see the damned thing fall.'

'It's only wounded. Any second it'll charge. Get back.'

'No. I want to see it fall.'

The buffalo charged.

Kinskii managed two shots before it reached the American.

One bullet smashed the buffalo's shoulder bone. The beast swerved and hit the American sideways. Caught by the buffalo's haunch and tossed high in an untidy somersault he crashed into the undergrowth.

The buffalo, confused and wounded, charged a full circle and disappeared into trees and bush opposite. Kinskii heard it drive forward a few yards, snorting and coughing before falling silent.

Sakayo – waiting behind as gun bearer – ran forward to help Kinskii lift the American and examined him for damage. Bruised, winded and badly scratched he pushed them away, snarling, 'What the hell happened? I hit the damned thing three times. How did it manage a charge like that?'

'Sakayo will take you back to camp,' said Kinskii. 'I must find the buffalo and finish it off.'

'I'll come with you. I've got to kill the bastard. It's mine.'

'No. This one's wounded and dangerous. He's close by and probably watching, working out how to get back at us. Buffalo are clever devils. They never give up. They draw you into ambush. If we're lucky this one's alone. If he's with a herd, we must be extra careful. Go now with Sakayo.'

The American allowed himself to be led back into the bush, Sakayo forcing a path for him to follow. Over his shoulder Sakayo said in Swahili, 'When this stupid *kaburu* is safely in camp, I'll come back to help you *Bwana* Count.'

Kinskii followed the trail of blood, broken earth and snapped branches with care. Using ears, eyes and nostrils he scanned the trees and thicket for any sight of the buffalo: *It won't be far. By now, he's probably stalking me, the cunning bugger.*

The buffalo spoor curved right and back towards the clearing. Kinskii crept along, watching the clumps and thickets, ready to leap behind a tree if the buffalo appeared: *This one's clever. He may try and catch me from the side. While I follow straight down his path, he creeps round and waits off to my right. Classic ambush. We did it in the cavalry, old chap. I'm ready for you....*

In the silent forest Kinskii found himself sweating, surprised at feeling nervous: *The bugger's waiting somewhere. Where is he? Where's he gone?*

Kinskii came again to the clearing and peeped out. There waited the buffalo, out in the open standing side-on to Kinskii, head lowered as though examining the ground.

Kinskii took aim: *Damn. No clear shot. I'll have to make him move – show myself and turn him, so I can go for the heart.*

He lowered his rifle and checked his ammunition pouch: *Shit – Sakayo's carrying the spare ammo.*

He unclipped the magazine. Two bullets, plus one in the breech: *Oh well. Three will have to do....*

He clicked the magazine back into place – a slight sound, but enough to disturb the buffalo. Staggering on shaky legs, it turned. Kinskii knew he had won: *He's mine. Now – get his head up....*

He stepped into the clearing. The buffalo lifted and swung its head, sniffing and peering. A perfect target.

Kinskii took bead on the killing area of breast just below the shoulder and planted two bullets smack into the heart.

The buffalo collapsed forward onto its chin, folded its back legs under and slumped in a heap, mouth open in a spraying sigh of blood-red foam.

Kinskii considered using his last bullet in a brain shot but decided to hold on in case he met another buffalo.

Slinging the rifle over his shoulder, he walked forward....

Kristina, sipping a cup of tea and half-listening to the chatter of her companions, felt worried. Her husband rarely needed more than two shots to finish an animal, however big, fast or aggressive. But she heard four shots, then another two, then a few minutes later two more.

The women – sitting in a circle under a tree drinking tea and chatting when the first sound of shooting rolled down the hillside – cocked their heads to one side, and listened.

The men, resting after a day in the forest, rushed from their tents and ran to where they could see further up the mountain, calling to each other, 'Good old George. Trust him to find something to shoot at.'

The second burst of gunfire caused laughter. 'Buffalo or rhino – damn thing'll be like a pepper pot by the time old George has finished with it,' they shouted, slapping each other on the back. 'Wish we'd gone with him after all. George always finds the action.'

At the third rattle of shots the whole group fell quiet.

Kristina felt a stab of fear: *Why? I've heard him shoot before. What's different this time?*

The tycoon's wife said, 'You are quite pale, my dear Countess. Are you well? Are you worried?'

Kristina managed a smile. 'No,' she said. 'No. But I'm never happy when I hear guns in the forest. I saw so many accidents as a young girl in Prussia.'

Servants moved round bringing more tea. One bent to fill Kristina's cup and whispered in Swahili, 'Memsahib. The *Bwana* 'Mericani is coming with Sakayo.'

Kristina saw two figures emerge from the forest-line several hundred yards away. The large heavy American limped along, supported by the slim Nandi, who carried two rifles dangling from his shoulder. Kristina waited for Kinskii to appear. Her sense of foreboding increased when the grey-green wall of bush remained closed.

She sent several servants to run and help Sakayo. The tycoon's wife, a steely middle-aged woman, laughed as her husband eased his backside into a chair and said, 'I'm not sure if it's worse being hit by a buffalo, or carried along by that man. By God, he stinks. Still, he got me and my rifles back here.'

At first, only Kristina saw that Sakayo had collected another tracker and, still carrying the two rifles, trotted straight out of camp back into the forest.

When the American noticed, he interrupted his tale to complain, 'Goddam man's run off with my two best guns.'

Servants helped the tycoon up and took him off for a bath. The group settled to a pre-dinner drink under the trees, looking out over the plateau.

'My goodness, how beautiful it is,' said the tycoon's wife. 'See how fast the shadows move when the sun goes down. And what lovely colours it makes on the snow on Mount Kenya. I could stay here for ever.'

In growing fear Kristina could not concentrate on the small talk but heard the tycoon's wife say with a laugh, 'George will make a good story out of this, no mistake. By the time we're back in New York it'll sound like Custer's last stand all over again...Oh yes...He'll write it up in his papers. All America will hear how he stood up to a charging buffalo...'

Sakayo followed his own tracks back up the mountain through deepening dusk. To the other tracker he said, 'Hurry. I must return to *Bwana* Count before dark. He'll never find his way down the mountain without me.'

Sakayo pushed hard and made it back to the clearing in twenty-five minutes. He stopped at the edge and saw instantly what had happened. In anger and grief he howled at the sky, shouting, 'That stupid 'Mericani *kaburu.*'

For hundreds of yards around, startled birds took wing in a clatter of sound.

The tracker shook his head and said, 'That buffalo was more clever than our Count.'

Sakayo crouched to examine the torn earth and said, 'Go back and bring Memsahib Kinskii with more men. Tell them to come slowly. You hurry ahead of the Memsahib and get here first with blankets.'

While waiting for Kristina, Sakayo followed the buffalo's track, seeing how it drew Kinskii in a circle and into its ambush. The two bodies lay close together at the centre of the clearing. Sakayo could imagine how the animal kept just ahead of Kinskii making sure he followed.

In fading light, he traced five bullet wounds in the buffalo carcass, three across its shoulder and stomach from the 'Mericani, two neat shots placed into its heart by Kinskii.

'Oooh. Oooh.' Sakayo keened quietly. '*Bwana* Count. If I had been here we would have waited. That stupid *kaburu* took me away and you died…'

Gathering wood to prepare and set fires round the clearing Sakayo could see how the buffalo had won.

Kinskii came back to the clearing not realising the buffalo stood waiting for him. He thought it exhausted and unable to move further.

Sakayo could see where Kinskii stepped out into the open and planted two shots into the buffalo's heart. Any tracker would have told Kinskii to watch the buffalo's hind legs.

When the buffalo fell it dropped forward, tucking the hind legs under ready for use: *Bwana Count. Unless the buffalo falls sideways, legs out straight do not approach.*

Kinskii would have thought that two bullets in the heart will kill a buffalo: *Oh yes, Bwana Count – if the buffalo is ready to die. But this buffalo determined to stay alive long enough to kill you.*

Sakayo tracked and followed Kinskii's actions and the buffalo's response.

From the edge of the clearing Kinskii shot the buffalo and watched it fall. With one bullet left he walked forward but unprepared to shoot. The buffalo, not breathing, watched and waited until Kinskii came close then with a powerful heave of its hind legs, rose and rushed.

Kinskii, hit at full force by the great ridge of bone across the buffalo's brow, smashed backwards, broken and crushed.

Sakayo hoped Kinskii died before the buffalo knelt on him, full weight pressed down on Kinskii's chest and stomach.

Sakayo felt sure Kinskii must be dead by the time the buffalo hooked his horns beneath the body and flung it across the clearing. Not once, but many times.

Sakayo did not know where a buffalo with two bullets in its heart could find such strength. It must have smashed, crushed, rolled upon, tossed and dragged Kinskii around for several minutes, ripping every stitch of clothing from Kinskii's broken corpse.

Sakayo could imagine that the buffalo – victorious but dying – stood head down for several moments before collapsing sideways, its bullet-wrecked heart giving up at last.

Saluting the buffalo's steel will and enormous courage Sakayo lit four fires in a square enclosing the two bodies.

He untied the shoulder knot of his blanket, wrapped himself warmly and crouched down to wait and to protect both Kinskii and the buffalo from forest scavengers.

Chapter Twenty-Two

Paper and Photographs

Kristina trekked up the mountain, through darkening forest.

A tracker led, carrying an oil lamp that swung and flared as he forced a way through clinging bush and bramble. Banshee shadows flew among the trees, their imagined screams howling in her brain.

Kristina struggled upward through dank, damp brushwood. The smell of her own sweat mingled with greasy smoke from the oil lamp and the reek of a dozen or so porters who stumbled with her in the black night. Unseen thorns whipped and scratched at her face and dragged through her tangled hair.

Kristina walked in dread, unsure why. It had all been so fast. An hour ago in the cool dusk, as she sat with the group of guests under a tree, drinking wine, two trackers had come to her chair. In Swahili they whispered that the *Bwana* Count needed her up the mountain and she must come now. Kristina made a quick excuse to the tycoon's wife who expressed brief concern at Kristina going out in the dark then returned her attention to her husband.

Within minutes, Kristina started up the mountain. One tracker trotted ahead with several blankets and disappeared into the trees. The second tracker gathered and marshalled a group of porters then set off at a steady walk, calling Kristina to follow, swinging his lamp to show the way. The porters, carrying mattocks, *pangas* and blankets fell into line and wound along behind Kristina, calling encouragement when she stumbled.

Kristina felt confused and apprehensive: *I understand the pangas to cut a path in the forest, but why the mattocks? What will they dig at this time of night? And – mein Gott – one of them is carrying a chair. Oh Jesus. What has happened up this damned mountain...?*

Fear for Kinskii swept through her body.

'Is my husband safe? Is he far from here?' she called to the tracker.

'Memsahib, we will soon be there. Sakayo is with him. You will see soon,' he called back over his shoulder.

For almost an hour Kristina pushed and fought her way across dark ridges and slopes. Finally the ground flattened. Acrid wood-smoke seeped among the leaves.

In wild hope a series of thoughts flashed through her mind: *A fire. Kinskii lit a fire. He's sick of being with the Americans. He's called me up here to eat meat and spend the night camped out. I'll kill him for dragging me so far....*

She burst from the bush into the clearing and stopped, staring in shocked silence at a ghastly scene.

Four fires burned and crackled, wood heaped high, sparks flying off into the black canopy of leaves, thick smoke trapped and eddying in the cold, still air.

Wavering red-yellow firelight showed Sakayo and his tracker, sitting wrapped and still beside a long blanket-bundle. Their eye-whites gleamed in the flames, as they turned to Kristina.

'The *Bwana* Count is dead, Memsahib,' said Sakayo. 'He has gone.'

Unable to comprehend, Kristina stepped into the square of fires. She looked with curiosity at the tightly folded blanket-bundle, tied several times round with creepers cut from the forest.

Unsure she had followed Sakayo's Swahili she said, 'He is dead? The *Bwana* Count is dead?'

'Yes, Memsahib.'

Kristina heard a low sigh from the porters, crowding into the clearing behind her.

Bewildered, she wandered past Sakayo to where a huge black buffalo lay, stiff and dead: *How interesting that tiny bullets can destroy such a big thing....*

She turned again to Sakayo.

'Did the *Bwana* Count kill this?'

'Yes, Memsahib.'

'Are you sure?'

'Yes, Memsahib.'

She strolled back through the leaping firelight and looked thoughtfully down at the blanket-bundle.

'Is that the *Bwana* Count? '

'Yes, Memsahib.'

'And he's dead?'

'Yes, Memsahib.'

'So they killed each other?'

'Yes, Memsahib.'

'Shall I see him?'

'No, Memsahib. You will not want to see him.'

'Please untie the blankets.'

'No, Memsahib.'

Sakayo stood and led her to the chair, opened and ready near a fire.

'Please sit, Memsahib. We will bury the *Bwana* Count here. It is too far to take him down. Tomorrow will be hot. We must put him in a big hole. Please sit and we will work.'

Kristina sat, at last understanding the mattocks and the chair: *Kinskii's right. He always says how clever the Natives are in their own way. No-one seemed to actually say anything, but they all knew what to bring – even a chair for me....*

Silently she watched the porters dig a deep neat grave.

She considered their skill: *The Africans really are clever. What a lovely tomb. So square and tidy. It will fit him perfectly. And dug in the dark, with a few simple tools. How impressive....*

She worried about her hair. In the rush of leaving camp, she had left her hat and mosquito veil. She ran her fingers through long tousled locks, concerned that Kinskii would not like her untidy at his funeral.

She did not move when six porters lifted the blanket-bundle and with gentle care lowered it into the grave.

As her husband disappeared Kristina nodded to him once. No words came to mind so she stayed silent.

Sakayo wrapped blankets round her shoulders and legs. He crouched, African-style, beside her. Together they sat, wide-awake until dawn. Not moving. Not speaking.

The porters slept on bare earth, waking from time to time to add wood to the fires. In the pale cold hour before dawn, they rose and collected a pile of rocks. At sunrise they built a strong cairn of heavy stones over the grave.

When daylight drifted through the trees Sakayo stood and said, 'Shall we go down, Memsahib?'

Kristina shook her head.

'Please, Memsahib. You should go down.'

Kristina shook her head.

Sakayo spoke to his tracker. The man disappeared and returned in an hour with food and tea.

Ten minutes later the newspaper tycoon, his wife, guests and dozen servants appeared with a picnic breakfast. The clearing filled with noisy people.

'My goodness, George' shrieked the tycoon's wife. 'Is *that* the beast you shot. Oh *darling*.'

She hugged Kristina and cried, 'Have you been here all night, my sweet? How awful for you. Your *poor* husband. Is he under there? How romantic. My dear girl, you look a sight. Your face is all scratched. And you need a bath. My goodness, you smell of wood-smoke and heaven *only* knows what else.'

Kristina refused food. She sat sipping hot tea and watched without speaking. The tycoon directed his personal photographer to arrange the buffalo into a more aggressive pose. They checked camera angles.

The tycoon called for a rifle – 'Not big enough, for God's sake. Give me that long one….'

He stood over the buffalo, smiling fiercely. His guests crowded round applauding and shouting in loud congratulation. The photographer took pictures from this angle and that. His flash pan sheared bright light across the glade, blinding Kristina as she sat by the grave, ignored by the tycoon and all his guests.

Sakayo whispered, 'Now, Memsahib. Now is the time to go down. Please come with me.'

Kristina allowed him to take her from the clearing. She walked slowly off the mountain and back to camp. She bathed, ate breakfast and went with Sakayo and his small safari down to the army post at Nyeri where Adam waited with Musa.

Kristina gripped Adam's hand and whispered, 'How did you know what happened? How did you know where I was?'

'Bush telegraph,' said Adam. 'It's amazing. Before you were off the mountain we knew the whole story and Sakayo had arranged for us to meet.'

Adam paid off the porters and drove Kristina back to Mzito in a donkey cart, wrapped in blankets, her violet eyes dull; hair a tangled mess; face a pinched white picture of misery.

Kristina stayed ten days at Mzito, at first huddled in bed hardly moving. The sight of Kinskii wrapped and dead and dropped into a cold mountain hole plunged her into melancholy so deep she felt dead and in her own grave.

Several times Kinskii appeared from the blackness of her mind. Debonair and handsome as always he urged her to join him.

Although tempted she managed to resist. 'Not yet,' she whispered. 'Not yet…'

Finally he gave up and when he came no more, Kristina began to recover. With great effort she pulled herself out of the dark void in her mind.

On the sixth day, Kristina woke before dawn, feeling almost normal. She climbed out of bed and in weak grey light studied herself in the mirror, fighting back an urge to cry at the sight of her gaunt white face and greasy knotted hair.

In sudden frenzy she took a brush and pulled it through the awful tangle, dragging at twisted hanks until her scalp stung then slapped her face and bit at her lips to bring blood and colour: *That's better. Now I look more human....*

Knowing that Eva would be in her usual pre-dawn place, facing east, Kristina wrapped herself in a blanket and walked weakly out onto the veranda.

'Darling, you're up,' cried Eva jumping from her chair and hurrying to Kristina. 'You look wonderful. Come and sit with me. Have some tea. Tell me how you are.'

'Better. It was awful, but I'm better now.'

A few days later Adam said, 'I've made a copper plaque to carry up the mountain and mark Kinskii's grave. Tell me when and where was he born, so I can complete the inscription.'

'I don't know,' said Kristina.

'You don't know how old he was?'

'No. He never told me.'

'Where was he born?'

'I can't tell.'

'Did he never say?'

'Yes...In a way...He talked of estates in Hungary and Bohemia, but never mentioned at which he was born.'

'What about pictures or letters from his family?'

'I found none.'

'How odd.'

Adam completed the plaque with Kinskii's name and rank, the date and manner of death and vague reference to a brave soldier from Austria-Hungary. A few days later he climbed the mountain with Sakayo and stood by the stone cairn, thinking of his friend.

The headless buffalo skeleton lay nearby, the white bones home to hordes of insects. Long weeds grew up through the rib cage. Four piles of charred wood showed black in the grey-green grass. The cairn stones seemed unmoved and firmly in place. No hungry scavenger had found Kinskii, thank God. 'You did well, Sakayo,' said Adam.

Choosing a full-grown tree-trunk he secured the plaque with copper screws.

That's as permanent as possible. It marks the man, but who, apart from us will know where he is? And will we be able to find this place again...?

Eva found herself unable to believe that Kristina knew so little about Kinskii and with Adam away arranged a picnic by the river to try and find out more.

'Why do you not know where Kinskii came from?' she asked.

Kristina, drinking lemonade and eating cold chicken, rolled her eyes to indicate the difficulty of explaining.

'Kinskii felt that here in Africa we forget our past and live for the moment. He said that when we have enjoyed Africa, we return to Europe and start a different life on his estates. So we never talked about the past. I kept quiet about Berlin and he said nothing about Austria.'

'He never mentioned his family?'

'Only a few words. Next year I think I will go to Austria and find them.'

'Why wait?' asked Eva, 'Why not go now?'

'I can't,' said Kristina. 'It is an awful thing. The one family matter Kinskii talked about was that his parents wanted him to produce an heir. He said they worried at the dangerous way he lived. They wanted an heir to take over the estates. Now they'll get one. I'm having a baby.'

'Oh my God,' said Eva, turning pale. 'When?'

'In October.'

'Are you sure?'

'Of course I'm sure.'

Eva threw her head back and laughed harshly.

'Me too.' she said. 'At about the same time – or just before.'

'Does Adam know?'

'Not yet. I'll have to tell him soon.'

On a hot morning in early March, Adam arrived at H.E.'s government office and immediately felt on guard. He saw that H.E.'s blue eyes, normally relaxed and lazy, were cool and formal, his smile a politician's mask.

'A couple of matters to discuss. Mostly personal. Sorry about Kinskii, by the way. Had to happen I suppose – the damned man was always putting himself in danger. And now his wife's back in circulation the rest of us had better watch out.'

Adam said, 'Bloody hell, H.E.. He's only been dead a few weeks. Kristina's a widow *and* she's having his baby. For God's sake show some respect.'

H.E. waved a hand in apology. 'My dear fellow. Don't take on so. I'm only joking. I know about Kristina's baby. I hear you and Eva have similar news. Congratulations.'

From his desk drawer H.E. produced a fat brown file tightly tied in green tape and sealed with heavy red wax. 'This belonged to your friend Kinskii. He left it as security. It may tell you about him…or it may not. His widow should find it interesting. Look at it later. For the moment I have other important matters to discuss.'

Adam listened in growing irritation as H.E. said, 'First matter. The army's bringing extra officers from India and we need billets. Kristina's house seems free, so we want to rent it. Second matter. I intend to leave Government service and take up farming and plan to buy my share of our partnership. The land at Chania should just about cover it. I can set up farming there.'

Adam said, 'You can have Kristina's house for a year. She's staying with us at Mzito until her baby's born. But you know nothing about farming. What the hell are you going to do living alone in the bush at Chania?'

'I may not be alone, old chap. I have plans, y'know.'

'A woman. It's a woman. Christ…you're not talking about Beatrice?'

H.E. dropped his head and avoided Adam's eyes.

'You'll find out soon enough. I'll get deeds drawn up – for both the house and Chania land.'

Adam said, 'I'll not be sorry to lose Chania. The place is already costing me worry and money and Eva will be out of action for a year with the new baby. But, bloody hell H.E., there'll be terrible trouble if you take Beatrice. God only knows what'll happen when Stewartby finds out.'

H.E. smiled and shrugged.

When Adam handed over Kinskii's file he saw Kristina turn pale and nervous, her brow furrowed, her eyes fixed on the fat package in his hand.

'Open it.' she said.

'Why? It's yours. You open it.'

Kristina shook her head.

'I can't.'

Eva said, 'Then we'll open it.'

Adam called a servant to move the tea tray, cut the file open with a knife and emptied the contents on to the table. He separated the papers into three piles – official documents, several photographs and what appeared to be personal letters.

171

Kristina sat transfixed, staring at the papers.

'Read something to me.' she said.

Adam sifting through the official documents, said, 'These seem to be his army papers. You'd find them easier to understand – they're in official German. Look, they are all headed with the Austrian Eagle. Here – you read them.'

Kristina shook her head.

'I can't,' she said. 'It will be as if he's come back.'

Eva picked up one of the headed papers. 'This is his warrant as an officer,' she said. 'Same as in the German army. His first promotion as lieutenant in the hussars, though it doesn't say from what.' She held up a page of scrolled writing – 'And he won a medal for fighting the Serbs. Did he ever tell you that, Kristina?'

Kristina shook her head. 'He never told me anything.'

Eva riffled through several other papers.

'And he went to Berlin. I wonder why? This is a letter to him from the Austrian army...says he did good work in Berlin. Dated nineteen-oh-six and...orders him back to Vienna. That's strange Kristina – when did we first meet Kinskii, that night at the Norfolk? I think in nineteen-oh-seven, soon after you arrived. So perhaps he never went back to Vienna. I wonder what happened to bring him here?'

Adam spread the papers over the table. He picked through the letters, Eva studied the official documents while Kristina compared several photographs. When Kristina spoke, both Adam and Eva jumped. In sharp excitement Kristina said, 'I think this must be Kinskii with his nurse. Look.'

She laid two grey-grained photographs side by side on the table.

One picture showed a woman with a small boy. They stood, holding hands, before a big grey-stone house, set on flat ground, among sparse trees, stables at the rear. The woman, slim and strong, was dressed in an apron. Her face was dominated by deep-set dark eyes, undimmed by the old, faded picture.

Aged about five, his sharp-boned face already formed, Kinskii stared hard at the camera. Impatience and energy radiated down the years.

Adam whispered, 'Bloody hell. Add a moustache and it's him. He never changed....'

'What about this one?' said Kristina.

The second picture showed the same couple in the same place.

'I'd say he's about fifteen here, so it's ten years later,' said Adam.

The woman, now plump and homely had lost her sharp beauty.

Only the strong dark eyes mirrored the first photograph.

Eva said, 'She must have been his governess. An educated peasant I would say. We had Poles like that who worked for us in Berlin.'

Adam saw in this youth the Kinskii he knew – slim, muscular and confident.

'He wrote on the back,' said Kristina, pointing at three words scrawled across the greasy spotted paper of the first photograph,.

'What language is that?' asked Adam.

'Magyar. But it's Kinskii's writing. I *think* he wrote 'My father's house', but I'm not sure.'

'And the second? What does that say?'

Kristina held the photograph up to the light. There are several words I recognise – 'itthon', 'hazmester' and 'lovak'. They mean 'home' or 'at home', 'servant' or 'caretaker' and 'horses'. The last word I'm sure of. Kinskii used it a lot.'

Adam said, 'It must be his father's house and Kinskii's personal servant. I suppose his father held the camera. What else do we have? What about the other pictures and the letters?'

Kristina passed over more photographs. Two showed Kinskii as a soldier dressed in dirty campaign clothes, standing by a horse in a muddy field and sitting by a tent with a group of comrades.

Kristina said, 'The only word I can read here is 'Serbia'. Why is he dressed like the other soldiers? Why is he not dressed like an officer?'

'They all look alike in the field,' said Eva. 'What about this one. It must be Vienna when he was in the Emperor's bodyguard.'

Adam looked in admiration at Kinskii dressed in glittering uniform and tall plumed helmet, sitting straight and elegant on a beautiful white horse. Handsome, confident – great sweeping moustache waxed and perfect – Kinskii stared across the years with arrogant black eyes.

'A fine man,' said Adam. 'You have to admit it. He was a fine man.'

Kristina stared closely at one last photograph. She raised her head. In the golden lamplight, her eyes shone bright and hard.

'When we were together I thought the same – most of the time. But he was also a strange man. I'm sure he came to Africa to be killed. He planned to die here, where no one knew him. That's why he never spoke of the past. Then he met me and changed his mind – I think.

'Do you really believe that?' asked Eva.

'I'm sure. Then he had that silly accident. Now I've seen these papers, I have two questions. The first is – would he ever have returned to Europe?'

'And the second?' asked Adam.

173

'Ask Eva about the army papers and letters then I'll tell you.'

Eva said, 'The army papers are strange but the letters stranger. Kinskii seems to have left the Hussars and gone to Berlin in nineteen-oh-three. He writes to a friend called Ermine in Vienna about everyday things – visits to the zoo, walks around parks and odd scraps of conversation. The friend's replies are just as odd. It is almost as though they are writing one thing, but saying something else – a code perhaps. Could it be that the friend was a woman? She may have been his mistress – perhaps her husband found out? Is that why he left Vienna so suddenly? And never went back?'

Kristina began to gather the papers together and push them into the file. She gave Adam the last photograph.

'This picture bothers me,' she said.

Adam took the picture and holding it so Eva could see, studied a different Kinskii. This Kinskii had short hair and no moustache. Dressed in a dark servant's suit with white braid at cuff and lapel, he stood in a city street, peaked cap in hand, head bent, smiling at the camera. A tiny blond woman stood at his side, her arm linked in his, fingers resting on the back of his hand.

On the reverse Adam read, 'Mariska – 1904'.

Eva said 'That's Berlin. I know that street. It's Berlin.'

Kristina sighed – a harsh abrupt wheeze.

'Yes. I recognised it. Now my second question. Who is that woman – and who is the man?'

Adam said, 'Kinskii. That's Kinskii. Dressed differently, but definitely him.'

Kristina laughed. 'Definitely the man we *knew* as Kinskii. But that does not tell us *who* he was. Nor do these papers and pictures. I must go to Europe. I must find out. I'll track him down. I'll find his family and ask them who he was. As soon as my baby is born....'

Chapter Twenty-Three

Cuckoo

When Adam handed over the Chania land deeds he said, 'I can't understand it. The bank released these documents without a murmur – although you're making no payment.'

H.E. chuckled and said, 'I told 'em you'd be paid from my inheritance in due course.'

'But it'll be years before that comes,' said Adam, laughing.

'If ever, m'dear man. Three healthy brothers ahead of me and a father built to last a century. Never mind. Nothing works so well as a promise from the nobility. However vague, it'll get things done. Let's go and celebrate.'

At the Norfolk, H.E. became quickly drunk – 'God, this stuff hits me hard these days,' he wheezed. 'You'll have to get me home. Stay for dinner.'

Adam loaded H.E. into a pony cart and for the first time realised that H.E.'s large body had turned into a soft lumpy mass. Greasy strings of long blond hair fell about his ears and neck. Ugly blue veins formed tracks across his blotched red-white cheeks. Vague pale-blue eyes struggled to focus.

'You look such a bloody wreck, H.E..' said Adam, 'You're going down fast.'

'Not yet, old chap,' mumbled H.E.. 'Heading for the rocks, but not quite on 'em. Change of course will help. You'll see. A good farm and a good woman – that'll do the trick. Out of this bloody madhouse of a town before it kills me.'

Helping H.E. from the cart, Adam saw lights in Kristina's house.

'Someone staying there already?' he asked.

'Couple of military fellows – officers. Nice chaps.'

When Eva heard what H.E. had said she found Kristina and whispered, 'How much do you think Adam knows?'

Kristina shrugged.

'It depends what H.E. told him. You must be careful. Adam can be more dangerous than you realise. He had you in his gun-sight at Namanga. That evening when you and Christy were out on the hill together.'

Eva put a hand to her mouth, and said, 'No. I don't believe it – he had his gun on me? Are you sure? How do you know?'

'He told me. On the train last December. The night I travelled with him to Mombasa. He got drunk and told me.'

'*Mein Gott.*' whispered Eva, 'It's true he was upset. We didn't speak for weeks after Namanga. I knew he was angry – but not angry enough for murder'

Turning back into the room, her mind full of what she had just heard, she missed the gleam of excitement in Kristina's violet eyes.

Three weeks later Kristina returned from a visit to Nairobi in a state of high excitement. 'While Stewartby went on safari H.E. took Beatrice to Chania and she's come back with malaria or black water fever. She's really ill and the whole town's waiting for Stewartby to return and find out. Oh what a wonderful scandal.'

In mid-June, Adam took a herd of cattle down to Damu and went to the bank.

'Sad about Mrs Stewartby,' said John Martin.

'What happened?'

'She died. Two days ago. Didn't you know? Caught some bug in the bush. Thought she'd recovered, but it came back and carried her off. They buried her yesterday.'

When Adam told Eva, she bit her lip, and said, 'Poor Beatrice. It's H.E.'s fault. He should never have taken her to Chania.'

He said, 'Beatrice went with H.E. of her own free will.'

'Yes. But it's still H.E's fault.'

The next day, Kristina went to the doctor in Nairobi and returned with more news of the developing scandal. 'Stewartby blames H.E.. There's terrible trouble. Before Beatrice died she must have confessed.'

'Oh God,' said Eva, tears starting in her eyes.

'Listen to what happened,' cried Kristina. 'Stewartby walked straight into H.E.'s office and without a word hit him three times across the face with a cane. Twice one side, and once the other. H.E. just stood and allowed it. He didn't move or speak.'

'How do you know?'

'The doctor told me H. E. came in bleeding and needing stitches. What do you think?' Her eyes shone with excitement.

Eva covered her face and whispered, 'What trouble we bring on ourselves....'

'What do you mean?' snapped Adam. 'What else has happened? What do you know'

'Nothing. I know nothing. What I mean is…a simple trip to the country…that's all…and look – Beatrice is dead – Stewartby attacks H.E…when men fight who knows how it will end? Why do we *do* these things? Why?'

Adam saw Kristina staring at him, her face bright with excited malice.

'That's enough,' he said. 'Whatever happened will blow over. Go and lie down Eva. I'll send in some tea.'

On the second day of July, an army runner arrived at Mzito carrying a message from H.E.: *Please be at my office on Monday sixth of July at ten a. m. I have official business to discuss with you. Captain Stewartby will attend….*

'*Captain* Stewartby?' said Eva, 'I didn't know he was a soldier.'

'Perhaps he'll bring a gun and shoot H.E..' said Kristina, laughing.' You'll be a witness Adam. How exciting.'

Adam arrived at H.E.'s office thirty minutes early.' Why are we meeting with Stewartby?' he asked, eyeing the red weals across H.E.'s cheeks.

'You know what happened?' said H.E.. 'The bloody man thought I was tupping his wife.'

'Were you?'

'No. Well…sort of. But only as especially good friends. She was such a sweet little baggage. He had no need to take on so. I wonder what she told him?'

'Are you worried at meeting him again?'

'God, no. Hitting me seemed to quieten the little bugger down. He's been no trouble at all since. Like a mouse. Got it all off his chest in one go. Saw me as a target. Poor little sod felt like hitting someone and I seemed handy.'

'Why are we meeting?'

'One of those crackpot Balkan bomb-throwers shot some royalty in Austria last week. Killed a Duke and his wife stone dead. Balkan politics are such a mess. Never understood them. Wish Kinskii were still with us. He'd explain it.'

'Does it affect us in Africa?'

'I'm not sure yet, but Europe is all stirred up. Ah – here comes Stewartby.'

H.E. rose from his chair with a nervous shuffle. Stewartby marched into the room, scowled at H.E. and nodded to Adam.

H.E. said, '*Captain* Stewartby, and *Lieutenant* Early. I am directed to tell you that from this moment you are called to the Colours and under military orders.'

In the silence that followed Adam studied the three sharp red scars etched across H.E.'s pink cheeks: *Christ. Stewartby must have been on tiptoes to reach up and hit him that high....*

With an abrupt snort, Stewartby said, 'Are you going to tell us why?'

'Of course,' said H.E., becoming the smooth civil servant. 'Please sit down. Matters have taken a dangerous turn in Europe. Austria and Russia are squaring up over Serbia. Germany supports the Austrians, Turkey supports the Germans, France supports the Serbs. God knows who we support, but it looks serious.'

'I don't see what it has to do with us?' snapped Stewartby.

'This'll help you find out,' said H.E., tossing two heavy brown envelopes on to the desk. 'Sealed orders. Quite dramatic, don't you think?'

One week later, Adam sat with Thinman at a secret army camp in the bush near Mombasa.

Thinman asked, 'What did your wife think of you being whipped away by the army at such sort notice?'

'She's furious.'

'When's the baby due?'

'October.'

'So you have plenty of time.'

'That's what I said. Now I'm here, what do you want of me?'

'I think you've exported your last wood to Germany for a while.'

'Are things that bad?'

'Worse. Trains are being prepared all over Europe.'

'For what?'

'To carry troops. Europe wants war. It'll start soon – within the next two or three months. Perhaps earlier, now they have an excuse.'

'What am I supposed to do about it?'

'Same as before – you take a patrol along the German border and sniff around. Don't cross – if war starts they'll grab you and never let you back. May even shoot you. You are to check the area from Taveta to Namanga. Note any activity from the German side – traders or farmers coming across, that sort of thing. And if you meet any Englishmen going towards German territory, turn 'em back. We don't want the Hun to get any of our people. We'll need 'em soon enough. Stewartby's doing the same thing between Kajiado and the Lake.'

Thinman introduced Adam to a smart group of askaris led by a bright young Nandi sergeant.' I'm giving you a company from the KAR,' Thinman said.' Train and lead 'em right and they're the best you'll find anywhere. You'll get on well with this lot.'

Three weeks later Adam sat at his camp table in cool colourless dawn. First sunrays of a new day tinted the Kilimanjaro snow-tips pink. He prepared to complete his journal of yesterday, and wrote the date as 4th August 1902, smiled at his error and corrected it to 1914.

From scribbled survey notes, he checked position against a map. A chill passed through his body: *Good God. This is almost the place I sat the morning we found Eva. Bloody hell. Twelve years ago. Am I reliving it? Is that why I wrote nineteen-oh-two?*

He shivered and sipped at a mug of hot tea.

He took up his pen to write, but stopped as Abdi came from the askaris' lines, with an Army runner.

'*Bwana* Adam. This man has just arrived with a message from the small man.'

The crumpled paper, written in Thinman's hurried scrawl, timed and dated at nine a.m. on Friday 31st July 1914, read like a telegram: *Return Mombasa urgently. War imminent. Abandon patrol and leave border area immediately.*

Within an hour, Adam led his men east at a smart pace, arriving at Voi Station, mid-morning on sixth of August. The Indian station-master ran out to meet him waving and shouting, 'Telegrams for you Lieutenant Early – I am holding two telegrams for you.'

The first, from Thinman dated 5th August, read: WAR DECLARED AGAINST GERMANY YESTERDAY 4TH AUGUST STOP TOOK LIBERTY OF READING TELEGRAM TO YOU FROM MZITO STOP UNDER CIRCUMSTANCES TAKE IMMEDIATE LEAVE STOP SEND YOUR PATROL REPORT WITH SERGEANT STOP RETURN HOME AND AWAIT FURTHER ORDERS END

The second from Kristina, dated 4th August, said: EVA GAVE BIRTH THIS MORNING STOP A SON STOP COME HOME END

In surging excitement Adam called the station master back and snapped, 'What's moving on the line?'

'One up train arriving Voi four to five hours, Sahib. One down train arriving seven to eight hours. Will your soldiers stay here to save me from the Germans, Sahib?'

'My soldiers must go to Mombasa.'

'Oh-my-God,' said the station-master, rolling his eyes.

Adam spent three impatient hours at Voi, pacing in the hot sun, his mind full of conflict: *A premature birth. Is he healthy? How is Eva? Why did Kristina give me no detail? Is something wrong? And war. Everything happened on August the fourth. Bloody hell. Whatever next.*

The train arrived early – 'You are lucky man, Sahib.' Adam's company of askaris, excited at the news of war, lined the track side, waving and shouting goodbye. Their sergeant stood to solemn attention, saluting, Adam's report held firmly under his free arm.

Adam forced his way through a larger than usual crowd at Nairobi station.

'Go to Damu and fetch our horses,' he said to Abdi. 'Bring them to the Government Office. I'll see you there.'

'Why so many people in town today?' he asked his rickshaw man, as he dragged through a throng of men, horses and mules in Government Road.

'The war, *Bwana*. They've all come from their farms to fight the Wa-Germani.'

Shaking hands, H.E. said, 'Welcome to the madhouse. Everyone's crazy.'

'What are they all doing?'

'Joining up. Going to war. Have you ever seen such a rag-tag and bobtail lot? They're coming from everywhere.'

'Looks as if they just grabbed what was near, and left the farm.'

'Exactly,' said H.E.. 'They're a bigger headache than the enemy. We're trying to form 'em into some sort of force, but they're making up their own groups. Bloody amateurs. God help us all if they get anywhere near the Hun.'

'Never mind about that. What's the news from Mzito?'

'What news do you expect? You had a telegram from Kristina. That's the news. Eva had a son.'

'I know, but that's all the telegram said. What else? How are they? How's Eva? How's the baby?'

'I saw Kristina in town yesterday. She said they're well.'

'No problems?'

'Not that I hear of. Why should there be problems?'

'Oh for God's sake, H.E.. The baby arrived eight weeks early.'

'Mmm…,' said H.E.. 'Sit down. I'll order some tea.'

'Abdi will be here soon with my horse, and I want to get on to Mzito.'

'Sit down anyway. I need to talk with you.'

'Your face looks better,' said Adam.

H.E. touched and stroked the three faint scars, now blending into his pink cheeks.

'That little bugger Stewartby came back yesterday, just in time to cause more trouble.'

'What trouble?'

'Now the little sod's a captain, he's throwing his weight about. He's been told to arrest all enemy nationals. He's chasing round like a bull with a bee up its arse. You should get home and be ready for a visit.'

'Why?'

'*Why*. Wake up man. Your wife and sister-in-law are Prussians and related to the enemy commander. And Kristina's an Austrian Countess. I'm surprised they're not in the bag already.'

'Christ. I never thought of that,' said Adam.

Jumping from his horse Adam ran up the veranda steps. Kristina appeared, calling, 'They're here in the bedroom. Hurry.'

As he passed she brushed her lips across his cheek. A warm, sisterly kiss. Just right. But why the excitement in her shining violet eyes?

Eva lay half upright on a pile of snow-white pillows cradling her son, swaddled in a bright blanket.

'Darling,' she said.' How lovely to have you home.'

Adam leaned across and kissed her – a long soft kiss on the lips.

'Sorry I wasn't here, but you didn't expect him yet. Was it difficult?'

'No,' she whispered.' Not at all. Here – hold your son.'

Adam took the baby, saying, 'Eight weeks early – he's heavier than I thought.'

He pulled the blanket back and....murderous anger surged through his body as he looked down at the tiny head.

A beautiful boy. A handsome boy. Golden glowing skin, bright blue eyes and a lovely head of white-blond hair.

In agony, Adam looked at Eva. She smiled – a slight hint of nerves in her grey eyes. 'Isn't he lovely?' she said. 'Isn't he beautiful?'

'Isn't he handsome?' trilled Kristina, her violet eyes alight with malice. 'And born with all that lovely hair. Most unusual....'

With gritted teeth Adam threw the baby into Eva's arms, pushed past Kristina and ran from the room. He jumped on his horse and rode in high fury through dusk and early dark to Nairobi. He took a room at the Norfolk, and stayed inside for three days, drinking, brooding, and dreaming bloodthirsty revenge.

Early evening of the third day, Adam opened the door to a servant and H.E. pushed into the room saying, 'I was bloody determined to find you. Someone said you'd bunked off to Mombasa, but I didn't believe 'em.'

'Bugger off and leave me alone,' said Adam.

'My God you look awful. Eva and Kristina have been worried sick.'

'Sod 'em both.'

'Kristina took a risk coming into town to tell me you'd disappeared.'

'What risk?'

'Stewartby's detained everyone who's German or Austrian or speaks with a funny accent. Worse still – they'll all be interned in India.'

'India? The little bastard's sending Eva and Kristina to India?'

'It's a possibility. But since I let him hit me, I reckoned he owes me a favour. He agreed they can stay at Mzito – provided they write no letters to anyone here or abroad. That solved I promised Kristina I'd find you and tell you to go home.'

'Have you seen that baby? He's blond. He's blue-eyed. He's a cuckoo – a bloody cuckoo. He's not mine.'

'My dear chap – most European children born in Africa are blond at first. Both you and Eva are fair – so are your first two children. Why should the new baby be any different?'

'Have you seen him? Is that little blond bastard my baby or Christy's?'

'My dear fellow – never ask a civil servant a direct question.'

'Bloody hell H.E.. At least tell me *something*.'

'Nothing to tell. I'm not going to be involved in your family wrangles. Shall we change the subject? What about you? What next? You have a farm, a business; a family. On top of that, you're an army lieutenant, and we're at war. You can't stay here. You can't abandon everything. What will you do?'

'I've been thinking of nothing else for three days. For the time being I'm shackled to that German woman.'

'Eva?'

'Yes. She tricked me into marriage and she's tricked me ever since – as *you* know, but won't say. Now she's come a cropper trying to pass off that baby as mine.'

'You won't accept him?'

'I've been thinking about that too. If I don't the poor little bugger'll have no chance in life. So until a better idea comes along I'll accept him. I see no choice. She's won again. But all the time I'll be waiting.'

'Waiting for what?'

'To get my own back…when the time is right.'

Chapter Twenty-Four

A Battle at Longido

November 1914

With an hour to go before sunrise the Colonel cantered up shouting 'Captain Christy. Halt the column please. Where are we? How far to Longido?'

'Perhaps another hour,' said Christy, stretching in the saddle and lifting his aching buttocks from the stiff leather: *Bloody hell. What a night. What an idiot marching us twenty miles in the dark....*

The Colonel said, 'We'll stop at first light for Orders. Keep going slowly till then; I want the column to close up.'

At Namanga the day before, the Colonel said, 'You've been chosen to lead us across the plain to Longido Mountain. Understand you know the area. Was told you've done it before both ways. Good. Capital. Just what we need. Thank God you're with us.'

Christy had smiled his confident soldier's smile, and saluted as his heart sank: *Oh Christ. I'll be right at the sharp end.*

When he heard the battle plan, his mood improved. Two infantry columns to attack the mountain from different angles; while a cavalry group swept behind and cut off the enemy's inevitable retreat. Christy saw several promising gaps in the order of attack that allowed him to disappear if need be.

His spirits fell again when the force he'd been ordered to lead assembled at Namanga. A column of twelve hundred young sepoys from the Indian Army commanded by a British major and three captains shambled in, the sepoys sweating and fearful in this strange country.

'Christ. Look at them,' muttered the Colonel. 'Absolutely useless. What the bloody hell have they sent me?'

The major had shrugged and said, 'I don't know, old boy. First time I saw them was when they were shovelled off a ship at Mombasa. Poor bastards need a good rest. How long do we have?'

'Until tomorrow afternoon. Thank God I have some cavalry coming.'

The cavalry cantered into camp at sunset. Seeing them, the Colonel shouted, 'They've sent me a bloody circus. Cavalry? They're a bloody joke.'

'Bowker's Horse, Sir,' said Christy. 'Settlers formed as mounted rifles. I know some of them. Fine fellows.'

'God help us. Look at them. More mules and donkeys than horses. Not a uniform among them. And look at their guns. Hunting rifles. Not one man has a proper weapon.'

'Most of them are hunters, Sir. Crack shots.'

'Hunters? *Hunters?* I need soldiers, not bloody hunters. Do they realise what they shoot at may shoot back? God help us all.'

Christy spent the next twenty-four hours hanging around headquarters, watching in dismay at the frantic rush as the Colonel prepared his force for a night march – 'To catch the Hun by surprise, and push him off the bloody mountain,' he snapped.

At sundown on the second of November the column straggled out of Namanga. As far as Christy could tell, it comprised about fifteen hundred souls, in varying degrees of excitement and fear. At the rear dragged four field guns, and six machine guns. One hundred mules, loaded with water *dhebis,* followed, herded along by handlers.

Christy rode nervously half a mile ahead of the main column, commanding a smartly turned out KAR company, led by a bright young Nandi sergeant.

'You're taking the lead and scouting ahead so I've given you the proper soldiers,' the Colonel said. 'If you run into trouble, they'll know what to do. It'll give warning to the rest of us.'

As darkness drifted across the plain his Nandi sergeant trotted up alongside Christy and said in Swahili, 'Do not worry, Sir. I know this area well. My father is a tracker. He brought me here many times. I shall take you to Longido.'

At daylight, thick white mist covered the plain and hillside, silencing the usual clamour of dawn chorus. In the eerie quiet, Christy became nervous. Ordering his sergeant to keep going, he rode back to find the Colonel.

'Shall I send a patrol forward to find the Hun?' he asked.

'Good God no, man. You'll give away our position. They don't even know we're here. But we know they're up the hill. We'll just keep going forward till we find 'em. I've sent a runner to bring in the officers for Orders. Return to the point and halt our march then come straight back. From here we'll attack.'

The Colonel's eyes glowed with excitement. Christy could see the scent of battle had brought on a dangerous mood.

Arriving back at the point, Christy listened to bad news from his

185

Nandi sergeant. 'We chased a Chagga – a scout for the Wa-Germani, Sir, but he escaped up the hill into the cloud.'

'Say nothing or the sepoys will panic,' said Christy. 'I'll tell the Colonel.'

Pale milk-coloured sunlight struggled through the mist. The Colonel called his British and Indian officers together for a breakfast of tea and bread. With his stick, he drew a rough map in the dust.

'Major, this is where we split the column and march in two curves, approaching the mountain like this…'

He scratched at the dust.

'Three machine guns to each column. You go with the right column, and climb until you meet the enemy. He has no idea we're here, so you'll probably catch him at ablutions or breakfast. I'll go with the left column. We'll meet at the summit or over the other side when we've chased them down to Bowker and his men.'

Christy lifted a hand and started to say, 'My KAR sergeant–'

The Colonel said, 'Shut up please, Christy. I'll come to you later.'

The Colonel continued, 'Bowker – you set off with your men as soon as they've had breakfast. Damn this fog, but it'll hide you from the Hun. Get round the back between them and the Moshi road. We'll hurry 'em down the mountain in your direction. Kill or capture every one. Your men and horses need a rest? Bugger that Bowker. Do as I say. Get riding within the hour. We'll attack the hill at ten. By eleven the enemy will be retreating towards you. Make sure you're ready for them. Where are they now? Up the bloody hill, man. They're up the bloody hill in front of us. Now do as I order and get your men ready to go.'

Christy again lifted his hand and began to speak.

The Colonel said, 'Christy. Will you please shut up until I've finished. The field battery will stay down here and give supporting fire if necessary. The Hun has no idea we're here. We'll take him completely by surprise. Yes Christy? Now. What were you so anxious to say?'

Christy smiled – annoyed at the patronising little bastard: *Sod him. Let him find out for himself.*

He said, 'Nothing important, Sir. I was going to suggest that you may need a company act as reserve and stay here to protect the guns from counter attack.'

'Right. I was coming to that. You and your sixty men will make little difference to our attack, so you stay to protect the guns and water mules. I'll send runners down when we need water, and your men can bring it up to us. It'll all be over by noon.'

Christy saluted, triumphant: *Done it. No need to advance. I'll stay at the bottom and watch...*

He leaned on a field gun, smoked a cigarette, and waved at several friends, as Bowker's Horse mounted and rode out into the mist: *What a joke. Look at the silly buggers. They think it's a game.*

He watched the two columns curve off into the mist, removed his heavy sun helmet, and settled under a tree with a cup of tea. Half an hour later, the cloud rose, dispersed, and showed the steep sides of Longido.

Christy sent forty of his men a few hundred feet up the slope to set defensive positions, then rode downhill and inspected the water mules, grazing in a gully. Satisfied, he returned to the guns, where the Sikh subadar saluted, and said, 'Captain, Sahib, this is not a good place for my battery. We have no range. With your permission, Captain, Sahib, I will move to that small ridge. Can your men help?'

Christy tied his horse to a tree, and sat back to watch the guns being dragged to their new position. For a few moments he dozed in the pleasant early sunshine, then remembered the letter in his tunic pocket. Now creased and damp from his sweat, it had arrived the day before, at Namanga: *Christ. How could he have forgotten a letter?*

In her spiky German script, Eva wrote: *I hope you are well and not in danger these awful days. You may not yet know that my baby was born on the fourth day of August. He is a beautiful boy, and looks just like his father. I am so happy. In my heart I named him Christopher Timothy, but cannot say it out loud. To everyone else he will be Jonathan Oswald but I call him Johann after one of my Prussian uncles – a fine and handsome soldier. To me he will be Johann Christopher Timothy.*

On the fifteenth day of October, Kristina's twins were born – a boy and a girl. She has named them Miklos, and Mariska. She chose Hungarian names for her late husband's memory.

Christy sighed and raised his eyes to the sky: *Bloody women. They're either mad or romantic, or both...*

He read on – a few words about the farm...some lines on the difficulty of being German in Nairobi just now: *Good God. What do you expect, madam? You are bloody German, and your lot is the enemy....*

As the thought passed through his mind, the sound of gunfire filtered down the hill. At first, sharp popping crackles – the noise of fireworks and fun. Then the deeper roll of a volley, followed by the hard clatter of a machine gun.

Christy jumped on his horse, rode up the ridge to the battery and shouted, 'Get the rest of my men up the hill into line. I don't want to be surprised by the bloody Germans.'

'The shooting is far away from us, Captain Sahib,' said the Sikh subadar, saluting.

'Bloody-well do as I say.' shouted Christy. 'Get them up the hill.'

He waited for half an hour, listening to the sound of battle. When it came no nearer, he climbed the steep slope on foot, forcing through thick bush. After ten minutes of sweat and struggle he found a KAR askari leaning against a tree, staring upwards, rifle at the ready.

'Where's your sergeant?' asked Christy, in Swahili.

The askari pointed up the hill with his chin.

'Where?' said Christy. 'Up there? What the hell is he doing up there?'

'He went to look at the *Wa-Germani*, Sir,' said the askari, keeping his eyes firmly on the thick bush above.

'What the bloody hell for?'

'You want us to kill them, Sir. We must know where they are, Sir. He will be back in two minutes.'

'How do you know?'

'I can hear him, Sir. He's coming down the hill.'

'Bloody nonsense. All I can hear is shooting. Where are the rest of our men?'

The askari pointed left and right with his chin.

'As you said, Sir. Guarding the guns. We made a line covering all paths down.'

Christy crouched, listening in mounting anxiety to the gunfire. He wrinkled his nose, at the smell of his European sweat, mingling with the sharp wood-smoke smell of the askari. A minute later, the Nandi sergeant came skipping downhill. He moved in sideways hops, covering the ground at speed, and passing through the dense bush as though it did not exist.

He said, 'There are about fifty *Wa-Germani* and five hundred askaris in long holes waiting for our soldiers, Sir.'

'In long holes? You mean trenches?'

'Yes, Sir. Trenches. I just finished counting them when our soldiers arrived. The Wa-Germani has machine guns, Sir, and they will win, because they are ready. Our Indian soldiers are struggling in the bush, Sir. Shall we take our men up and help, Sir?'

'No. Bloody-well stay where you are. Guard the hill. Stop any Wa-

Germani or their bloody askaris coming down. I'll go back and warn the subadar.'

As Christy arrived at the battery, all four guns fired a loud salvo up the mountain.

'What the bloody hell are you doing?' he shouted at the subadar, who saluted and said, 'Orders from the Colonel Sahib to shoot. A runner came with orders for you also, Captain, Sahib.'

Christy read the message, scrawled on a scrap of paper: *Urgent you inform Bowker I need his men up in support. They must climb their side of the hill, and attack the German lines from behind. Send up water mules. Act immediate.*

Christy scribbled a return message, and sent the runner up the hill with instructions to tell his Nandi sergeant to come down for orders. The battery fired another salvo. Christy ran to his horse, pulling and plunging at its tether. Beyond, in their gully, the water mules moved in confused braying circles.

As Christy mounted, half a dozen shells came back down the mountain, and exploded in a line across the battery, throwing up a cloud of thick red dust: *Bloody hell. The Germans have guns too. Christ. I'd better get out of here…*

He cantered down through the dust towards the water mules. A second German salvo whistled in, straddling the battery in noise and red dust. Two stray shells exploded downhill, near the mules. Flayed and blinded by a blizzard of sand and small stones, Christy grabbed the saddle and hung on, as his horse reared and thrashed in fear and pain. Regaining control, he raced into the gully to find the mules stampeding out onto the plain and scattering.

He chased and caught four, tied their muzzle ropes to his pommel, and led them back towards the ridge. Most mule handlers had fled. The two or three left, caught several mules and pulled them back into the gully.

More German shells landed, exploding round the ridge. From the centre of the red dust cloud Christy heard the battery reply with steady fire: *He may be a bloody Indian, but that Subadar knows how to work his guns.*

He dragged the four mules into shelter behind a pile of rocks, until the German bombardment eased, then called his sergeant and the *Subadar* down from the ridge.

To the sergeant he said in Swahili, 'Take those water mules in the gully up to the Colonel with forty of your men. I will take these four water mules to the horse soldiers and give them the Colonel's orders.

If the Colonel does not need you up the mountain, come back here and stay with the guns. I will find you when I return.'

In English, he told the *Subadar* the same, adding, 'Move your battery. The Germans know where you are.'

As he spoke another line of shells flew in, crashing and thumping into the mountainside. Christy jumped into the saddle, and dragged the four water mules downhill, out of range. Looking back, he saw the *Subadar* and sergeant scuttle up the ridge, and disappear into the new red cloud covering their position: *Rather you than me, fellows. See you in Namanga....*

For two hours, Christy struggled round the mountain, his face smarting and weeping from hundreds of small cuts and grit holes. The thump and clatter of battle, rolled and echoed down the mountain, as he rode. *They're all too busy up there to bother me; thank God....*

Bowker's column of mules and horses had left a clear track in the bush – a wide swathe of flattened grass, broken branches and dung. The trail he followed, skirted the lower gullies and ridges of Longido on ground riddled with holes and gullies.

When Christy came upon a fifty foot high pile of bare rocks, easy to see and identify from a distance, he stopped. After a short search, he found a wide crevice, hidden from view. Twenty minutes later, he rode on, checking as he went that the water mule left tethered in the crevice was invisible from prying eyes – human or animal.

The sun was high and hot before he found Bowker and his men, huddled together on a tree-covered rise, between mountain and plain, listening to the gunfire above.

'Thank God you've brought water,' said Bowker. 'We thought it would be over by now. What happened? We've been waiting for the Germans, but no-one came. Good God, man. Look at your face. Are you wounded?'

'It's nothing. Caught in an artillery barrage, that's all. What you'd expect in a battle.'

Bowker's men crowded round as Christy passed on their orders. 'Can we take our horses up?' asked one.

'As far as you can. The rest will be on foot. You must hurry. The Colonel called for you two hours ago.'

'Are you coming with us?'

'Wouldn't miss it for the world,' said Christy with a gallant smile. He removed his heavy military sun helmet and wiped his brow, as Bowker's men admired his brave, bomb-blasted face. He ran a hand through his sweaty, white-blond hair, and said, 'Come, gentlemen. Shall we mount up and go to war?'

After several hundred feet, heavy undergrowth broke the cavalry column into scattered groups, and the slope became too steep for horses. By the time they were forced to dismount, Christy had managed to drop behind.

'Bloody animal won't go. He's tired after dragging those damned mules here,' he called.

He struggled on up the hill and came across a cluster of young men standing by their exhausted mules. A cheery voice said, 'Can I help you at all, Captain Christy?'

'Bloody hell Martin – what are you doing here? You're a bank manager.'

'I joined up with the others,' said John Martin, his young friendly face streaked with sweat and dust. 'Couldn't stay behind, could I? I'd have missed all the fun.'

He smiled at Christy from beneath a wide brimmed hat.

Christy smiled back and said, 'We'll kill our mounts if we push them further. Let's leave 'em here, tied to these bushes and collect 'em when we've whipped the Hun.'

Two hundred feet further up the mountain several bullets whipped past Christy. Realising the Germans had him in their sights, he dived into a thicket and lay petrified: *This damned helmet. It'll be the death of me. Stands out a bloody mile....*

Around him, several young men stood on tiptoe trying to see where the shots came from. Christy shouted, 'You bloody idiots. Get down. You're telling them where we are.'

The firing increased. He whimpered, and pushed his sweating, stinging face into the dust, as heavy bullets rushed through the leaves around him. Several young men fell, hanging off the ground, held by thick bush as tough as barbed wire.

A hat. Now I'll get a hat.... In a lull, as some of Bowker's more experienced hunters found targets, and returned fire, Christy crawled from the thicket. He tossed his sun helmet into the undergrowth, wriggled across, and snatched a wide brimmed hat from the nearest body.

As he crawled backwards down the hill, John Martin's blank open eyes stared after him, the friendly smile replaced by a cold dead grimace.

Silly bugger. You should've stayed in your bank....

191

Christy slithered down to his horse. Rode slowly off the mountain, away from the sound of battle. Found his water mule among the rocks. Rode off across the plain in the afternoon sun, and set course for Namanga.

He was not alone on the plain. The retreat from defeat at Longido had already started. Whenever he heard or saw other stragglers, he changed course. Water was precious and not to be shared. Oh no. Not a drop....

Near Namanga, he stopped in a gully and waited till dark, watching and listening as shattered groups of soldiers staggered by. When he knew several British officers had made it back, he released the horse and mule, and limped slowly into camp, leaning on a stick found in the gully.

'Thank God you survived Christy,' said the Colonel. 'What happened to your face?'

'It's nothing. Caught in an artillery barrage, that's all. What you'd expect in a battle.'

'Good man,' said the Colonel.

Chapter Twenty-Five

Countess in Custody

Kristina sat in a small stifling room wondering why the hell she was under arrest. This must be a cell. Hardly any furniture – just two chairs, one small table and an oil lamp casting soft yellow light. The twins slept quietly in wicker cots on the floor.

Outside in the dark, bare feet padded along the wooden veranda in slow regular beat. Round and round they went, regular as a clock, leathery foot-pads slip-slapping on hard wood planks. *Askaris* patrolling – guarding. *Is this a prison or a police station?*

Kristina, with nothing else to do, counted the number of steps to complete a full circuit. The sound of pat-patting feet receded round the corner; marched across the rear veranda; swung with effortless rhythm down the side then back across the front in perfect symmetry. She knew the men looked in at her each time they passed – two black outlines sliding across the fly-screened windows, eye-whites catching the lamp-light.

This is terrible. Am I a peep show for damned Africans...?

Mosquitoes droned and zipped against the window mesh. One forced through and headed straight for the babies. With a slap of her hand, Kristina squashed it against the wall. She slumped back in her chair nearly spitting in anger and humiliation: *God, what an awful day this has been....*

Kristina remembered the shock when, at noon, a small column of police *askaris*, led by an embarrassed European constable arrived at Mzito.

The constable said, 'Sorry ladies. I must take you into Nairobi for questioning. Captain Stewartby's orders, I'm afraid. Please come quietly. Yes Madame, you may bring whatever children and servants you want, but please hurry.'

Kristina said, 'But my sister's husband is away at the war and my babies are only three weeks old.'

'Yes, Madame. Please hurry.'

Crowded in the small donkey cart with Eva and her children, Kristina rattled and bumped down to Nairobi through the hot afternoon, escorted by the constable and his men. Kristina's babies slept the whole way, swinging along in their wicker baskets, carried by *ayah* and wet nurse, walking alongside the cart.

At dusk they entered a compound among trees on the edge of town. The European constable led Kristina to this room, ushered the *ayah* and wet nurse out and locked Kristina in. Shocked to silence, she forgot to ask about Eva. By the time she shouted, he had gone.

Christ, why are they doing this? How long will I be in here...?

One of the twins began to cry. *Oh for God's sake. Which one? The little devils looked so alike I can't tell.*

Annoyed, Kristina leaned over the two wicker baskets. One baby lay serenely asleep. The other yelled loud and shrill: *The girl, I think....*

She checked. Yes. The girl. Is she hot or hungry? Sunset, an hour ago, had made little difference. The room remained uncomfortably humid.

Kristina took up the child, opened her blouse and offered a breast. Slick lines of sweat ran down her back and formed in beads on her chest. The baby, a hot wriggling little doll, pulled hard, drawing milk: *No one told me these damned children are so bloody demanding. Where's my wet nurse? Why did they take her away? Why do I have to do this...?*

She heard the clatter of boots on wood. The door opened. Stewartby stepped in and stared down at her. She glared back: *Bloody little man thinks he's wonderful in that stupid uniform....*

She snarled, 'Why are you holding me? When do I go home? Where's my sister? Why do you keep us apart? Where are my *ayah* and wet nurse? Bring them to me now. Why are you keeping me in this room?'

The baby, stuffed with milk, rolled its eyes and fell asleep. Kristina stretched forward and dumped it into the wicker basket. Her sleek damp breasts swung out, glowing slippery golden-wet in the lamplight.

Stewartby's eyes widened and narrowed to sharp points; glowing with an inner heat she knew so well in herself.

Got the little bastard....

She turned towards him, fastening loose blouse buttons with slow insolence; fingertips sliding across damp skin, leaving one milk-slick nipple negligently bare. Turning the full force of her violet eyes on him, she whispered, 'Please let me go home.'

For a moment she saw him waver then with obvious effort he pulled his gaze away and dragged the other chair forward to sit stiffly upright; ankles together; hands cupped on kneecaps; elbows locked straight – a stiff policeman's pose. His eyes looked at and past her, fixed on a point alongside her head – the pose of an interrogator; neutral and disturbing. He began to ask questions.

For ten minutes she felt completely bemused.

A battle? And the British lost. *Two* battles? At Longido and Tanga? And you lost them both? Who did you fight? The *Germans*? But that's in Europe. What does it have to do with me? Yesterday? The battles were *yesterday*? You brought me here and locked me up because of that? Of course I know nothing about them – I've been weeks out on that damned farm with no news of anything. Did I send information to Moshi? What information? What would I know? How could I send information? This is all so silly. Where is my sister? Why do you humiliate me like this? What on earth are you talking about you stupid man...?

She sat up in her chair; waved a fist at him, her body tense with anger. His eyes dropped to the soft wet nipple, peeking from her blouse. She leaned back and took a deep breath. Through lowered lashes, she watched his jaw muscles tighten to hard lumps and his colour rise.

'Shut up and listen to me,' he snapped. 'You are German *and* Austrian – an enemy national twice. Your late husband served as an officer in the enemy army. If he were here now which side would he be on? Which side are *you* on? We know about his background, and we know about yours. We know he was a spy and think you may be a spy also.'

'What nonsense. Why should I spy? *How* would I spy? What do I know? This is ridiculous. Where is Eva? Is she here in another room?'

'Your sister is released. As an Englishman's wife we cannot hold her. *You* we can hold and intern for as long as we want. *You* we can deport to India along with the other foreigners.'

'*India?* I don't want to go to India. Where is my sister? Back at Mzito?'

'No. We released her to the custody of Hocklyffe-Evans until her husband returns and takes charge.'

'*Hocklyffe-Evans?*'

A brilliant idea swept through Kristina.

'How wonderful. Hocklyffe-Evans is my fiancé. I can go to him also.'

'Your fiancé?'

His eyes switched from neutral to angry – to bitter and baffled.

'Your fiancé? He didn't say.'

'No. We're keeping it secret until a year after Kinskii's death. But it makes me almost English, so you can let me go also.'

Stewartby jumped from his chair and stood to attention, jaw muscles clenching and releasing.

Kristina smiled into his eyes: *My God, he's quite handsome. Pity he's not taller....*

Stewartby marched from the room, slamming and locking the door. She heard his boots stamp down the veranda steps, and march away, thumping into the hard-packed dirt across the compound.

She waited for the slip-slap of bare feet to restart their patrol. Instead, she heard the tiptoe shuffle of leather soles on wood planks – up the steps and across the veranda.

Mein Gott. The bloody man's creeping back to peep at me....

She opened her blouse to the waist. Leaned across and picked up a baby. Made sure the yellow lamplight shone across her face and chest. For the next ten minutes she cradled, cuddled and suckled her babies. As they fed she fondled them and herself; turning and preening; giving full view of her magnificently shining profile to the golden lamplight, and to the still small silhouette in the window.

An hour later, H.E. opened the door, and said, 'I hear we're engaged.'

His huge bulk filled the room.

Kristina said, 'I've always wanted to be engaged to you. I thought it would help if we did it now.'

'It may help you – I'm not sure it'll help me.'

'Are you angry?'

He laughed, running a hand through his long blond hair.

'I should be, but I'm not. I suppose I can rescue the occasional damsel in distress. Stewartby's released you to me under house arrest, until we work out a proper parole arrangement. Come on. With Adam away I'm responsible for you now. Let's go home.'

Under a sky filled with small bright stars, Kristina and H.E. rocked up the hill in a small horse-drawn rickshaw. The twins followed with their *ayah* and nurse in the donkey cart.

At H.E.'s house Kristina said, 'I need a bath.'

'Sit and have a drink first,' he said. 'Remember we're engaged and you're under arrest, so do as I say.'

Kristina sipped her wine and remembered Eva.

'My sister. My God, I'd forgotten her. Where is she? We made enough noise arriving. She must have heard. I'll go and find her. Which room?'

'In the guest wing fast asleep. She'll not hear a sound from us whatever we get up to.'

Grunting with effort H.E. stumbled to his feet, his blue eyes sharpened in speculation.

'Come on. Now it's time for a bath.'

With a shiver of anticipation Kristina said, 'Good. I'm hot and sticky. A splash in the bath is just what I fancy.'

Chapter Twenty-Six

On Licence

In the cold dawn, Kinskii came again. He appeared from the dark outer limits of Kristina's mind, looking down with a sad smile, shaking his elegant head.

Annoyed, she shooed him away saying, 'Leave me alone. I'm not ready to come yet. Go back to your damned mountain....'

He bowed and retreated into the deep melancholy surrounding her soul.

To speed his departure Kristina forced herself awake and ran her hands across her naked body, relaxing at the soft luxury of her fingers fluttering over breasts, thighs and buttocks. Oh, such pleasure it gave to feel herself each morning and confirm she remained still firm, still interesting: *Almost perfect. Who'd think I gave birth only a few weeks ago....*

She stroked and pulled at the silken mat covering her lower stomach. Smooth. Soft. Her hand lingered and played. The bliss of being alive returned and pushed Kinskii further into a darker distance.

Beside her, H.E. stirred, his huge bulk rocking the bed. In the grey light he looked as blond and beautiful as the first time they met. *Oh how I fell in love with him then. When was it? Ah yes...Kilindini in 1905. My God. Nine years. It took me a week to get him into bed then. Why did he wait so long to come back?*

The instant and complete love she felt on the Kilindini dockside those years ago swept through her again: *Stupid man. We could have been together all this time. What a waste.:...*

On the veranda outside, she heard the pad of bare feet. Her jailers? Come to reclaim her?

No. Eva's voice and the clink of teacups: *Of course, it's dawn. My silly sister must sit out and watch the sun rise.*

Taking H.E.'s dressing gown, Kristina slipped out on to the veranda. Eva, wrapped in a blanket, sat on a wicker chair sipping tea.

Eva said, 'Come and sit down. Have some tea. There'll be toast in a moment.'

'Eva, darling. You look tired,' said Kristina.

'So do you. When did they let you go?'

'Late yesterday evening. And you?'

'As soon as I saw Stewartby. Stupid little man. He's never forgiven me for hitting him and stealing his whip. He'd have loved

198

to send me to India.'

'So he gave you to H.E. who brought you here?'

'Yes. You too?'

'Yes.'

Eva sighed and murmured, 'I can see your house is empty now. How sad. I hope the fighting will end soon. It's ruining everything.'

'You're thinking of Christy?'

'Yes. I can't help it. He fascinates me. What about you? Did you sleep with H.E.?'

'Darling. Of course I did. I've waited for years. I couldn't give up the chance.'

Eva laughed and said, 'Just how it was in Berlin. Different houses; different men.'

'No,' said Kristina, her violet eyes gleaming. 'This is different. Here we do it because we want to choose our own men. In Berlin we did it because father ordered us and he chose the men. I prefer it here. House arrest is much more fun.'

Eva said, 'Be quiet. Here's sunrise.'

Kristina sat in silence and watched clear sharp shards of light break through the trees, dappling the red earth. Eva sighed and hugged Jonathan.

At breakfast H.E. said, 'I'll speak to the Governor today and try to arrange your return to Mzito. You'll be safer there than here.'

'Why safer?' asked Kristina.

'For God's sake woman. Use your bloody head. Everyone knows you're German and your damned people have killed some good men in the last five days. On Friday I saw the casualty list from Longido. Several of your friends – and mine – were killed in the damned battle. We're still waiting for news from Tanga. Heaven only knows what that'll tell us.'

'Killed?' said Kristina. 'Who was killed?'

'Sandbach-Baker, for one.' snapped H.E..

'Oh no,' moaned Eva, 'Poor Queenie. Are you sure?'

'Of course I'm sure.'

'Who else?'

'It'll all be published soon, then you can read for yourself but your friend Christy is listed as slightly wounded so he's safe.'

'And Adam?'

'Not on the list so he's safe or he may have been at Tanga. We're still waiting for full news of that disaster.'

199

The sisters stared at each other, grey-faced and silent.

H.E. said, 'Take my advice and stay here. Germans are not popular in Nairobi, just now. No wandering about, or you may find yourself in far worse than Stewartby's friendly little jail.'

As H.E. prepared to leave, a runner arrived, loping through the trees. H.E. read the message and grunted.

'Thank God,' he said. 'This is a telegram from Thinman. Your husband survived the battle at Tanga and is on his way by train from Mombasa. Musa's wounded but your husband's safe. I'll meet him at the station and bring him here. He can take charge of you both.'

Forty-eight hours after leaving Musa wounded and seriously ill in a Mombasa hospital, Adam found himself reliving the horror of the past week. Exhausted by battle and travelling companions who talked of nothing but war, he felt great desire to see his wife and children – even Jonathan.

Seeing Adam off at Mombasa, Thinman said, 'You read the message from H.E. – your wife and her sister arrested as spies. Go up to Nairobi, sort it out and recover from the battle. Spend Christmas with your family then come back here with Abdi and a dozen or so Somalis. I need you to form an intelligence unit along the German border.'

At Nairobi station Adam found H.E. in the crowd and asked, 'Where's Eva?'

'At my house. Good God man, you look awful. Why's your arm in a sling. What happened? No one said you'd been shot. Musa too? At Tanga? You fought there? Bloody hell. Where will it all end? Follow me. I have a pony cart. We'll swap stories on the way.'

As the pony cart travelled up Government Road and along Sixth Avenue Adam said, 'Tell me what's been going on here.'

'Things are not good. The casualty list from Longido was a horrid surprise. Our lads expected war to be a jolly lark. You know the sort of thing – pop off at a few Huns, then back to the club for a sundowner. Then came the ghastly news of our disaster at Tanga – what could the military mind do? Easy. Blame German spies and arrest everyone with a foreign accent. Your two lovelies are obvious suspects – so into jail they went. I claimed privilege and rescued them from Stewartby yesterday but only on licence until you returned. After that, you can tell me your adventures....'

Eva heard the pony cart first. She jumped to her feet and called,

'Kristina. I think this is Adam. What shall I do?'

Kristina laughed. 'Pretend he's Christy. That should do the trick.'

Eva hurried to the veranda steps.

Watching the pony cart come through the trees Eva felt an unexpected thrill of affection. *How odd. I must have missed him. A sling? His arm – it's bandaged? He's been shot. My God, he's been shot....*

Eva intended to wait on the veranda with Kristina and greet Adam with a calm hug and kiss. Instead she ran down the steps calling, 'Here I am, darling. Adam. Darling. I'm here.'

He waved and smiled.

Overcome with relief – *Thank God, he smiled* – she threw her arms round his neck and kissed him hard.

'Darling, you've been wounded. Is it bad? What happened?'

'Nothing much. How are you? I heard you'd been arrested. Where are the children? Mind my arm.'

'Darling, I've missed you so much,' cried Eva, surprised to find herself meaning it.

She caught Kristina's mocking gaze and H.E.'s sceptical smile.

Damn them. Damn them both. I did miss him. He's my husband....

H.E. returned immediately to Nairobi – 'I need to see the Governor about you two women.'

To Eva's relief, Adam pleaded exhaustion and went to bed – 'I must rest. I'm useless now. I'll be better this evening. We'll talk then.'

'But your arm, darling – what happened to your arm.'

'I'll tell you this evening. I'll tell you everything.'

She resumed her seat on the veranda and sat brooding through the afternoon heat, face blank, eyes dark with worry. Kristina joined her for tea. Eva, reverting to the close intimacy of their girlhood, started a whispered conversation.

'I'm confused. I missed my husband more than I thought. When he left after Jonathan's christening I felt he may never come back. I've been awful to him.'

'Do you love him?' asked Kristina.

'Probably.'

'And Christy?'

'I've told you – he fascinates me. Did you love Kinskii?'

'Not when he was alive.'

'Why did you marry him?'

'To stay in Africa. To avoid Berlin.'

'I married Adam for the same reason.'

Kristina chuckled.

'Does anyone ever marry for love?' she asked.

At dinner, Eva tried to draw Adam into telling of the fight at Tanga.

'Later,' he said. 'I'll tell you later. I'm still trying to sort it out in my mind. More important is how H.E. arranged to keep you two out of prison.'

H.E. explained. 'We've stopped that bloody little popinjay Stewartby taking you back into jail. After all, he can't deport Englishmen's wives and fiancées. I spoke with the Governor this afternoon. He agreed you can stay out on two conditions. You ladies can return to Mzito provided you set up an officer's hospital there. That is one condition. The second is that you have no contact with Germany or any Germans or Austrians, including your relatives. You will be completely free to run the farm and come or go as you please, provided you agree.'

Kristina threw her arms round his neck and kissed him.

'I will be the perfect English lady,' she shouted. 'God save the King.'

'Get off me woman,' growled H.E.. 'I've had enough of you.'

'But I'm your fiancée.'

'Only while we're at war. Make the most of it.'

Eva led Kristina out to the warm darkness on the veranda, leaving the men to smoke cigars and drink brandy. She sighed and looked through starlit trees, towards the lifeless black bulk of Kristina's house.

Kristina whispered, 'How was Adam? When you were alone?'

'Quite happy,' Eva whispered back. 'He's changed. He even cuddled Jonathan. He'll be here for Christmas, then back to the army.'

'Will you see Christy again.'

Eva felt helpless tears sting her eyes.

Christy, oh Christy – what shall I do about you...?

'Probably not.' she said.

Chapter Twenty-Seven

Mzito Hospital 1914-1915

December 1914

In the heat of late morning, Adam sat alone on the veranda drafting a note to Churchill. He stretched and rubbed his arm where the healing wound still ached.

Churchill had written: *Pray tell me about Tanga. Did you take part in the action? By what means did so few Germans achieve such complete victory over our superior numbers? Your reply may have bearing on our campaign in France....*

'This is deadly secret,' H.E. said the day before when he brought Churchill's note to Adam. 'For God's sake keep prying eyes away – especially your two Valkyries. If they see it and word gets out you'll be shot at dawn. And so will they.'

Adam stretched again, distracted by the sound of Eva's voice shouting at Anwar again, he raised his head and smiled. Poor Anwar. He came down from the Kinangop to help Eva design the hospital *bandas* and stayed to supervise construction. Now, with the work progressing, she almost sat on the poor fellow's shoulders, checking, measuring and instructing.

The children played and laughed with their *ayah*, running and hiding among trees on the other side of the house. And Kristina? Not a sound. Probably crouched in a corner somewhere, shuffling through Kinskii's papers....

Adam sighed and picked up his pen to be distracted again, this time by the sight of a young African limping towards the house. Dressed in smart military tunic and shorts he crabbed through the trees on a rough wooden crutch; his right leg wrapped in a dirty blood-crusted bandage.

He dragged himself to the veranda steps, face grey with pain and exhaustion, stiffened to attention and saluted, balancing on his good leg.

'*Bwana* Lieutenant, I am here to see my father,' he said.

'I know you,' said Adam. 'You were my sergeant last July when we patrolled the German border. Where were you wounded?'

'Longido, *Bwana*.'

'Who is your father?'

'Sakayo, Sir. Your tracker. I am Kiptumi.'

'Sakayo? Good God.'

Adam pulled a chair down the steps.

'Sit here. I'll bring water and a new bandage and send for Sakayo. Then you must tell me about Longido.'

'He's wounded?' said Eva, in delight. 'Good. He'll be my first patient.'

She cleaned and bandaged Kiptumi's leg – 'He arrived just in time. Look. The wound's beginning to fester. I'll put him in the first *banda* – it'll be ready in an hour. When Musa arrives the day after tomorrow, I'll have a *banda* ready for him, too.'

'You must move them out before the officers get here.'

'Of course I will, darling. But we can practice on them before the officers come.'

In the hospital *banda*, Sakayo crouched on the dirt floor beside Adam's chair, while Kiptumi told his story of Longido.

When he finished, Adam said, 'So you led your men up the mountain alone? Where was your commander?'

'Gone.'

'Shot?'

'No. He went.'

'Went? Where? Who was he?'

'An English captain with white hair. But he was not old. He was young. I don't know his name. We called him *Nyoka*.'

'Snake? Why did you call him snake?'

'Because he slithered into the bush when he saw trouble. Like a snake on its belly. He left us to fight alone.'

Sakayo turned silent knowing eyes to Adam.

'*What* has your mad wife done?' asked H.E. when Adam delivered his reply to Churchill three days later. 'Put two Africans in the hospital *bandas*? Good God. The bloody army will go mad if they find out.'

Adam said, 'What difference does it make? Musa came off the train on a stretcher yesterday. His head's better, but the throat wound is a problem. He can hardly speak but now he's in proper care he should recover.'

H.E. pushed the heavy sealed packet into his wall safe.

'Did you say you'd added some notes about Longido to this?'

'Yes. Sakayo's son told me a lot about that battle of real interest to Churchill.'

A few days later an army runner trotted into Mzito with a telegram.

204

Adam said, 'Thinman needs me at the Coast. I'll go next Monday. I'm ready and so are the horses. I can't stay here much longer.'

For the next four days and nights, Eva pushed Christy deep into the darkest dungeon in her mind – *stay there, damn you* – and managed to give Adam full attention.

On Saturday she drove her pony cart to Rowbas village asking Adam to join her, saying, 'You can say goodbye to Musa and Kiptumi while I change their dressings.'

In Musa's hut Eva cleaned and bandaged his wounds, listening to his new rasping voice. When he returned to Mzito only two weeks ago she felt sure Musa would die. Now he sat up and asked when he could join Adam.

'I must be with you soon, *Bwana* Adam.'

'No. Stop here with your family. Don't come to be shot again.'

'I cannot be shot again. God has shown he does not want me yet. You, too. We are both safe.'

Eva looked at Musa's wife sitting quietly in the background – a slim nut-brown Kikuyu girl with her hair in delicate plaited ringlets: *Poor woman. Why should her husband fight someone else's war...?*

4th January 1915

Eva stood on the veranda and waved goodbye as Adam cantered up the slope, leading fifteen Somalis off to war. She breathed deeply – almost a sigh at his going. She waved again, hoping he would look back.

Without warning, Christy took over, wriggling his way up from the secret depths of her mind. Tears of frustration blurred and stung her eyes. Since that last night together she banished him to the sidelines of her conscience – *forget him, you fool* – but he refused to stay. She struggled to send him back – *for God's sake, not while my husband's still here* – but his merry blue eyes challenged her resolve.

'What next, little sister?' whispered Kristina. 'Who'll come riding in to see you, oh-so-soon?'

'Shut up, damn you.'

Eva turned, ready, almost, to hit her sister to find the veranda empty except for echoes of guilt.

Topping the slope, Adam twisted in his saddle for a last goodbye just as Eva turned away – probably looking for Kristina.

He shrugged and kicked his horse into a canter, dipping over the ridge and losing sight of Mzito: *What relief. Back to the simplicity and freedom of war, thank God....*

Eva struggled through thick mud on her way back from the cattle pens. Exhaustion gnawed at her bones. Depression clouded her mind.

Everyone's deserted me. No news from Adam. No sign of H.E.. And Christy...? Disappeared completely. Not a word. Not a hint of where he's gone or when he may come again. I'm stuck out on this damned farm with my sister, six stupid officers for patients and thousands of cattle. Oh God, these last two months have been hard....

Last week the heat of March turned into cold April rain. Life seemed nothing but work. Great herds had flooded in from the north, unannounced. Crowded pens broke. Cattle spilled across surrounding land, trampling crops and coffee trees and wandering into the bush – easy prey for hyena or Kikuyu from the forest.

She passed the empty hospital *bandas*. Yesterday all six officer-patients had left. Tomorrow a new batch would arrive. Just like a bloody hotel.

More work. More worry. Her shoulders sagged and she felt beaten down at the prospect.

Eva disliked the hospital but knew that Kristina loved it, spending most of her time with the patients – 'Supervising, darling, just supervising. Nursing's much more fun than farming. Now I'm nearly thirty, I like being with younger men – especially when they're in bed. It's hard work but I manage to spread myself. '

Eva often heard Kristina creeping back into the main house late at night. Did she have a favourite among the young officers? Eva never asked, but suspected that Kristina spread herself in many different ways in the *bandas*.

Climbing on to the veranda Eva called for tea and settled to paperwork in the office, losing track of time. She checked records of cattle sent for slaughter to Damu, against records of meat sold; read telegrams from the cold store at Mombasa; checked wood production at Anwar's; calculated coffee yields; wrote lists of needs for the hospital. So dull and boring. So necessary.

Damn Kristina. Why can't she help and do some of this work. She's nothing but a damned parasite....

At dusk, exhausted by a day of heat and dust working among her coffee trees and cattle, Eva climbed on to the veranda, fell into a chair, kicked off her shoes and called for a drink.

Thank God for Kiptumi. What would I do without him as headman now Musa's rejoined Adam. He's young but by God he keeps discipline around the house and farm.

'He is a soldier, Memsahib,' Musa said before leaving. 'He will look after you until I am back.'

Lights from the hospital *bandas* shone through the trees. *Oh God. The new patients.*

She peered through the trees trying to see signs of activity.

I should go down and see them but I can't. I'm too tired. I'll go tomorrow. Nothing I can do tonight....

She lay back sipping at a glass of cold lemonade, relaxed and secure in the peace of evening and the sounds and smells of home. From the kitchen *banda* a delicious aroma of roasting meat. From the dining room the clink and rattle of table laying. From the bathroom the giggles and splashing of her daughter being bathed.

Should I see the children yet? No. Leave them to the ayah. I'll cuddle Jonathan later. Before bed....

She dozed for several minutes until woken by the shuffling pad of bare feet. Kiptumi limped up the veranda steps with a letter – 'From Memsahib Kristina,' he said.

Oh God. Kristina. I've ignored her. I should have gone to the bandas to help.

Kristina scrawled: *I know you're back. We have an emergency patient in Banda Four. Come straight away.*

Eva jumped from her chair, scrabbled into her shoes, dashed through the trees to *Banda* Four.

Breathing hard she peered round the darkened room.

No sign of Kristina.

She squinted, adjusting her eyes to the shadows. On the bed lay a man, still and silent as a mummy, one arm flopped through the mosquito net, fingers trailing the floor.

An emergency? How is this an emergency?

She tiptoed forward. Pulled aside the mosquito net. Bent to study the patient.

Loose bandages swathed his upper body and wound over his face and head. A sheet covered his stomach and legs. Eva could see no sign of blood or injury. An internal wound perhaps? Or is he dead?

She ran her fingers down his arm, seeking a pulse beneath the hot damp skin.

The man sighed then gulped and gasped. The sharp heave of breath dragged bandage into his mouth. Spluttering, he sucked savagely for air and yanked more lint down his windpipe.

Eva snatched at the material covering his face. Piles of linen came free with surprising ease, falling in white curls about the bed.

His chest pumped and shuddered – his whole body shaking without control.

My God. A seizure. I'm killing him. He's dying. It's my fault.

In panic she grasped and pulled at the bandage, hauling him free of its deadly embrace.

A final tug brought him clear. Silky white-blond hair flopped out across the pillow. Tears streamed from merry blue eyes. A gale of repressed laughter burst out across the room. His limp trailing arm swept up and pulled Eva down on to the bed.

'Christy,' she screamed in shock. 'What are you doing here?'

'Shut up and I'll show you,' he shouted. 'I'm here for a month. Clear the decks for action....'

Chapter Twenty-Eight

A Golden Month

May 1915

Christy wheeled his horse in to a graceful canter and waved a bronzed arm to Eva. From among the coffee bushes she waved back, using her broad-brimmed hat as a banner.

He saw a sheen of sweat glisten across her brow. *Bloody farming. Why spend all day out here grubbing the dirt? What a filthy waste of time.*

Swaying in perfect harmony with the horse he kicked in to a gallop, leaning with the swerve across rocky grassland. He felt young, strong and alive.

God, this is great.

He flashed another wave at Eva, turning in the saddle to show the ripple of his chunky muscles.

Bloody hell. Look at the woman.

Instead of watching and admiring she had turned away, calling orders to her work gang digging and weeding along the lines of coffee.

His horse careered over a ridge. Christy pulled hard to slow down, dragging with angry strength at the bit. Hunched and sullen he rode at a walk towards the river.

Damned if I can take another two weeks of this. Fun at first but now it's so bloody boring.

He allowed the horse find its own way along the riverbank while his mind roamed over Eva. That damned village must be along here somewhere – and the place he had first shown her how a good man can make a woman happy.

She really enjoyed that. She's never been able to get enough since....

The saddle rolled in friendly motion between his thighs. Arousal came as no surprise.

Damn me, that feels good. Should I go back and give her a tumble in the coffee trees?

He wore light shirt and shorts – not suitable for horseback, but easy to whip off. *You never know. She may fancy it.*

On the other hand he needed to keep his strength up for the difficult task of serving two voracious women. Eva and Kristina – a couple of bloody tigresses – one during the day the other at night. *Between 'em they'll wear me down to a shadow. Christ. If Eva knew.*

Grinning at his devilry he rode round a bend and saw a slim nut-brown Kikuyu girl washing clothes in the river. She straightened and stared at him, wet shift clinging against every detail of her neat young body.

By God. Just what I need to get rid of this....

He urged the horse in to a cavalry canter, clattering across the riverbank rocks.

How wonderful to see fear start in her eyes.

She turned and ran, bunching her skirt in tight fists; racing up the slope, her plaited hair ringlets bobbing; her long brown legs flashing a delightful pattern through the sunlit grass.

Within seconds he caught up, leaning out to grasp and pull her off balance. Leaping from the saddle he tipped her to the ground with a thump and dived on top.

Holding her down with the weight of his body he wriggled free of his shorts, then ripped her shift from neck to hem.

She fought like a trapped leopard – spitting, biting and clawing.

His mind howled in glee. *So much better when they struggle.*

He hit her twice in the face. Not too hard. Just enough to shock her towards submission.

She plunged and heaved, banging her fists against his head and chest, flailing her legs with frantic strength as she tried to dislodge him.

He hit her again. This time with a masterly punch to the chin. Her resistance broke. She sobbed and relaxed; allowed him in.

This was a most satisfactory rape – one of his best ever. He took complete control of her slippery, sweaty body with its heavenly smell of village wood-smoke. His toy. His plaything. *Damn the rest of the day. This is the game for me.*

He slithered and rolled, so deep in excruciating pleasure he missed the turn of her head towards the sound of feet shuffling through the grass.

A hard blow crashed across his spine.

Howling in pain and fear he ripped free of the woman, scrambled to his knees and saw a wooden club swinging down for a second strike.

He fell backwards and rolled in to a ball, throwing his arms up to protect his head. The club cracked across his forearms.

In shock and agony he unrolled and scrabbled backwards on hands and heels, scuttling like a crab, stones and thorns digging at his bare buttocks. His attacker – a young African – followed, stepping over the prostrate woman, club raised for a third strike.

Through his pain and confusion, Christy saw the African limping – dragging a heavily bandaged leg and losing ground to the speed of Christy's frantic retreat.

Panic and the need to survive brought Christy to his feet.

Oh God. His boots felt heavy as lead, his short shirt flapped round his waist. Naked between shirt and boots, his fast cooling testicles swung free in the breeze.

The African hesitated – eyes wide at the sight of a bare-arsed European.

Christy's natural instinct as a bully led him straight to the African's weak point. Skipping forward he swung a kick. His solid leather toecap thumped in to the bandaged thigh.

The African gasped in pain; dropped his club and staggered back. Blood flowed immediately, spreading a bright red stain throughout the bandage.

Christy kicked again. The African collapsed across the woman, writhing in agony. Christy grabbed the club to hit him twice across the body and once on the wounded leg.

'That'll teach you to attack a white man, you black bastard,' he shouted. 'Move and I'll bloody-well kill you. Understand?'

The African groaned, holding his wounded leg, pulling at the bandage – pulling and pulling to keep it tight.

Keeping a wary eye for trickery – *You can't trust these buggers* – Christy scrambled in to his shorts.

He looked again at the African.

Damn it, I know his face.

'I know you. You're Kiptumi. You're my bloody sergeant. You were with me at Longido. How dare you assault an officer?'

He smashed the club across the African's leg.

'If I see you in uniform again I'll have you bloody-well arrested.'

For good measure he whacked the naked woman on her kneecap. She wailed in pain – an echoing howl that rolled along the valley. From towards the village Christy heard an answering call and the sound of feet hurrying through the bush. Time to go.

He ran and found his horse cropping grass nearby. Climbing up he dragged the animal round and threw his club at the screaming woman. Kiptumi rolled forward and took it full force across his shoulders.

Twenty or so Africans burst from the bush along the riverbank, running fast, waving spears and *pangas*.

Christy whipped the horse to a gallop and raced away from the river, followed by the woman's wail and a strange hissing shout from

Kiptumi – *'Kwaheri Nyoka.'*

The chasing Africans took up the phrase in chilling rhythm.

'Kwaheri Nyoka. Kwaheri Nyoka. Kwaheri Nyoka.'

The horse easily outpaced following warriors. At the ridge-top Christy slowed and looked back. The Africans stood waving their weapons and singing in deadly chorus, daring Christy to return.

He rode on, the chant ringing in his head.

Goodbye snake. What the bloody hell do they mean by that? Goodbye snake. Never heard that before....

As he galloped, excitement and fear wore off. Worry took over.

Bloody hell, what next? By God, these bruises hurt. How the hell do I explain 'em? And those bloody niggers. I'll have to watch myself in the dark. Definitely time I moved on....

He told Eva, 'There I am at full gallop. Head down, belting along and – wham -straight in to this low branch. Lucky I saw it at the last minute and got my arms up or I'd have lost my head. Bloody horse galloped on while I tumbled over backwards and bashed myself on some rocks. Thank God this is a hospital. Just shows how lucky I am. Rub some more of that cream over my back. Lower. No lower still. Now forward a bit. There. That's better. See what you do to me? Oh that's much better. Come round the front now, my sweet....'

Christy thought about what to do next and saw a way out. At breakfast Eva had said, 'Darling, tomorrow I must go to Chania for H.E.. You can come with me. Cretikos will be with us. He'll be our chaperone. We'll only be away a few days.'

Early this morning Christy felt little enthusiasm for going to Chania. Now it seemed a good idea – an escape from all those spears and *pangas*. But why the hell must Cretikos come?

Cretikos – not to be trusted, I think. Oily little Greek. Just like a lizard with that black hair smarmed back and held in place by grease. Crafty little bugger watches everything....

A plan trickled through his mind – *A few days at Chania then find a reason to slip away. Leave her there. Back to the regiment. Back to sanity.*

Christy nibbled Eva's ear and whispered, 'I've been thinking about Chania. I *will* come.'

But afterwards I'll be glad for a rest from her and her sniffy Prussian ways. Christ. She won't even let me sleep with her in the house. 'It is not right, darling. It is my husband's bed. You and I are comfortable here in the hospital.'

In his head he mimicked her German accent – 'It is my husband's *bett.'*

Comfortable? You may be comfortable madam, but I'm bloody-well not. Especially with a village-full of bloody Africans after my gizzard....

'Oh darling,' said Eva, 'I'm so happy I want to cry. This is a golden month. Having you with me here has made this my golden month.'

He licked salt tears from her face and whispered, 'Mine too, darling. Mine too.'

Chapter Twenty-Nine

Collision Course

1st June 1915

Adam rode out of Namanga and led his twenty-one men across the German border carrying only rifles, ammunition and whatever fitted into a saddlebag.

Before leaving he stood in early sunlight chatting with Mayne, the District Commissioner, in his Government compound. 'Are you really going over there?' asked Mayne.

Adam said, 'My orders are to patrol the border. No one said which side.'

'Good God man. You could be writing your own death warrant. How many men do you have?'

'Twenty-one. Me and my man Musa, along with fifteen Somalis and your four Masai scouts.'

'Twenty-one men? Bloody hell. Not many to take on the Germans.'

'They won't know we're there.'

'I hope not. Look how the Hun bashed up two thousand of our lot at Longido last November. I watched 'em go out at dawn and saw 'em stagger back at dusk. A sorry sight I can tell you.'

'They weren't Somalis. I'd bet Somalis against any odds. They'll fight and win or fight and survive to win later. They're absolute buggers in a scrap.'

'Absolute bandits, you mean.'

Adam shrugged.

'Just what I need. They'll be here soon. I sent Musa to fetch 'em.'

Mayne laughed and said, 'By the way. Remember that odd bugger – the chap that ducked out of the lion hunt at Delamere's place then pretended he'd shot the beast ten minutes later?'

Adam clenched his teeth and turned away, looking for his men. *Where the hell are they?*

Mayne said, 'What was his name? Christian...no...Christy. That's it. Christy. Was at the scrap last November, y'know. I'm told he went all the way to Longido and all the way back and never set eye on the enemy.'

Adam heard the sound of horses nearby. *Thank God.*

In a rush of dust, hooves and fluttering coloured robes Adam's Somalis galloped into the compound, shouting and laughing in absolute exhilaration.

Mayne said, 'For God's sake, tell 'em to stop waving those rifles about. Someone'll get shot.'

The Somalis hauled on their reins, swung in a dusty circle and settled abruptly, eyes and teeth flashing at the fun of being alive, armed and going to war.

Musa cantered into the compound and said, 'Sorry we're late, *Bwana* Adam. They had not finished praying.'

'Bloody hell,' said Mayne, 'I hope prayers never coincide with a battle.'

Adam said, 'Time for us to go.'

Mayne shook hands and said, 'Good luck with your band of brigands. Rather you than me.'

Adam said, 'Thanks. Telegraph that message I gave you to Thinman in Mombasa as soon as I've gone. A coded reply will come back. Hang on to it until I return – it'll be my orders to enter German territory.'

'You mean you don't have orders to go over the border?'

'I will have when you've sent my message.'

'Good God man. Be careful. You're likely to be shot by one side or court-martialled by the other.'

Adam and his raiding party passed Mount Longido and disappeared into the wide grassland along the foothills of Kilimanjaro. Recent rains had left plenty of water on the plain, so they moved between waterholes and lived off game.

For five days, patrolling from dawn to dusk, Adam tracked south then east in a curve across enemy raiding routes.

Each morning he sent Masai scouts out before sunrise. They ranged ahead of the column, loose long legs carrying them easily across the rolling plain.

Near sundown on the sixth day, a scout found tracks of a large party moving north towards British territory – 'They passed here yesterday, *Bwana* Adam. About thirty men with tents and heavy boxes. Two Europeans. No horses. They are slower than us.'

Adam said, 'Find the nearest waterhole. We'll camp now and catch them tomorrow.'

The enemy left a wide well trampled trail. Next morning, following slowly, biding his time with a hunter's care and calm, Adam felt he could see into the German commander's mind.

Feeling safe in his own territory, so near his own mountain, *Herr Kapitän* will take no precautions until across the border. Looking over his shoulder will not occur to him – or to his *askaris. Why should anyone be following? The danger's ahead, not behind. They'll still be relaxed. I'll let them stay that way. Let them camp. Let them settle. Let them cook dinner. Dusk. That's the time to attack. We'll find 'em and wait until dusk....*

Through the heat of day, Adam tracked patiently after the enemy, despite grumbles and urgings to hurry from his Somalis. At three in the afternoon a Masai scout appeared out of the long grass and said, 'The Wa-Germani have stopped. They are close ahead. Four tents and no sentries. They are all resting. We can go down and kill them now.'

His words raced along the column. Excited Somalis urged their horses forward, ready to charge in an instant, showing great disappointment when Adam dismounted and waved them back.

'*Bwana* Adam. Let us ride down and kill them,' shouted Abdi, waving his rifle above his head, 'My men are ready.'

'They're my men, damn you, and they'll do as I say. Get them off those bloody horses and tell them to shut up. Stay here until I return. Musa. Come with me. We'll go forward on foot with the scout and see what's there.'

Adam crawled to the top of a low ridge above the German camp and lay in a fringe of long grass. Hot afternoon sun burned his back as he checked the area through field glasses.

Four tents – two sleepers and two for storage – set among thorn trees in a shallow valley. Twenty or so *askaris* lounged about in the shade, dozing, chatting and smoking. No sign of guns or sentries.

Outside one of the tents, a plump European sat in a canvas chair, reading, drinking from a tall glass and wiping his large moustache with the back of his hand.

Not very military. If it weren't for the uniforms, I'd think him a hunter or trader....

Musa wriggled into position alongside.

Adam whispered, 'The scout is right. They're not expecting trouble.'

He swung his field glasses in a slow arc across the hollow and decided his plan of approach: *Slowly down the slope through the long grass, then fast into the trees and among 'em before they know we're there. That's the way....*

His whole being tensed at the thought of action.

Bloody hell. I'm looking forward to it. Shoot; survive; move. That was Tanga. That was battle. This will be different. This will be bush skirmish – like fighting the shifta. Get close. Face to face. See the man you kill. Watch him die....

He shuddered in fierce excitement and whispered to Musa, 'We'll attack in two parties. You and I will lead one group. Abdi will lead the other. They'll go for the *askaris*. We'll go for the officers and the two store tents. I want nothing destroyed. We need those stores.'

By sundown, Adam and his men lay on the ridge overlooking a tranquil scene. A cook prepared dinner at a large fire while two servants laid table. *Askari*s relaxed in casual groups about the campsite. The plump German appeared, wandered through the trees, spoke to the cook, and ducked into a tent.

'Still no sentries and no defences,' Adam whispered to Musa. 'But where is the other European?'

'Maybe in his tent resting before dinner, *Bwana* Adam. We'll find him when we go down.'

Adam said, 'I'll take the fat man. You go for the other.'

The sun dropped out of sight. In fast fading light Adam gave the signal – a quiet click of his fingers. With barely a rustle the two groups moved down the slope and stopped in long grass a few paces from the camp.

Adam crouched and listened. No reaction from the enemy. Their gentle evening seemed almost too pleasant to disturb.

He checked his men. *All in position. They're impatient to go. We all are. I am. Wait. A few more minutes till dark. Hold back and keep quiet....*

He held his breath. *Surely, one of these headstrong Somalis will break ranks and charge.*

To his relief no one moved.

The campfires glowed red as pearly dusk turned to warm black night. The German *askaris* moved closer to tend their steaming food pots. Some began to eat.

Now.

Adam stood and rushed forward, hearing only the swish of feet as his men rushed with him, twenty ghosts appearing from the grass – moving so quietly they seemed to float into the ring of firelight, falling upon the German *askaris* without mercy, hacking and spearing at any who moved.

Adam sprinted straight for the tents, jumping fires and recumbent *askaris* in his dash through the camp. Musa raced alongside, splitting at the last moment to dive into the other sleeper. Adam burst into the first tent, knocking over the canvas chair as he went.

The plump officer lay on a cot, body and face stiff with shock. Adam aimed his rifle, shouting in German, 'Hands up. Stay still. You're a prisoner.'

The officer scrambled round, grabbing a pistol from under the pillow. With a twist of his body he brought it to bear.

Adam shot him through the chest.

The man flopped back across his cot. A fountain of blood sprayed out over the tent, covering Adam's face and shirt in a greasy sheen.

He reeled back in horror. Spitting and wiping at his face and eyes he stumbled out of the tent into a hellish scene. Leaping fire-flames threw crazy shadow-patterns on a graceful ballet of slicing and stabbing as his men moved among the trees, killing in eerie silence. Their victims, frozen by terror, died without sound.

Thrilled and stunned by the savage tranquillity, Adam stood rigid, appalled that his orders could cause such slaughter.

The horrid yellow-red firelight flashed and sparkled on silent spears and swinging *pangas*. Galvanised by the soft wet thump of steel on flesh, Adam ran forward shouting, 'Stop. Stop. I want prisoners. Stop, damn you.'

Deafened by bloodlust no one heard.

Adam grabbed a flaming branch from the fire and laid about him, hitting at any Somali in range, shouting, 'Stop. I said stop.'

Nearby Abdi took up the call. Round the camp – and in the long grass beyond – the terrible bloodshed ceased. The Somalis dragged surviving *askaris* into the firelight and pushed them into a crouching frightened group, eye-whites shining in terror.

Adam heard Musa's new harsh voice in a grating call from the second tent.

'*Bwana* Adam. Come quick. Hurry.'

He ran across and pushed through the flap to find Musa guarding a German captain.

The officer said in English, 'Good evening, Adam. You have become a skilled soldier.'

'Bloody hell,' said Adam. 'What are you doing here?'

'Same as you,' said Paul von Ansbach. 'Fighting a war. Are you injured? You're covered in blood.'

'Oh for Christ sake, get out of here,' said Adam. 'Go. Go now. I don't want to see you. Bugger off. Run away. Musa – take him out into the bush. Point him back the way we came. Don't let the Somalis see him.'

'But I'm your prisoner,' said Paul.

'No you're not. Go. Musa get him some water for him to take.'

Paul said, 'Why do you do this?'

'Don't bloody quibble, Paul. Musa – cut a hole in the back of the tent. Take him out that way.'

'Adam – are you injured?'

'No. Not my blood. Your friend wouldn't surrender. I had to shoot the poor bugger to stop him shooting me.'

'Reserve officers never know when to give up,' said Paul.

Musa returned carrying a water bottle and with a sweep of his *panga* slit the rear tent wall from roof to floor.

Paul shook Adam's hand and speaking German, said, 'Don't stay here too long. Your old friend Weiss is following with a column. Don't try an ambush. He has a hundred men. He'll wipe you out.'

Musa growled, 'Come with me, *Bwana* Paul. Hurry or you'll be seen.'

'Clever coming up behind us from our own territory,' said Paul. 'We never thought of that.'

12th June 1915

In the heat of late afternoon, Adam and Musa rode into Namanga and made their way to the Government compound.

'So my runner found you,' said Mayne.

'Yes, thank God,' said Adam, dismounting. 'Just in time to stop us making for Mombasa.'

'Where's the rest of your patrol?'

'Following with prisoners carrying captured stores. They'll be a couple of days yet.'

At sundown Adam sipped his drink and told Mayne the story of his attack on the enemy camp.

'So there were two German officers,' said Mayne. 'You shot one and the other escaped. How did he get away?'

'Cut his way out the back of a tent,' said Adam. 'Musa followed and tried to track him, but he disappeared in the dark.'

'He'll probably die of thirst in the bush,' said Mayne.

'Probably.'

'What happened next?'

'Not much. We bandaged the wounded and did our best with the dead – covered 'em with branches and put up a marker. Then we ate their dinner, took three of their tents and moved out with all their stores.'

'You left the dead German in his tent?'

'Yes. I thought it best.'

'And ate the poor bugger's dinner?'

' Seemed a pity to waste it.'

'Bloody hell, man. How terribly cool.'

Adam managed to turn a shudder into a shrug: *How the hell did I manage it? Killed the man then sat next to his corpse and ate his supper....*

Mayne said, 'I really must admire you. I never thought you'd have it in you.'

'Nor did I,' said Adam.

'What modesty, my dear chap.'

After the action Adam moved his patrol back into British territory and made for an area of rocky hills remembered from his days as a surveyor. Here he set up camp in a defensive position among boulders and set watchers on a peak to scan the plain. His Masai scouts slipped out to find their tribesmen and gather news. Adam allowed his men and horses two days rest while he interrogated the prisoners and sifted through letters and papers captured at the German camp and wrote his action report for Thinman.

The Masai intercepted Mayne's runner and brought him into camp with two telegrams from Thinman. One, dated fourteen days earlier, read: *Patrol at will on either side of the border. Gather intelligence and engage the enemy wherever possible.*

The second read: *Abandon your patrol and pay off your men. Meet me in Kisumu on 19th June for a special operation.*

A special operation? During dinner he asked Mayne who said, 'It's a bash at the Hun across Lake Victoria. Hit the buggers where they're weakest. The whole thing is dead secret.'

'If it's secret how do you know about it?'

'Common knowledge, old chap. Everyone knows.'

Adam sipped his brandy and said, 'How secret is secret if everyone knows?'

Mayne laughed, his eyes shrewd and searching.

'You know what it's like here, my dear fellow. No secret is safe. Probably doesn't exist as a secret in the first place. Even our deepest personal conspiracies get out. A hint at the dinner table – a word from a house-servant. Everyone knows everything in the end.'

Before going to bed Adam scrawled a note to Thinman: *On my way to Kisumu I will spend a couple of days at Mzito.*

Next morning at dawn he gave the message to Mayne, saying, 'Telegraph this as soon as possible. When Abdi arrives with his prisoners, tell him to take the men back to Mzito and work with the cattle as before until I return. Tell Formby to return to his unit.'

With Musa, he rode out of Namanga and across the plain to Sultan Hamud, where two days later they loaded their horses and themselves on to a train for Nairobi.

16th June 1915

A damaged bridge – enemy action – delayed the train's arrival at Nairobi station until just before dusk. Despite the danger of night riding, Adam, consumed with unexpected desire to see his wife, said, 'To hell with it, we'll get on home.'

Avoiding the main town he circled down to the river and rode out along the dark trail towards Mzito.

Damp low cloud blotted out moon and stars. The slowly rolling saddle and regular clop of hooves lulled Adam into a state half-asleep and half-awake, his mind floating free, drifting between dream and memory.

A special operation. What the bloody hell does Thinman mean? New danger? Death nearly got me three times. Will it try again? No one ever talks about four times lucky....

He groaned.

If I'm killed...what about Christy? Will he move in? No. That's finished. He's gone. She promised....

At ten o'clock his horse climbed the last rise, sensed home, and clipped into a trot over the ridge. Lights from Mzito glowed through the trees.

The horse swerved towards its stable, nearly unseating Adam. He hung on, laughing. Musa followed, cursing and struggling to control his mount as it hurried to keep up.

Overcome by the need to see his wife Adam pulled his horse to a halt, jumped from the saddle and gave the reins to Musa saying, 'We're here for two days. Make the most of it. See you tomorrow.'

He hurried back towards the house, passing near the hospital *bandas*. Golden slabs of light spilled out of doors and windows, forming square panes across the dark earth. Adam walked swiftly through the shadows, his legs flashing yellow in passing from pane to pane.

Framed in one open doorway an officer-patient sat drinking, damaged leg propped on a stool. He waved his glass and called, 'I say. Is that Tim the tiger? Back from your jaunt up-country already? Tail still twitching I hope. Not fallen off through overwork? Come and have a drink old boy.'

His crisp British voice struck chill. Adam stopped and said, 'Tim the tiger? Who's Tim the tiger? Who do you think I am?'

He stepped into the light, staring at the officer who stared back and said, 'I say. My dear chap. I'm terribly sorry. Thought you were someone else. Come and have a drink.'

'Who's Tim the tiger?'

'A chum of mine. Army captain. Everyone's looking for him to go to Kisumu. He seems to have disappeared. In the dark, I thought you were him. You're obviously not.'

'No,' said Adam and marched on to the house.

Running up the veranda steps, he listened for noise. None. The house seemed deadly quiet – even the kitchen.

He checked the living rooms.

Empty. Lamps out. Dinner table cleared. *Where the hell is everyone?*

He hurried to the nursery. *Thank God.* He could see the children tucked safely in bed, vague shadows behind mosquito nets.

He peered through. Thomas, Alexandra and…. Jonathan? *Where's Jonathan?*

The *ayah* dozing in a chair didn't move until Adam touched her shoulder and hissed, 'Where's Jonathan?'

She half opened her eyes and mumbled, 'With the Memsahib.'

Of course. He would be. Eva liked to keep him with her when she could. *Her youngest. Her favourite. Her….*

He thrust the thought aside and went to the bedroom.

Deserted. The bed not even ready.

Baffled, frustrated and puzzled he stood in the dark doorway. *Surely, they're somewhere.*

From along the veranda he heard the splash and gurgle of water.

Joy surged through him.

The bathroom. They're in the bath. She's playing with him in the bath.

'Eva, I'm home,' he called and ran down the veranda. Her voice echoed in sweet reply. He burst through the door into a swirling golden mist of damp steam and yellow lamplight. Kristina stood in the bath, long hair straggling down her wet back. Pearls of bright water shone on her shoulders and slid into the towel held loosely round her body.

'Darling Adam,' she cried with a brilliant smile, 'You're home.'

'Kristina. What are you doing?'

'Bathing, darling. I've just finished. But I'll start again if you'll join me.'

'Where's Eva?'

'Chania, darling. She's gone to Chania.'

'Chania? Again? Why?'

'I don't know, darling. She never said.'

'Did she take Jonathan?

'Yes.'

'Did she go alone?'

'No. With H.E.'s man Cretikos,' but Kristina's shrug and happy smile cut through Adam like a spear.

'That's it,' he hissed. 'Christy. She's with bloody Christy.'

Transfixed by cold hate and thrilling thoughts of murder he knew he must go to Chania and kill them. All three. Eva, Christy and Jonathan. In an instant. Without further thought. And be happy to hang....

Kristina broke his spell of death.

In a graceful swirl, she tossed the towel aside. Her beautiful wet body gleamed gold and brown in the shifting steam. Trickles of shining water traced patterns across her breasts and stomach.

Violet eyes glowing in excitement she opened her arms and from deep in her throat whispered, 'Darling Adam. Don't be angry. Why bother about Christy? What if she's with him? What do you care? You have me. Look. Look what I can give you.'

Those amazing eyes changed from innocence to whorish calculation and sparking sexual electricity.

He paused.

'Come on, darling,' she whispered. 'Come in the bath....'

Desire swept murder aside: *Sod it. Sod Christy. Sod Eva and Jonathan. Sod the lot of 'em. Make the most of what's here. Next week I could be dead....*

He ripped off his clothes and climbed into the warm slippery water.

Kristina held him close, her strong wet body cleaving to his. She whispered, 'Darling Adam. Sit down. I'll bathe you, then you bathe me....'

He lay back in the deep warm water and watched as she knelt between his knees, leaning forward to massage him with a soft soapy sponge. He groaned with pleasure and played with her breasts then with his fingertips traced the water trails down her stomach until she groaned with him.

She dropped the sponge and shifted forward, guiding his hand, wriggling against him, nibbling at his ear and sighing, 'I'll bathe you later....'

Adam slipped and slid in the soapy water. Eva and Christy faded from his mind. Murder went with them. *This wonderful woman is saving my life. To hell with anyone else....*

Chapter Thirty

Collision at Bukoba

Heavy afternoon sun filtered through low damp cloud and pressed a yellow-grey blanket of sticky air down on the lake, trapping a wet stench of rotting vegetation along the shoreline.

Adam stood by the ship's rail searching for a hint of breeze to sweeten the afternoon; his starched khaki-drill uniform wilting in to a sweat stained rag in a bloody awful day made worse by a bloody awful headache.

He lifted his binoculars and peered at files of troops marching down from town to lakeside, swinging briskly along the dirt road, half-hidden in a rolling mist of kicked-up red dust. Impossible to identify the units yet. Better to wait and check them off when they arrive on their jetties.

Stinging runnels of perspiration trickled in to his eyes blurring the scene even more. He cursed and shook his head, wincing at the noise of Thinman marching along the hard teak deck, the thump of his heavy boots driving drumbeats through Adam's aching skull.

'For God's sake Thinman, do you have to be so noisy?'

'Military precision, old chap,' said Thinman. 'May I join you?'

Adam stared out across the lake. Sullen iron-grey water heaved oily reflections of heavy thundercloud billowing from the Nandi hills. His headache worsened.

He turned back to the lakeshore jetties. *Christ, what a sight....*

Six small lake steamers – *they look like bloody toys* – made up the invasion fleet. Hardly strong enough to take the men and equipment jamming aboard – *they'll tip over if any more are shoved on* – he could not see how such tiny ships would frighten anyone, let alone the Germans.

On the other hand, the Punjabi sepoys filing aboard looked tough, confident and well equipped. On the next jetty he saw twelve gleaming machine guns lined up, ready to load. And further along, a group of Indian gunners hauled at ropes, hoisting two neat little field pieces aboard the *Rusinga*.

'Part of a mountain battery,' said Thinman. 'Damn good little guns. Did well at Longido, I understand. But I'm glad we're taking the Loyal Lancs. They'll stiffen the line. And we have the Royal Fusiliers. Good fellows all.'

'How soon before we sail?' asked Adam.

'A couple of hours – about sundown. Why? Do you want to go below for a rest? You look tired.'

So would you, my dear fellow, if you'd serviced Kristina for two days and three nights....

Adam grinned to himself, lost in the unreality of his time with Kristina. From the time he slid in to the warm soapy bath he spent almost every moment with Kristina, ignoring the outside world. At first entranced by her skills and able to meet all her demands, he spent the three nights and two days touching, stroking, canoodling, whispering, giggling and making love in every room, on every possible piece of furniture.

She seemed insatiable and so did he but when, two days ago, Adam left Mzito, riding up the slope with Musa, a great weight lifted from his shoulders. Free of Kristina, free of the farm, free of Eva and Christy. No more responsibility. *Thank God. It's over. Life's simple again. Back to war.*

Thinman said, 'Wake up, Early. Here is the Lancashire Regiment. For heaven's sake stop dreaming and log them on board.'

Adam dragged his attention back to increased activity along the lakeside. The thump of heavy British boots echoed as the first companies of Loyal Lancs marched on to their jetty, red faces sweaty and cheerful.

He scribbled their arrival on his pad and peered at the line of rugged young men through his binoculars.

Thinman said, 'By God, they look ready for this scrap. No doubt about it – we're taking the best this time. Look. Here come the KAR.'

Adam turned his binoculars on to two companies of African soldiers marching down the road led by two British officers, their faces shaded and hidden by sun helmets.

Thinman said, 'I say. Where's your man Musa going?'

Adam leaned out, surprised to see Musa moving with speed and purpose along the shore.

Thinman said, 'Oh I see what he's up to. He's meeting the KAR. Probably spied a friend or two.'

Adam watched Musa disappear in to the crowd of African soldiers pushing forward on their jetty. He reappeared by the gangplank, staring at the two British officers climbing up to the ship moored alongside. Adam focussed his binoculars on Musa's taut face and said, 'What the hell is he doing?'

Thinman said, 'I say – It's that terrible cad Christy across there with the KAR. Look. There. At the top of the gangplank, counting his men on board.'

Adam's jaw clenched – he heard his teeth grind – as he swung the binoculars and closed up on Christy's handsome face.

Thinman chattered on, 'So they managed to find the bloody fellow. I'm not sure whether to be glad or not. We sent several runners searching for him. He disappeared upcountry with some floozy, y'know. Pity they found the damned man.'

Disappeared upcountry with some floozy? That's my wife, dammit.

'Thank God he's not on this ship with us,' said Thinman. 'I'd cut him dead in the mess if he were.'

And I'd cut him in pieces....

'Oh hell, he's seen us,' said Thinman. 'Ignore him.'

Christy doffed his sun helmet towards Adam and bowed – a slow mocking greeting made worse by every magnified detail of his merry blue eyes and cheerful smile. Tendrils of white-blond hair, damp with sweat, trailed in graceful pattern across his bronzed brow. The picture of a handsome young colonial soldier going to war. Adam's fingers tightened round the binoculars, trying to strangle the image.

Thinman said, 'Ignore the bounder. He's nothing to do with us.'

Adam dropped his binoculars and turned away quivering in rage.

Thinman said, 'All units are on board now. We've nothing left to do here. Come on. We'll go to the wardroom and make our plans for tomorrow.'

22nd June 1915: Bukoba, Lake Victoria

At dawn, refreshed and ready to go, Adam joined Thinman on deck and sniffed the damp calm air. Thin high cloud spread grey shadows across the lead-coloured lake. *Winifred* led the fleet of toy ships slowly towards a flat shoreline backed by low hills.

'Anything happen?' asked Adam, sweeping the scene with his binoculars.

'You'll never believe it,' said Thinman. 'During the night we steamed right up to Bukoba with all lights blazing. The Hun sent up a rocket and half a dozen flares so we promptly turned back and steamed away. Have you ever heard anything like it?'

Adam turned his binoculars along the line of ships to check which might be carrying Christy. He swung back and studied the shoreline. Completely deserted. Same with the town about three miles to the south.

'Small place,' he said, checking for movement among a scattering of white buildings round a solid looking fort and a surprisingly large church. 'Looks empty.'

'So did Tanga,' growled Thinman. 'And what happened there? They sucked us in and spat us out. If we're not careful they'll do the same here.'

'Remind me how many troops the Germans have here?'

'About one thousand five hundred in the area – *askaris* with European officers. Half in Bukoba, the rest nearby.'

Adam lowered his binoculars and asked, 'How are you so sure?'

'Military intelligence, my dear fellow. While you were riding in circles near Kilimanjaro and resting at home with your lovely wife, we were working. We sent a couple of Arab traders through this province, trading tobacco and whisky. They wandered round making profit from the Hun and spying for us.'

*Resting at home with your lovely wife...*Adam clenched his teeth, lifted his binoculars again and focussed on a nearby ship. *Is that Christy on deck? Is the bastard up and about? Will he finish the day, or will the day finish him...?*

'Look over there,' said Thinman. '*Usoga's* moving in to land her troops. This is where our work starts. Remember. You and I stay out of the fighting. We're here to observe, record and take a party to destroy the enemy wireless station when the battle's over.'

Adam laughed. 'Sounds easy,' he said.

Thinman said, 'I'm going ashore. You stay on board. Log all ship and troop movements until the landing finishes then come and find me.'

Adam saw Thinman off in a small boat and settled to his task, spending the next few hours sitting on the officers' deck, sipping tea, eating breakfast and recording the landing from his perfect view of the whole shoreline.

'Comfortable way to fight a war old chap,' commented a passing naval officer. Adam waved a teacup in reply.

At sunrise, *Winifred* and *Usoga* landed the Royal Fusiliers without opposition. Through his binoculars Adam watched the troops move smartly inland and occupy a low hill, driving off a small German outpost.

Around nine o'clock he saw *Nyanza* detach from the fleet and hurry towards Bukoba. From somewhere near the town a heavy gun thumped twice, sending a couple of badly aimed shells out across the clear morning. *Nyanza* turned in a cloud of diamond-bright spray and scurried back.

A naval officer snatched Adam's binoculars, swearing and shouting, 'Damned Hun has artillery. Get a bearing so we can bang back at the bugger.'

Signal flags fluttered between ships. Heliograph messages flashed to and from the shore. The ships lobbed a few shells and the German gun fell silent. Adam noted and timed the action and returned his attention to the landing.

Just before noon *Rusinga* ran in to disembark the Loyal Lancs and mountain guns. The soldiers formed up and moved inland. The mountain battery took position on a low crag.

Adam logged times and positions and watched the Royal Fusiliers hurry from their hill, swarming after the Loyal Lancs with a rattle of rifle fire, followed by the heavier thump of machine guns. The mountain battery began to shoot. The German gun banged an occasional reply. The action settled to a regular roll of musketry.

'Sounds as though it's well alight,' said the naval officer. 'When do you join in?'

'Soon,' said Adam. 'I'll follow the KAR.'

'There they go now,' said the naval officer, pointing.

Adam swung his binoculars and focussed on the African soldiers scrambling down in to long boats; calling and yodelling to each other at the exciting prospect ahead. He studied each boat, searching for Christy, finally spying a tall sun helmet from which escaped a few strands of white-blond hair. He followed the boat all the way to shore watching Christy hunch lower and lower as he headed towards the gunfire. Adam grinned and whispered, 'Bad luck you bastard....'

By early afternoon with the KAR landed and moving off the lakeside towards Bukoba, Adam completed his diary entry and said to the naval officer, 'Time for me to go. Arrange a boat please.'

Half an hour later Adam waded with Musa through knee deep water to reach the flat grassy shore. Apart from a few African porters unloading supplies, the area seemed deserted and the battle inland seemed settled to only occasional bursts of rifle fire.

From towards Bukoba Adam heard the deep clatter of a German machine gun. The mountain guns continued to shoot, the whip-crack of their light shells bringing a heavy thump of reply from the German artillery piece.

Adam looked round, wondering where to go.

Musa said, 'There is the small man.'

'Where?'

'On the hill. By the guns.'

Thinman stood at the edge of the rocky crag, sweeping his arms in urgent signals that said, 'Get up here fast.'

Adam and Musa dashed across the open grass shore and up the slope, clambering over or round huge granite rocks scattered across the hillside. Thinman ran down and met them halfway, his bony face white with anger.

'Thank God you're here,' he shouted. 'We've got to get this damned battle moving. Our bloody general's letting it all slip away. He's at the top of this hill watching the Hun do what they want while we're sitting on our arses. It's Tanga all over again. Come with me.'

Adam followed over the rise to see a group of staff officers standing at the crest, studying maps. A line of KAR *askaris* lay along the hill brow covering any approach from Bukoba. Nearby the Sikh gun crews worked smartly, sending a stream of small shells out across the shallow valley.

Thinman said, 'Thank God we have the mountain guns. They're after an enemy machine gun on the ridge opposite. The damned thing's so well hidden and in command of the approach to Bukoba our whole advance is halted.'

He pointed up and down the valley.

'The Loyal Lancs are on our right. The KAR are to our left by the lake with the Fusiliers and Indian troops in the centre. Trouble is that none of 'em is doing anything. The Fusiliers reached to within a mile of the town at noon but halted and took cover when the machine gun hit their flank. Been stuck ever since. That leaves the KAR stranded along the lakeshore – can't move unless the Fusiliers move too – and the Loyal Lancs are sitting on their backsides instead of pushing in the enemy left wing. So that one bloody machine gun has stopped us dead. I've been waiting for you so we can get across and find it. I'll go and tell the general. Check your rifles and ammunition. I'll be back in a minute.'

He hurried across the hilltop and pushed in among the group of staff officers, starting an immediate argument of loud angry voices.

Adam waited, regaining his breath after the steep climb and watching the Sikh gunners. They seemed almost alone in keeping the battle going, sending shells whistling across the valley to raise stones and dust on the other side.

Both gun crews, drilled to perfection, moved in a ballet chorus dance from ammunition pile to gun breech, keeping time with the deadly music of their trade. Shells clanged in the breech and blasted from the barrel in a shivering explosion of flame and dust. Every discharge drummed shock waves through Adam's rib cage.

He raised his binoculars and followed the barrage creeping across the hillside opposite. The hidden enemy machine gun continued to shoot short bursts from a position but Adam saw neither movement nor gunsmoke.

Apart from the noisy game of hide-and-seek between machine gun and mountain battery, action along the line had died down to single rifle shots echoing through the hot afternoon.

Thinman came rushing back, and said, 'Come on. I have a couple of smoke bombs. In a few minutes our battery will hold fire so we can get up the opposite side and find that bloody machine gun. Follow me. Hurry.'

In a crouching run he raced off down the slope, ducking between granite boulders for cover. Adam followed, slipping and sliding, kicking up dust and stones in a helter-skelter dash to the valley. Halfway down his heavy sun helmet flew off and bounced away to God knows where. Covered in dust and sweat, heart pumping, he reached the bottom and dived flat to join Thinman behind a rock. Seconds later Musa arrived, sliding in to bushes a few yards away.

Several bullets whipped past. Thinman snapped, 'Bugger. They've seen us.'

'Can you see where they come from Musa?' called Adam.

'From the left, *Bwana*. They come from the left.'

'A bloody sniper,' said Thinman. 'Not the machine gun. It's a bloody sniper.'

Adam crawled round the rock and peeked out, studying the banks of a marsh about one hundred yards away. A telltale ripple sidled across the muddy water from a clump of reeds.

'He's in that swamp. Across on the right. I can't see him but I know he's there.'

'We'll go after the bastard,' said Thinman.

'What about the machine gun?'

'The sniper first. He's seen us, so he's more danger. You and I'll do that.'

He fished in his pockets and said, 'Sergeant Musa. Here are the smoke bombs. Get up that hill and find the German machine gun. Mark it and retire quickly. If you survive, meet us back here when we've killed the sniper.'

Musa took the bombs, nodded to Adam and moved off across the valley at a fast crouching trot.

If you survive....

The words rang through Adam's head. He felt a surge of fear for Musa. *Bloody hell. I may never see him again....*

From beyond the swamp came a heavy burst of rifle fire. Adam crawled round the rock and through his binoculars saw a line of KAR *askaris* hurrying across a small clearing, shooting as they ran. Several shots echoed reply from the swamp. Two *askaris* fell. The others ran for cover, scrabbling back the way they had come.

Adam swept the swamp banks with his binoculars and again saw the revealing water ripple edging out from close-packed reeds on the German side.

He needed a better view so stood, leaning against the rock and in a surge of fear saw every small detail of a rifle barrel swinging towards him.

With instant reaction he ducked and fell flat. A heavy bullet smashed in to the stone above his head, spraying needle-sharp chips of granite. Grovelling in the dust he heard Thinman fire twice in reply.

'Did you get him?' he shouted.

'No,' growled Thinman. 'Stand up again. I'll have another go.'

Adam swore, scrambled to a kneeling position and from behind his rock fired four bullets in to the reed clump. Four waterspouts shot up around the sniper's hiding place.

From across the swamp, the KAR joined in, shooting a long volley that shattered the water in to a chaos of spouts and waves and whistled in a windstorm through the reeds.

Thinman shouted, 'Wonderful. You marked the bloody man beautifully. Well done, Early. He'll never survive that.'

The shooting faded and stopped. At the same time the mountain guns ceased fire. For a moment silence fell. Then from the reeds came a shot. Just one. Aimed in defiance at the bank opposite. Adam saw a splash – heard the bullet slap in to the mud, and laughed.

'He's playing with us. The bastard's so confident he's playing with us.'

'Right.' snapped Thinman. 'It's up to us. This is how we'll do it. You go left and wait. I'll go right and push him out. Between us we'll sandwich the damned fellow....'

Five minutes later Adam lay silent and still in long grass on the marsh edge – a perfect ambush position with full view across the swamp ahead and the clearing to his left. His nostrils filled with dust-dry grass pollen and the sour stench of stagnant water. Humid swamp air sucked sweat from every pore. Hot sun roasted his unprotected scalp and a cloud of marsh insects droned and buzzed about his head and neck, landing to nipping and stinging. He dared not move or sneeze. Dared not slap or wriggle to ease the torment.

Behind him the KAR started a skirmish towards thick bush blocking the approach to Bukoba. The enemy replied with heavy fire but gave ground. The Fusiliers, further up the line, started shooting and a rolling battle developed along valley and lakeshore.

Deafened and excited, Adam found it hard to concentrate on the opposite bank. Thinman should appear soon to flush the sniper out.

Keep watch damn you. Keep watch. In this noise Thinman will move fast....

He waited, forcing himself to be patient as a sniper must be patient. Match the man on the other side. Wait. The chance will come.

Two plumes of yellow smoke rising from the hillside three hundred yards away took his attention. Almost immediately the area seethed in smoke and flame, bracketed by shells from the mountain guns.

Bloody hell. That wasn't to plan. Thinman said two minutes. They forgot the two minutes for Musa to get away.

Anger rose. Adam forgot Thinman and the sniper. He dropped his rifle, lifted his binoculars and focussed on the maelstrom of explosions halfway up the valley. No sign of Musa but he could see a German officer with half a dozen *askaris* struggling to lift and move the machine gun.

Within seconds another salvo fell. The officer and his men disappeared in a cloud of flame and dust. Amazingly most survived to reappear, scrambling away up the slope, leaving the gun and two bodies thrown together in a mangled pile.

The mountain guns ceased firing. Along the line battle faltered and faded. Adam could hear the KAR a short distance away, chattering in excitement and saw a company of KAR *askaris* settling in to new positions among trees on the far edge of the clearing.

Adam turned back to the swamp. A clump of reeds opposite parted and a German, chest deep in mud and water, moved out, wading cautiously along the reed-line towards the new KAR position, holding his rifle high.

With a deep breath, Adam took bead on the man's thick neck. Something familiar in the shape of head and shoulder made him hesitate. He lowered his gun, lifted his binoculars to check and saw....

Weiss. Bloody hell it's Weiss. What's he doing here? He's too old to fight....

Adam snatched up his rifle, aimed at Weiss's skull, squeezed the trigger to first pressure – and paused, gritting his teeth in frustration. *To save a man's life thirteen years ago and kill him now....*

Ten yards behind Weiss, the reeds swayed. Thinman slid out, in a snake-like wriggle, head and rifle barely above water.

Adam eased his trigger finger and emptied his lungs in a slow sigh. *Thank God. Thinman's here. He can do it. He can kill the bugger....*

Thinman brought his shoulder above water, preparing to shoot. At that instant Adam saw a head and gun barrel appear from the cover of a half-submerged log six feet to Thinman's rear. Adam swung and fired, smacking a bullet in to the rotting wood – six inches off target but enough to distract the sniper who ducked, leaving the crown of his sun helmet protruding.

Adam jumped up and sent two shots down in to the helmet. Particles of head and hat flicked across the swamp. The sniper fell back and sank in the dirty water.

Both Weiss and Thinman, startled by shooting from behind, jerked round, bringing their rifles up in unison. Weiss shot Thinman through the body and plunged for cover in the reeds. Thinman threw up his arms, falling sideways in a thrashing of foam and bubbles. From his new cover, Weiss fired twice at Adam, the bullets whacking in to the bank a yard away.

Adam dived in to the long grass, rolled away from the swamp edge and scrabbled on hands and knees to the edge of the clearing, heart thumping. Thinman reappeared from the water, trailing a filthy blood coloured slime. Weiss broke cover and splashed out in to the swamp, lifting his rifle to finish Thinman off. Adam snatched two ill aimed shots; the bullets spraying plumes of water in to Weiss's face.

Weiss flinched and missed.

From their position in the trees, the KAR started shooting wildly across the swamp. Half a dozen *askaris* jumped up and galloped down to the marsh edge. Howling in excitement they loosed off a storm of shots at Weiss and Thinman, raising a blizzard of spray. Adam saw Thinman fall in to the scum, roll over, pull upright, and wallow back in to the reeds. Moments later he dragged himself on to the bank and lay face down, covered in filth and blood, legs twitching.

A German machine gun opened fire hitting at the KAR along the bank. The survivors fled yelling in fear. A stream of bullets hosed after them clipping at their heels.

Taking advantage of the confusion, a company of German *askaris* led by two hatless officers burst from the bush. Shouting and shooting, they chased the KAR in to the trees, rolling up the KAR right wing. The Fusiliers sent a hail of supporting fire along the valley, cutting through the German attack.

Pinned down by the storm of bullets from both sides Adam kept his face pressed to the ground and followed the action with his ears, heart thumping in eagerness as the battle swung towards him.

Any moment now and they'll be in the clearing. Let the bastards come. They may get me, but I'll get some of them first....

Tense and sweating; ready to kill or die he rose to a crouch and checked his rifle.

Seconds later a European raced from the long yellow grass opposite, running like a sprinter; head back; mouth open; arms pumping.

Adam whipped up his gun. A split second before firing he recognised his target.

The bullet struck Christy full in his chest with a loud thwack, flopping him to the ground.

He slid in to an untidy pile of bent arms and twisted legs, hunched up on his right shoulder, head pushed sideways in the red dust facing Adam. His heavy helmet skipped and rolled away across the clearing. Scarlet blood pumped from a neat hole below his breastbone, mingling with the dirt, drying immediately to a pink-brown delta shaped stain.

He lay dribbling a mixture of spittle and bright red foam, his tanned handsome face contorted in fear and shock. His eyes opened. Beautiful clear blue eyes, framed by white-blond brows. His boyish silky hair ruffled in the breeze.

'Early...help...,' he mouthed, unable to make himself heard through pain and the sound of battle.

Spittle-foam floated free from his lips sparkling prettily in the sunlight.

'Early...help me....'

Adam raised his rifle. Took careful aim on that hated handsome face. Squeezed the trigger.

Christy's head exploded as a bullet smacked in to his left eye; pulped his brain; scattered the shattered rear of his skull in shards across several square yards of grassland.

Adam's own shot flew wide – jerked sideways by the shock of a gun exploding alongside his ear.

He flung himself down, turning, reloading and aiming in one movement.

Musa stood behind Adam, rifle barrel smoking, his uniform ripped and dirty, his face covered in bleeding cuts. Ignoring Adam, he stared at Christy's oozing corpse, hissing, 'Kwaheri Nyoka.'

'Bloody hell, Musa,' shouted Adam. 'Why did you do that?'

Musa said, '*Bwana* Adam. It is time he died. Come. The small man is in trouble. We must go and help him'.

Musa stepped back and disappeared in to the bush.

Adam scrambled up. To savour the moment, he paused, looking back at Christy. *Definitely dead. The bastard's definitely dead.*

Hidden in the sound of battle a cloud of heavy machine gun bullets whispered across the clearing. Two hit Adam. One passed through his thigh, taking out a great chunk of meat. The other smashed in to his stomach, throwing him out in to the clearing. He fell in full view of six German *askaris*, charging from the long grass opposite.

At first, the pain felt far away. Sure he was dreaming, Adam watched the *askaris* rush forward, chattering at him in German. He replied in the same language, with no idea what he was saying.

He felt them grab and lift him and race back towards their own lines, his body jerking when they stumbled. All at once the pain came in impossibly great waves that turned to shock and agony. He screamed and fainted into merciful lifesaving oblivion….

Chapter Thirty-One

Tabora

Dragged from the battlefield, Adam's horribly wounded body made strategic retreat to its core, leaving pain at an outer boundary.

Drifting in deep coma, without notion of passing days or weeks some small section of inner brain stayed aware of life, regulating his recovery and floating him occasionally up towards a surface of understanding. At these times he came close to seeing or hearing but never quite broke through – recoiling from a barrier of agony that racked his body when nearly conscious. Overcome, he sank back, seeking the calm of death, surprised at each revival that he still survived until one day, abruptly and without warning, he woke.

His eyes opened. Light flooded into his brain, recognising he must be ill and in hospital but not knowing why. His memory, blank as white paper, refused to help.

Laying on his back in a small bed, staring at whitewashed walls and ceiling, he allowed his mind to roam, seeking some idea of time and place.

Nothing.

His head remained empty. No name. No history. No inkling of what brought him here in this state.

Feeling desperately weak he tried to lift his head but failed. By rolling his eyes he managed to see most of the bare white cell. Tiny windows. Heavy wooden door. No furniture. Only this bed and the mosquito net rolled back. No chair. No table. No hint of comfort.

He lifted an arm and saw a skinny wasted stick where young muscles should be.

Why?

His mind remained blank.

Gritting his teeth at the effort he moved a leg.

So that's working.

He moved the other leg.

Christ that hurt.

Running a hand down to check why, he found his stomach and thigh swathed in bandage. The shock jerked his brain into action...bullets thumping...Thinman twitching on the bank of a filthy swamp....

Thinman. That's it. I remember. A battle. We were in a battle....

Shaken by the awful scene he scrabbled at his fractured memory trying to see more. Nothing. Absolutely nothing. *Bloody hell....*

The door opened. An African servant looked in and left without speaking. Adam called after him – but managed only a feeble squeak.

The door opened again and an army officer hurried through, a white coat flying open to reveal his uniform.

He smiled and said in German, 'So. You are awake at last. Do you know who you are yet?'

Bewildered, realising he didn't know who he was, Adam replied automatically in the same language, gathering strength to whisper, 'Where am I?'

'Tabora. You are here with us in Tabora. I am Doctor Fischer. You have been here since June. How do you feel?'

Adam whispered, 'I'm not sure. How did I get here?'

'Our army brought you. I'll talk about it while I examine you. It may help you remember, *Herr* Early.'

Early.

A spark jumped in Adam's mind. *That's it. Early. My name's Early....*

Fischer pulled back the sheet and removed Adam's bandages, murmuring, 'Very good. Very clean. The wounds are healing well.'

The African servant returned with a table, a bowl of water and clean bandages. Adam lay still and listened while Fischer worked, chatting quietly. He seemed a kindly man; pleasantly middle aged; carefully competent.

He said, 'Our *askaris* pulled you from the battlefield thinking you German because you shot a British officer and wore no hat. In that action our officers fought without hats so their men could recognise them in the bush. You were dirty and covered in blood so no one realised you were English. Our men threw you on a boat to Mwanza then carried you here to our hospital in Tabora. Not until later did we discover you are English. That's enough for now. You must rest. From tomorrow I shall see you regularly. We'll talk some more....'

For several days, Adam felt terrible, alternating between sleep and half-awake. His left leg and lower body ached abominably. Any activity – even simply drinking water – brought shattering exhaustion. He lay in bed, undisturbed by voices and footsteps passing his room, concentrating on regaining strength and overcoming the awful pain.

While Adam's body mended, memory started returning in disjointed fragments. He felt his mind searching and delving, revealing scattered chunks of his past in confusing disarray. One fragment led to another, the brain following leads – sniffing out a name here, an incident there, until a picture of previous life began to emerge.

At times he found the experience harrowing – were the awful scenes of depravity and destruction flooding his mind true? Or visions from dementia brought on by fever and the death that so nearly claimed him?

'Don't worry about terrible dreams experienced under coma,' said Fischer, his friendly face easing Adam's mental discomfort. 'They are just as likely due to shock and to the morphine we gave you.'

'You're probably right,' said Adam. 'But how long did it go on?'

'Your coma? Almost four months.'

'Four months? My God.'

Adam settled to the hospital routine of his little white room and let it carry him along. Two African servants washed and fed him – at first a light soup then thin meat gruel.

Better health brought boredom. With no company – other than his daily hour with Fischer – and nothing to read, Adam passed time by trying to identify and catalogue the noises outside his door and soon built up a picture.

Feet thumped or clattered at a regular pace. Voices murmured – not quite loud enough to gather words, but his ear picked out intonations of German, Swahili and Arabic. The whole place sounded disciplined – under control. *It must be a military hospital.*

A move to solid food increased Adam's strength. One morning he overcame pain and with effort dragged himself up to a position half-sitting and half-lying against the wall, his legs hanging over the bedside, feet touching the floor. Fischer laughed in delight, clapped his hands and said, 'The time has come for exercise to rebuild your muscles. You'll soon be walking. First round the room then outside.'

Adam started a painful journey towards recovery, at first sitting up and laying down, supervised by Fischer then standing up and, supported by two African servants, shuffling a few steps until he made it halfway round the room.

Every improvement brought pain and exhaustion but his strength increased until one day Adam found himself strong enough to stand and walk without help. He said to Fischer, 'Now is the time for me to walk outside.'

With a servant holding each arm, he shuffled through the door into bright sunlight, surprised to see the parade ground of a small fort.

'What's this?' he asked. 'I thought I was in hospital.'

'Oh no,' said Fischer. 'You are a special prisoner. We couldn't keep you in hospital.'

'A special prisoner? What does that mean?'

'Concentrate on walking then we'll sit in the shade and talk.'

Gritting his teeth, Adam managed about twenty slow, painful steps before giving up. Fischer called for chairs and they settled beneath an awning.

Adam stretched and eased his wounded leg, running a hand along the wasted thigh muscle, tracing two great bullet craters on either side. *In and out. That's what Fischer called them last week. 'In at the front, out at the back. The bullet passed right through, ripping out muscle but missing the arteries and bone. Fantastic luck. Same with your stomach – terrible mess and badly mangled but somehow the main organs survived.'*

Now Fischer asked, 'Do you bleed from the exercise?'

'No,' said Adam. 'But I need rest.' He relaxed in his chair and studied the fort.

Thick stone walls bordered a hard dirt parade square – red dust scuffed by his twenty dragging steps. Rooms and offices built into the walls. A heavy wooden gate, open to show a tree-lined dirt road sloping down towards houses and other buildings a mile or so away. Several *askaris* lounged round the walls and leaned from gatehouse windows, watching.

My guards...?

A German captain came to an office door and looked at him without speaking.

My jailer...?

'Why am I a special prisoner?' asked Adam.

'For several reasons.'

'What reasons?'

Fischer's friendly face became troubled. He said, 'I cannot say. I'm sorry – it is not for me to tell you.'

'Who will tell me?'

'*Herr* Weiss. He will tell you.'

'Weiss? Is he here?'

'Not now. But he will come. He is our District Commissioner.'

'Bloody hell,' said Adam in English.

Weiss. After all these years the damned man's following me around....

Adam remembered the exchange of shots with Weiss at Bukoba – or did he? Was it real? Or part of his coma-induced dementia along with the other shooting and killing his mind kept repeating in awful detail?

Thinman wounded and struggling in a swamp…a sniper shot and sinking into filthy water…Christy's skull flying in pieces across a clearing? These terrible images that invaded his mind along with so many others in the past four months?

Four months?

'Is this true?' he asked Fischer. 'My coma lasted four months? All those awful dreams seemed to pass in no time.'

Fischer said, 'Oh yes. The coma helped you survive by handling the mental shock of your terrible wounds. The dreams, whether real events or fabrication from your deep subconscious were part of your mind ridding itself of the dreadful things you had seen and done.'

That night Adam lay in bed trying to separate the real and imagined but found it too distressing so gave up. *When I get home I'll find out who's dead and who isn't….*

During November and December he concentrated on daily exercise on the parade ground and found his strength returning. On the morning of Christmas Day Fischer appeared with a cake and walking stick. 'Your presents,' he said, 'And today I take you outside the fort.'

Together they passed through the gate, Adam limping slowly, watched by the silent sentries. A feeling of intense excitement and freedom possessed him as he stepped beyond the walls. Strength and energy flowed through his body.

'This is wonderful,' he said. 'I feel I could walk all the way home.'

'Ah no, my dear friend. You are still our special prisoner.'

'Then why am I allowed out of the fort?'

'Because there is nowhere to go. You are almost a thousand kilometres from the sea and the same from your own people. This whole town is your prison, not only the fort. This is why we never bother to lock you in.'

Adam laughed to dispel a feeling of isolation.

'Then I must find a way to escape,' he said.

Fischer shook his head. 'Not possible. You are watched all the time. Please do nothing hasty and dangerous. For the moment you are safe here.'

For the moment? What the hell does that mean…?

By the end of January, Adam's strength returned to almost normal. He discarded the walking stick and concentrated on correcting his limp. He felt almost without physical pain but his mind remained in awful turmoil.

His memory seemed fully returned, bringing a different agony. Eva's affair with Christy – and its terrible consequences – clashed with satisfaction at the bloody man's death. *I got the bastard in the end – one way or another. Now what shall I do about her....*

His mind worked on many plans, some so murderous and shocking he wondered at his sanity. *But I must remember – everything is her fault. She had the affair. She had his bastard. She drove me to Kristina. She caused Christy's death and my capture. If I'd not lingered to gloat....*

Every day Fischer walked with Adam for up to an hour and one morning spoke of the battle at Bukoba – 'Your people pushed us out the day after you were shot. We withdrew during the morning and your soldiers burned our fort then looted every building – a disgusting and most unmilitary practice – and by evening sailed away and left Bukoba in a terrible mess. Of course, we went back and rebuilt everything. We are not sure of the reason for the attack. It seemed quite pointless.'

Another day Fischer said, 'Your army in East Africa will soon have a new commander – a South African Boer called Smuts – and your friend Churchill has resigned from the British government. His attack through the Dardanelles on our gallant Turkish allies failed and your prime minister dismissed him.'

'Who told you I know Churchill?' asked Adam.

'We have spies, too,' said Fischer with a laugh. 'You are not alone.'

'What does that mean?'

Fischer laughed. 'Nothing, my friend. I am joking. I think you told me. Please relax and enjoy your stay with us.'

Relax. The doctor's right. Relax and recover.... After two harrowing years, Adam found life as a solitary prisoner congenial. The fort – a haven of peace – allowed rest and recuperation no hospital could provide.

Yet a growing worm of independence began to stir in his gut. For three months no one but Fischer spoke to him or even acknowledged his presence. German officers around the fort looked the other way whenever they passed. The servants smiled and nodded if Adam addressed them, but never uttered a word.

'Why?' he asked.

Fischer shook his head with a sad smile and said, 'I've told you. Because you are a special prisoner. Please do not ask again. I can say no more. *Herr* Weiss will tell you when he comes.'

Bloody Weiss. What's the man playing at...?

The worm shivered deep inside bringing thoughts of escape.

Despite being alone, Adam never felt lonely. He spent time in his cell, or sitting in the shade sketching. When Fischer first brought paper and pencils Adam said, 'Good, I can write some letters. Will you send them for me?'

Fischer shook his head and said, 'No. You may not write or receive letters. I must go away for a week. I am worried that without me you will be bored. This is for you to pass time by drawing pictures.'

Adam said, 'I don't draw.'

'But you do,' said Fischer. 'Major Kreuz showed me your excellent painting of the beach and harbour at Tanga. He said you made sketches of the harbour and took them away to paint. Please draw some pictures of our fort for me. I shall take them back to Germany when the war is over. My wife will be interested to see where I served.'

'I'm not very good but I'll do my best. What do you want drawn?'

'Just the walls and gates and a few figures – *askaris* and some natives – and perhaps a few scenes from the battlements. Give a general view of the place. You may go outside if you wish to keep up your exercise but stay away from the town. An *askari* will accompany you everywhere.'

Kreuz? So he's involved too. Do I smell a rat? Are the bastards setting a trap...?

Puzzled and distrustful of the easy attitude to his imprisonment, Adam tested how far he could go. At sunset he made a few sketches of the inner fort, cursing as he tried to entice soft evening shadows on to paper. A sentry glanced in his direction and turned away, yawning. *No reaction. So far, so good.*

Next morning he sketched the gatehouse and sentries, making sure the *askaris* saw what he was doing, then moved towards the battlement steps and paused.

The sentries showed no interest. Heart thumping, back muscles tense and cringing – *Is this the trap? Shot whilst trying to escape? Allow me halfway up, then bang* – he hauled himself, one step at a time, up to the battlement above his cell. He arrived sweating and nervous, his wounded thigh aching from the effort. Blinded by bright morning light he looked back into the shaded fort.

Completely peaceful. The sentries stood by the gate chatting. A German officer walking across the square glanced up but ignored the sight of his special prisoner standing atop the walls.

Adam relaxed, sketching and drawing for two hours until the sun became too hot. During the afternoon he rested and in the cool of early evening decided on the biggest test. Holding his sketchpad in full view he strolled across the square and out through the open gate. The sentries watched, making no effort to bar his way.

Unsure where to go, he turned right and strolled down the track towards Tabora. An armed *askari* marched from the fort, rifle held high.

Adam's whole body tensed, waiting for a shout or a shot.

Nothing.

He heard nothing but soft evening sounds of Africa and the shuffle of bare feet through dust.

He looked back. The *askari*, rifle slung casually over his shoulder, keeping pace ten yards behind, seemed quite at ease.

With conscious effort, Adam began to relax. *So. It looks as though they're not going to shoot me in the bush either....*

After a few hundred yards he calmed enough to turn and make a quick sketch of the battlements – sharp contours outlined against the setting sun. The *askari* leaned against a tree looking bored before following Adam back towards the fort.

So that's it. I really am free to roam....

One morning Adam ignored Fischer's warning and wandered to the outskirts of Tabora. Sitting under a mango tree he drew a large grey-stone building with wide verandas, fancy pillars and many windows. German officers, servants and messengers hurried along the verandas and from room to room.

Adam scribbled furiously, pencil flying, trying to capture the energetic scurrying. Seeking contrast he shaded in the slow-waving white and black imperial banner flying from a tall flagpole. *Still not right. It needs depth.*

Seeing a small building hundred yards or so beyond he soon added it to the picture along with the curving road and squat mango trees.

As Adam bent over his picture working on small imperfections, a thrilling and familiar sound destroyed his concentration – the groan and rattle of a railway train. To his delight an engine pulling six freight wagons hissed through the trees and squealed to a stop alongside the small building, belching clouds of white steam.

A railway. I've found a bloody railway....

His stomach churned. The worm of independence twisted and lurched in sudden excitement.

The way out. Right in front of me....

Striding back to the fort, mind tumbling with wild plans, he counted each pace as a second. Thirty-five minutes. That's how long. Thirty-five minutes to a chance of freedom....

Chapter Thirty-Two

Make For The Congo

Sitting outside his cell in the warm evening air checking through a pile of drawings Adam looked up to see Fischer hurrying into the fort, calling, 'It's good to see you after so long.'

Fischer shook hands, perched a chair alongside Adam and said, 'What have you been up to during my absence? Running around the countryside I hear. My people saw you in so many places I wonder if some of the sightings are rumours.'

He laughed but Adam saw tension in the normally friendly face. Fischer seemed guarded and worried; prey to an underlying strain.

Adam asked, 'Are you well?'

'Yes, yes,' said Fischer avoiding Adam's eyes. 'I am very well. Very well indeed. Thank you.'

He reached over to lift the sheaf of drawings, saying, '*Mein Gott*, you've been busy. How many pictures have you made? There must be twenty here.'

He shuffled through with rippling fingers; head bent; crouching over the sketches, talking all the time in a half-whispered singsong, 'Oh I like this one. And this. Oh, this is very good. I'll take this one. Oh, and that.' – his voice raised – 'Ah, I see you found our Kaiser's shooting lodge. Wonderful. What a lovely picture. And the railway station. Exactly what we need.'

He held the drawing up, twisting to run light across the paper.

'Such detail. Excellent. Perfect. This is an important building. Thank you so much. If ever our Kaiser comes to hunt elephant or lion, this is where he will stay. Perhaps we shall see him after the war. He may even see your picture and hear your story.'

'Story? What story?' asked Adam. 'What do you mean?'

'Nothing,' said Fischer. 'Just a figure of speech.'

He dropped his eyes, fussing among the pictures, saying, 'I'll take these and see you tomorrow afternoon. Please make sure you are here.'

Next morning Adam made to leave the fort for a walk. Two sentries stepped from the gatehouse and barred his way. Looking round for an explanation Adam caught the eye of a German officer watching from a shaded doorway. With the slightest of movements, the officer shook his head. Adam turned back, wondering what had changed.

He found out at precisely five in the afternoon when Fischer marched through the gate. Normally Fischer ambled into the fort with a soft civilian step, a pleasant nod at the *askaris*, a courteous wave to Adam.

Today he marched stern and upright; a real military man. No more the amiable doctor embarrassed at the need to play soldier.

Today he stamped across the square with martial precision, clattered to a halt before Adam and said, '*Herr* Early. Into your cell, please. We have business to discuss.'

Adam set aside his work for the day – a drawing of Mzito from memory – and squinted up.

'Why on earth are you standing to attention?' he asked. 'It doesn't suit you.'

'*Herr* Early. Do as I say. Into your cell. Immediately.'

Fischer shut the door and handed Adam an unbound file, saying, 'Please read and sign this deposition. I will wait.'

Mystified, Adam sat on his cot, opened the document and read the stark black heading, 'CONFESSION'.

'What the bloody hell is this?' he asked.

'Read and sign,' said Fischer. 'Please be quick.'

Adam flicked through half a dozen official typed pages, his brain taking in great gulps of text with increasing astonishment....

Lieutenant Early first came to our notice when surveying our border in 1902, using the pretext of helping a German hunting party in distress to ingratiate himself with our authorities.... Used visits to Moschi and Tanga to spy on our military installations and draw plans of our harbour at Tanga (copies are with the court).... Used an invitation to Berlin to spy on and report back on our national railway system (copies of his letters are with the court).... Is known to send regular reports to senior British government ministers (documents with the court).... Is a known associate of the confirmed Austrian spy passing under the name of Kinskii, with whom he made a reconnaissance of our installation at Moschi in 1910 (full documentation of Kinskii's activities in Berlin are with the court).... Lieutenant Early is a member of a British Intelligence, reporting to the spymaster Thinman with whom he operated behind our lines during the battle at Tanga.... He led a terror attack while on a spying mission near Longido in June 1915 resulting in the murder of a German officer.... Was captured behind our lines at Bukoba, passing himself off as a German officer, a pretence kept up for many weeks during captivity.... Whilst a prisoner at Tabora he continued spying by leaving his place of detention and drawing plans of important buildings and railway installations (copies of drawings are with the court....

'This is all bloody nonsense.' said Adam. 'Whose joke is it?'

'We do not joke,' said Fischer. 'It is all fact compiled by *Herr* Weiss. You must sign this document now for presentation at your trial tomorrow.'

'Trial? What trial?'

'You will be tried for spying and shot if found guilty.'

'I'm not going to sign this nonsense.'

'You will be found guilty anyway and shot.'

'Bloody hell.' said Adam. 'This is crazy.'

'No. You are a British spy. *Herr* Weiss returned yesterday with a full dossier of your years of spying against Germany. Do as I say and sign.'

'Bugger off.'

'Very well. I leave you with the document. Your refusal will act against you and confirm your guilt in court tomorrow.'

Fischer marched from the cell, smashing the door closed and clanging the heavy outside bolt into place. Adam clenched his fists and breathed deeply: *Think. Calm down and think.*

For an hour in mounting alarm he read and reread. Laid out in dry official language the carefully selected material hung together as a damning indictment.

He went through the dossier again, trying to find a way out. Instead he found damnation and guilt on every page – in every paragraph. The words and phrases raced round and round his brain in a pattern of awful logic, ending with a firing squad. He could see no reply; find no defence. Even the pictures drawn for Fischer were part of the trap.

Damn those drawings.

He groaned at his stupidity.

Every bloody day I looked for traps and missed the most obvious. Bloody Fischer tricked me. What did he say? 'And the railway station. Exactly what we need....' I fell straight into it. How bloody stupid. How can I argue against it...?

He paced from wall to wall, sweating at the effort then sat and read through the dossier again in angry frustration.

Sod this. I can't sit here worrying any longer....

He undressed and climbed into bed. With effort he emptied his mind, forcing away visions of the awful prospect facing him tomorrow. Drifting into the state of relaxation that heralds sleep he heard the door-bolt slide back and his cell door open followed by a soft slap.

Jumping awake he sat upright, and heard the door close. 'Who's there?' he hissed in German, peering through the folds of his mosquito net. He waited. Listened. Heard only the sounds of revelry from the officers' mess.

He slid from the bed, crouched and ready to fight. Free from the mosquito net his eyes adjusted and he saw through the gloom that someone had dropped a small bundle by the door. It lay on the floor showing black against the white wall. *Another trap?*

Keeping low he crept across the floor half expecting the door to burst open. He reached the bundle and studied it from six inches. He reached out and touched a bundle of rough material. He felt buttons and a belt. The material, wrapped round a hard centre, felt like…a uniform.

Sitting in the dark, realisation dawned – *Fischer. It must be Fischer. He wants me to escape….*

He crept towards the door and tried the handle. The door opened.

He peeked out. Across the square lights and drunken songs blared from the officers' mess. Apart from that the fort seemed deserted. No sign of night sentries guarding the gate or patrolling the walls.

This seems too easy. A new trick? A new trap? Can I trust Fischer?

He lit the oil lamp and carried the bundle back to his bed. It contained the bush uniform of an infantry lieutenant – khaki drill jacket and trousers, rough shirt, sun hat and puttees. *Damn puttees. They're so difficult to put on….*

A small piece of paper fell from the hat. He held it to the light and found a note written in spiky German script that read: *Railway station, tonight. Ten thirty. Train for Kigoma. Make for the Congo….*

Adam sat on his bed, considering two options – *Stay and be shot? Or run and be shot?*

He shook out the jacket and tried it on. A perfect fit. The hat settled on his head as though specially designed. In a flash, he knew what to do.

That's it. I'll go. Rather die moving than standing still….

Shaking with excitement or fear – he couldn't tell which – Adam clambered into the uniform.

Chapter Thirty-Three

Oberleutnant Früh

Adam slipped from his cell into the warm starlit night. He paused, heart thumping – *Is this another trap?* – before creeping round the square close to the dark wall shadow.

From the officers' mess drunken songs and lamplight spilled from the open window. He pulled the heavy hat low, straightened his back and lengthened his stride. Concentrating on not limping he marched past the mess, across the square and out of the fort, surprised at the ease with which he escaped.

In a nervous moment at the gate he deliberately passed through a pool of light to show his officer's badges but the sentries, snug in their guardroom, did not even look.

He snatched a glance at the gatehouse clock. *Almost nine-twenty. Plenty of time. Thirty-five minutes to the station. Sneak on to the train. See what happens next....*

At first he walked slowly fearing ambush from the darker shadows, pausing to listen for pursuit. Enough starlight filtered through to guide him past the Kaiser's shooting lodge and into bushes by the railway.

Sweating with effort and tension, he checked the station. Narrow shafts of lamplight from two windows threw yellow rays across the low gravel platform. No sign of crew or station staff.

A small locomotive sat ready to pull eight freight wagons. Adam crouched, squinting into the pitch-black crevices between freight wagons, looking and listening for the snare.

Apart from gentle steam-swish – and clouds of night insects whining round the lighted windows – the whole area seemed silent.

The place seemed empty. Really and completely empty.

Too easy. All too easy and neatly arranged....

He checked back up the road, cupping his ears, listening for pursuers. Not a sound. Complete quiet. Not even a breeze to rustle the trees and cause fright.

He stepped from the bushes, waiting a second to calm himself with a deep breath before strolling across the dirt road, hands behind his back – an inspecting officer on duty.

He reached the low platform, wincing at the crunch of boots on gravel. Steeling his nerves and keeping to his inspecting officer's steady pace he moved along the train checking each wagon door.

Through the first lighted window he saw two Arabs and two

Africans – obviously the stationmaster and train crew – sitting at a table eating steaming stew from a big pot.

Opposite the second lighted window he found an unlatched wagon door.

A quick pull and the warm dusty smell of grain blew out into the night air.

Perfect. Sacks to hide behind and sleep on.

He clambered up, dragging the door shut, cursing the clatter of metal as the latch clacked into place.

Desperate to hide he shuffled down the wagon in stifling darkness, feeling his way by fingertip along the narrow corridor between maize bags and wagon wall. His foot caught an empty bag on the floor. He tripped and fell forward, thumping on to the sack pile. A spicy mixture of grain-dust and hemp particles swirled up, stuffing his nose and catching his throat in a vice.

A door banged and he heard the train crew walk along the platform. Fighting back an enormous cough-and-sneeze, he lay hunched across the sacks, gulping and straining – his whole body convulsed with the effort to stay quiet while outside the train crew shouted farewell to the stationmaster.

With clenched teeth and streaming eyes, entombed in dust and darkness, Adam listened, frantic with impatience – *For God's sake get on with it. Let's bloody-well go. Start the damn train so I can sneeze....*

At last the train lurched into motion, clanking and squealing out of the station allowing Adam to explode into a sneezing fit, hacking and gagging and almost overcome by the pain to his stomach scar.

The train settled to a regular rhythm, clickety-clacking over rail joints. Pushing the wagon door open he thrust his head out, gulping sweet night air into his lungs.

Exhausted, he sat on a maize sack, head bent into the fresh clean breeze, recovering and considering his plight: *Throat and mouth dry as dust. No water until Kigoma in twelve hours or so. Best to get through that by sleeping as long as possible – and risk the open door, rather than suffocate with it closed....*

His spirits rose at the thought of sleep. Working by touch in the pitch-black wagon, he began pulling sacks down and building a bed alongside the door. The train ran into a curve. Thrown off-balance he stumbled, dropping a heavy maize bag. He skipped back to avoid injury, catching his heel on a loose sack and almost falling.

He cursed and regained balance, kicking the loose sack away. Using his last reserve of strength he finished building his sack-bed and within seconds fell asleep.

Shortly after dawn a shaft of intense sunlight flashed across Adam's face, searing through his closed eyelids, bringing him instantly awake and aware of his surroundings. The open wagon door framed grey-green bush and thorn trees in a changing pattern as the train rattled on at about fifteen miles an hour.

He groaned and rolled over, cursing the lumpy maize sacks. Every bone and every muscle ached. His mouth and throat tasted foul. He sat up and tried to spit out the bitter dusty grit coating his teeth and tongue. Nothing came but a painful croak.

He stood to ease his stiff muscles and – 'Oh for Christ's sake,' – stumbled again over the loose sack. He turned to kick it out the door and found a small canvas bag. Thrusting a hand in he felt…a water bottle. He opened the top and sniffed then sipped. *Christ. What luck. Some porter's done me a favour….*

Clean cool water slid down his throat, drawing a silken trail all the way to his stomach. In delight, he took a great gulp, clearing his gullet of grain-dust and hemp particles in a drenching rush.

Scrabbling round inside the bag, he discovered two paper-wrapped packages and a square leather pouch tied with a thong. He opened the packages and found bread and several strips of rubbery dried meat. *Bread? Dried meat? More luck. Someone's left a complete picnic. Bloody hell.*

Puzzled by the pouch – *Not something a porter would carry* – he sat on a maize sack picking at the leather knot with a fingernail until the pouch unfolded like a wallet showing neatly folded papers tucked into different sections. Good quality paper. Stiff and crisp. *What the bloody hell is it?*

In a pocket behind the papers he felt half a dozen hard discs. *Metal? Money? Surely not….*

Pausing to think he lifted the bottle and swilled and gargled, using as little water as possible before allowing it to trickle down – *Waste not a drop. Plenty more hours in this box with the heat of day yet to come….*

Lubricated by the water he tried the stale bread and dried meat but gave up after choking on the first mouthful. *Later. I'll eat later….*

Instead, he explored the pouch, finding two folded papers and six silver Maria Theresa dollars. *Bloody hell. Enough money to buy half this train.*

With shaking fingers he opened the papers and found…a set of Army orders to Oberleutnant Früh, instructing him to inspect and report on the waterfront defences at Kigoma on Lake Tanganyika.

He laughed aloud at seeing his name translated directly into German before realising – *Bloody hell. This is no coincidence. Oberleutnant Früh. By God, I'm a proper German officer….*

In mounting disbelief he skimmed through the document.

Stamped with the German Imperial Eagle and signed by Colonel von Lettow-Vorbeck, it read: *We expect the British or their Belgian allies to attack by ship from the Congo. You will hire a boat and approach Kigoma from the Lake. You will study and report on how best to repel an enemy landing similar to that at Bukoba with special attention along the northern shoreline for possible landing sites and defence positions….*

Unsure of his grasp on reality, Adam went slowly through the orders again, checking every word. He examined the stamp and signature – held the paper up and squinted at the watermark. No doubt about it – the Imperial Eagle again.

All correct. This bloody document is genuine. It must be. But how? And from whom?

The second paper turned out to be an unsigned note scrawled with a blunt pencil. For several seconds he struggled to decipher the angular Gothic script before recognising the handwriting.

Excitement and relief welled up in a loud shout – 'Paul. You clever bastard. It was YOU. Not Fischer.'

Paul von Ansbach wrote: *At Kigoma go straight to the lakeshore. These orders and your perfect German will get you past any questions. On the shore you'll find plenty of Congolese fishermen to take you by boat to Uvira at the north end of Lake Tanganyika. Pay no more than one Maria Theresa – it's as much as they earn in a lifetime. The other five Marias should get you through the Congo and safely home. Destroy this note. It is the only direct evidence against me.*

Laughing with excitement, Adam ripped the note into confetti and shouting, 'Goodbye Tabora,' tossed it through the door.

Elated, he leaned out and watched the small paper shards form a dynamic white tail, twisting and swooping, flickering in the sunlight, before settling and disappearing into the bush.

The train settled into a siding at Kigoma just after noon. Adam closed the door a few miles out. Sealed in his wagon, roasted by the mid-day sun, he lay panting and sweating, half-suffocated by maize dust.

He heard the crew clatter away and waited until the station and yard fell silent before opening the door and shoving his head out to drag in great gulps of dust-free air. Once recovered, he jumped down and pulled the door closed, patting the wagon in affectionate gratitude.

He crossed the lines and stopped in the shadow of a wall. Ahead lay a narrow red-dirt street lined by white painted mud-and-brick houses. A few hundred yards away, beyond the last house, sunlight sparkled off bright water. The lake. Freedom.

The street – completely empty – reeked of danger and ambush. Gritting his teeth – anxious to get it over whatever the cost – he cocked his helmet at a military angle, tucked the leather pouch under his arm and marched down the street, head held high.

His confident step and straight back hid the absolute fear and certainty that each dark doorway held an armed sentry ready to step out and make the arrest.

To his surprise and relief he reached halfway to the lake without challenge. The whole town seemed deep in slumber under the mid-day heat. He strode along, soft dust muffling his boot-fall past a dozing dog.

Unable to believe the ease of escape he reached the lakeside and paused in silent tension. Sweat flooded from his back and armpits, collecting in great black blotches on his tunic.

Behind him the town slept on. No movement. No pursuit. No sound of human activity. *What next? What do I do now?*

To the right a straggly line of African fishing boats clustered on the grassy shore, half in and half out of the water. Some seemed little more than dugout canoes. Others, larger and built from planks, seemed to be small sailing dhows.

Fishermen lay sleeping in the shade of their boats, arms thrown over their eyes to dim the harsh noon sunlight.

Adam chose the largest dhow and shook the fisherman awake.

The African jerked to a sitting position grasping Adam's sleeve with bony fingers, his thin face taut and annoyed. Before he could speak, Adam whispered in German, 'Are you from the Congo?'

The African rolled his eyes in fright, whispering back in a mixture of German and Swahili, 'Please don't arrest me. I'm only a poor fisherman trying to make a living.

In Swahili, Adam hissed, 'You're from the Congo?'

'Yes, *Bwana*, yes, but please don't put me in jail. I've done nothing wrong.'

'I'm not a policeman. I'm not arresting you. I need your boat. Take me to the north shore and I'll pay you well.'

'How much?'

'More than you'll earn from fishing. Provided we go now and provided we go without noise.'

Fear left the African's face. 'Wait here,' he said, 'I'll fetch my brother.'

Within five minutes, the two Africans launched their boat, lifted Adam on board, poled out to deeper water and set sail – almost without sound. Still fearing pursuit, Adam removed his helmet and lay back on a pile of dry fishing nets, hidden to anyone chancing to look from Kigoma. A wave of elation swept over him. *I've done it. I'm bloody well free....*

With casual expertise, the fisherman caught a light breeze that carried the boat quickly out into the lake then turned north along the shoreline. Adam raised his head and asked, 'What's your name?'

The fisherman frowned, his eyes suspicious and said, 'I have many names. It depends where I am and what I'm doing.'

'Tell me your name for here and now?'

The African spat over the side and said, 'You can call me Samaki. My brother you can call Ndege.'

Adam laughed. 'Fish and Bird. Good names. I'll call you Samaki and Ndege. Where do you live in Congo?'

'Near Uvira.'

'Uvira is where I want to go.'

Samaki scratched his head and screwed his eyes in concentration.

'Uvira will cost more than the north shore.'

Adam plucked one Maria Theresa from his pocket and held it high, silver sunlight flashing from its bright surface. Samaki's eyes narrowed and his thin face tightened. He leaned forward, staring at the coin. Adam felt the boat rock. Tensing his muscles he turned to defend himself and saw...Ndege on his knees praying.

Samaki suddenly howled – a high pitched screech that made Adam jump in shock. He swung back, fists raised to see...Samaki leaning back and singing in a loud high voice, eyes raised to heaven. Beating the side of his boat in perfect time he wailed over and over, 'Thank you, Jesus, you sent this man. Thank you, Jesus you're taking us home.'

In the bow, Ndege stopped praying and joined in, singing and drumming on the hull with a wooden paddle. The awful noise rolled across the lake. A flock of birds scared into clattering flight along the shoreline.

255

Adam snapped, 'For God's sake shut up, you'll wake the whole of Kigoma.'

In apparent ecstasy Samaki wept and cried, 'Oh *Bwana* – we want to go home and Jesus has sent you to take us. We are singing to thank Him.'

'Well, for God's sake, thank Him quietly.'

Samaki raised his eyes to heaven and hummed, 'Thank you Jesus.'

Adam whispered, 'Hear-hear....'

Chapter Thirty-Four

Welcome to The Congo

At dusk Samaki beached the boat on a small island. After a wonderful dinner of fish stew and vegetables – *How the hell do they do it?* – Adam slept on jute sacks stuffed with grass, unworried by dreams or mosquitoes.

Next day the boat made tranquil progress, pushed by gentle southern winds. Adam lounged on his fishing-net couch and dozed through the heat of day until he saw the western lakeshore appear as a stain on the horizon. Samaki hummed words of praise to Jesus and turned northwest on a diagonal course towards land.

Approaching the Congo Adam felt a change of mood in the two Africans. By the time Samaki turned to run a parallel course to shore about two hundred yards out, both men seemed sunk in nervous gloom, their cheerful smiles and happy banter gone.

In mid-afternoon Samaki steered into a small bay, ran the bow on to a soft mud beach and said, 'Give me the money now *Bwana* and leave my boat. This is Uvira.'

Ndege jumped from the boat and held his hands ready to help Adam down.

'Where is Uvira?' asked Adam, 'I see no town.'

Samaki pointed along the lake and said, 'Uvira is a short walk that way.'

'How far?'

'Not far.'

'Then take me by boat.'

'No, *Bwana*. This is as far as we go. I cannot take my boat to Uvira town.'

'Why not?'

'I cannot. Give me my money and leave us. Now.'

Adam looked at Ndege. The man seemed apprehensive, hopping from foot to foot and staring over his shoulder into the bush a few yards away. Samaki stood in the stern, hand outstretched, his face hard and unfriendly.

'Why are you frightened?' asked Adam.

'This is not our area,' said Samaki. 'Our home is with the European Christian brothers in their mission half a day south. The people here do not like us. Go now, *Bwana*. Through the bush is a small road. Follow it to Uvira. It is not far. Keep the lake on your right hand.'

Adam jumped to the beach, plucked a Maria Theresa from his pocket and tossed it, spinning and flashing into Samaki's hand. Ndege immediately shoved off, scrambling aboard in a flurry of arms and legs. Adam called goodbye and waved but the two men, straining to pole the boat round, ignored him.

The sail flapped and filled, swishing the dhow smartly away leaving Adam feeling dumped and deserted.

In a surge of anger he shouted, 'Where am I? Where the hell have you dropped me?'

The two Africans took no notice until, sixty yards from shore, Samaki spilled wind and slowed, holding Adam's sun helmet high, calling; 'You left this, *Bwana*.'

'Keep it,' Adam called back. 'I don't want it.'

Samaki clapped the helmet on his head at a jaunty angle, his white teeth flashing for the first time since he entered the bay. Then he hunched over his tiller, picked up the wind and swept round the point.

Overcome by a shock of absolute loneliness Adam watched the boat disappear. These two bloody men had thrown him off and run. He felt abandoned and threatened by this silent shore.

He shivered and turned away from the lake. Pushing into the bush he forced a way through long grass and clinging thorn branches, unsure what he would find. After a few yards he thrust out on to a small red-dirt track, just as Samaki said.

The road – an airless channel lined both sides by thick undergrowth that trapped the suffocating afternoon heat – felt hot as a furnace. Sweat burst from every pore in Adam's body, soaking his clothes and rolling in great rivulets into his eyes, stinging and blurring.

Bloody hell – they've left me in the middle of nowhere....

He knew he had to do something, so turned right and moved along the track, his boots stirring fine red dust into a following swirl.

Straining to see or hear any hint of movement in this godforsaken place, for the first time in his life he felt nervous and vulnerable to the wilderness. Without the company of bearers and guns, the awful danger of Africa bore down – an almost tangible weight on his body and soul.

He kept steady pace for several hundred yards, blinking and rubbing at the blinding sweat in his eyes, snorting and spitting to clear red dust from his nose and mouth. Unable to see properly, he stopped in surprise when a tall African stepped from the bush a yard away. *Oh God – am I hallucinating?*

The African grinned, showing fierce teeth filed to sharp points. He wore a greasy grime-covered semblance of military uniform and a French-style army kepi, stained and bent. He balanced a heavy rifle across his shoulder, barrel facing forward.

Before Adam could speak the African swung his rifle out and down to smash at the side of Adam's leg just above the knee. In agony, Adam crashed to the ground, shouting 'Stop,' in Swahili.

The African swung his gun again, hitting Adam's ribcage in an echoing thump that drove all air from his lungs.

Through waves of pain Adam saw half a dozen more uniformed Africans leap from the bush. Within seconds they stripped him naked and trussed his arms hard with rope, binding his elbows together by his spine and looping a thong round his neck. Hauling him to his feet they danced about, throwing his clothes from one to the other, bending to peer and point, jeering, screaming with laughter.

One African took a knife and slashed Adam's upper arm, leaning forward to lick at the blood, howling in delight. Others pushed the man away and started dragging Adam along the road.

In terrible pain but regaining some breath Adam shouted in Swahili and received a heavy rifle butt to the kidney. He fell in the dust, hauled along facedown for several yards before two captors grabbed his arms and pulled him upright.

Adam lost count of how far they dragged him and how many times he fell rolling in the dirt. They kicked and pulled him along the track until, through pain and confusion, Adam felt hope rise when he saw the mud huts of a village and excited Africans running out to watch him being dragged past. Hope plunged and disappeared when his captors slammed him to the ground in front of a rough thorn fence.

Flopping into a disgusting slick of cow dung and urine he tried to struggle up but fell again, twisted in a painful heap unable to move; arms almost ripped from his shoulders by the rope, half-strangled by the loop round his neck. One of his captors pulled the loop-end tight and stood with a foot on Adam's neck, pressing his face into the filth. The rest lined up shuffling to attention.

Adam heard the thump of heavy boots and screwed his eyeballs round to see a tall European dressed in military khaki and kepi striding through a gate in the fence. *A Belgian officer. At last. Rescue.*

'Thank God,' he croaked in English. 'Get this damned savage off me.'

The officer marched forward, drew his boot back and kicked Adam in the stomach. Adam howled in pain and disbelief. The officer drew his foot back to kick again but stopped when Adam yelled, 'For God's sake, you're supposed to help me. I'm a British officer. What the hell are you doing kicking me like that?'

The officer stepped back and laughed. In perfect German he said, 'That's how we welcome filthy Hun spies to the Congo. First we kick them. Then we shoot them. Now I kick you. Tomorrow I shoot you. So welcome. Welcome to the Congo.'

Chapter Thirty-Five

Chameleon

After spending an awful night in this filthy hut chained to a post by a heavy slave link round his ankle, Adam lay naked on a lumpy wooden cot watching grey light of daybreak force through holes in the thatch roof and mud walls. Now newly awake from surprisingly deep sleep he tried to sit up.

Groaning at the pain from yesterday's beating he managed to twist enough to run fingers over his body and leg.

What luck. No rifle butt or boot had hit the scars left by German bullets and Fischer's surgery. He lay back, hissing at the agony of cracked ribs.

How to make that Belgian brute listen? Last night the bastard laughed at Adam's attempts to explain and laughed again when the *askaris* dragged Adam through the cow dung and chained him up. As a concession the Belgian released Adam's arms and arranged for a cot to be brought, saying, 'I think you should be comfortable for your final night on earth. See you at dawn for the firing squad.'

Adam moved again, trying for relief from the misery of his bruised chest. The foul covering of dried mud and cow dung cracked, giving off a disgusting odour.

Adam managed a grin – *I may smell awful but at least it kept the mosquitoes away....*

The hut door opened and the tall Belgian strode in. He set three bananas and a tin mug on the floor beside Adam, shouting in German, 'This is your last breakfast, you filthy Hun. Enjoy it. See you at sunrise for the execution.'

'You bloody sadist.' Adam shouted back in the same language, unsure if the man spoke English. 'You can't shoot me without a military trial.'

'Oh yes I can.' shouted the retreating Belgian.

Adam hurled his tin mug at the closing door and fell back in anguish – *God, how stupid. I've wasted all my water.*

He swilled saliva round his mouth and tried to eat a banana. As he forced it down, two *askaris* burst in, tied his arms, looped a rope round his neck, unlocked the slave link and dragged him to his feet. Determined to go to his death unaided, Adam pushed them aside. As steadily as his condition allowed, he walked from the hut in to a sunrise of breathtaking beauty.

Squinting in the sudden brilliance Adam saw the Belgian officer sitting at a table, flanked by two African orderlies holding large buckets. To the right a file of armed *askaris* stood in a casual line, watching and giggling.

The Belgian officer pointed to a spot a few yards in front of the table. Adam stopped where indicated and the officer waved his hand at the two orderlies. They stepped forward and, swinging their buckets doused Adam in a flood of water. Adam staggered back.

'Stand still you filthy devil,' yelled the Belgian in German. 'Move and you'll be shot on the spot.'

'You Belgian bastard,' Adam shouted, 'Shoot me if you like but at least give me some clothes.'

To his surprise, the officer stood up, saluted, and, in a complete change of mood, said mildly in English, 'I'm Danish, not Belgian. Danes are tall and blond like me. Belgians are short and dark and fat because they eat too much. I am Major Hansen of the Force Publique and commander of this area. Why do you insist on speaking English?'

'Because I'm a British officer, you bloody dodo.'

Hansen walked round the table and bent forward to examine Adam's scars. 'Big wounds,' he said. 'Where from?'

'Bukoba. The Germans hit me with machine gun bullets. Now get me some clothes. I'll tell you nothing else until I'm dressed.'

Hansen nodded and spoke fast French to the orderlies. One ran to a hut and returned with a shirt and *kikoi*. The other brought a chair. 'Sit down,' said Hansen, 'I want to hear your story.'

Hansen's mild mood continued as he politely asked questions, listened carefully and scribbled notes of Adam's replies.

An hour after sunrise the heat of day began in earnest. Hansen dismissed his *askaris*, saying to Adam, 'It's too late to shoot you today. Perhaps tomorrow. Depends on what you tell me. Meantime let's go inside for some tea. It's too hot out here. Follow me.'

He led the way to a cool stone house and sat at a desk, saying, ' Please make yourself comfortable.'

Adam's feeling of unreality increased when a white-robed servant brought tea with a plate of English biscuits and Hansen waved a hand to indicate Adam should help himself. Adam poured milk from a jug, added tea and ate a biscuit – what delight after so long – while Hansen continued questioning and scribbling. The servant poured for Hansen.

Adam, now quite sure he was in cloud-cuckoo land, continued his story.

Finally, Hansen stopped writing, leaned back with a sigh and said, 'Enough. I need to think.'

He ran a hand over his face and sighed. 'Are you *really* telling me the truth?'

'Yes,' said Adam. 'I know it sounds far fetched but it's all true.'

Hansen peered at his notes. 'Let me get it right. Your name is Adam Early and you are a lieutenant in the British army wounded and captured at Bukoba?'

'Yes.'

'And you're married to a German woman related to the Hun commander. Her cousin – a German officer – helped you escape to avoid execution as a spy?'

'Yes.'

'And you expect me and others to believe this story?'

'Yes.'

Hansen' face froze in anger. His eyes squinted to hard points as he snatched a crumpled paper from his desk drawer. Thrusting it forward he snapped, 'So am I expected to believe this is true?'

Adam's heart sank. The Imperial Eagle waved in front of his eyes.

Sod it. Those orders. Stuffed in an inner pocket and forgotten. I should have ditched the bloody things in the lake.

Hansen leaned forward, snarling through clenched teeth, 'I found this in your tunic, damn you. If you are Lieutenant Early who is *Oberleutnant Früh*? I think Lieutenant Early died at Bukoba and *Oberleutnant Früh* took his place to spy on us. I think you're telling me a pack of lies. I may not wait until dawn. I think I'll shoot you in the next five minutes.'

In desperation, Adam cried, 'For God's sake man, who'd invent a story like that? It's too complicated to be anything but true. I'd never remember it all. Hold me a couple of days and ask every question again. You'll get all the same answers. You made notes. You can check.'

Hansen frowned and growled, 'What should I do? What should I believe? You speak English like a Lord, German like a Berliner and Swahili like a coastal Arab. I don't know what to think. I'm not sure whether to shoot you or ask you to lunch.'

On impulse Adam said, 'I'll only accept lunch if the food is good.'

Hansen leaned back and laughed – a gulping hooting guffaw – and said, 'Only an Englishman jokes at a time like this. And only a damned Englishman pours milk first and tea second. You're either genuine or a wonderful actor. Yes. I'll keep you for a week and keep asking questions. Then if I'm not satisfied I'll shoot you. Meantime you must stay here as my guest and companion in this filthy place. We are two Europeans in the bush and should live as civilised gentlemen.'

Adam could not believe the topsy-turvy world he had fallen in to. From naked prisoner to honoured guest in one hour. For the next week Hansen exuded courtesy, except during interrogation when his mood could change at startling speed. Twice a day Adam went through his story while Hansen checked and queried, picking ferociously at small inconsistencies.

Otherwise, Hansen seemed anxious that Adam should live in comfort and ease, pampered by two personal servants, sleeping in a soft bed and eating good food.

On the second day Hansen walked in carrying several sets of clothes and threw them on the bed, saying, 'You can't stay in that bloody *kikoi*. Try these damned Belgian uniforms. Bad but better than nothing.'

Adam sorted through the pile, selecting outfits of reasonable fit. At dinner Hansen chuckled and said, 'Look at you – a bloody chameleon. Dressed like that you could pass for a Belgian officer. What do the English say? A master of disguise. That's what you are. Now I'm sure you're a bloody spy.'

Adam laughed, feeling better at the banter.

The days passed in rest and recovery – Adam's bruises spreading and turning yellow, the pain of his ribs easing. Each day he ate lunch and dinner with Hansen, who complained constantly about the Belgians and his posting to, 'This damned dirty outpost of someone else's empire.'

'Why are you here?' asked Adam.

'Money. I'm a bloody mercenary. This is the Belgian colonial army. The Belgians call it the Force Publique and it's a joke. Very few Belgians serve. The officers are mainly Danes like me. We command the worst scum from the worst tribes in Congo. Some are cannibals before we take 'em into the Force. We try and wean them on a different diet. Sometimes we succeed.'

Adam ran fingers along the knife slash on his upper arm and said, 'I think one of the buggers tested me for flavour.'

Hansen laughed and said, 'Yes, I saw that. You're lucky they brought you to me. In a different mood they'd have popped you in the pot and had you for supper.'

After five days Adam became angry during further interrogation and said, 'For God's sake, why do you continue this? I've answered everything a hundred times. Why the hell don't you give up? There's nothing more to tell.'

Hansen said, 'You're right. I'm bored with it too, so I sent signals asking for a check on your story from the British. We'll have the answer in a few days. Have another cup of tea.'

Two days later Hansen said, 'The British are intrigued. They have you listed as killed at Bukoba. They're sending detail – questions for me to ask – to identify you absolutely. When it comes we'll have the final story.'

Adam said, 'Thank God. At last I'll be able to get out of here.'

Hansen laughed and said, 'Exactly. I'll shoot you or release you as soon as I know the truth. What shall we have for dinner tonight?'

Freed from interrogation Adam spent his time resting, trying not to anticipate what may happen next. Four days later, afternoon heat drove him to his bed. He lay half-dozing and half-thinking, his past and future life floating through his head in no particular order. A thump of boots and Hansen's voice broke in to his dream, shouting in German, '*Früh. Oberleutnant Früh*. Where are you? Identification has arrived. Come and face it.'

Adam jerked awake and scrambled from his bed, head swirling at the sudden change from sleep to activity. Snatching a *kikoi* he rushed to the living room, where Hansen stood holding a large envelope, fierce excitement creasing his face in tense lines.

Hansen bellowed, 'Stand still. Don't move. Now we'll find out who you are.'

Adam halted, unsure of this part of the game.

Hansen turned away and shouted, 'Come in now.'

The veranda door opened. An African stepped through.

Adam's jaw dropped in shock. Tears welled in his eyes. 'Musa. My God. Musa. What are you doing here?'

Musa's broad calm face crumpled and he too started crying. He opened his arms and ran forward. The two men fell in to a long embrace, weeping and hugging. Musa wailed, '*Bwana* Adam. We all thought you were dead. God has saved you. Thank God, thank God, thank God.'

Behind him Adam heard Hansen laugh and say in English, 'There's the answer. My chameleon shows his true colour at last. When you two finish dancing, we'll talk.'

Sitting on the veranda after dinner, Adam still quivered with shock at the news from Nairobi. He fought to calm his nerves as Hansen took a long drink of brandy and said, 'So all that nonsense you told me was true. And now you have a new twist to the adventure. Who would have thought it?'

Adam frowned, took H.E.'s letter from the large envelope, held it up to the lamplight and read it for the tenth time.

H.E. wrote: *My dear old fellow – if it is really you – When we heard you had turned up in the Congo we just did not believe it. You were dead. Killed at Bukoba. Thinman saw it all. We even held a funeral and buried a casket. I suppose we'll have to dig the bloody thing up now.*

The news from here is that your farm is still in good fettle. The two ladies keep it going with help from my man Cretikos. Abdi keeps Damu and the cattle turning over and Stewartby runs both the cold store in Mombasa and military security in Nairobi. He's a major now and a dangerous sod. He's after your blood over Christy's death. There is some hint that you were involved and talk of an enquiry – statements and depositions and suchlike. So it's probably best that you stay away for a while.

I'm secretary to the War Council – a position of amazing influence – so I've wangled you a liaison post to the Belgians. Stay with them as long as you can, or until the dust settles. No letter from your wife – too shocked at Christy's death and shocked at your possible survival. With this I send your official orders.

I sent Musa to identify you – who better? He'll stay there and look after you, as always. Do keep in touch and let me know what those bloody Belgians are up to. I don't trust the buggers an inch....

The orders transferring Adam to the Belgian army under their commander, Colonel Olsen left no doubt that Adam must remain with the Force Publique until at least the end of hostilities.

'You'll like Olsen,' said Hansen. 'Fierce bugger but a great soldier.'

The next day Adam left for Olsen's headquarters at the northern end of Lake Tanganyika. Before shaking hands and saying goodbye, Hansen produced Adam's leather pouch and the set of German orders signed by von Lettow-Vorbeck. He said, 'You should frame these and hang them on the wall. Great souvenir.'

Adam checked his pouch and counted six Maria Theresa.

'I should only have five,' he said. 'I paid one to come across the lake.'

Hansen waved a hand and said, 'My *askari*s got it back for you.'

'How?'

'They caught the boat ashore a few kilometres away from where they found you.'

'What did they do to the two fishermen?'

Hansen shrugged and said, 'Probably ate them.'

Chapter Thirty-Six

The Column

Stamping with impatience, Adam stood at the edge of a dirt road winding through thick bush outside Abercorn. The clattering hum of a million insects and the screaming whine of nearby tree-crickets bore down on him. All just too bloody annoying.

He told no one of his secret decision to come out and be first to meet the column. Now, the devils were late and with hot near-noon sun raising itchy sweat on his scalp, it didn't seem such a good idea.

Lifting his kepi, he ruffled at his hair, cursing the heavy discomfort of full dress uniform at this time of day. Sweating and swearing, he stamped again, staring up the track. *Where the bloody hell are they...?*

He flicked his swagger stick at grains of red dust settling on his immaculate calf-length boots. *Musa worked hard to get that shine. Better not spoil it.*

He turned his head at the sound of footsteps and saw a British officer coming round the corner from Abercorn.

Damn. He turned away hoping the man would ignore him, but no, the bloody fellow halted and said in French, 'Excuse me, major. Any sign of them?'

Adam turned in fury to snap in French, 'Of course not, you cretin. If I could see them so would you,' but stopped and said in surprised English, 'Good God. I know you. Mayne, isn't it? Remember me? Last time we met was at Namanga in nineteen fifteen. What the hell are you doing here?'

'Heavens above,' said Mayne, his long nosed English-gentleman face showing equal surprise. 'Early, isn't it? Adam Early. I remember very well. You murdered a whole German patrol then ate their officer's dinner while the poor bugger lay dead in his tent. Never forgotten it. What on earth are you doing dressed up like a Belgian music hall singer?'

Adam laughed and said, 'It's a long story. Started at Bukoba.'

Mayne's smile froze and faded. He said, 'Ah yes...Bukoba...I remember...Something happened...I heard....'

Adam felt Christy's ghost rise. The word *murdered* hung in the air.

To help Mayne through his embarrassed mumble, Adam forced a laugh and hurried into his story – 'I was press-ganged. The Belgians needed officers so they grabbed me and held on....'

Press-ganged.

Hansen howled in glee at Adam's return to Uvira, shouting, 'I told you Olsen is a fierce bugger. He saw you and caught you. Like your English navy. What did they do? Press-gang. That's it. Olsen did the same. He press-ganged you. And now you're a bloody mercenary like me. We're blood brothers so you must move into my house. We'll mess together and get drunk like proper soldiers.'

Hansen sent Adam and Musa north to Olsen's headquarters with an escort of six file-toothed *askaris* – 'They'll make sure no one eats you in the bush.' – and a packet of despatches for Olsen – 'Hand them over personally. Give them to no one else.'

Olsen – so like Hansen they could have been twins – shook Adam's hand, said, 'I heard you were coming,' and invited him to dinner – 'after you've bathed and rested.'

Warm dusk settled across the lake and servants in long white robes served a civilised meal on Olsen's veranda – 'One thing about working for Belgians,' said Olsen, 'The food's always good.'

Along the shoreline hundreds of cooking fires sparkled to life. A sharp-sweet aroma of wood-smoke and roasting meat drifted on the evening breeze.

'How many men do you have?' asked Adam.

Olsen said, 'Almost five thousand. We're ready to fight the Hun. You're here to help with information.' He leaned forward, blue eyes shining in the yellow lamplight. 'I'll include what you to tell me about the Germans in Tabora to the despatches you will carry back to Hansen. You return to Uvira the day after tomorrow.'

'But I'm not going back,' said Adam. 'I'm posted to you as liaison officer.'

Olsen's blue eyes hardened. He snapped, 'I need fighting officers, not clerks. You're under my orders and I'm sending you back as second in command to Hansen. You will help us capture Tabora. Today you are a British lieutenant. Tomorrow morning you'll be a Belgian captain….'

Mayne said, 'Good God. Is that how it happened? Did he have the authority to steal you away?'

'It seems he did,' said Adam. 'Anyway, I couldn't argue. I became a Belgian officer and that was that.'

'And you fought through their whole campaign?'

'I did.'

'How was it?'

'Difficult. A battle of columns. No lines, no trenches, nothing like Tanga and Bukoba. Just columns moving and searching. Trickery and ambush. Trap and counter trap. Bloody dangerous.'

Mayne raised an eyebrow and with a faint smile asked, 'Why did you stay with the Belgians so long?'

Adam said, 'No one asked me to come back.'

Hansen read Olsen's dispatches and said, 'Someone doesn't want you at home. You are to stay with us for the whole war. What have you been up to? Don't tell me. I don't care. We're like the Foreign Legion here. Hide for long enough and whatever you did is forgotten....'

Here on the roadside at Abercorn, Mayne's sardonic expression proved Hansen wrong. At Namanga, three years before Mayne said *'Our deepest personal conspiracies get out....*

Adam's mind raced, fearing the next question but Mayne simply smiled and asked, 'How did you become major in such a short time?'

Relieved, Adam replied, 'The death of my commander. No one else to take over so I was shoved into the job.'

'What happened to him?'

'A bloody clever ambush held us up on the approach to Tabora and he lost patience.'

Adam watched in horror as Hansen lost his temper, jumped from cover and raced howling with fury towards the German position. His crazy charge must have shocked the enemy. For a moment they slackened fire then hit him with a wall of fire from three machine guns at once that smashed him down and broke him apart.

Adam knew that the silly bugger wanted to die in battle. 'Why wait?' Hansen would ask. 'I don't want to be old. I'll go as a soldier or not at all. I'm not going to wait for malaria or syphilis.'

Adam buried his friend alongside the railway line and took command. Olsen summoned him to headquarters and said, 'You know Tabora. I'm placing your battalion at the front. I rely on you to lead us in.'

Fighting from water point to water point, Adam struggled along the railway and approached the town in early September. The Germans settled into prepared positions and battled hard for ten days before abandoning Tabora and retreating southward. Olsen let them go – 'We have our objective. We've regained our territory and chased the

Germans from theirs.'

Adam settled his men around the fort, delighted to sleep again in his little cell.

'So you saw no more action?' asked Mayne.

'Some,' said Adam. 'The Germans split their columns. One went south into Portuguese territory, the others moved east and west then split again. We chased the buggers for almost two years, catching one column then another. Lots of skirmishing – small stuff in the bush – until we'd eliminated them except von Lettow-Vorbeck himself. He was too clever.'

'Ah yes,' said Mayne. 'He'd gone south. And now he's come north again to surrender.'

'He may not see it that way,' said Adam. 'He's never been beaten.'

'I hear we're allowing him to march in.'

'Yes,' said Adam. 'To acknowledge his skill and bravery.'

'Bloody nonsense,' said Mayne.

'Not at all,' said Adam. 'He's the only undefeated German general of this war.'

'Is it true your wife is related to von Lettow-Vorbeck?'

'Yes.'

'Strange situation for you?'

'I suppose so.'

Mayne said, 'Well here comes your relative, the German commander. Now's your chance to congratulate him personally.'

Two hundred yards up the road a column of troops swung into view, marching smartly between the trees in perfect step, spurts of red dust spitting up at each precise boot-fall.

Mayne turned away towards Abercorn, saying, 'Must get back to warn the Brigadier. He'll want to be ready to welcome the Hun. See you at the victory celebrations.'

Adam recognised von Lettow-Vorbeck immediately: *When did we last meet? January nineteen-fourteen. Mombasa. Just before the war...My God, he's lasted well....*

The strain of four hard years of war and disease showed in von Lettow-Vorbeck's face and stringy body but he marched with an air of self-assurance and strength. Adam could see the bold eyes and confidence of an undefeated soldier returning to barracks.

Adam straightened into a salute and von Lettow-Vorbeck flicked his hat-brim in reply. Adam saw several of the following officers look in obvious surprise at the lone Belgian officer standing by the roadside.

One man in the centre rank slowed and stared in such concentration he lost rhythm and broke step causing those following to stumble and swear. To Adam's surprise the soldier called, '*Herr* Early. Is it you?' and pushed his way out of the column, tripping and losing his helmet.

'My God,' said Adam. 'Fischer. What are you doing here?'

Fischer ran across the road, white hair flying and shouting, 'Herr Early. You survived. Thank God. You survived. How wonderful. I heard no news and thought you died.'

Adam looked into Fischer's delighted eyes and fought back the urge to hit the bloody man – to smash his nose and stupid damned smile right through to the back of his head. Instead, he accepted a hug and fierce handshake, trying to forget that this little bastard had been happy to plan his execution….

Fischer cried, 'How terrible if you had died after I saved you in Tabora. My dear *Herr* Early. You were so clever, escaping and disappearing completely. I don't know how you did it and thought of you often, hoping you survived. Your cousin Paul von Ansbach is also safe. He is further back in the column. Wait here and he will pass. What a terrible business this war has been. I must go now but please come and see me in Abercorn. I am sure we have much to speak of together. Now the war has finished we can be friends. I must go. Wait here and Major von Ansbach will come.'

Before Adam could speak, Fischer dived back into the column and disappeared. Seconds later, Paul stepped out of the passing ranks and shook Adam's hand. 'Thank God you're here,' he said. 'I thought you may be dead.'

At noon, Adam stood on Abercorn parade ground watching and listening. British troops stood guard at every angle, dominating the German column, now drawn up in a hollow square.

Fear tweaked his gut at the sight of these *askari*s in their odd high hats and tight leggings. Here – only yards away and fully armed – stood the bastards who'd been trying to kill him for the past four years.

But along straight stern ranks, Adam saw disease and fatigue. Most officers thin and weak; some *askari*s, grey and ill, swaying under the weight of their shouldered rifles.

A murmur passed across the parade as von Lettow-Vorbeck stepped forward, saluted the British flag, pulled out a notebook and read a formal statement of surrender in German and English.

Complete silence followed. Adam held his breath and crossed his fingers. The whole parade ground seemed frozen, waiting for tension to break.

Adam felt almost unbearable stress – every muscle in his body tight as wire. He looked along the rigid lines and with a jolt, realised.... *Christ. No one knows what to do. The war's finished. What now...?*

He looked round wondering who in hell knew the rules.

At last – after what seemed an hour – von Lettow-Vorbeck acted snapping sharp clear orders at his troops to lay down their arms.

A sigh passed through the German ranks. Not one man moved. For a second or two, Adam thought they would refuse, then – in a last fine act of discipline – every man in the German force bent forward and placed his rifle neatly on the ground.

A feeling of relief swept across the parade ground with intensity that made Adam almost stagger. *It's over. Bloody hell, it's over. I survived.* In those few magic seconds, he realised the same thought struck every man at the same time.

A crisp British brigadier stepped forward and accepted surrender in the name of King George.

Von Lettow-Vorbeck exchanged formal salutes, nodded to a whispered instruction and turned to face his men. He stiffened to full attention, drew in a deep breath and paused. All attention focussed on the small straight figure. Adam could hear not a sound across the whole parade ground. Two thousand men waited – eyes fixed on von Lettow-Vorbeck.

The little general held them transfixed for seconds more then in a clear confident voice, bellowed, 'German Forces in Africa. STAND DOWN.'

The neat German ranks collapsed into swirling rabble. *Askari*s ran and danced, whooping and shouting and laughing and skipping over neat lines of abandoned rifles as they raced from that place. In less than a minute the parade ground emptied, except for a forlorn group of German officers around von Lettow-Vorbeck.

Adam hurried to where Paul stood, surveying the ranks of rifles. He turned stricken eyes to Adam and said, 'I never thought we would see this. Defeat and surrender. It is too much to bear.'

'Come with me,' said Adam. 'We'll find some food.'

Adam took Paul to the mess where he ignored stares from other officers and found a table under an awning. Speaking German, Adam said, 'Pay no attention. I can do this because they think I'm a foreigner.'

Paul slumped on to the chair and coughed – a hollow hacking sound. Blood flecked a corner of his mouth. His face twisted in pain and turned a bluish grey. With hunched shoulders he drew deep rattling breath, whispering. 'Pardon me. This cough came last night and hurts. It will go.'

'You look awful,' said Adam. 'Shall I fetch a doctor?'

'No. Order some soup. That will help. And tell me why you're dressed as a Belgian major.'

Adam said, 'It's your fault. You got me out of Tabora. When I reached the Congo the Belgians held on to me.'

Paul managed a weak smile. 'Oberleutnant Früh. That was a good plan. I'm glad it worked and saved your life.'

Paul dragged in more air and said, 'Weiss summoned me to be your defending officer. He thought it a great joke – his humiliation on us and both our families. He wanted me to argue your case but see you shot anyway. With the detailed evidence against you we had no chance.'

'I saw the evidence. Weiss made it all up. What does the man have against me?'

'You humiliated him in nineteen-two by saving his life...by saving *our* lives. To him the story is different. *He* would have saved us had you not come along and taken his glory. That's how he remembers it.'

'I could have killed him at Bukoba. I had him in my sights.'

'I know. I heard. He knows also. Even more reason to see you dead.'

'He had the power to execute me?'

'Absolutely.'

Trying to say more, Paul fell to a bout of coughing, leaning forward in obvious pain, groaning and gasping, his face turning purple.

Adam said, 'Christ Paul. Don't go on. You're too ill. I'll find a doctor.'

With the help of another officer, Adam carried Paul to the wooden hospital building, pushing through into hot airless wards crowded with soldiers from every unit in both armies.

'He'll probably be dead by morning,' said the British doctor, 'This strain of 'flu usually turns to pneumonia in twelve hours or so and carries 'em off. I'll do what I can. Leave him here and go.'

Adam looked round in shock. The hospital – a cavern of sweat, fever and vomit – was jammed full. Men of all ranks lay scattered about – on beds, benches and stretchers or wrapped in blankets on bare board floors.

'Bloody hell. What's happened?' he asked.

'An epidemic. It's sweeping the world. God only knows where it came from but it's a killer.'

'I want to stay.'

'Not a good idea. This bloody 'flu travels like wildfire. You and I are lucky not to have it yet. My advice is that you bugger off before it grabs you too.'

'When can I come back to see how he is?'

'Try tomorrow morning. Now get out of here.'

Adam returned at dawn with Musa. The doctor said, 'Your friend managed to get through the night. Not much more we can do for him here and I need the space. Take him to a comfortable bed somewhere. Keep him fed and watered and hope for the best. It'll be touch and go for a few days but he may survive.'

Musa found a stretcher and two *askari*s to carry Paul. Adam went ahead and prepared a bed in his tent then passed Paul into Musa's care.

A few hours later the brigadier gave Adam new orders.

'We're sending the Hun officers back to Germany. You'll go with them to Dar-es-Salaam as interpreter. First, go through the Hun camp and count how many we have – officers, *askari*s and followers. Then come back with a dispersal plan. You're the only one with enough languages to cope. I'll give you whatever staff you need. Get on with it and be done in a week. I want to go home, too.'

The Lake Steamer: 4th December 1918

Shortly after sunrise, Adam sat in chill morning air alongside Paul on the after-deck of a small steamboat travelling north along Lake Tanganyika towards Kigoma.

Adam leaned across to adjust the blanket round Paul's shoulders and smiled at the sight of several German officers strolling the deck like tourists taking air before breakfast. A captain nodded and said, '*Bon jour.*' Adam replied in the same language, touching the brim of his kepi.

Paul opened one eye and said in German, 'Don't treat me like a baby and why do you still wear a Belgian uniform?'

'Because a Belgian major has more authority than a British lieutenant – which is what I really am. How do you feel this morning?'

'Better. How do I look?'

'Better. But still too thin. You're a bag of nothing. You must eat more.'

Paul opened his other eye and said, 'What will you do now? Return to the Congo or go home?'

'No one's told me. I suppose I go home. The Belgians won't care.'

'Eva will be happy to see you. How is she?'

'Difficult to tell,' he said. 'Post never caught up in the bush. I haven't heard for a while.' – *Not since Bukoba. Three bloody years. A few notes from H.E. at the beginning then they dwindled to nothing. Not a word from or about my family. They could be bloody dead for all I know....*

Adam glared at Paul's gaunt profile and joined his tense silence. Nearby a hunting fish-eagle passed in graceful flight. Adam watched it go and realised his feeling of blessed peace had gone too....

On The Beach: Dar-es-Salaam , 9th December 1918

Adam walked with Paul along a perfect curve of white beach. Clear blue water lapped at his bare feet. Damp sand squidged between his toes in a sensuous warm trickle.

He looked at Paul, his long bony face dark with worry at the news from Germany, and said, 'Don't leave Africa. Come to the farm and stay with me. You'll be safe and well there.'

Paul shook his head. 'I must go home. My country is broken. This news of the past few days is horrible. Our Kaiser is gone, our government collapsed. I am needed in Berlin. I cannot imagine what is happening.'

'It can't really be as bad as we are hearing,' said Adam.

'It may be worse. We were so deep in the bush we had no news from home for several years. Only now we realise how terrible was the war in Europe. Those trenches are beyond our imagination. So many millions dead. Now we hear this awful 'flu is killing millions more. Our families are dying and the Bolsheviks taking over our cities. All our men are frightened for the future. We need to get home.'

'What effect can you have. Don't go. Stay with us. You'll be with family – Eva, Kristina and me.'

'No. I cannot. I must go home. You sail for Mombasa tomorrow. If I join you I will desert my comrades and my country. I have no choice. Only a new army can keep order in Germany. I must return to Berlin.'

On The Dockside: Dar-es-Salaam , 10th December 1918

In damp late-afternoon heat, Adam stood with Paul on the crowded dock waiting to board ship for Mombasa.

'So.' said Paul. 'You are ready to go. What is your plan?'

'Musa and I will stay a few days at the Creek House to sort

ourselves out before going on to Nairobi.'

Adam dug into his pocket – 'Here are your six Maria Theresa dollars. I never used them....well I used one, but it came back.'

Paul took the small pouch and tipped six shining coins onto his palm. 'Are you sure,' he asked, frowning. 'Will you not need them?'

'You'll need them more than me when you arrive home.' Adam clutched Paul's arm – 'Why go? Why not come with me now? Come and live with us on the farm. There's room on the ship. I'll get you on board. Please.'

Paul shook his head. 'I told you yesterday – I am needed in Berlin.'

He slipped five silver coins into his pocket and handed one back to Adam, saying, 'Keep this as a souvenir. Remember how we saved each other's lives so many times.'

Embarrassed at the emotion in Paul's eyes Adam took the coin. 'Christ, I must go. They're taking up the gangplank.'

Paul shook hands and said, 'I forgot to tell you. Weiss turned up yesterday. I thought he'd been killed but he survived.'

Adam shrugged and clambered up the steep steps, stopping and turning at the top. Paul waved. Adam waved back, holding his Maria Theresa aloft between finger and thumb. It sparkled in the sun and seeing a small blemish he looked closer and found...a dull patch on the queen's breast.

Blood. *Christ.* A tiny fleck of dried blood.

Tears pricked at his eyes and from deep in his soul Samaki and Ndege called greetings....

Chapter Thirty-Seven

Return To Mzito

That chance meeting with Mayne outside Abercorn planted a worm of anxiety in Adam's gut – a vague niggling apprehension, dormant at first but stirring at odd moments in the weeks since then growing

Settling in at the Creek House, Adam's worm of worry grew into a devouring monster. Immobilised by depression, his mind a swirling stew of anxiety, he sat for five days on the Creek House veranda, unable to move or consider life beyond the moment.

Each wretched sweaty night he half slept, wrestling endless dreams of war pain and adultery until dawn brought rescue.

Each wretched dismal morning he dragged himself to a place where shade and breeze made the heavy heat of day bearable, to sit grey-faced, dull eyed, his whole mind turned inward.

From depths of hopeless melancholy, he hated Eva, hated Christy, lusted after Kristina, relived death and destruction; saw... Greasy blood spraying across a moonlit tent. A sniper's shattered skull flicking dainty patterns across filthy swamp water. Spittle and bright red foam sparkling in the sunlight....

With Adam lost in misery, Musa took charge of the Creek House servants, who showed no surprise at Adam's sudden arrival after so many years. Musa cared for Adam – fed and dressed him, insisted he bathed and shaved – talking all the time, trying to relieve Adam's deep despair.

On the fifth day, Musa came to where Adam sat staring at nothing and said, '*Bwana* Adam. It is time we went home. We must return to Mzito.'

The words broke through. *Return. Mzito.* Adam dragged himself back from despair. The sight of home lifted his fog of gloom. His children running to greet him in shrill excitement. Eva standing stern but welcoming, ready to restart their life together. A surge of energy flooded through his body. He pulled himself upright and for the first time since arriving at the Creek House felt able to think properly. *Thank God. Thank-God, thank-God, thank-God.*

Without hesitation he said, 'Tomorrow. We'll go tomorrow. Start packing.'

The act of making a decision cleared Adam's mind. All worry disappeared. *Sod it. Bugger Christy. Bugger the Congo. Bugger everything. If there's trouble I'll go home and face it....*

Adam sent a telegram to H.E. asking that news of his homecoming be passed on. H.E. replied: I'LL MEET YOU OFF THE TRAIN IN NAIROBI STOP URGENT WE SPEAK BEFORE YOU GO TO MZITO OR SEE ANYONE ELSE END

At Nairobi station Adam hung on to the door-jamb and leaned out, peering across the excited swirl of heads, trying to see through the noise, the pushing and shoving. *Where's H.E.? Or Eva? Where the hell are they?*

No sign of them or anyone else he knew, except Musa offloading luggage from a rear wagon. Deflated, Adam dived into the mob and forced a way through. Over the noise he heard his name. 'Mr Early. Wait. Please, Mr Early. I am here. Wait.'

A small olive-skinned man with bright black-button eyes popped from the press of bodies and clutched Adam's sleeve.

In a quiet sweet voice that barely carried over the general hubbub he lisped, 'Please, Mr Early. I am Cretikos. You know me. I made your bed. I am here to meet you. Please come. Please.'

'Made my bed? What the hell do you mean.'

Adam tried to free himself but with words, gestures and insistent fingers, the man persuaded Adam through the crowd and out of the station, his soft attractive accent easing his force of personality – 'Don't worry about your luggage, Mr Early, or your man, Musa, Sir, he will be cared for. I am here for his Lordship. He has sent me to bring you. Don't worry, Sir, I am taking you to his Lordship.'

'Who the bloody hell are you?' snapped Adam, annoyed at finding himself unable to resist this little man's will.

'I am Cretikos, Sir. I am Greek. I work with his Lordship. Into my Model T motor car please, Sir, yes, there into the back. You will be comfortable. I will drive you carefully, Sir. You will be with his Lordship in a few minutes, Sir.'

Cretikos? Cretikos. I remember. This is the man H.E. sent to Chania with Eva....

Adam climbed into the spindly black machine and stung his buttocks on seat leather fried hot by the sun.

The little Greek skipped forward to crank the engine then hopped in behind the steering wheel, his hands fluttering over the controls. The car spluttered and jerked into motion swerving through a crowd of donkey-carts and set wavering course up Station Road. Adam held on, wriggling to ease his stinging backside. Over his shoulder he saw Musa loading luggage on to a donkey-cart, helped by two other Africans.

'Don't worry, Sir. Your luggage will follow, Sir. It is all arranged.'

Adam looked at the raven-wing curve of oiled-shined hair over Cretikos's ears. *How the hell did he know I looked back?* Cretikos turned his head and smiled, black-button eyes sparkling in his olive face. *Christ, he can hear me think. I'll have to watch this bugger....*

Cretikos led Adam along cool corridors to a large door and ushered him through, saying, 'Here we are, your Lordship.'

H.E. heaved up from behind a huge desk and bellowed, 'Bloody good to see you old fellow. Take a seat. Sit down and we'll talk. My God, you look well. Slim as a whippet – more than can be said for me, hey?'

Taken aback by H.E.'s huge bulk, Adam could only stare. H.E. had slipped into heavy middle age, his nose and cheeks a boozer's child-scribble of purple veins on red and yellow skin. The smooth plump affluence and dramatic sweep of lush blond hair remained, along with the easy charm but H.E. seemed expanded to twice the size and weight Adam remembered.

Adam shook hands – his fingers disappearing into the pillow of H.E.'s great soft mitt – and from the corner of his eye saw Cretikos slip out of the room. Still unsure what to say, he asked, 'Who's Cretikos? He says I know him.'

'Cretikos? You don't remember? The little bugger made that bloody great marriage bed for you. All those years ago when the lovely Eva first arrived. I'm sure you made the most of his handiwork then but I'm afraid there's little welcome at home for you now. You're very much in the dog-box, old fellow.'

Adam frowned but felt confidence return at this direct challenge. He considered and rejected pretence.

In a bold voice he said, 'What? After all this time?'

'Yes, my dear fellow. And not only at home. We both know what I'm talking about. Sorry to say your little fracas at Bukoba is still a big subject – you're in some trouble I'm afraid. A possible military enquiry, old chap.'

'An enquiry? Why? Because of Christy?'

H.E. nodded, his shrewd blue eyes blank in their slits of fat. Adam saw no sympathy in the hard civil servant's gaze. Here was no friend. Here was an official doing his job.

'Bugger that. The war's over. I'm not a soldier any more.'

'Afraid you are, old chap. Not released until that little matter's cleared up. Sorry, old fellow. That's the situation.'

280

Adam said, 'I didn't kill Christy.'

H.E. shrugged. 'Save it for the enquiry, old fellow. For the moment, no one else knows you're here so I can let you out to see your wife.'

'Let me out?'

'Yes. Orders are to arrest you on sight'

'Arrest me? What the bloody hell for?'

'Don't argue. I'm doing the best I can. Cretikos will take you to Mzito. See your wife and make what arrangements you can. I'll arrest you tomorrow and sort it out so you'll be free to live a normal life until the enquiry.'

'Free? Normal life? I should bloody-well think so.'

H.E. laughed and said, 'Off you go. I'll see you in the next twenty four hours or so. And by the way – welcome home, old boy.'

In the car Adam thrust the thought of arrest from his head and concentrated on meeting Eva. *I'll be friendly and careful...let things take their course while I settle in. It'll be good to see the family again – and Kristina.*

Shortly before sunset the car shuddered over the crest and rolled down towards Mzito. Adam's stomach tightened at the sight of his farmhouse through the trees. *What's different? Not much – it's hardly changed.* He felt reassured. *It's still home. I'll be safe here....*

Cretikos said little during the drive, struggling with steering wheel and brakes, trying to avoid ruts and potholes. Now his soft voice lisped, 'There's your wife, Sir. On the veranda, waiting for you. How beautiful.' He fought the car to a halt in a cloud of red dust ten yards short of the house.

'Thanks,' said Adam. 'You can go now,' but Cretikos waved a weary arm, closed down the engine and slumped back in his seat.

Adam clambered out, glad to be rid of the bone-shaking machine. Through clearing dust he saw Eva standing by the veranda rail, alone and absolutely still. His heart thumped at this first sight of her for how long? *Christ. January nineteen fifteen – nearly four years. But why is she wearing black?*

He waved.

She turned and walked into the house.

Adam ran up the steps and halted, his hand resting on the rail. *Where the hell's she gone? Didn't she see me?*

The house seemed empty and silent. He checked both ways – down towards the kitchen then along the veranda to the line of bedrooms.

No sound or movement. No clatter of servants in the kitchen, no children playing or running to greet him. Puzzled, he followed Eva through into the darkened room....

An hour later Adam jumped from the car, still quivering in anger and fear at how close he'd been to violence. He stormed through gathering dusk into the Muthaiga Club. Cretikos called, 'His Lordship will be waiting for you in the bar.'

Adam burst in to find H.E. sitting in a large wing chair sipping from a big glass.

'You absolute sod,' snarled Adam. 'You told her I was coming. You arranged all this.'

H.E. squeezed his face into a smile and said, 'Didn't think you'd be long. Have a drink.'

'Drink with you? I could kill you.'

'Don't talk like that. You're in enough trouble over killing already.'

With a grunt of effort H.E. stood up and said, 'Come on. Dinner time. I've booked us a private room. Follow me. We'll swap news. See how to sort things out.'

Adam followed to a bedroom arranged with a table set for dinner and clenched his teeth at seeing his luggage present and unpacked – clothes set neat and tidy on shelves and hangers.

'Christ, H.E.. You planned this. You knew I'd end up here.'

'Obvious, old boy. Obvious she'd kick you out. Trying to help. Not interfering, you understand, just trying to help. Sit down. Relax with some brandy and tell me what happened at Mzito.'

Slumped in a soft chair Adam swigged brandy in great slurps, matching H.E.'s astonishing intake glass for glass.

Neither man spoke until after half an hour of silent drinking Adam said, 'You're right. She kicked me out.'

'I thought she might.'

'She was waiting on the veranda. Soon as I arrived she disappeared.'

'What happened?'

'I followed her into the living room....'

Eva stood stiff and straight and barely visible in early evening shadows – the damned black dress making perfect camouflage.

Adam said, 'I'm home. Don't you recognise me?'

She stared, her face a white blank patch in the gloom. His words dropped in to dead silence.

Confused, he stepped forward.

She raised a hand and in a harsh voice said, 'You killed him. You are not welcome here. Go.'

H.E. grunted and said, 'What did you do?'

'I lost my temper. What a bloody thing to say. Not welcome in my own house? How the hell can she tell me that? I shouted at her. I just kept shouting. After all, she'd been carrying on with bloody Christy behind my back. Who's in the wrong here? Certainly not me.'

'What did she say?'

'Nothing. She just stood. Absolutely still. Then the door opened and that little bastard came in.'

Eva flinched as the door creaked and a small boy trotted into the room, white-blond hair shining in the half-light. Adam stopped in mid-shout. Stunned to silence he watched Eva bend and lift the tot to her hip, where he hung, looking at Adam with bright blue eyes.

In a surge of fury, Adam lurched half a step towards Eva and the brat then, straining for control, stopped and stepped back. *Christ, if I get near I'll strangle them both.*

Eva and the little boy clung to each other. Across the darkened room Adam saw fear in their wide eyes. He snarled, 'Where are *my* children? I want to see them. I want to talk with them.'

Eva lifted the boy and held him out. 'This is your son,' she hissed. 'Will you not speak with *him*?'

Adam waved a hand – Eva flinched again at the abrupt and aggressive movement.

'That little bastard's nothing to do with me and you know it,' he shouted.

She pulled the boy back, holding him tight, saying, 'So you do not accept your son. I know you are wanted for murder already. I think you have come to kill us.'

'What did you say to that?' asked H.E..

'Not much. She took the wind out of my sails. She just stood there with that little bastard, refusing to move or tell me where my children are. In the end I promised to leave if she agreed that I can come back from time to time to inspect the estate and see my children – after all the bloody place is mine, not hers.'

'What did she say?'

'Nothing,' lied Adam. 'So I left.'

He gritted his teeth, remembering how Eva became agitated. Swaying from foot to foot she hugged and gripped at her son and whispered, 'Did you kill Christy?'

'No.'

'Were you there when he died?'

'Nearby.'

'Did you see?'

'Yes.'

She gulped – a great sobbing intake of breath.

'How did he die?'

Christ. How do I answer...?

'Tell me. Tell me how he died?'

'In battle.'

'I know that you fool. I know that. I want to know that he died like a soldier.'

Of course he did you silly bitch. He had his head blown off....

'He was shot,' snapped Adam. 'That's the nearest you can get to dying like a soldier.'

Eva cuddled her son and wept. The boy clung on and began to cry.

After a moment she said, 'I don't believe you. I think you killed him. You must go now. You can only come back to stay when we know you are not a murderer. If you killed him you will hang. If you go free you can come back and live here but not as my husband.'

'Bloody women,' said H.E..

Adam said, 'Does she know I'm to be arrested?'

H.E. belched and chuckled and filled Adam's glass, saying, 'Everyone knows. But don't worry about the small things. We'll work it all out tomorrow.'

A comforting brandy-glow settled on Adam, drawing a velvet veil across his anger and humiliation. He looked at his drunken drooping friend H.E. and felt the need to speak before the bloody man fell asleep.

'Why does Cretikos call you Lordship?' he asked.

H.E.'s face screwed into a ghastly grin – the purple map of broken veins wriggling on his yellow skin. He said, 'Didn't you hear? The worst thing that could happen. My three brothers – all killed last year. In France. One shell got 'em all.'

'One shell? How?'

H.E. giggled, sucking at his brandy.

'Can you imagine. The silly buggers gathered for a birthday treat. In a trench of all places. A damn great Hun bomb landed on 'em. All three. Gone in a flash – quite literally.'

'Bloody hell.'

'Gets worse. The shock did for my old Pater. Within a week he'd popped off leaving me all his damned debt. So now I'm Lord-sodding-Taunton. Last bloody thing I wanted – all the expense and bother – all that change. My whole bloody life's changed. The whole bloody world's changed.'

Adam nodded, feeling wise and philosophical, forcing words through the velvet veil. 'You're right,' he said. 'Everything's changed. Except that Prussian woman's accent.'

'What Prussian woman?'

'Eva. My bloody Prussian wife. She sounded like a bloody Prussian recruiting sergeant. Christ. What a way to speak. Why have I never noticed it before? Do you know she wouldn't let me see my children or tell me where they are.'

'Difficult to see them, old chap. There's another change. Your sprogs are in England. Gone to school. Best thing for them.'

Adam felt his face rearrange itself into a deep frown. He gave several minutes calm consideration to the thought of his children at school in England before asking, 'When did they go?'

'Last month. They went with Queenie. She's settled 'em down near Taunton so the people on my estate can keep an eye on 'em. They'll go to Queenie in the holidays.'

After more careful thought Adam decided this seemed a good idea and mumbled, 'Dear old Queenie'll look after them.'

Ten minutes concentrated drinking later, H.E. pulled himself upright and said, 'I've remembered another change – bloody Kristina's gone too.'

'Gone? Where?'

'Off to Europe to find Kinskii's fortune – fat chance.'

H.E. giggled and said, 'Here's another thing to make you laugh – some silly bugger arranged a memorial service for that sod Christy. What a hoot. Funniest thing you've ever seen. Half a dozen women at the back wailed and howled all through. You wouldn't believe it – three nurses, a couple officers' wives and two Goan girls. Quite spoiled the singing.'

'Was Eva there?'

'Oh yes. She came with me. Ignored the noise and cried all the way through'

'And Kristina?'

'Good God, no. She had long gone on her way to Europe, thank heaven. She'd already diddled with half the men in Nairobi and was just starting on the other half when the war ended and she went like a shot....'

Chapter Thirty-Eight

Anyuka

Hungary: January 1919

In late afternoon with uncertain daylight fading, Kristina clambered from the train, twisting and sliding on hard-ridged ice, grabbing at the door handle, wrenching her shoulder.

Freezing wind flicked tiny pellets of snow into her face, flaying at her skin, stinging her ears. She glared at the bleak grey clouds in anger. *God. What an awful country....*

She regained balance, dragged her trunk from the train, gathered the twins – handed down by a helpful but smelly peasant – and moved to the part shelter of a small tile canopy held up by splintered wood beams.

Unsure she had been wise to leave relative warmth and safety in Budapest, she straightened and looked around; wondering whether she preferred the disgusting heat and odours of the crowded train – with its risk of the terrible 'flu – or this fierce fresh air.

The station – a small wayside halt made up of a signal box and this canopy – seemed unconnected to the rest of the world. No other passenger disembarked and Kristina stood alone on the rail-side. The engine hauled out, shunting and grunting, throwing a shower of sparks into the spinning snowflakes, leaving Kristina in sudden panic. *Christ. What do I do now...?*

She pulled up the long collar of her fur coat, tipping tiny flecks of ice down her neck. Swearing, she turned to heave her trunk onto the wooden bench as a windbreak for the twins and hissing, 'Don't move till I say or you'll be whipped.'

They stared back – two four year old tots with heavy wool scarves wound round their faces and wide eyes barely visible under fur hats a size too big. She almost laughed at the sight of them wrapped and stuffed into so many clothes. Two little sausages sitting completely still, seeming stunned by the cold, thank God. *At last, I've found something to keep them quiet....*

A door banged. Kristina jumped and looked round to see a man climbing down from the signal box. She ran towards him dredging a few words of Magyar from deep memory and called, 'Can you help us? Where is the town? How do I get there? It'll soon be dark. Please help.'

He stood, eyes squinted against the snow and wind and in slow German said, 'Where do you want to go?'

287

Realising his German was little better than her Magyar, Kristina said, equally slowly, 'I am Countess Kinskii. I want to go to my husband's estate. Is it nearby?'

The man frowned and looked past her at the twins, his lined face softening.

'Please help me,' she said. 'This is our first time here. We don't know where to go.'

The man looked her up and down and stared again at the twins. Kristina, unsure he had understood, said again, 'I am Countess Kinskii.'

'Countess Kinskii?' he said and for some reason, seemed puzzled, then speaking slowly in a mixture of Magyar and German he said, 'Yes. I can help you. I go that way. Wait.'

He disappeared behind the signal box and returned leading a small horse pulling a farm cart. He wrapped the twins in a blanket and placed them in the back with the trunk, handed Kristina up onto the wooden seat and clambered alongside, throwing another blanket over Kristina's knees. He picked up the reins and paused, hunched forward against the wind. 'Countess Kinskii?' he asked. 'Did you say Countess Kinskii?'

Kristina nodded.

He frowned again and said, 'Which Countess Kinskii?'

Kristina controlled a surge of anger – *Damned questions* – and said in slow Magyar, 'I am Count Otto's wife.'

'Count Otto?' said the man. 'Count *Otto*?' He flicked at the reins and guided the horse in a curve away from the station. Kristina stared at him in sharp annoyance, sure that he chuckled. But his face remained calm as he checked the road and looked back over his shoulder at the twins.

'How long to the estate?' asked Kristina.

'An hour,' said the man and sat quiet for the next thirty minutes while the horse pulled them through soft snow across a flat plain.

His silence and the slow plodding journey gave Kristina time to think of her awful shock on landing at Marseille – this terrible winter and the awful chaos of war and disease.

And now look what she'd come to – dragging on a farm cart to God-knows where across a freezing snow-bound plain… *Oh Kristina. Why did you ever leave Africa.*

She glared over her shoulder at the twins. Once ashore on the frozen dock at Marseille, Kristina found that, for the first time since their birth she must care for them alone and without help. No servants at all. Not one.

God. What a bore. The unspeakable things children do. And such hard work. She'd no idea. The little devils were never still; never quiet; never clean; always hungry; forever disappearing. They wore her to a frazzle and worse – none of the men she tried to charm along the way showed interest in a tired woman with two small children however beautiful and available she made herself.

She found being from the beaten nations no fun. As soon as the French and Italians heard her German accent or Austrian name, they turned away – women ignoring her and men refusing help. She spent four terrible days in Milan, cold; alone; harried by those dreadful Italians and her own children's constant demands. Each day she spent hours at the main station, pushing and arguing to get seats on a train to Vienna or cooped up in a tiny hotel room with her bored, bickering children. She tensed at their every sniffle – *If either of you catch 'flu and pass it to me, I'll kill you....*

She found Vienna a city grey with fear, grey with cold, grey with defeat; devastated at the collapse of empire.

It took her five depressing days to get out – finally obtaining precious tickets on a crowded train to Budapest that wound along the filthy grey Danube under a filthy grey sky taking two days to complete a six hour journey.

She found the stink of defeat lay even heavier on Budapest. Kristina did not understand the politics but could see that the new republic was a mess – unable to import food or handle its enemies, internal and external. She saw Bolsheviks fighting in the streets; heard of Rumanian armies massing on the borders; workers refusing to work; peasants refusing to bring produce into the city. The whole damn place seemed to be falling apart and it took her three desperate days to discover where Kinskii's estate lay.

She sighed and glanced back again at the twins, hidden and silent under their snow-covered blanket. Her movement brought the driver to life. He turned his head and in his mixture of German and Magyar said, 'You are a fine lady but the Kinskii's are a big family. I'm not sure which one you married.'

Kristina scrabbled in her overnight bag and found her packet of letters and photographs. 'Here,' she said. 'Take a look.'

First she passed over the picture of Kinskii aged about five; then the older Kinskii – about fifteen – then the wonderful picture of Kinskii the hussar on his horse; glittering uniform, plumed helmet, sweeping waxed moustache.

The driver pulled the horse to a halt and held each square of faded card up to the sparse light. At the first he nodded and murmured, 'Yes. I thought so. That's him – that's Otto.' At the second he said, 'What a strong young man.' At the third he smiled and said. 'So that's what he became. Well done, Otto.'

With a surge of excitement, Kristina said, 'Did you know my husband?'

'Oh yes. We all knew Otto. He was a brilliant horseman.'

'But you didn't know he became bodyguard to the emperor?'

'No. After he left we never heard again.'

'He never came back? Never wrote?'

'No. We missed him. He was such a brilliant horseman.'

'You've already told me that.'

The driver studied each photograph again and said, 'Why are you alone? Where is Otto?'

'Dead. I'm his widow.'

The driver turned and Kristina saw tears start in his eyes.

'Dead? Where? How?'

'Before I tell anyone I must tell his mother.'

'And these children? Are they Otto's?'

Annoyed at his distress and the delay, Kristina snatched back the photographs and snapped, 'Of course. Please start moving again. How long before we're there?'

'About ten minutes.' He brushed tears away and pointed at snow-covered trees ahead. 'We are on the estate. Soon you'll see the house.' He flicked the horse into motion.

For the first time in this long journey Kristina began to think about what happened next – *What if Kinskii's family doesn't accept me? They must. I'm his wife – his widow. These are his children. Why did he never contact his family – did they survive the war...?*

She clutched at the packet and asked, 'Do my husband's family still live here?'

'His mother,' said the driver.

'Just his mother?'

'Yes.'

'Where is his father – or brothers?'

The driver shrugged.

'Don't you know?'

The driver shook his head.

'Are they dead in the war?'

The driver shrugged again.

'But his mother lives here?'

The driver nodded.

Kristina settled back, satisfied. The damned peasant had more or less said what she needed to know – if only the mother remained, the uncles and brothers must be dead; shot or blown up in the War. *Good. That'll make me an heiress. They'll thank me for bringing Kinskii's son to carry on the line....*

She peered through snow-flurries at a large house set on flat ground in a grove of trees. She pulled out her photographs and checked. *Yes. This is it. At last. The trees are taller and thicker, but it's the same house – grey-stone, stables at the rear. Oh God, I've found it.*

Kristina shaded her eyes and squinted, better to see through the falling snow and gathering dusk. The house seemed closed and shuttered. *Why should this be?* She turned to ask the driver but he jumped from the cart and took the horse's head, guiding towards the stables.

'Please take me to the front door,' called Kristina but he ignored her, shuffling through the snow shoulders hunched. Kristina could see no sign of life at the house. *Perhaps Kinskii's mother lives in the opposite wing?*

The cart drove into the stable-yard under an arch headed by a carved coat-of-arms made up of two rearing horses and the name 'Kinsky' laid out in flowing old-fashioned script.

Before Kristina could think of this her attention transferred to the stables as several half-doors swung open and heads popped out, swivelling to watch the cart pass towards a small cottage. Behind the heads she saw furniture, stoves and oil lamps. *My God. People live in there....*

The cottage door swung open framing an elderly woman in yellow lamplight. Kristina managed to follow the Magyar as the woman said, 'Who is this you've brought home, Imry?'

The driver helped Kristina down, whispering, 'This is Otto's mother.'

Kristina hissed, 'Bring the twins and luggage,' and with as much grace as possible slithered across icy snow to the cottage, nervous and unsure but wearing her brightest smile.

She began to say, 'Madame Kinskii, I am Kristina – ,' but the elderly woman raised a hand and in clear, educated German, said, 'Come in. Hurry. You'll die of cold out there. And children? You have two children? *Mein Gott,* we must get them in here by the fire.' Switching to Magyar she shouted, 'Imry. Bring those two poor things in here before they freeze.'

Kristina hurried into the warm cottage. The woman bustled past to take the twins from Imry and carry them into a small well furnished room. She dumped them on a huge soft chair by a blazing log fire, saying, 'There – that's better. You'll soon be warm again.'

To Kristina she said, 'You seem a fine lady. I don't know you but you and your children are welcome.'

In the few seconds it took to compose herself and begin again on her prepared introduction, Kristina looked deep into the elderly woman's strong dark eyes and handsome face and in a thrill of recognition saw Kinskii staring back. *My God. They look so alike....*

She took a deep breath and said, 'Madame Kinskii. I am Kristina. I am Otto's wife. These are his children. We have come home to you.'

Kristina expected shock or surprise but saw only a veil of dignified sadness settle across the woman's face and blur the deep dark eyes.

'Otto's wife? You are Otto's wife...?'

The woman's voice faltered. She lowered her head and whispered, 'I have waited years for news. Now a fine lady comes to tell me she is his wife and I know he is dead or he'd be with you.'

Kristina nodded and said, 'He died a hero. You should be proud of him.'

The woman straightened and looked at Kristina, her face sombre, her eyes clear once more. She said, 'And these are Otto's children? My grandchildren?'

Kristina nodded, full of admiration. *Here is a true aristocrat. Show a stranger no emotion, however hard or tragic the moment....*

Kinskii's mother knelt on the floor and studied the twins dozing in the big chair, their faces pink and pretty in the fluttering fire-glow. Kristina saw light of love pass over the old woman's face as she whispered, 'Twins. How beautiful. And so like Otto at the same age....'

Kristina peeled off her gloves, wincing at the sharp tingle of returning circulation in fingers and face. *God. It was colder than I realised....*

She said, 'Madame Kinskii. It is wonderful for us to be here. I hope the twins and I can stay and get to know you.'

Kinskii's mother rose to her feet with a strange sad smile and said, 'Oh, my dear lady. I am not Madame Kinskii. I am Anyuka, her maid. Madame Kinskii is in Vienna.'

Kristina shook her head – a sharp snatching movement.

'No. You don't understand. That man – Imry. He told me Otto's mother lives here. Now you tell me she's in Vienna.'

The woman said, 'Madame Kinskii *is* in Vienna – or perhaps near

Prague on one of her other estates. But Imry is right. Otto's mother does live here. I am Otto's mother.'

Chapter Thirty-Nine

Otto

The words pierced Kristina's heart. In a daze of confusion and shock she grabbed a wooden chair-back so tight her knuckles cracked. She whispered, 'Impossible. You can't be Otto's mother. You're a maid.'

With pained eyes, the woman whispered back, 'And what was Otto, my fine lady? Otto was a stable boy.'

Kristina squealed, 'A stable boy? My husband was a *stable boy*?'

She pointed at the twins in pure hatred – 'Are you telling me that these are the children of a *stable boy*?'

The woman nodded, 'Until he left here with the circus my son was a stable boy.'

With the circus? The CIRCUS. Oh God. Oh God in heaven. What did I marry?

Kristina slumped on to the chair in disbelief, whispering, 'But he was a nobleman – Count Kinskii. His family owned estates. He told me....'

Unable to say more, she stared in silent shock.

The woman shook her head and in a voice so quiet Kristina could barely hear said, 'I don't know what Otto told you or what he became but here at home Otto was Otto – nothing more.' Her fine dark eyes blurred with tears and she too sat down, head bowed.

Kristina glared without sympathy at the woman's distress then in sudden hope dragged the packet of photographs from her bag. 'You must be wrong,' she cried. 'We *can't* be talking of the same man. Look...I'll show you.'

With shaking fingers she dealt out the first picture like a playing card – Kinskii and this woman holding hands in front of the house. Kristina leaned forward pointing and said, 'There. He wrote on the back. 'My father's house.' *This* house. It belonged to his *father*.'

She dealt the second picture almost shouting, 'And *here* he wrote.... Oh damn. I'm not sure what he wrote but I think it says 'At home with a servant and the horses'. *You* are the servant.'

Finally she threw her trump card forward – Kinskii the hussar; straight, elegant and arrogant on his beautiful white horse; every inch the noble cavalryman. In triumph she snarled, 'There. How can *you* be his mother? He could *never* have been a hussar with a *maid* for a mother....'

The woman's dignified face crumpled and she wept, rocking back and forth, moaning, 'Oh my darling son. Oh Otto. How wonderful. Look what you became. Oh my darling son. How handsome….'

Fear clutched at Kristina's gut – *Mein Gott she means it. She's telling the truth….*

Down the years she heard the echo of so many questions turned aside – Kinskii's smile, his casual shrug….and his introduction on the night they met: 'I am Kinskii. Spelt with three 'i's' please. One in the middle and two at the end. No 'y'. Otto Kinskii. Count Otto Kinskii….'

The stable arch. Oh God. That name on the stable arch….

Weak with dread she whispered, 'Tell me…please tell me. What was Otto's family name?'

Through tears, the woman smiled her sad smile and whispered back, 'He had none. He was Otto. Just Otto.'

Stunned, Kristina felt her whole life and personality shatter. She sagged in the hard wooden chair, head down, deep in despair, not responding when Kinskii's mother pulled herself together, hugged Kristina and said, 'I'll attend to the children.'

For an hour Kristina sat without moving – struck rigid by depression so black; so awful; it killed all will.

She watched with blank eyes when Kinskii's mother took the children – *To where? Who cares.*

She listened without interest to the splashing and shrieks of delight from a bathroom somewhere in the house – *Whose children? A bloody stable boy's children, that's whose….*

She sat sweating and sick in her fur coat and hat, unable to act or to think beyond destitution; unable to see a way forward – *I'm lost. Oh God, I'm lost….*

She made no effort to help when Kinskii's mother dragged the heavy coat and hat from her back and head and pulled her away from the fire, crying, 'Oh my fine lady, you'll die of heat-stroke.' – *Fine lady? Me? No. I'm the wife of a damned lying Hungarian stable boy….*

Crushed and defeated, Kristina collapsed deep into a hole without past or future. Existing only in these awful moments and this awful place, she felt her soul die – wished to follow but could not summon the energy.

She remained hunched and silent until Kinskii's mother started feeding thick delicious soup into her mouth. Unable to resist, her lips fastened on to a soft chunk of beef. She sucked it in and licked around the spoon, greedy for more.

Kinskii's mother leaned forward with another spoonful and whispered in her soft educated German…. 'Otto was such a beautiful baby – just like your lovely twins. He was born in this house and from the first loved horses. By his fifth birthday….'

…By his fifth birthday Otto – already a brilliant horseman – knew his skill brought him privileges denied the other estate children.

For instance why did *he* – little Otto – live in a proper house by the stables with proper beds and chairs and things when the other estate children lived with several families jammed together in wooden huts, or partitioned barns, sleeping on hay bales. And why was *he* – little Otto – treated with such respect by all the estate workers and allowed to play where he liked – even in the big house when Madame was away?

Until the age of five this seemed quite natural, because of his fantastic skill on horseback. He often explained this to the other children – 'If you learn to ride like me, you can live in a house like mine.' – until his mother heard and scolded him. 'Don't say such things,' she hissed. 'You'll get us both into trouble,' but never explained why.

On his fifth birthday a tall handsome man with lovely dark hair, beautiful clothes and a big black moustache came to the estate and made Otto stand in front of the big house with his mother and look at a small black box. This seemed silly and Otto – anxious to ride and test a new horse that appeared in the stable that morning – had no time for such nonsense. But his mother, dressed in her best apron and for some reason nervous, held his hand so hard it hurt, hissing at him to be still and turn his face towards the box.

Oh, how annoying but the man was clever – he understood; laughing and saying, 'Let him go. He's far more interested in the horses than in me and I want to see how he rides.'

Otto felt sorry when the man left – he seemed so kind and when alone hugged Otto, saying, 'You're a clever boy and a brilliant rider. Your mother and I are proud of you.' But Otto had other things to think of and soon forgot him.

Oh, Otto knew he was clever and more intelligent than those around him and for his mother this became a problem. Although the other servants and estate workers tried their best to keep his mother's secret, by the time Otto reached ten years old he had a fair idea of why he lived a better and different life than the other estate children.

But over the years, although no one in the close-knit estate society ever dared say anything definite, the occasional whispered word or ribald comment helped Otto work out his background and his mother's place on the estate, but could not identify his father – until his fifteenth birthday when the man returned.

Otto's mind raced back to when he was five. Then he had thought nothing of the man, but this time revelation came in a flash of kinship that passed between them the moment he looked into the man's eyes. He almost blurted out the word but managed to hold back.

His mother said, 'Otto. This is Count Karl. He is visiting the estate and wants to meet you and see you ride.'

Count Karl?

Count Karl…. Count Karl *Kinsky*….

Otto had heard the name – whispered…*whispered*….but never spoken.

This is the man…. this *man* is the one who…. Otto looked at his mother in anger at her soft acceptance at what this man – this Karl *Kinsky* – had done.

Otto blinked in shock and glared without speaking – knowing his strong self-confidence intimidated most people – but this man simply smiled and patted Otto's shoulder, saying, 'I understand you are in charge at the stables,.

Otto nodded.

'You are young to be in charge. I'm proud of you.'

Otto's mind snarled, *If you're proud, why don't you stay here with us?* – but he didn't speak. Instead, he shrugged.

The man asked Otto to stand with his mother in the same place as ten years before. Otto stood straight and firm, showing his strong arms and slim-but-solid body to the camera, chin raised, eyes direct at the lens using his imperious look – his independent look that said here is no common worker.

The man took several pictures then shook Otto's hand, saying, 'Now we'll go to the stables. Bring out the best horse and show me how you ride. I've heard you're very good.'

To oblige his mother – and the sick look of pride on her face – Otto leapt on to the largest, most difficult horse in the stable and set to, galloping back and forth on rough ground behind the house. For half an hour he rode – *performed* – with great daring and perfect control.

He swerved and swung the horse through a ballet of spectacular frenzy; twisting and dancing; jumping impossible obstacles; sliding tight dramatic turns so sharp he heard his audience gasp and applaud his courage and control.

He leapt out of and into the saddle at speed – skipping from stirrups to ground and back again or grabbing the horse's mane to dive forward over its shoulder and neck; somersaulting back into the saddle from the other side.

With a long lance he rode down standing and moving targets from every angle, picking them with astonishing ease – in between, performing every trick he knew or had seen or had heard of.

For a dramatic finish he tipped under the horse's belly and hanging on by one leg hooked to a stirrup, head only millimetres from the dirt, he swooped at full gallop down a curved line of coloured handkerchiefs hidden in the grass. Snatching with both hands, he missed not one and – my God. – felt good showing off to this man; whoever he was.

Amazed at his own performance, Otto hauled the horse to a skidding halt; arms held high; head back; lungs pumping; heart thumping with conceit.

Mother looked overcome with pride, but the man simply clapped – a restrained polite tapping of palms – and said, 'Very good. Now I must speak with your mother for an hour. Please excuse us.'

Otto's fists clenched as the man touched his mother's arm and led her towards the big house. In the look on her face Otto understood his own origins with a mixture of pride and hate....

Revived by the combination of soup and story, Kristina gathered together enough shards and tatters of her personality to glare at Kinskii's mother in contempt. She tried to snarl an insult: *You stupid woman. You've ruined us all...*but her throat – so dry it hurt – managed only a hoarse rattle.

To Kristina's annoyance Kinskii's mother mistook the sound for a sob. She patted Kristina's shoulder and said, 'Rest a little more, my fine lady. There's more to the story.'

Kristina croaked again, trying to interrupt but the woman carried on with a sad smile....

'Poor Otto. I know he hated seeing his plump middle-aged mother mooning over a bald elderly man but Otto didn't know us when we were young. Oh, the handsome Count Karl thought me so pretty and we were as foolish as all young people. When Madame realised what had happened she banished the Count. Almost six years passed before he took advantage of Madame's absence and returned for Otto's fifth birthday. Oh she was so furious when she discovered he had been to see us – so angry she banned him from ever coming to this estate again. But ten years later he came again. He knew what a fine young man Otto had become and wanted to see him, so took the chance. Of course it turned out to be a mistake....'

...Otto found himself unable to forgive either his mother or the Count. Why had they done this to him? Why had they made him meet the Count in such a way? Why could Mother not have warned him...prepared him for this abrupt meeting. Seeing his mother's simpering acceptance of this man and the way she disappeared with him into the big house caused Otto great shame and anger.

Although none of the estate workers said anything in his hearing, for days afterwards Otto imagined the sniggers and comments in half whispers that struck him like arrows.

Over the next few weeks Otto withdrew into himself, becoming sullen and rude – to his mother and to everyone else. When the photographs came by post Mother showed him with such pride but he glanced at them and in anger threw them down on to the table. He said nothing. Not a word. He just tossed them skidding across the polished wood and walked out....

...Kinskii's mother wept and said, 'But when he ran away I found two of the pictures missing – those that you brought back. They must have meant something to him or he would not have kept them all those years.'

Kristina's voice returned enough for her to croak, 'Where did he go?'

'I don't know. For all these years I have never known. When he left, he went with a circus that stopped here for a few days. The owner heard of his riding tricks and asked him to perform. He never said goodbye. He just disappeared. I heard no more of him – not a word – until you came through my door to tell me he is dead.'

Kristina shuddered.

Dead. Oh God. What a horrible word....

Kristina flew again to the terrible vision of Kinskii's death. That awful night high in a forest clearing. Her dead husband, bundled and bound in stained blankets; his dead killer, a pile of buffalo meat awaiting butchery. Wavering red-yellow firelight flickering a ghastly dance....

Sick with the horror of it all, Kristina could stand no more.

'I must sleep,' she whispered and Kinskii's mother wrapped her in a soft eiderdown on a wide bed in a warm room. Sure she would never sleep – if she did Kinskii would come and mock her – Kristina lay curled and confused, listening to snow pellets flicker against the cottage in rising wind. How could she survive all she had heard?

Oh God, this is worse than when Kinskii died....

As the thought ended she fell into deep abrupt dreamless sleep until next morning when she woke completely recovered; surprised to find her head had worked out a plan fully formed.

Chapter Forty

Kristina's Plan

My God. How brilliant....

Kristina saw with amazing clarity what to do next. Whilst deep in sleep the far reaches of her brain had sorted itself out; banishing depression and bringing her fully awake primed with energy.

Resisting the urge to leap from the bed she forced herself to curl up in her eiderdown and analyse the plan, running it back and forth through her mind.

The pictures.... Those pictures.... They're the clue.

Gathering the eiderdown about her shoulders, she swung her feet on to the floor, toes curling at contact with cold stone. Retrieving her bag from a chair, pausing to throw a log on the almost dead fire-embers she dived back under the blankets and piled pillows behind her shoulders.

Sorting through the photographs she selected Kinskii as a soldier in the field and as a fine hussar on his tall white horse; lay the pictures across her eiderdown and dug Kinskii's official army papers from their hiding place in her bag.

Leaning forward she ran half closed eyes over the images and words...pondering...probing – *How the hell did a Hungarian stable boy turn himself into an Austrian Count...?*

She shivered at the hint of an answer whispered from beyond the grave.

Vienna. That's where it happened. Vienna. Soon as possible I must get to Vienna....

A clatter of feet and excited voices – the damned twins – broke her concentration. Cursing, she swept the pictures and papers out of sight but the noise faded as the twins raced off to somewhere else in the house.

She lay back, heart thumping; determined to escape this place fast. But first she faced three problems. The plan showed simple solutions for two, but the third....

Unable to resist a surge of energy, Kristina jumped from the bed and laughed to find herself fully dressed – stockings and all. *My God, what a state I'm in....*

She stripped naked, wrapped herself in the eiderdown and wandered out to find her luggage and clean clothes.

The aroma of roasting coffee drew her into a large kitchen where

Kinskii's mother turned exhausted eyes to Kristina and said, 'I haven't slept all night thinking of Otto.'

'What a terrible night for us both,' said Kristina forcing tears from her eyes and folding the woman into her arms. She even managed a reasonable sob in the old lady's ear and felt her hug returned.

She remained entwined until Kinskii's mother whispered, 'Where did my son die?'

'In Africa – killed by a buffalo.'

The old woman jerked upright and thrust Kristina away.

'A buffalo? In Africa? How did he get to Africa?'

'That's what I hoped you'd tell me,' said Kristina. 'But since you can't, let me tell you *how* he died.'

For twenty minutes Kristina told the old lady of Kinskii's life in Africa and Sakayo's account of the buffalo hunt. After a pause to gather courage she ended her story with Kinskii's death and burial and the plaque Adam set up to mark the spot.

To Kristina's surprise, Kinskii's mother listened without emotion in complete silence. When the tale ended she passed a cup of coffee to Kristina and said, 'I guessed at the time why Otto left – and his words on those pictures confirms I may be right. But I still find it difficult to forgive him.'

'Why did he leave?' asked Kristina.

'I think he blamed me for his shame and left here to confront his father.'

'But that would be in Vienna. Why did he go to Africa?'

The old woman shrugged. 'Who knows? Perhaps his father banished him.'

'So you think they met?'

'Perhaps. I cannot ask because I never saw his father again either.'

Kristina pulled the two photographs from her bag.

'What *did* he write,' she asked. 'I couldn't read the Magyar properly.'

Kinskii's mother turned the two photographs over. 'On the first showing him as a small boy he wrote, 'The house of my father', and on the second when older, 'At home I am only a caretaker of horses'.'

'What did he mean?' asked Kristina.

The old lady shrugged. 'He must have written those words after he left here. In the first I think he's claiming his position – showing he is son of the landowner. In the second he's showing what he has become – a lowly caretaker of no importance in his own father's house. Why he should write such things I don't know.'

Kristina said, 'I'll go to Vienna and find out.'

'From whom?' asked the old lady. 'And why?'

'I came to find my husband's family and claim his inheritance. It gave me great shock to meet you and hear the truth. Now I'm determined to discover what happened to him after he left here.'

'You may bring trouble on yourself.'

'I don't care. I must know. I'll go tomorrow.'

Kinskii's mother said, 'Impossible. Look out the window. It started last night.'

To Kristina's horror snow swirling out of dirty grey cloud, covered flat ground up to the waist of a man struggling towards a barn.

'My God. How long will this last?'

'Days or weeks – even perhaps a month. We can never tell. It's a present from Russia.'

'What shall I do?'

'My dear fine lady – you must stay here. You have no choice. Nothing can move in snow like this – no trains, no horses and certainly no people. Imry may struggle to his signal box to look for telegrams, but that is all. There are many times when even *he* can't make it.'

'Telegrams?'

'Yes. Imry is stationmaster and postmaster. He does his best but sometimes it's impossible.'

'So I can send or receive a telegram?'

'Yes. If Imry can get to the signal box.'

Kristina said, 'Where are the twins?'

'Safe and warm in the barn, playing with the other children. We always keep them inside during winter.'

'What a wonderful idea,' said Kristina; her brain racing through all possibilities.

She made a decision – 'So we can stay with you?'

'Of course. To take my grandchildren away in this weather and at this time would be criminal. Apart from the snow and ice we have an awful 'flu throughout our land and those terrible Bolsheviks everywhere just waiting for fine ladies to fall into their hands. God knows what they'd do if they caught you.'

Kristina smiled and nodded, doing her best to control a surge of excitement – *Perfect. Absolutely perfect. She's taking charge....*

For the next few weeks Kristina placed herself in the care of Kinskii's mother and settled to the quiet comfort and warmth of the house. The old woman looked after Kristina and the twins with all the skills of a born servant allowing Kristina to relax and apply full concentration to the first part of her plan – making friends with Kinskii's mother and being kind to the twins.

She found both tasks easy – especially being kind to the twins as she hardly ever saw them. Each morning Imry lifted them over new snowdrifts and into the barn where they joined a dozen other estate children for a day of play and lessons. Within a week the twins began to speak Magyar. Within a month their astonishing fluency delighted Kristina and the third and most difficult part of her plan began to work itself out in her mind.

But first she needed money.

Now, for the first time in her life, Kristina felt panic at a lack of money. She struggled to bring her mind to bear and give deep thought to what she realised could become a desperate problem.

Her family in Berlin? *Probably all dead.*

Eva? *No help – she's as broke as me and God knows where Adam is.*

H.E. seemed to be her only chance – *I may have been rude to him before I left, but after all – the bloody man is my fiancé* – so she prepared a careful telegram, asking him for help.

She couldn't think of a figure so requested enough to cover her return with the twins to East Africa plus a little extra to pay for the second part of her plan – a week or two in Vienna tracking down Kinskii's past. Surely he had left traces such as property or bank balances she could claim as his widow.

'Can you send this telegram for me?' she asked Imry.

'Certainly, Madame. As soon as the storm ends.'

Snow continued to howl in from Siberia and brought with it the 'flu epidemic – so the estate workers believed. The illness passed Kristina by but struck hard at the close-packed families in the stables and barns – and Kinskii's mother.

The old lady went down with fever so awful the estate workers turned for leadership to Kristina. Using sturdy Prussian methods she took control, organising those in reasonable health to nurse and feed the sick. She slaved and supervised night and day, working as doctor and matron, surprised to find deep satisfaction in the work.

She kept special watch on Imry, worried that if he fell ill and died her telegram would never go and she'd be imprisoned in this place.

Some 'flu victims died within three days, their phlegm-filled lungs failing in an agony of pneumonia. Others struggled through fever and delirium, to recover slowly at first, then to regain strength enough to help nurse to those newly ill.

After two weeks Imry managed to reach his signal box through the diminishing storm. 'I sent your telegram, fine lady,' he said on his return. 'Next week I'll go back for your reply.'

Kinskii's mother began to recover – thank God – and Kristina basked in the glory of her approval. 'Having you here is like being with Madame again,' croaked the old lady through her rasping sore throat. 'I want you to stay for ever.'

'Of course,' said Kristina. 'The twins and I love it here. This is our home.'

A week later Imry returned from another journey to his signal box. 'Your reply, Madame,' he said, passing over a twisted sliver of paper.

The cramped print read: ENOUGH MONEY TO GET YOU HOME SENT ACCOUNT OF BRITISH EMBASSY BUDAPEST STOP USE NAME ADAMS ESTATE TO UNLOCK SAFE STOP DON'T ASK FOR MORE AS I'M BROKE STOP HURRY BACK END

Kristina gritted her teeth in triumph. Her spirits lifted and she laughed. Typical H.E.. Clever sod; cunning spy; crafty diplomat. No sign of his name or title. Just a simple riddle meaningless to anyone else.

In a flash, part three of her plan became obvious. *My God, I'm clever. This solves everything....*

Chapter Forty-One

Budapest

Kristina strode along the railway platform, her boots squeaking on dry packed snow. How much longer before a damned train would come and get her out of this God-forsaken place?

Last night the storm died and disappeared. Today a pale yellow sun-disc hung low in the eggshell sky, sparking diamonds across the ice-covered plain. Kristina squinted east along the line, looking for a smudge of smoke or a black dot or *anything* that would show movement in this shining white wilderness.

She stamped her freezing feet in disappointment. If a damned train didn't arrive soon she'd need to get down to the village and find a place for the night – or worse, return to the estate. *Oh God, no.*

Several days ago she prepared for travel; enough clothes for a week chosen and packed. She decided not to take her big trunk so Kinskii's mother found a small tooled leather valise – 'Make sure you bring it back. It belongs to Madame' – and Kristina filled it as tight as possible with suitable clothes and linen. *Enough to be going on with....*

This morning, as soon as she saw clear sky Kristina roused Imry and ordered him to bring his horse and cart. Before climbing onto the hard wooden seat she hugged Kinskii's mother and kissed the twins.

She chuckled and settled for the cold bumpy journey alongside Imry, quickly dismissing her last sight of the twins in their heavy boots and lumpy clothes running through the snow to be with their friends. *They're Kinskii's children in Kinskii's home. They're safe and well. I've done my best.*

Now Kristina marched along the station platform trying to keep warm and thinking only of how soon she would be gone from here. For two hours she waited; sitting with Imry in his cold signal box or striding up and down the tiny platform trying to keep warm, feeling more and more frustrated and annoyed.

From the signal box she heard Imry banging his levers and the big signal arm clatter down to its stop position. With lifting hope, she saw a smear of black against the white horizon.

Thank God. She grabbed her valise from under the canopy and watched the train materialise from the ice-mirage and haul into the station on a bow-wave of powdered snow.

It dragged to a squealing halt and a thousand eyes stared at Kristina. As far as she could see the damned train seemed completely full –

every carriage and every inch of spare space stuffed with farmers and peasants and their fat women.

Kristina looked in dismay at the disgusting tableau of beards, fur hats and heavy cheap cloth. How the hell could she force her way on? And how safe will she and the children be with these terrible people? – probably all Bolshevik murderers.

Along the train a compartment door banged open. A man leaned out, calling in Magyar, 'Come in here, Madame. We have a place for you.'

Uncertain, Kristina looked up at Imry. He waved at her – an urgent pushing movement – and shouted, 'Hurry. You'll delay the train.'

She slithered along the icy platform and clambered into the compartment, surprised to find it occupied by only two men, both well dressed – clean-shaven and wearing well made suits and shoes; expensive Russian fur coats folded on top of their luggage. No smelly peasants, thank God.

Speaking German, she said, 'You're very kind. How do you have a place to yourselves like this?'

'Ah, you are Austrian,' said one of the men, ignoring her question. 'Please sit down, Madame Kinsky.'

Startled, Kristina said, 'How do you know my name?'

He pointed to her valise. For the first time she saw the Kinsky coat of arms repeated in a small design throughout the tooled leather.

She laughed – her tinkling little flirty laugh – and gave him full force of her violet eyes. 'How observant.' she trilled. He winked and lifted her valise into an overhead rack, saying, 'I am Béla Kun. My colleague is Tibor Szamuely.'

Both men stared at Kristina as though expecting some reaction and she didn't know why. To fill the awkward silence she said, 'I am Countess Kinskii. My late husband came from a branch of the family with different spelling – three 'i's' – one in the middle and two at the end. No 'y'. I borrowed this valise from my aunt.'

Béla Kun raised his black arched eyebrows, wrinkling his domed forehead. Szamuely stared with cold hard eyes, his skinny face unmoving. Kristina stared back, determined not to be intimidated.

The train jerked into motion. She removed her heavy coat and fur hat, fluffed out her long hair and arranged herself on the seat opposite and allowed them to look her over. She saw immediate effect on Béla Kun. The other cold bastard just looked away.

'Well now, Countess Kinskii with three 'i's',' said Béla Kun, 'Why are you travelling alone in these difficult times?'

'I have business in Budapest connected with my late husband's estate.'

'Your business must be important.'

'Of course.'

'Your husband died in the war? – or in some local conflict?'

'In the war. I prefer not to speak of it.'

'Naturally. But I must say you are brave to travel alone and braver still to go without protection to Budapest. What business could be so important that you take such risk?'

She frowned at the direct question – *The bloody man's interrogating me* – and said, 'I've heard news of Bolsheviks fighting in the streets and this dreadful 'flu everywhere. But it can't be *that* bad. People exaggerate so. Have you been to Budapest recently? Is it true?'

Béla Kun chuckled and said, 'Szamuely and I are returning after two months absence to find out for ourselves. We've been called back to help.'

'Ah,' said Kristina. 'You are doctors.'

'In a manner of speaking,' said Béla Kun.

'Specialists?'

'I suppose you could say that.'

Szamuely barked in sudden laughter – a harsh sound that made Kristina jump.

'So, my dear Countess,' said Béla Kun. 'Will you join us in some vodka? We are faced with a slow journey and should make the most of it.'

Kristina hesitated, studying this strange pair; frightened by the strength of will dominating Béla Kun's deep dark eyes but thrilled and attracted at the chink of weakness in his plump lips and sly approach.

Her mind moved fast. *This one seems a good bet. I'll stick with him....*

She giggled and said, 'Of course. Let's drink vodka and enjoy our time together....'

Next morning Kristina lay in a big bed, her head bursting with pain, trying to recall what happened on the train yesterday.

She groaned and swivelled her eyes round, wondering how she came to be in this enormous room – what the hell had she been drinking? *Oh God. That terrible Polish vodka....*

She concentrated hard and remembered several hilarious hours of reckless boozing with Béla Kun and a series of others who crowded into the compartment during the journey.

308

At some point she must have admitted ignorance of Budapest because in her mind wavered a vague picture of Béla Kun patting her hand – or was it her knee? – and saying, 'Don't worry. We have a big hotel. You can come with me. I'll look after you.'

That skinny cold fish Szamuely refused to drink and left the compartment. She and Béla Kun became giggling stupid – as did several burly young men who wandered in from the corridor and joined the drunken party. Only when two of them helped Kristina off the train and into a big motor car at Budapest did she realise they must be some form of police squad.

The car swept from the station through cheering crowds waving a forest of red flags and placards – written in damned Magyar so Kristina couldn't read them. Béla Kun acknowledged the mob with a wide smile and slow regal movements of his arm.

Kristina found this most confusing. Controlling her fuddled brain with difficulty, she asked, 'What's happening? Are you important?'

'Not yet,' he said, holding her up straight. 'But in a few days...well...you'll see.'

She leaned against him, grateful for the support, wondering how the hell he'd recovered so fast from all that damned vodka?

Working through the confusion of events, Kristina's mind produced pictures of Béla Kun jumping from the car – leaving her to be hauled out by his guards and half carried into the hotel. They guided her to a lift then along a corridor to this room and laid her on the bed. She tried to speak as they left but although words formed in her head, brain and tongue seemed disconnected so she gave up and allowed herself to float to oblivion.

Now she lay here in the half-light of this warm, luxurious curtained room with heavy wooden furniture and a large log fire, wondering how on earth her clothes came to be scattered all round and how she came to be naked in bed alongside Béla Kun. *Bloody hell....*

She lifted the bedclothes and peeked. *The damned man is naked too. I wonder if he....*

Trying not to disturb him she peered at herself down the tube of blanket; running her hands across breasts and stomach; searching for marks or bites; checking buttocks and soft inner thighs, her fingers sliding and lingering in a flush of pleasure. *Should I or shouldn't I?...No...I'll wait till he wakes....*

Shivering with deprival she forced her hand away, slipped out of bed and tiptoed to the window. Poking her head between curtains she looked down on...roadblocks and machine guns commanding a cobbled boulevard alongside the wide grey Danube and pointing across two bridges over the river.

Red flags waved over the barricades and a hundred or so men in grey uniforms crouched behind barriers, aiming rifles along the road.

Bolsheviks.

In shock she pulled back from the window, snatching the curtains shut. Béla Kun shot upright, shouting, 'What do you see?'

She squeaked, 'Armed men. All round the hotel.'

He said, 'Holy Christ.' and jumped up, racing past her to peek between the curtains. Kristina ran back, dived under the covers and hid her head in the warm safe dark. From the window Béla Kun gave a shout of laughter.

'Come here, you stupid woman,' he yelled. 'Come and see. They're ours. Look. They're all facing the other way. If they were attacking they'd be aiming *at* us. That idiot Szamuely put his men on guard without telling me. Christ, what a fright. I thought the right wing had taken over.'

She tiptoed back to where he held the curtains wide and peeped out.

'They're ours? But they're Bolsheviks.'

'That's right. They're ours and they're Bolsheviks.'

'*Mein Gott.* Are you a *Bolshevik*?'

'Of course. Today I'm a Bolshevik. And soon I'll be head of state.'

'Really?'

'Yes, really. For God's sake, woman – you still don't know who I am. Now come back to bed. You were too drunk last night and you owe me a rail ticket. Get into bed and get hold of this.'

In a state of quivering excitement Kristina dived back on the bed, took hold of what he offered and with all her skills and tricks set about servicing him.

Wonderful. A head of state.

She'd done all this before in Berlin with senior government ministers, but never with a head of state. *Oh father – you'd be proud of me. A head of state. Look how far your little daughter has come....*

But Béla Kun seemed in too much of a hurry to enjoy her attentions. After a few minutes he pushed her aside, leaped from the bed and disappeared into the bathroom calling, 'Get me out some clean clothes. Hurry.'

She fiddled with the straps of a big trunk and found a mixture of clothes – including dresses and ladies undergarments. She wrapped herself in a flowered robe and laid out shirts, ties, and clean linen on the bed. He rushed from the bathroom and began to dress, snapping; 'Socks. You've forgotten socks. For God's sake find me some socks.'

Kristina delved into the trunk, piling clothes on the bed, saying, 'These dresses – do they belong to your wife?'

'Yes.'

'Where is she?'

'Not here. That's all you need to know.'

'Where are you going now?'

'To the National Assembly. I told you – soon I'll be head of state. Now get out of my way. I'm in a hurry.'

'I'm trying to straighten your tie.'

'Oh for God's sake,' – but he stood and waited while she teased at his collar.

She said, 'When will you be back?'

'I don't know. Late tonight or tomorrow.'

'What do I do until then?'

'You wait here. Don't leave this room. My men are guarding the door. If you need anything – food or drink – bang on the door and ask. They'll attend to it. I'll be back later. Be ready for me. And wear your own damned clothes. That robe belongs to my wife.'

Kristina calmed her nerves with the luxury of a deep hot bath and the satisfaction of washing and brushing her hair and cleaning her teeth and dressing in fresh linen – some her own and some from Béla Kun's trunk, blessing the luck that brought her here. The alternative – searching the cold, snowy 'flu-ridden city for accommodation – made her shudder. She'd settle here for a few days, complete the third part of her plan then slip out to the British embassy to collect her money and disappear to Vienna.

Disappear. She pondered the word and decided it held surprising attraction.

Over the next week she enfolded Béla Kun in a cunning mix of wife and mistress, surprised at the speed with which he became used to her presence.

When he returned late at night, usually exhausted, she poured his drinks, ordered and served his food at a table near the window, and listened to long tales of his meetings and speeches and the trouble his men stirred up in the streets of Budapest.

Each morning she chose and laid out his clothes, chatting like a wife, watching his mood, feeling him become more and more relaxed in her presence. Then one morning he said, 'Get dressed. I need you with me to take notes at a meeting. You're the only one I can trust who speaks and writes good German. If you do well you'll come with me every day. Think you'll be able to do it?'

'Of course,' said Kristina in delight. *At last. A route out of this damned room and this damned town....*

Chapter Forty-Two

Two Telegrams

Fighting a yawn, Kristina looked round the room at these dull old men – every single one a gas-bag. Revolution by boredom. Mumble your way into power. Is this how they did it in Russia? *My God. What a farce.*

She managed to turn the yawn into a sigh and pretended to scribble a note. One of the speakers switched from Magyar to German and she turned her scribble into a real record of his words.

At least this dreary job kept her out of that damned room and sometimes in the last couple of weeks she even managed to get out of the hotel – always dragging two security men in tow. Béla Kun insisted on absolute control – never allowing her out alone. The security men stayed with her even in the corridors of the enormous hotel Kun's Bolsheviks had turned into the unofficial headquarters of his damned Soviet Republic.

She raised her head and looked round this collection of old fogies. The English phrase slipped into her mind unbidden; the words so exact – so neat- in describing this collection of elderly windbags.

Her slight inward smile brought an answering glimmer from across the table. Lowering her eyes – a brief flirtatious flutter – she peeped to see who the hell dared play games in a place like this.

Ah yes. Doctor Balogh. Youngest of the fogies. She reckoned him to be around forty. A heavy little man with thick brown hair and soft eyes. During break he sidled through the crowd and introduced himself, 'Ah, Madame Kun,' he said. 'I am Doctor Balogh, how pleasant to meet you.'

Kristina laughed and whispered, 'I am not Commissar Kun's wife. I am his...secretary.'

She saw embarrassment chase across his face at her delicate pause and raised eyebrow. She extended her hand. 'A natural mistake,' she said, smiling, 'I must say I have yet to see the lady myself so I've no idea what she looks like either. What are you a doctor of?'

'My dear Madame...I am senior doctor at the hospital. I am here to report on the 'flu epidemic. May I know your name?'

Senior doctor? 'Flu epidemic? Mein Gott. What luck.... This man slotted into her plan like a peg. Perfect. She held his gaze for several seconds, watching hope grow in his soft brown eyes.

'My dear Madame,' he whispered, 'I hope I did not embarrass you.'

She touched his arm, a story to tell him forming in her head.

'Think nothing of it. A simple mistake. You have no need to mention it again.'

'Oh thank you, my dear Madame. Thank you so much. But please…your name?'

'Eva. I am Eva.'

'Madame. I cannot call you Eva. Your husband's name…please…give me a name I may use.'

She lowered her eyes. 'I have no husband. I am widowed. Please just call me Eva.'

'A widow? Oh poor Madame, you are a widow. How long? Was it the war? Can I help in any way?'

'No. Not really. Although perhaps you could…. No. I must not impose. No. You cannot help me in any way at all. I am here in Budapest alone and lucky to have met Commissar Kun. He…looks after me quite well but….'

'Madame Eva. I see there is something. Allow me to assist. Please. I am at your service.'

'It is not possible.' – Kristina lowered her eyes – 'Commissar Kun watches me all the time.'

'But he is away now. I know it.'

'Yes…but…those awful security men…they follow me everywhere…but wait – I know. The 'flu. Tonight or tomorrow. Can you come to the Hungaria Hotel tonight or tomorrow?'

'My dear Madame Eva. The Hungaria is one place I cannot go. They will never allow me in.'

'They will if you have a proper reason. Listen. Tonight I will contract 'flu. I will call the hospital for a doctor and you must come. Please…It is so important to me.'

'Good. I am on duty tonight. This awful 'flu attacks fast so you must catch it this afternoon and call me this evening. I shall come immediately. Will we be alone in your room?'

'I promise.'

'Then I will surely come, dear Madame.'

Kristina found her security men and said, 'I feel ill. Take me to the hotel.'

Back in the room she refused food and ran an extra-hot bath, sitting in scalding water until her face turned blotchy red. Then, wrapped in a fur coat, she ran-on-the-spot by the fire until wet with sweat – great patches staining her dress and flowing from her neck and armpits and streaming down her face.

Breathing hard from the effort she threw off the fur and banged on the door. The two security men reeled back at the sight of her scarlet face and laboured breath and the great damp sweat-patches on her dress. She managed a hacking cough and groaned, 'Bring a doctor.'

Changing into a nightgown she arranged herself on the bed against a pile of pillows; her long hair fluffed out across shoulders and breast...and waited.

Within thirty minutes Balogh plunged into the room whispering, 'My dear Madame Eva – those poor men are so frightened of the 'flu. They pushed me through the door, swearing they'll come no nearer until you are cured or dead.'

He sat on the bed listening to her antics. 'You mustn't laugh,' she hissed, 'I'm supposed to be ill.' She leaned forward to pat his hand, allowing her gown to drop open, watching his eyes flick down then back to her face. She asked, 'How long do we have before they wonder what's happening?'

'About half an hour. That would be a normal examination, dear Madame.'

'A *normal* examination?' She raised her eyebrows and the poor man turned pink. She patted his hand again – 'My dear Doctor...you may *certainly* examine me ...but first...you offered to help.'

From under the pillow she plucked two slips of paper and said, 'These are two important telegrams. Can you send them? I am unable to do so myself.'

'Why not, dear Madame?'

'Commissar Kun never lets me out. I dare not ask his men to help. Do you read and write German as well as you speak?'

'Yes Madame.'

'Good. Then you can translate one into Magyar for me.'

'Of course.'

She said, 'Listen. My sister, Kristina, married a Hungarian soldier – a hussar from the Kinsky estate east of here. When he died in the war she sent her children to live with his mother on the estate and tried to find work in Budapest. A month ago she wrote to me in Berlin and asked for help. I was horrified to realise from her letter that in order to live she had become.... Oh I'm sorry I cry at the thought, but what disgrace on our family.'

She stopped and heaved a hearty swallow that passed as an agonised sob. She continued in a tragic whisper.

'I came to Budapest to find my dear sister already dead. Oh damn

– I'm crying again. But what do you expect? My poor sister…the most awful circumstances…in a hovel…and of God knows what disgusting disease.'

Kristina managed to break down and weep properly, covering her face in a large white handkerchief Balogh produced. She peeked out to check the effect so far and saw his stricken face. *Good.* She gulped and continued.

'Somehow I must tell her poor mother-in-law. But how? I have written a telegram but it is in German and useless. The poor old lady speaks only Magyar. Please, *please* help me.'

'Of course, Madame Eva. Of course I'll help. And the other telegram?'

'It is written in English.'

'I do not know English, Madame, but can send it anyway.'

'How?'

'At the main post office they don't know English either. They send many telegrams in foreign languages by copying the words exactly as you write them.'

Kristina relaxed – *Thank God.*

'Oh Doctor Balogh. How shall I *ever* repay you. But there's another very small thing – I'll be eternally grateful if you…. No. I can't ask. It's too much. I'm going too far….'

'Please, my dear Madame Eva. Tell me. I'll help however I can.'

'There *is* one other thing…but I hesitate to ask – you are already too kind. It is difficult…I cannot allow my sister's mother-in-law to know the true circumstances of Kristina's death. The shame would kill her. Please, *please* help a little further. I have written the telegram as though it comes from a doctor saying how poor Kristina died in the 'flu epidemic. Please can you sign and send it as though from your hospital? You will help so much and save terrible embarrassment….'

She fell to weeping again and for a moment she thought she'd overdone it. But the poor fish took the telegrams with a promise to send them straight away. That night.

'Please bring me copies after they've gone,' she said. 'I'll be ill for a few more days so you can come tomorrow. How much longer do we have for a normal examination?'

He checked his watch. 'Almost twenty minutes.'

'Good. Come close and I'll show you an *abnormal* examination.'

The next evening he returned, staying for half an hour. After he had examined her and left happy, Kristina smoothed out the telegram forms he handed over. He had followed her instructions exactly and sent Anyuka's to Imry at the signal box.

She could not read the Magyar but knew exactly what the printed strips said:

FOR ANYUKA AT KINSKY ESTATE STOP REGRET TO INFORM THAT YOUR DAUGHTER-IN-LAW DIED OF INFLUENZA AT BUDAPEST MAIN HOSPITAL STOP LAST WORDS WERE FOR HER LATE HUSBAND OTTO AND HER TWINS WHOM SHE COMMENDED TO YOUR CARE STOP I ATTENDED THE DEATH AND ARRANGED COMMON GRAVE BURIAL END

Balogh signed with his full title and hospital address. *Most impressive. Those stupid peasants will never find me now....*

Kristina lay the English telegram alongside and read:

FOR HOCKLYFFE-EVANS AT NAIROBI GOVERNMENT HOUSE STOP TERRIBLE NEWS STOP TWINS DIED IN FLU EPIDEMIC STOP THEY BURIED ON ESTATE STOP I NOW IN BUDAPEST ON WAY HOME VIA VIENNA SOON AS MONEY IN HAND END

She went to bed triumphant and lay awake, planning her next move and savouring the freedom that death brought....

Chapter Forty-Three

Red Interlude

Kristina scuffed through dirty snow on the deserted Danube boulevard. Grey water rolled by, whipped into curls and ringlets by a bitter April wind. Shoulders hunched against the freezing air, she pulled her heavy fur coat tight and glanced back at her security men. They grinned and waved.

She flapped a hand over her shoulder and heard them giggle. She knew they thought her dalliance with Balogh amusing and conspired to keep it hidden from the Commissar, thank God.

'Why do you have me followed?' she shouted at Béla Kun when he first allowed her out for exercise and fresh air.

'No choice.' he snapped. 'Szamuely thinks you're a spy. He wants you arrested and shot. My men make sure that doesn't happen.'

She half believed him and took fright, keeping away from the British embassy. She first started exploring these streets with the intention of circling nearby then diving into the building. On earlier walks she had sauntered past and saw the heavy door shut fast – entry gained by shouting through a grille.

Impossible. Kun's gorillas would snatch her away before she got past '*Help.*' If that happened, Kun wouldn't wait for Szamuely. He'd shoot her himself.

She shuddered, weighed down by the fear and tension of four weeks juggling between Balogh and Kun. Oh the relief at being almost free.

Just one more task for Balogh and I'll be rid of this awful entanglement.

Kristina checked the time on a church clock across the river. Just gone three. Surely by now the poor fish must be in the British embassy with her note. This evening he'd bring the money and she'd be ready to escape.

'*Berlin,*' she promised Balogh. '*We'll go to Berlin.*'

'*Anywhere,*' he whispered. '*Anywhere but here. Away from these damned Bolsheviks before they kill or starve us all.*'

Kristina walked down to the bridge roadblock, stopping to joke with Szamuely's men. They would report her visit, confirming time and position – nowhere near the damned British embassy.

Nervous and impatient she returned to the hotel and for the rest of the afternoon paced her room, smoking cigarettes, her mind full of

Balogh and his task. Now she regretted her strict instruction – *'Don't come straight here from the embassy. Go back to work. Hide the money for a few days. When I'm ready I'll let you know.'*

For once he showed anger – *'Of course not, dear lady. Do you take me for a fool?'*

Kristina spent the next four days following Béla Kun around Budapest in a rolling drone of political verbiage. She became alarmed on the fifth day when a doctor she did not recognise rose to report on the 'flu epidemic and unrest caused by the latest food shortage.

That night she asked Béla Kun, 'Where's Doctor Balogh? I haven't seen him for a few days.'

'Balogh? That capitalist hyena? He's dead. Szamuely had him shot.'

'Shot. Why?'

'Szamuely's men caught the snivelling spying bastard leaving an imperialist embassy with a pocketful of their filthy money.'

Kristina coughed and swallowed and managed to say, 'When was he shot?'

'Two days ago. He'll be tried and found guilty next week.'

'Next week? But you say he's already dead.'

'Yes. But we still must try him or his execution isn't legal.'

Almost overcome by this topsy-turvy world Kristina squeaked, 'How did you catch him?'

'Szamuely's men followed him to the British embassy last week and arrested him as he came out. His imperialist paymasters must have been pleased with his work – they'd paid him well.'

'How much?'

Kun laughed – 'Enough to get him halfway round the world, I would think.'

Oh God. He knows.

'Was he interrogated?'

'Naturally.'

'Did he confess?'

'Of course. He'll have told Szamuely's men everything – absolutely everything – then begged for a bullet in his brain.'

Kristina's blood turned to ice and her heart almost stopped. She managed to ask, 'What did he say?' then – sure she would faint – held on to a chair.

Luckily, the Commissar – bored with the subject – did not notice. He turned away to pace the room, saying, 'I haven't seen the report yet. Nor has Szamuely. He's away in the country suppressing counter-revolution. We'll discuss it when he gets back. Now. Enough of that hyena Balogh. Let me tell you what happened in parliament today....'

He droned on into the night while she sat, trying to control her nerves – *He must not notice. I mustn't let him realise....*

For the next two months Kristina lived in the shadow of arrest and execution. Men she knew well and saw every day disappeared to be shrugged off by Kun as, 'Another dead hyena.'

Sure her turn would come she cursed Balogh's stupidity at getting caught – especially with her money – and kept out of Szamuely's way whenever he came to the hotel.

Gradually Kristina's fear diminished. Szamuely seemed too busy building his private army and murdering political opponents: *He can't be bothered with small fish like me....*

Her life continued in a dreary round of meetings. For several confusing days she acted as interpreter between Kun and a small South African general called Smuts, who spoke in fractured English difficult to follow and translate into German. These negotiations seemed to get nowhere. For the first time, Kristina detected despair in Kun's voice.

In early June Kristina noticed Szamuely was missing. Hoping he'd been shot – along with so many others – she asked Kun, 'Where's Szamuely? I haven't seen him for a few weeks.'

'Moscow. He's run off to Lenin to complain about me. I'll arrest the little bastard when he gets back. He's beginning to defy me in everything.'

When Szamuely returned, Kristina waited in hope but Kun took no action.

Her self-confidence began to revive, only to be shattered again by an incident one hot afternoon in June while Bela Kun dictated to her in the hotel room when a huge explosion shook the building, followed by hammering small-arms fire.

Kun hurried to the window. 'Counter revolution,' he shouted. 'The bastard counter-revolutionaries are shooting at me.'

'Shooting at *us*,' Kristina screamed.

Béla Kun rushed from the room, leaving Kristina helpless with fear.

Regaining control she peeped through the window to see a small warship on the Danube shooting shells at buildings on the bank. From vantage points on both sides of the river Szamuely's men replied with machine-guns and rifles.

Fascinated by this grandstand view she watched the engagement for almost two hours until the ship drifted downstream and the river fell silent.

'Where have you been?' she asked, when Béla Kun turned up two days later pale and exhausted.

'Trying to keep the army on my side,' he said. 'Come with me. We have work to do.'

For the next eight weeks Kristina raced around Budapest at Béla Kun's side, watching his Bolshevik revolution lurch from crisis to crisis. She felt danger all round and shared his fear of assassination. Wherever he turned for help there seemed no way to overcome the problems piling up on his ramshackle government.

By the last week of July Kun's spirit seemed broken. She knew he had lost all support – his Red Army beaten in battle and disintegrating; a White Army marching towards Budapest; Lenin ignoring frantic telegrams for economic help and military intervention; a coup by his own supporters discovered just in time and quashed.

'I must escape,' he told Kristina. 'The rightists will kill us all when they arrive.'

'What about me?'

'Find your own way out. What do I care about you?'

'You can't abandon me. Where are you going? You must take me. Even to Russia. I've supported you since the day we met.'

'That's not what Szamuely says. He has proof you're a spy.'

'How can you say that? You know he's lying.'

'You're all liars,' he shouted and stormed from the room.

Kristina stayed alone in the hotel for three days and nights while gunfire echoed through the city. Although her security men disappeared along with Bolshevik clerks from their offices throughout the building the near-deserted hotel continued operating as normal so she ate well and remained calm and her fear subsided.

On the last day of July she lay in bed dozing to escape the heat of afternoon when Kun burst into the room shouting, 'Clear all the drawers. Give me any papers you have here. I need everything. Hurry.'

She jumped from the bed, wobbly with sleep and cried, 'There's nothing here. You've already cleared the place.'

He pushed past and pulled out every drawer; opened every cupboard; dived to check under the bed; pulled out pictures and mirrors in a frantic scrabbling search, sweating and breathing hard.

Kristina sat on the bed watching; making no attempt to help. She said, *'Mein Gott.* You look terrible. What's been happening?'

He flopped down beside her on the bed. 'I'm leaving. I've resigned. Tomorrow I go to Vienna then to Russia.'

She grabbed his hand.

'Am I coming with you?'

'No.'

'Why not?'

'No room.'

'What do you mean?'

He pulled his hand away and stood, moving to the centre of the room.

'We have a train. It's full. Only special people are allowed on.'

She stormed forward and slapped him – a hard palm across the face and a backhand that left knuckle marks on his cheek. She screamed, 'You *will* take me with you. I will come on your damned train whether you like it or not.'

He stepped back, turning to go. Kristina ran round and blocked his path to the door.

'You can't come,' he said. 'It's a diplomatic train arranged by the French and British. They want us out of here without bloodshed. You need a special pass.'

She held out a hand. 'Give me a pass.'

He shook his head.

She wiggled her fingers. '*Give* me a pass,' she said.

He shook his head again. 'There's a list. You're not on it. If you're not on the list or not a journalist you're not allowed on the train.'

She said, 'I'm a journalist.'

'How?'

'You used my notes in your newspaper. That makes me a journalist.'

His head dropped. He frowned. Kristina could see his resolve fading. She returned to the bed and sat down keeping a hard-faced stare directly at him.

He grunted; pulled a card from his pocket and threw it on the floor.

'That'll get you on,' he snapped. 'It makes you a journalist on Red News.'

She picked up the card and tucked it safely away.

'When does the train leave?'

'Mid-morning.'

'Where are we going? Russia?'

'No. Vienna.'

Her heart sang. For once in her life she prayed. *Vienna. Oh thank you, God. Thank you; thank you; thank you....*

322

Kun moved to the door and glared over his shoulder.

'Make sure you get into the rear coaches. If you come near me I'll have you thrown off. And if you see Szamuely, tell him nothing.'

'Does he have a ticket?'

'No.'

'You're leaving him here?'

'Yes.'

'But he'll be shot.'

'That's what I'm hoping.'

Chapter Forty-Four

Welcome To Vienna

Kristina raised her head and glared at the tall Austrian officer stepping into her cell. Light from the corridor showed his immaculate uniform and badges of rank and a row of bright medal ribbons. A beautiful moustache curved perfect arcs across his cheekbones. Removing his stiff peaked cap he patted thick brown hair back into place and bowed, clicking the heels of his long shiny riding boots.

At last. An officer.

Kristina snapped, 'Why are you keeping me here in this filthy room? Your men snatched me from the train and dragged me through Vienna like a common criminal. I don't know where I am or who you are. I am a German citizen passing through your country. How dare you treat me like this.'

Her voice choked on the dust floating round this disgusting cell. She felt dirty and defiled and determined that this officer – so smart; so self-assured; so well *groomed* – would feel the hard edge of her tongue.

Completely unruffled he smiled and said, 'Welcome to Vienna. May I bring you a more comfortable chair? That old wooden thing looks hard. Is it digging into your back?'

'Why am I under arrest?'

The officer bowed. 'Let me assure you, dear Madame, that you are not *technically* under arrest. You are...detained...under our care, so to speak. We feel the need to protect you...to ensure your safety in these difficult times.'

His hands waved a graceful arc. Kristina felt the force of his undoubted charm and the apology in his gesture and believed not one word.

The same elegant movement conjured up a soldier carrying a new chair and turned into another perfect bow. 'Allow me to introduce myself. I am Colonel Ebenstein. May I please know your name?'

Kristina fought against a stir of interest – *Mein Gott this one's attractive* – and said in her coldest voice, 'If I'm not under arrest, why am I in this cell? When will I be allowed to go?'

Ebenstein settled himself into the hard chair, made a face and raised an exquisite eyebrow – 'By God, this *is* uncomfortable. You'd think our great new Austrian Republic could do better, wouldn't you?'

Doing her best not to be entertained Kristina stared, trying to work

324

out – *Is this man stupid or clever? He has me in this awful cell with one stupid chair and one filthy table and makes jokes? What is he up to...?*

Ebenstein smiled and said, 'On the other hand, I suppose we're lucky to have two chairs. I hate standing, don't you? Now. Circumstances throw us together. Only for the moment, you understand...until we clear up a few points. So why don't we make friends? May I please know your name?'

'Very well. I am the Countess Kinskii. My name is spelt with three 'i's' – one in the middle and two at the end. No 'y'.'

Kristina expected a flicker of recognition – *Surely this man knew Kinskii* – but Ebenstein retained his polite smile and asked, 'May I enquire, dear Countess, how a high born lady such as yourself came to be travelling with a trainload of Bolsheviks? Acknowledged ruffians and criminals fleeing their country. How did you fall in with them?'

'By accident.'

Ebenstein's eyebrow raised again in that attractive way. He ran a hand through curly brown hair; leaned back in the hard wooden chair and crossed at the ankles.

Kristina studied his muscular calves – shown to perfection by his gleaming boots – and decided to tell her story – or as much as she felt to her advantage....

She talked for an hour, starting with Kinskii's death. Ebenstein listened in silence, making no notes but when she finished took Kristina aback by repeating her long tale word for word, checking a point here and a name there. Impressed at his ability to remember every small fact – *Thank God I didn't mention Anyuka or the twins* – she felt surprise that he showed no interest in her search for Kinskii.

'Did you know of my husband?' she asked. 'He served in the Emperor's bodyguard.'

'My dear Countess. Your tale is absorbing but you must forgive that my true interest is in the Bolsheviks and their workings.' Despite the awkward chair he managed a quite stylish bow. – 'I'm sure you understand. Please tell me more about Béla Kun. For instance, how was he in his humour?'

'What do you mean?'

'I ask about him as a politician, as a leader and as a man. Pardon my intrusion but, being his...*personal* secretary...you held a unique position – in many ways, if I may say so,' – an eyebrow raised. 'You probably knew him better than his wife. How was he during the time

325

you spent with him? In a general sense, of course.'

At last Kristina smiled. Several of the positions she tried with Béla Kun were certainly unique.

'Excited. All the time excited at being in charge. That is until the end when even *he* realised his theories for proletarian dictatorship were rubbish.'

'How did he work? How did he spend his time?'

'Talking. All Bolsheviks talk. And talk. And talk. You cannot believe the hot air. You could run a whole fleet of Zeppelins on the gas from one day in parliament. But the peasants. They thought Béla Kun an arsehole. No one bothered to follow his orders and over four months the whole country collapsed just like Russia – no food, no transport; fighting and murder in every city and throughout the countryside.'

'Did you see or have first-hand knowledge of murders?'

'Oh yes.'

Kristina talked for another hour detailing the disappearance of so many men she knew and the story of Balogh – without mention of her part in his capture and death.

This time Ebenstein took notes on a pad – 'I need direct evidence against Kun and his men. Your agreement to sign this document as a statement will assist me in providing you with better quarters. This dreary place is not for a high born lady and I look forward to making you much more comfortable. When? In the next hour, dear Countess. As soon as you sign this statement.'

Kristina did not bother to read the text he presented. More interested in keeping her sleeve from trailing across the filthy table, she scrawled her signature and said, 'Can I go now?'

'Of course, dear Countess but where? Do you have money?'

'No.'

'What are your plans?'

'To find a place for the night then decide tomorrow.'

'How will you find a room if you have no money?'

'I'll manage. Please return my luggage and I'll be on my way.'

Ebenstein stood and smiled down his long nose at Kristina. 'Please allow me to suggest a solution to your difficulty. You mentioned that your late husband served in our Emperor's bodyguard?'

'Yes.'

'My dear Countess. The regiment always takes care of a comrade's widow. May I offer you dinner? We can relax together and consider arrangements of help in your time of need. Please take my arm so I may escort you from this army barracks to a place more suited to a lady such as you.'

Having no choice Kristina agreed and shortly after midnight found out what Ebenstein meant by his phrase, 'a lady such as you'.

First he took her to a large well-furnished apartment alongside a wide road full of evening traffic; automobiles and horse drawn carriages. 'This is the famous Ring,' he said. 'Truly a sight after dark – a river of lights flowing both ways even in these difficult times.'

Kristina saw her leather valise waiting just inside the door. Ebenstein murmured, 'I took the liberty of delivering your luggage earlier. Such a beautiful well tooled piece.'

'So you planned to bring me here?'

Ebenstein shrugged and said, 'Please – make yourself comfortable. I shall leave you for an hour to find your way around. Relax and take a bath. I am sure you need it after the past few terrible days.' He bowed, clicking his heels. 'Please don't look so surprised. As I said – we must care for a comrade's widow....'

Once again Kristina could not believe her luck. She bathed and perfumed and stood naked before the mirror, appreciating her pink, damp, firm, *luscious* image. Fascinated by the mounds and mysteries so attractive to men she twisted and turned; checking and studying herself from every angle. *Not bad for thirty-three.*

Oh, she could have stayed here for hours, admiring and playing; trying new ideas with the soaps, sponges and oils so strangely plentiful. But she sighed and dragged herself away to prepare for Ebenstein. *The damned man's sure to be punctual.*

So a few minutes before the hour she posed by the window, framed against soft evening light. When Ebenstein stepped in without warning she turned her head and smiled with lowered eyes, blessing the low-cut evening dress from Budapest she had squeezed into the valise for emergencies such as this.

Ebenstein bowed and murmured, 'Charming, dear Countess. Charming indeed,' and took her to a wonderful restaurant where she drank red wine and ate lobster and a delicate ice-cream and loved the attention from a stream of handsome army officers who came forward to be introduced. 'My friends, my comrades,' said Ebenstein. 'All fine men and happy to meet you. In the next few days I hope to introduce some very useful senior officers.'

Overcome by the wine and the warm crowded room Kristina took Ebenstein's hand and said, 'You are so kind but where will I stay? How shall I live?'

Ebenstein leaned close and whispered, 'The apartment belongs to our regiment for the use of…special guests. I have arranged that you may stay for a few months on….easy terms. Only if you wish to, of course, dear Countess. Naturally you will need money to live. There are certain…dispositions. I shall explain on our return to the apartment.'

Ebenstein explained an hour or so later in the warm glow of the bedroom, lit only by the golden light of a flickering log fire. But he waited until Kristina lay drunk, naked and exhausted watching Ebenstein fit his hard-muscled body into that lovely tight-fitting uniform. What beauty. What tailoring. What style. *These Austrians may have lost a war and an empire but, by God, they know how to dress.*

Ebenstein laughed. Kristina realised she had spoken the words aloud and giggled with him; pleased at the girlish sound. No wonder he found her so alluring. How many other women offered a man such combination of experience, beauty and youth? *Oh why is he leaving now? Why can't he stay the night?*

She rolled over and patted the pillow. 'Stay,' she whispered. 'Stay with me. Don't go.'

Ebenstein sat on the bed and pulled on his boots. 'Staying is not part of the contract,' he said.

'What contract?'

'My dear Countess. The contract is that you may remain in this apartment for two months exactly – no longer. During that time you enjoy full hospitality and company of our regiment – officers only, of course. In return you are asked to be discreet and to…entertain…myself and some of my comrades. Here. In this apartment.'

Trying to concentrate – *Damn this alcohol.* – Kristina worked slowly through his proposition and with a wriggle and a giggle and said, 'You want me to be your prostitute for two months?'

'Not our prostitute, dear Countess – our *courtesan*. A high grade appointment held by ladies of quality. Most recently a Russian duchess – like you fleeing Bolshevik terror and in need of help.'

'A Russian duchess? Stayed here?'

'With delight and gratitude.'

'What if I say no?'

He bent and kissed her hand – oh, how she enjoyed the feathered brush of his moustache – and said, 'You need say nothing. Tomorrow morning the maid will come at nine to tidy up and prepare breakfast. I shall come at ten. If you are here...we have breakfast together and discuss arrangements for the day. For instance you are short of clothes so I shall take you shopping – at the regiment's expense, of course. If you are not here...I have breakfast alone and that is that.'

'And I am free to go?'

'Yes. Until ten tomorrow morning. If you are here when I arrive at ten...you are accepting our contract.'

Kristina smiled. Snuggling under the silken sheet, she blew him a kiss.

'See you at ten,' she whispered.

Exhausted and sinking towards sleep, she barely heard the clink of coins and the clicking closing door.

Chapter Forty-Five

Kinskii's Trail

Prompt at nine a maid shook Kristina and whispered, 'Breakfast at ten, my lady.'

Kristina dragged herself awake and hurried to bathe and beautify herself for Ebenstein's arrival, laughing when he stepped through the door at exactly ten. 'Every church bell in Vienna rings when you arrive. You do it on purpose.'

'Punctuality is a virtue of the regiment.'

'That's what my husband used to say,' she lied watching for reaction.

He smiled, lifting an eyebrow – 'Then he must have been as pompous as the rest of us.'

She smiled with him, hoping for more – *Surely he'll say something* – but no.

Disappointed, she said, 'You dropped money last night. Twenty crowns. Here.'

He reached forward and curled her fingers over the coins. 'That's part of the contract,' he said. 'Every time you entertain an officer he leaves a gift.'

'A gift?'

'Yes. A gift.'

'Not payment?'

'No. A gift. Paying implies commerce. Such a thing should not exist between a lady and a gentleman.'

Kristina turned her face away. Should she accept? Did she have choice?

She turned back with a brilliant smile. 'I understand. A gift each time I entertain. Each time I entertain any of your officers?'

'Correct. A gift as each officer sees fit. In your case I am sure each officer will see *very* fit.'

Ebenstein's words came back to Kristina at some unknown hour past midnight six exhilarating weeks later. During a pause in her nightlong session with two young officers she searched the bathroom for more body oil and caught sight in the mirror of... a glowing handsome woman – primed and ready and exuding sex and desire.

She laughed and blessed Ebenstein's contract. – *What a change from that poor skinny thing in Budapest. My God, I'm enjoying every minute of Vienna.*

She found the oil and slithered back into her orgy; eager to serve these two rich young blades. They'd pay well for her energy and expertise. The more she took out of them – so to speak – the larger their gift. *A little extra work now – a flood of silver crowns before dawn. Just what I need....*

When Kristina's young lions departed at first light she lay wrapped in stained, rumpled sheets trying to remain awake long enough to calculate. Dazed by alcohol and limp from hours of continuous sex, she clutched at the money they showered on her stomach; counting and recounting; her addled mind trying to tally this stream of silver with the pile hidden under a floorboard.

Thank God for Ebenstein. He'd been right. Since that breakfast six weeks ago the gifts rolled in. *Surely by now I've enough money to reach Berlin.* She whispered, 'From now, my dear Ebenstein, *you* can come free.'

She giggled at her pun and drifting into sleep, realised... *Only two weeks left in this place. Mein Gott, I'll need to work hard....*

For the first time in years Kinskii returned from the dark edge of her mind during a dream so clear Kristina thought him real. She kept him buried deep along with her children and felt annoyed that he came unbidden.

'Why are you here?' she asked.

'To remind you why *you* are here,' he said, frowning.

'Why do *you* care? You died and left me. I expected to be married all my life. But you chased alone after that stupid buffalo. Anything I do now is your fault. *Anything.* Come close so I can touch you.'

He shook his elegant head and retreated to the dark edge, whispering, 'Don't forget you are trying to find me. Don't forget why you are here. Don't forget me....'

She woke grinding her teeth in frustration. Look at where Kinskii's lies and posturing had brought her. *And now he blames me.*

Consumed with fury she hissed a fierce Prussian oath and snatched his photographs from their hiding place. Throwing them across the bed she glared down at Kinskii's gray image.

There's the lying hound. Look at him. Look at the devious bastard. – *God. If only he'd come back I'd spit in his face.*

His face. His face. That face. *Christ. Why didn't I see before?*

She picked up the two photographs of Kinskii as a soldier in the field, standing by a horse and sitting with a group of comrades and for the first time studied the other faces. Of course, the dirty campaign clothes did not help but that half-seen man behind the horse…and that same man sitting near Kinskii by the tent….

Her mind spinning, she lit a lamp. Holding the pictures as close as she dared to the hot mantel she peered at the man's face…twisting the picture to catch better light…almost certain….

She sat back knowing what to do next. *Kinskii's right. I've come here to find him.* She shook her head at how she had forgotten her true task — her motive for coming to Europe in the first place. This wonderful whirl of restaurants, parties, shopping and sex had taken over. *But for some reason Kinskii came to remind me….*

When Ebenstein arrived for breakfast Kristina – bathed, dressed and perfumed – poured coffee, passed over small sweet cakes and agreed to go shopping. 'But first I have something to discuss that troubles me.'

Ebenstein set down his coffee cup. 'Has one of my officers let you down in some way?'

'I suppose he has. He lied to me – by silence.'

'By silence?'

Oh that delicate raised eyebrow. Oh that wary tilt of in his head – *He doesn't like my riddle….*

She said, 'I have several times mentioned my husband, Count Kinskii, to you but…by your silence you profess not to know him.'

Ebenstein's polite smile remained steady but Kristina saw the wariness in his eyes turn to full-blown suspicion.

She said, 'How can this be? You are the same age; the same regiment – probably served together in the Emperor's bodyguard…?'

She allowed her voice to trail away into a question….

He frowned.

Kristina plucked the two photographs from her bag, placed them on the table and said, 'I know you are an intelligence officer. How do you – as an *intelligence* officer – analyse these. Because you appear on them both next to my husband.'

He lowered his head – *Hiding his face, the clever sod* – and studied the pictures.

In a calm voice – quite friendly really – he said, 'You are lucky. We arrested and held every other soul on that train from Budapest. Some are imprisoned in terrible places. I spared only you.'

'Why should I care about them? Tell me about the photographs.'

He said, 'We put Béla Kun in a lunatic asylum.'

'The right damned place,' she said. 'Now – the photographs, if you please.'

After a moment of deep thought Ebenstein said, 'When your husband first joined our regiment we saw him as a smart young Magyar with great ability but no background. After a few months of fighting the Serbs he became – through skill and charm – our most popular officer. We'd never seen such a brilliant rider; such a crack shot; such a first class leader. We'd never seen an officer so loved by his men; so respected by his superiors....' He shook his head and sighed.

'But?' asked Kristina.

Ebenstein smiled. 'But. You are right. *But*...to us – his fellow officers – he seemed unreal...never spoke of family or background *but* moved through the ranks too fast from lieutenant to captain then major – all in less than a year. Such smooth advancement implied strong patronage – *but* from whom? What contact in high places gave such backing to an unknown young Magyar?'

'Surely being first class leader brings promotion?'

'True. And so does bravery. Your husband showed amazing bravery – he fought always in the line of fire and thick of fighting, almost as though he sought glorious death against impossible odds.'

Ebenstein held up the picture of Kinskii standing by his horse.

'This picture shows Kinskii a few minutes after he returned from a crazy solo charge against a whole Serb company to save a captured Austrian officer. Kinskii raced across the battlefield at full gallop, tipped from the saddle with one foot hooked in a stirrup, banging away from under the horse's neck with a rifle.'

Ebenstein shook his head.

'My God, what a horseman. The best in our army.'

Ebenstein picked up the second photograph and said, 'This picture two weeks later celebrated Kinskii's promotion to captain. We held a small party and drank vodka. This seemed to go to his head and he changed after we returned to Vienna, causing a return to our original suspicion and distrust.'

'Distrust?'

Ebenstein nodded. 'Shortly after the regiment returned to Vienna the Emperor heard of your husband's valour and demanded his appointment to the bodyguard. This elite group of hussars attend special occasions. During one ceremonial your husband saw a senior minister and became convinced....'

'That he'd found his father?'

'Exactly. This caused your husband to begin a...*campaign*...of vilification against one of Austria's senior families. In particular he directed venom at the senior minister whose name you may find easy to guess.'

'Kinsky?'

'Yes. We discovered later that, in fact, your husband made contact with the minister *before* joining the army. The minister refused open acknowledgement but offered help. Your husband took the name Kinskii and joined our regiment.'

Kristina said, 'With patronage from the minister?'

'Yes. We think the minister made a deal with your husband....'

'Along the lines of – 'Keep out of my way and I'll give you secret support'?'

'We think so.'

'Why do you keep saying '*We*' ?'

'My dear Countess. You *know* I am an intelligence officer. By '*We*' I mean the intelligence service.'

Kristina said, 'My God. It all seems so complicated.'

Ebenstein said, 'Let me end my story. On our return from war, your husband's obsession returned. He again confronted the minister – this time as a hero, rather than an unknown young Magyar – and began a campaign of embarrassment against him and began styling himself 'Count'.'

Kristina said, 'To force acknowledgement from his father.'

Ebenstein nodded. 'Impossible, of course. But your husband forced us to act. The regiment transferred your husband to my special section and I sent him to Berlin.'

'Why Berlin?'

'We sent him as far away as possible – and where he would be of value.'

'Value? In Berlin?'

Ebenstein said, 'The German Kaiser saw our Emperor growing older and weaker so offered clandestine support to certain Austrian political groups in favour of union with Germany. We kept close watch through an intelligence operation in Berlin. After some success our network began to fail for reasons we could not determine so sent your husband to find out why.'

'Did he succeed?'

'Beyond our expectations. All the energy and intelligence he applied to being a soldier he turned to spying and started a flow of reports that became a flood of information detailed beyond our experience. His work enabled us to control the pro-German party in Vienna and infiltrate several previously unheard of groups around Austria and in Berlin. Then overnight our network collapsed – fell completely apart.'

'What happened?'

'You may not wish to hear.'

'Tell me.'

'We discovered that your husband probably murdered a young woman who worked for us and betrayed our network to the Kaiser's secret police.'

'What do you mean – 'Probably'?'

'All our Berlin agents died at the hands of the Kaiser's interrogators – except your husband and the young woman. The civil police found her murdered an hour before the military police struck at our network. Your husband disappeared completely. The Berlin civil authorities concluded he killed the woman and escaped.'

Kristina pursed her lips in disbelief.

Ebenstein said, 'Until I interrogated *you* we had no true knowledge of his origin or fate. We really only knew him as a soldier – his middle life, so to speak. Your revelations confirmed his birthplace, his whereabouts after disappearing from Berlin and his death. This closes part of our file but leaves open the reason he betrayed our network. Will we ever know?'

'Revenge on his father?'

'A possibility made stronger by your information'

In a shiver of agitation Kristina asked, 'The woman. The dead woman. Was her name Mariska?'

'How do you know?'

'I've seen it written and wondered about her.'

Ebenstein said, 'Thinking of names – you can no longer be known as Countess Kinskii in Vienna.'

'Why?'

'To do so would perpetuate the scandal started by your husband.'

Kristina said, 'I married a Count and I remain a Countess. Kinskii is my name now – married or widowed – and is the name I shall continue to use.'

Ebenstein said, 'Impossible, my dear Countess. Vienna will not allow it. You may be called 'Countess' as a form of stage name so to speak but without the name Kinskii.'

'Stage name? What the hell are you talking about?'

Ebenstein raised a hand and said, 'My dear Countess. You have taken the regiment by storm. You are known as a delightful companion – fresh; active; cultured. But above all – *discreet.*

'What the hell does this have to do with a *stage* name?'

'Dear Countess. Your name – your *title* – is on the lips of every officer in the regiment. You are *famous*. But only within the regiment. Now think of the money to be made if your name – your *title* – became more widely known.'

'Oh for God's sake. What are you saying?'

'Your contract with the regiment ceases in only two weeks. It seems a pity not to capitalise from your success so far. I own a large apartment nearby – the perfect place for you…to set up and continue entertaining…just as your activity here but to a wider group of patrons. Think of the money we would make.'

'We?'

'Yes, dear Countess. We. As business partners. My apartment has room to include two or three other high class ladies. With four of you – imagine the variations of *pleasure* we can offer.'

'You're suggesting we open a brothel?'

'A salon, dear Countess. A salon. Discreet. Luxurious. Furnished and decorated in best possible taste to attract quality clientele from the cream of society. Almost every senior officer in the army for a start, plus government ministers, visiting diplomats. Oh think of what they will pay for our services….'

Ebenstein leaned back in his chair and smiled without hint of guile; his handsome face open, honest and clear.

Kristina stared; unsure whether to be shocked or interested – *By God, he means it.*

'I'll think about it,' she said, finding herself so aroused at the possibility she took Ebenstein to bed for an afternoon session of such energy and invention that after two hours he groaned, 'No more…you'll kill me. Save it for our salon. We'll make a fortune.'

That evening Kristina lifted the floorboard and counted her pile of silver. *At last. – enough to get to Berlin then on to East Africa….*

Next day she told Ebenstein, 'I refuse to give up my name and I don't wish to stay here waiting for the next grandfather to come through my door. I'm going to Berlin. I must find out what happened to Kinskii.'

Ebenstein showed no disappointment – *What self-control* – and said, 'The salon is ready and I have three ladies of quality eager to attend; two Russian and one Czech. All from excellent families and well educated in social graces. They'll do well for each other and for me. I previously refused one other well qualified lady also eager to join but your vacancy now allows her in. I'm sorry you are leaving but she will certainly be happy.'

'You're not angry with me?'

Ebenstein shrugged and said, 'Not at all. But you must leave Vienna when your contract ends in three days time. I shall escort you to the train with a first class ticket to Berlin as my going away present. Without you I would never have thought of the salon.'

Three days later Ebenstein carried Kristina by horse-drawn landau through a cold October day to the noisy Vienna-West Station. She stood with him on the platform alongside her carriage and surprised to be nervous at leaving his protection, held on to his hand, whispering, 'I'm sorry to be going. I really am.'

He bent and kissed her. She pressed forward, hugging him hard – a beautiful woman; a handsome soldier – oblivious to the hurrying crowd; the swirling steam; the clatter and clamour of departure.

He murmured, 'If you find what happened with Kinskii in Berlin write and let me know. Why he betrayed and killed Mariska and how he managed to escape to Africa. I need to close my file.'

Kristina giggled and drew back slapping a soft palm at his face – 'You're terrible. Always the intelligence officer.'

'Not for much longer I hope,' said Ebenstein, laughing.

He helped her on to the train and handed up her leather valise – 'Such a tiny piece of luggage. Why not take more clothes? The regiment certainly bought you enough dresses and things.'

She blew him a kiss and said, 'I leave Vienna as I arrived. With few possessions but as Countess Kinskii.'

Doors slammed; a whistle blew; train wheels squealed. Ebenstein saluted and said, 'Good luck,' then over the noise, shouted, 'My God. I nearly forgot.' He reached up holding a small envelope – 'This belongs to you. My people found it on Szamuely's body.'

'He's dead?'

'Yes. After escaping Budapest he tried to cross into Austria. When our border guards moved to arrest him he pulled a pistol and blew his own brains out.'

'Good.'

The train moved away. Kristina blew him a kiss and grabbed the envelope in one movement calling, 'What is it?' but could not hear his reply over the clamour of departure.

She settled into her seat, opened the envelope and pulled out a telegram from H.E. that read: HERE IS YOUR MONEY STOP COME HOME QUICK STOP ADAM TO BE TRIED FOR MURDER STOP EVA NEEDS YOUR SUPPORT STOP HOCKLYFFE-EVANS END

Shivering with excitement she read the telegram again – *Murder? My God. Murder? This came with the money to Budapest so the trial must have been…when?…March or April…or was it February? Stupid H.E. doesn't say. Who did Adam murder? Oh God. Christy. So it's true. Adam must have shot Christy….*

Consumed with delight she crushed the telegram to her heart and whispered, 'So you got the bastard. Well done, Adam. And what does my *oh-so-perfect* sister think about *that*?'

She closed her eyes, savouring the impact of Christy's death on Eva. *Will she wear black? How can I find out more? What happened? Did Adam hang? Which one does she mourn – lover or husband? Detail. Oh God, I want detail….*

Frustrated she opened her eyes and stared out the window. *Berlin. I'll telegram H.E. from Berlin – but wait. I don't want him to know where I am….*

Her mind flashed round a new plan – *Four weeks or so in Berlin and I'll have tracked down Kinskii – then it's off to Marseilles and a boat. Four or five weeks later I'll be back at Mzito and hear everything first hand. That's it. I'll wait. I'll wait for Eva to tell me every detail – every tiny detail….*

She closed her eyes again, imagining that wonderful moment….

Chapter Forty-Six

Twins

Thinman drove along the crude dirt road at furious pace without regard for potholes, rocks and clouds of harsh red grit spinning up from the wheels.

Adam spat out a mouthful of dust and shouted, 'Do we need to go so fast?'

Thinman appeared not to hear – probably because of the clatter and bash of their passage towards Mzito.

Adam tried again – shouting louder – but Thinman took no notice, his bony face set in the same angry cast as last night during the celebrations for Adam's acquittal. What a wet blanket he'd been. And for the first time in Adam's experience pretty drunk.

Adam hunched down in his seat, decided to endure the journey as best he could and tried to remember everything that happened after he heard the news of his acquittal yesterday.

God, what an evening it had been. As soon as the court president passed verdict Thinman hurried Adam from the courtroom and back to the mess where every officer stood and applauded. Then H.E. appeared, pushing his great bulk forward and booming, 'Well done, old chap. Come on. I've organized a bash at the Norfolk,' and with Cretikos at the wheel rushed Adam in this same car to the Norfolk Hotel. The party went on until after midnight with a crowd of those so-called friends who'd ignored him for a year buying Adam drinks and slapping his shoulders, yelling, 'Congrats, Early. Knew you'd get off....'

This morning at dawn Adam struggled awake, unable to believe he was free and in the Norfolk instead of jail; his mind echoing with Thinman's drunken mumble last night – *'By God Early you're lucky. In a proper court martial you'd have swung from the gallows. I'm ashamed...to be part...of such...travesty. Such absolute bloody travesty. No written statements. No proper cross examination. Complete absence of credible evidence. And what a mess that cretin Stewartby made of the investigation. I'll never be involved in the like again. Not at any price.'*

In the optimism of sunrise Adam felt sure Thinman didn't really mean it. Now at noon, with the damned man driving like an avenging apocalypse, face taut; eyes glittering; Adam's certainty faded. To ease tension he leaned over and shouted in Thinman's ear, 'Why did you decide to drive? Why not use Cretikos?'

'Needed us to be alone,' Thinman yelled back and a few minutes later hauled on the brake, dragging to a stop among a group of trees on the rise overlooking Mzito. Their dust cloud caught up and collapsed a choking red shower into the car.

Thinman hawked a gob of purple mucus from deep in his throat and sent it curling into the roadside bush, growling, 'God, these machines are damned uncomfortable. Prefer a horse any time.'

Adam rubbed stinging dirt from his eyes. He stretched forward, peering over the windscreen and down through the trees. 'I've been coming here – to the estate- for the last year,' he told Thinman. 'But never to the house. Never by this track. I haven't seen her for almost twelve months. She'd never allow it. I've always gone down to the village or the cattle pens. So I'm not sure what welcome I'll get.'

Thinman said, 'Only yourself to blame. I saw everything that happened at Bukoba. You should have hanged for what you did. And Musa. The two of you should have swung.'

Adam said, 'Did you bring binoculars? I can't see properly from here'

Thinman said, 'Damn it, Early. Listen to me. I saw you take part in the murder of a brother officer. You're guilty as hell but won't admit it.'

'Oh for God's sake, Thinman. You'd been shot through the gut. What could you see face down in the grass a hundred yards away?'

'I managed to roll over. I watched everything happen. You shot Christy plumb through the chest. Knocked him straight down then prepared to shoot again. We both know you did.'

'But I didn't kill him.'

'You intended to. I saw you take second aim and squeeze your trigger. You're all but a damned murderer.'

'So why defend me? Why save me?'

'I didn't save you. Lack of witnesses and Stewartby's damned incompetence saved you. No one but me saw what actually happened and the idiot never questioned me. If he'd asked for a statement I'd have been duty bound to tell him exactly what I saw.'

'So why didn't you go to him and speak up?'

'How could I? It'd have meant the gallows for you and Musa. The two of you. No reprieve. No mercy. How could I do that? You both saved me from death three times in a few minutes. You by shooting that damned sniper who jumped me from behind a log then by chasing Weiss away before he could finish me off. And Musa by coming across and carrying me from the field when he could have bolted and been safe. Without him I'd have bled to death on that swamp bank.'

'So you kept quiet and we went free.'

'And God forgive me, I was wrong. I should have spoken up.'

Adam shrugged and sat in silence, staring through the trees at Mzito.

Thinman said, 'I heard rumours that Christy had an affair with your wife. Is this true?'

Adam nodded without turning his head.

Thinman said, 'I heard other rumours – difficult to believe – that I suppose offer some justification for your action. But why did Musa join in? In God's name why did he come up behind you and blow Christy's head off?'

Adam said, 'Don't ask me. Ask Musa.'

Thinman jumped from the car, his bony face red; eyes glittering in anger and shouted, 'I damned well shall.'

He cranked the engine with furious energy until it spluttered and fired then hopped back in, jerking the car forward at such speed Adam shouted, 'Bloody hell, Thinman. Slow down, can't you. Musa's not going to run away.'

Sure Thinman would kill them both, Adam hung on, bouncing and swaying in his seat until the car burst into open space by the house and skidded sideways in a cloud of dust, stopping just short of the veranda steps.

Adam jumped down, spitting grit and cursing. *Christ. This is just how I came home a year ago. Same car, same red dust. And now the same terrible welcome.*

Last night at the Norfolk, during the drunken party, H.E. used his great bulk to push through the crowded room and edge Adam into a dark corner, mumbling, 'Got a letter for you, old fellow. Two letters actually but I can only give you one.' He pulled two crumpled envelopes from his pocket and peered at them through brandy sodden eyes. 'Must give you the right one,' he burped with a giggle. 'God-awful trouble otherwise.'

Adam dragged out a note written in Eva's spiky Teutonic handwriting and read, *'You may come home.'*

'Is this all?'

'What did you expect?'

'At least she could have signed it.'

H.E. giggled again – 'Think yourself lucky, old chap. If you'd gone down the other letter's a bloody-sight shorter.'

'Show me.'

'No.'

'Bloody-well show me.'

H.E. closed one bleary eye in a wink – 'Only if you never tell.'

'Not a word.'

The second note read, '*Hang.*'

'See what I mean?' said H.E..

Now Adam looked up through clearing dust at Eva standing by the veranda rail, alone and absolutely still; just as last year but this time dressed in high-necked white blouse with patterned skirt.

He hesitated. *This is the woman who hoped I'd hang. Do I really want to live here?*

Three Africans he didn't know trotted from the kitchen area.

Eva said, 'The servants will take your luggage.'

Strain in her voice and anxiety in her grey eyes surprised Adam – *Christ. She's nervous....*

He marched up the steps.

She turned away, 'I'll see the servants get it right,' and hurried along the veranda. The Africans hoisted Adam's trunks on their heads and followed.

Over her shoulder Eva called, 'Major Thinman. Will you stay for lunch?'

'Thank you kindly but no.' Thinman called back. 'Must return to barracks and pack. Off on tonight's train to Mombasa and boarding ship for Palestine tomorrow.'

Eva waved and disappeared. Thinman blew air from puffed cheeks and said in a low voice, 'Not too warm a welcome.'

Adam trotted back down the steps and said, 'Stay if you like.'

'I think not. Better you're left alone to sort things out. Before I leave I must speak with Musa. Have him called.'

Scampering in the soft dust, a small boy ran round the house. He skidded to a halt and stared at Adam with bright blue eyes, white-blond hair shining in the sun.

Adam said, 'Hallo Jonathan – I'm home.'

Thinman stiffened in surprise and said, 'Good God. The rumours are true.'

'That's only the half of it,' said Adam.

As he spoke a slim nut brown Kikuyu woman appeared, calling in Swahili, 'Jonathan. Come back. You must eat.'

Adam said, 'This is Musa's wife. She'll know where he is.'

With a giggle and a howl, another small boy shot into view. Adam turned in time to see shock and outrage flush across Thinman's face as he glared at the sight – a small handsome boy; African in features but with light tanned skin, almost-blue eyes and frizzy yellow-blond hair.

Without a word, Musa's wife shooed both boys back round the house, clucking like a mother hen.

'That's the other half,' said Adam.

'I can't believe it. How long have you known?'

'Since last year when I came home.'

'So Christy....'

'...raped Musa's wife. That's the result.'

'Good God. Those boys are half brothers..

'Exactly.'

'They could almost be twins.'

'Almost.'

Thinman shook his head and whispered, 'No wonder Musa shot the bastard. I'd have done the same.'

'I thought you might say that.'

Thinman said, 'This is the biggest shock I've ever had. To think...a British officer... How does your wife cope?'

'Ignores it completely. Refuses to acknowledge anything. As far as she's concerned, one boy is my son and the other is Musa's – probably a throwback to some Sudanese Arab ancestor. She's blind to anything else.'

'And Musa?'

'The boy is his wife's so Musa accepts him.'

'What's the boy's name?'

'Kristofa.'

Thinman barked a sharp laugh. 'Who the hell thought of that?'

'Musa.'

Thinman laughed again – 'What sense of humour. Never thought I'd hear the like from an African. Look – I must go now. Tell Musa I'm sorry I missed him. I would have loved to have shaken his hand and thanked him.'

Chapter Forty-Seven

A Conversation At Muthaiga

Six months later Adam rode through a fragrant morning from Mzito to Muthaiga and found H.E. sitting on a rear veranda squeezed into a creaking wicker armchair, waving a hand and calling, 'Thank God you've arrived. Now I'll be able to have a drink and some lunch. How did you travel? By horse? No wonder you look hot. Come and have a cold beer.'

Adam sat looking out over green lawns towards a grove of flat-topped trees. 'Why are we here?' he asked. 'What do you want me for?'

'Just a chat and to swap news. How are things at the farm?'

'Not bad. Eva's friendlier now. Getting used to having me around.'

'Sleeping together?'

'Of course not.'

'Think you will?'

'Doubt it. She has her part of the house and I have mine. We rarely meet except for meals. I've started to join her at dawn for breakfast on the veranda to chat about the farm. But that's about it.'

'How about Jonathan?'

Adam paused; sipped his beer and studied the flat-topped trees: 'Difficult to say.'

How to explain the odd bond he found developing with the small blond boy? One morning a couple of months ago Jonathan stumbled from his room in the early light of dawn, pyjamas rumpled, hair a tangled white-blond web, eyes damp with sleep. Trotting down to the breakfast table he avoided Eva's outstretched arms and clambered on to Adam's lap, mumbling, 'Want to be with Daddy.'

Overcome by an unaccountable flood of affection Adam snuggled the small curled body against his chest and smiled at Eva who turned away – a tear starting in the corner of her eye.

H.E. asked, 'Do you get on with the little bugger?'

'Quite well. He comes with me to the cattle pens – I carry him on my horse – and sometimes we go down to the village. He likes to play with Musa's son.'

H.E. nodded, his eyes gleaming, 'Ah yes. Kristofa....'

Adam said, 'I don't want to sit here discussing my domestic arrangements. If you've nothing else to talk about I'll go.'

'Sorry, old chap. I do have several bits of news for you. And I think

344

you'll be pleased to know that Stewartby's gone to Europe for a couple of years to help the new League of Nations in Geneva. He went on the same ship as Thinman. I saw them both off.'

Adam said, 'So that's why I've been asked to buy out his share of our cold store in Mombasa. I'm negotiating with his lawyer. I knew Stewartby was away but thought he'd gone on leave.'

H.E. laughed and said, 'I reckon he went to avoid you. Everyone knows he made a terrible bog of that investigation. He felt such a fool he jumped at a job he'd refused a month earlier. God knows how he'll get on. Those European politicians will chew him up and spit him out before he's even noticed.'

'What's the job?'

'African expert. The Allies are squeezing the Hun dry of money and industry so the buggers will never be able to break out and start another war. Not ever. At least for a couple of centuries. We're getting their African territories and Stewartby will advise on that – if ever he gets a word in edgeways. I don't envy him. Did I tell you I'm getting out of politics?'

'To do what?'

'Same as you. I'll move to Chania and run the farm as soon as I find a woman to come with me.'

'Do you have anyone in mind?'

'Several. But they're all married.'

'Oh for God's sake, H.E..'

'Honestly. They all want to come but not one of 'em dares tell her husband.'

Adam laughed. 'You don't need a woman to help on the farm. You have Cretikos.'

'No more, I'm afraid. He's leaving me to build a hotel in Nairobi. And who is his partner? Damned Stewartby, that's who. Probably so he'll have a place to live when he comes back.'

'Bloody hell,' said Adam. 'Stewartby's like a cancer affecting us all.'

'So that's why I need a woman,' said H.E.. 'Which reminds me. Have you heard any more from Kristina? She's supposed to be my fiancé after all.'

'Not since Budapest a year ago although we heard from Kreuz that he met her in Berlin – bumped into her in the street.'

'What did he say about Kristina?'

'Not much. They had only a brief chat. She told him her parents died in the 'flu epidemic and she planned to start out for Nairobi

345

within a couple of weeks. That's the last we heard. She's probably found someone or something in Berlin and decided to stay. Eva's not worried and thinks that one day Kristina will turn up here as though nothing's happened. Meantime she'll have found a way to survive in Berlin.'

H.E. laughed and said, 'I'll bet she has – and heaven help Berlin....'

Chapter Forty-Eight

Ticket To Africa

Berlin: March 1922

Kristina raced round her small flat, hurrying to prepare for another night of earning money and caught sight of her puffy eyes and straggly hair in a mirror – *God I look awful. Why do I always oversleep? Must get out of here before the maid arrives....*

In panic she glanced at the clock. Nearly eleven? Impossible.

She rushed from perfumed bathroom to disorderly bedroom, scrabbling through cupboards and drawers for two important packages from last night's work. She found the money first then – with a gulp of relief – her cocaine. Pouring a small pile on to the dressing table she leaned forward and sucked the wonderful white powder in to her nostrils and waited; groaning in ecstasy until the euphoric rush subsided, leaving her exhilarated but able to continue.

She dropped to her knees and crawled under the brass bedstead. Careful not to split a fingernail she lifted the loose plank, pulled her cash box out from behind a joist and pressed last night's earnings on to the pile of money already tucked away. She pushed the box back in to place and scrambled out. No point in counting and calculating. Inflation in this crazy new Germany wiped out her profit within days no matter how much she earned.

How different from two years ago when she first started work in Berlin. In the small hours of each morning after clients had departed she used to sit, still excited by hours of alcohol and sex, riffling through her wads of banknotes working out how soon she could afford her ticket back to Africa.

Now – in these difficult days – money of any value came only from occasional foreigners newly arrived in Berlin; the ones who paid in dollars, sterling or francs. But you need to catch them fresh. They don't stay wet behind the ears for long. Within a week they work out how to change their currency for profit and pay in useless marks – saving a fortune and laughing when you complained.

Damn inflation. And damn this stupid country. Thank God for cocaine. Without it life wouldn't be worth living.

Resisting another snort she hid her precious package under a tile in the bathroom and came back to choose what to wear for tonight's activities, running her hands along the row of expensive dresses hanging neat and tidy in the wardrobe; enjoying the feel of luxurious soft material sliding through her fingers. Still floating in the bliss of cocaine she blessed her luck – *Rich clients, a good maid and a good apartment. Things could be worse.*

She could have hunted for years to find a flat of this quality and a landlady stupid enough to believe that Kristina worked in the theatre and her constant late night visitors came from the cast.

Kristina giggled – *Well…I am in an entertainment industry of sorts* – and again considered her maid; Polish but a pretty little thing and grateful for a job despite late night hours and odd circumstances. *Look at how well she cares for my clothes….*

Still buzzing from the cocaine Kristina grabbed the long black dress and drew it on then discarded it for the shorter low cut pearl-grey that always showed a hint of nipple. She looked in the mirror, twisting and turning and returned to the black, checking the fall of material over her buttocks, seeking the attractive curve that made men look. Should she wear the short pearl-grey with no knickers or the more sophisticated high necked black tonight?

In the end she decided on the black with silk knickers – a smoother line and defence against the cold March wind. She scrawled a note to the maid: *Clean and tidy well in case I bring a friend home,'* and drew on a short fur coat, calling goodnight to the landlady.

She trotted in darkness along the narrow deserted street, heels clicking and echoing until she burst in to the light and noise and crowds of ogling men in Oranienburger Strasse. She pushed across and plunged in to quieter streets down towards Hotel Adlon. A cold breeze spun off the Spree. She shivered, pulling the fur coat tight and blessing the knickers.

She arrived at the Telephone Box just after midnight and must have looked anxious because the doorman said, 'Don't worry. Boss is out the back.'

Kristina said, 'Busy yet?'

'No. Big dinner at the Adlon is keeping them late. Be ready for a rush around one.'

Kristina pressed a few cigarettes in to his hand and slipped in to the dressing room to check her makeup and tidy her short fashionable hairstyle. A pity she'd cut it so short but the tangle of long tresses didn't suit the tangles of her new life.

Satisfied at her looks she passed down the plush purple hall – purple wallpaper; purple hangings; purple furniture glowing in purple lamplight – and in to the main bar making sure she sauntered through the door as though returning from a visit to the washroom.

Relieved that no one noticed her entrance she stopped by a balcony to look down on the room – an amphitheatre of half a dozen levels set with tables curving round a small dance floor. On each table a tall brass telephone gleamed in the dull light. Not many customers yet – just a few younger men eyeing up the girls – and the place seemed flat and dull as always when empty with its ingrained smell of cigar smoke, alcohol and sweat and lighting so low she could barely see through the gloom. *God, how dreary. I really must find somewhere better....*

On the other hand she always felt like this before the drink, the band and – perhaps – a sniff of cocaine livened things up. She sighed and moved with care down the steps, holding on to the brass railing, checking the room as she went. *How many girls in tonight? More than forty? Boss must be expecting big business....*

Seeing her two friends at a table on the second tier up from the dance floor she threaded her way towards them.

'Good evening, Duchess. Good evening, Condesa. You've claimed a good position.'

'Good evening, Countess,' said the Duchess, inclining her handsome head, trying to focus eyes already dazed by heroin.

'You're late, Countess,' said the Condesa, scowling. 'And you owe us a hundred marks for your share of the table.'

Kristina said, 'Let me sit down and settle in first.'

The Condesa held out a hand. 'Sit down and settle up now.'

Kristina plucked at her purse and passed the money over. The Condesa stuffed it down her corset without a word, her olive face and black-button eyes set and angry as always. What a wonderful act these two made – the Duchess so graceful, the Condesa so arrogant. It always amazed Kristina how many clients they snared acting as a team.

Kristina laughed and said, 'Relax. We have an hour before the fun starts.'

'We know,' said the Condesa. 'Once the Adlon empties we'll start fishing properly.'

The band shuffled on to their small stage; fiddled with their instruments until the notes sounded about right and attempted a few slow melodies as prelude to the howling jazz to come. Kristina relaxed, sipping fruit juice; enjoying this relatively quiet period before the night degenerated in to a brutal brew of noise, alcohol and God-only-knows what hell-stew of male humanity to be cosseted, cajoled and served as their pleasure demanded.

During the next hour the shiny brass telephone on their table rang twice. Each time the Condesa snatched up the instrument and bellowed, 'No.' at the mouthpiece without even checking to see which table may be trying to make contact.

Around one o'clock Kristina watched the younger men drift away to be replaced by older – richer – gentlemen in black evening suits and stiff collars who called for drinks and cigars and settled to survey the flesh.

Some she knew – Government officials; a steel baron with a shipbuilder; several financiers, a couple of politicians in a party with several senior policemen.

'Stand by for boarding,' said Kristina. 'The Adlon's turning out.'

The Condesa grunted and nudged the Duchess, 'Wake up darling. You'll be working soon.'

The Duchess inclined her elegant head and turned her dreamy gaze round the room. Kristina tried to work out how much the Duchess had taken so far and wondered if she'd last the night.

Telephones round the amphitheatre jingled and girls drifted between tables to join the rich and famous as the night's work began in earnest.

Their own telephone began to ring more frequently but the Condesa continued to refuse all offers. Being Spanish and a cunning negotiator she spun a delaying mixture of argument and lewd enticement until her suitors became so frustrated or drunk they would agree almost anything to get their hands on her and the Duchess.

Now, as Kristina listened to a developing discussion in which she seemed to be included, her eye caught a group of men shuffling in to chairs on a top tier opposite. She recognised the elegant and urbane Harry Kessler, recently returned ambassador to Poland and a couple of the other men she knew as Government officials. The others must be foreign visitors from the Adlon dinner.

She blinked and squinted through rolling clouds of cigar smoke. A short handsome man leaning forward to peer over the balcony looked familiar. The quality and cut of his formal dark suit and stiff wing collar marked him as one of the foreigners.

'Who is that with Kessler?' she asked.

The Condesa finished her call, glanced up and said, 'Why ask? If he's Kessler's friend he's no good to you or any of us.'

Kristina looked again but the man sat back and turned away to accept a match being held to his cigar. Something about that hard profile echoed in Kristina's memory – 'My God. Give me your opera glasses.'

The Condesa grunted and dug in to her evening bag.

The man blew a cloud of smoke and turned to again survey the room. Kristina peered through the small binoculars; fiddled with the tiny focus wheel and caught his face in an arc of light from the bandstand. She gasped and sat back, humming with delight, a plan – *Oh such a clear and simple plan* – flashing through her mind.

The Condesa asked, 'Do you know him?'

'Yes.'

'Where from?'

'My past.'

'Is he rich?'

'No.'

'Then why are you so happy?'

Kristina snatched up the telephone. 'Connect me to table eighteen,' she commanded.

The Duchess came alive and asked, 'Who is he?'

'Who is he?' said Kristina, her voice harsh with excitement. 'Who is he? He's my ticket to Africa.'

351

Chapter Forty-Nine

The Countess and the Colonel

Kristina watched Kessler bend to the telephone and said, 'Let me speak with the Englishman.'

Without a word Kessler passed the instrument over.

Holding the opera glasses tight against her eyes with one hand and the earpiece hard against her head with the other, Kristina leaned across to the mouthpiece and speaking Swahili said, 'Hallo *Bwana* Stewartby. What are you doing here in Berlin?'

She shrieked with laughter, her violet eyes sparking delight, as Stewartby leapt up, his obvious shock magnified through her binoculars.

'Who the hell is that?' he shouted, his voice made tinny and weak by the telephone.

Switching to English Kristina said, 'One of your prisoners. Look across the room. I'm waving.'

Stewartby said, 'Good God.'

He dropped the telephone and turned to Kessler in agitated conversation, pointing over the balcony.

Kessler smiled and bowed towards Kristina. Into the telephone he said, 'Dear Countess. I wonder if you could persuade the Duchess and the Condesa to join us. We are only here for an hour and would enjoy your company.'

'Harry, darling. You're such a diplomat.'

Kessler bowed again and said, 'You are very kind.'

'Why must we join damned Kessler?' grumbled the Condesa.

'Because half his party are foreigners,' said Kristina. 'That means real money. Come on girls.'

The Condesa swirled her shawl, smoothed her silk dress and set off across the dance floor in a haughty Spanish stride. The Duchess rose and stood for a moment to check balance and bearings until Kristina took her arm and whispered, 'Come on darling. We'll go together and have a wonderful time.'

Kessler's party stood to receive them. The Duchess gripped Kristina's hand and whispered, 'I count nine men. Do we satisfy them all? Three each?'

'I don't think so Duchess. Some of them will prefer boys.'

'A pity,' said the Duchess.

Stewartby stepped forward, his stern face breaking into a smile of unexpected charm. 'Well damn me. It *is* you. I couldn't believe it – short hair and all that makeup.'

In an inexplicable reaction Kristina leaned forward and kissed him. To her surprise he dragged her into an embrace and returned the kiss.

'I didn't recognise you,' she said. 'In formal clothes and with such a white face.'

'We diplomats rarely get out in the sun. My God this is a shock. What the hell are you doing here?'

She spread her arms, palms up, in a movement that encompassed the whole room with all its sleaze and debauchery.

'You work in this place?'

'Yes.'

'As a hostess.'

'Yes.'

She watched his pleasure fade into calculation, his eyes hardening and roaming down the line and curves of her black dress.

He said, 'Shall we sit down?'

'Only if you buy champagne.'

'Kessler's already ordered. Come and sit here away from the others so we can talk.'

Kristina joined him at the next table, sitting straight-backed to show her figure and crossing her legs.

His eyes roamed again and he asked, 'Are you a prostitute?'

'Of course not. I'm a courtesan.'

'What's the difference?'

'Am I on the street accepting any drunken sailor or cheap clerk? No. I'm here entertaining high officials and rich men.'

'But you sleep with them.'

She lowered and widened her violet eyes and from under long lashes whispered, 'If they can afford me.'

'What does that -?'

Kessler interrupted to call, 'Countess. How do you know my guest Colonel Stewartby so well? He only arrived from Geneva this afternoon.'

'Last time we met he arrested me as a spy.'

'Did you Stewartby? How ungallant.'

'Different place and different time,' snapped Stewartby. To Kristina he hissed, 'Can we get away from this group?'

'Only by dancing.'

'We'll never get into that crowd.'

'I'll find a way. Come on.'

She took his hand and pulled him down the steps into the thicket of entwined couples shuffling and sweating on the darkened dance floor.

She slid into his arms, wrapped herself round him and giggled at the immediate effect. Her lips caressing his ear, she whispered, 'The last time we met you had me completely in your power. Remember?'

He clutched at her then pulled back, his face hard. 'You were an enemy alien. I did my duty as an officer.'

'Don't be so pompous. You peeked through the window and watched me half naked. You enjoyed it. You know you did.'

'And I know you saw me watching. We both enjoyed it.'

She swayed forward, rolling her hips and whispered, 'Are we both enjoying this?'

He almost laughed – a strangled gurgle – and said, 'Stop teasing. Then you were a Countess and I was a colonel. Now you're a whore but I'm still a colonel. Stop this, or we'll never know where it may end.'

She wriggled, caressing him with hips and breasts, murmuring, 'Oh colonel, do we *want* it to end. There's a lot more here than you saw the last time.'

He threw her arms away and stepped back; jaw muscles clenching. He snapped, 'I can't put up with this. I'm leaving.'

'But darling, I'm just starting. Please don't go.'

He marched up the steps. Kristina trotted behind and called to Kessler, 'Oh Harry, Colonel Stewartby must leave. Please bring him again. I enjoyed his company after all these years.'

Kessler said, 'I'm afraid we must all leave. Come on gentlemen.' He slipped a wad of money to the Condesa and bowed to the Duchess as she unwound herself from one of the foreigners, deftly rearranging her clothes before standing to curtsey.

'What did you do to frighten the little Englishman?' asked the Condesa.

'Offered him what he wanted years ago but didn't get,' said Kristina.

'And he ran away?'

'Give me the binoculars,' said Kristina.

Stewartby strutted to the main door and paused. Kristina focused on his face and caught the wet gleam of lust in his eyes as he looked back.

She waved and after a slight hesitation he nodded.

'He'll come again,' she said.

Next night Kristina wore the short pearl-grey that showed her nipples and sat alone at table eighteen, refusing all offers. To keep a clear head she avoided cocaine and alcohol and – *Mein Gott. What a difference. How much worse this place looks when you're cold sober....*

Shortly after midnight she saw Stewartby slip through the main door alone. He made his way straight to Kristina and said, 'I couldn't concentrate properly last night with Kessler and his crew hanging round.'

She said, 'Why have you come again? Last night you called me a whore and left.'

'Think of my shock at seeing you here like this. I knew you as a Countess in Nairobi. Now you're a whore in Berlin. No point in saying otherwise.'

'But now I'm a whore and available you came back for me.'

He frowned and said, 'You may be right.'

She laughed and said, 'And I was right last night. You don't want it to end.'

'It hasn't started yet.'

'Oh yes it has – or you'd not have come back. It started when you watched me through that cell window in Nairobi. I don't want it to end either, darling, but life is difficult. I must earn a living.'

She shrugged and smiled, leaning forward as though pleading, watching him struggle to keep his eyes off the pearl-grey stretching across her nipples.

He said, 'I'm in Berlin for a month. Perhaps we can...meet? In the day. Away from this place.'

'Impossible.'

'Then how do I get to know you?'

'Simple. Pay to sleep with me. You think I'm a whore so treat me like one.'

'I can't do that.'

'Then go. You're wasting my time.'

He didn't move.

Lifting a cigarette from her bag Kristina leaned forward. 'Do you have a light, darling?'

In the two-second pause before Stewartby reached for matches she watched him surrender – saw his inner resolve wither and die. Blowing a delicate trickle of smoke, she raised an eyebrow and with a twist of her hand signalled a passing waiter. He nodded and skipped away to the bar.

Kristina said, 'What are you doing in Geneva?'

'League of Nations. I work in a section tidying up after the war. My contract's almost finished thank God. Another two months and I'll be back to Africa.'

*Back to Africa...*Kristina's heart thumped...*Two months? Not long....*

The champagne arrived and so did the Condesa. Kristina said, 'Where is the Duchess?'

'Following.'

Kristina held out her hand, palm upwards. 'Two hundred marks if you want to sit here.'

Stewartby stood and said, 'Introduce me to your friend.'

The Condesa said, 'Doesn't he speak German?'

'No. He speaks English.'

The Condesa said, 'Then let the Duchess have him. She speaks English.'

Kristina said, 'No. He's mine.'

'Just as well. He's a bit short for the Duchess.'

The Duchess sailed up inclining her handsome head and Kristina made introductions in English and German.

Stewartby frowned and said, 'Kristina, who are these people? Why can't we be alone?'

'They're my friends. Let them stay for a few minutes.'

The Condesa laughed and pointed across the room. 'Look. There's *Herr* Schwanz. I'll bet he's looking for you, Countess.'

'Where is he?' said Kristina.

'Over by the door. Ha! He's seen you. He's coming this way.'

'Oh God – not Schwanz,' cried the Duchess hiding her face. 'Not that awful boy.'

The three women fell to frantic giggling as a tall gangly young man burst from the crowded dance floor and stumbled up the steps shouting, 'Countess, I'm here. Come and dance with me.'

'I can't,' said Kristina, indicating Stewartby. 'I'm with him.'

Stewartby stood and said. 'Good evening, Herr Schwanz.'

The Condesa and Duchess fell again into helpless giggles.

The young man stepped back and stared down his hooked nose, arrogant blue eyes sparking with anger. 'What did he call me? What did he say? What are you laughing at? Are you drunk? Is he mad?'

'No. He doesn't speak German. He misunderstood a joke the Condesa told us. I'll introduce you.' Speaking English, she said, 'Colonel Stewartby, this is our young friend Reinhard. He's a naval cadet on leave in Berlin.'

Stewartby offered his hand and the young man took it with a stiff bow and said, 'Heydrich.'

'Heydrich?'

Kristina said, 'His name is Reinhard Heydrich. Don't say the other word.'

The young man stiffened to full height and said, 'You promised this evening and night to me. I already paid a deposit. Kick this damned Englishman out.'

'I can't. He's an old friend. Take the Condesa.'

The Duchess rose and said, 'No. Take me. It's my turn to have someone young blond and handsome. Tonight I'm yours for half price.' She took Heydrich by the arm and led him down the steps.

'Who the hell is that?' asked Stewartby.

Kristina said, 'A damned nuisance – a young boy from a country town throwing his savings away on a wild holiday in Berlin. He's on his way to join the navy in Kiel. This is the last fun he'll have for a year so he's making the most of it.'

'Bit of an odd fellow with that high voice, long nose and big hips. He's very blond but is he Jewish?'

'Perhaps. Who cares?'

'He seems angry with you.'

'He is.'

'Why?'

'He booked me for the night.'

'Booked you?'

'Yes. And paid a deposit.'

'A deposit? Good God.'

'How else should I run my business?'

'You make it sound like a taxi service.'

'Isn't that what we're called in America – taxi dancers?'

Stewartby clenched his fists and teeth in obvious anger.

Kristina laughed and said, 'Stewartby, darling. Look round. Everywhere here you see business – alcohol; drugs; sex. This is how we make our living.'

Stewartby shook his head. 'I must get you out of here,' he said.

'Are you booking me for the night?'

'If that's the only way we can leave this damned place.'

'Then give me five hundred marks now.'

'Why?'

Kristina pointed to the dance floor where Heydrich's sweep of blond hair and sweat-shining sloped forehead stood like a beacon above the other dancers.

'I must return his deposit.'

357

Chapter Fifty

Spider Web

Kristina hurried Stewartby into the street, linking arms and pulling him along, laughing when he said, 'For God's sake – what's the rush?'

'Darling Stewartby. Think of all the years to catch up on in one night.'

'Where are we going?'

'My flat. I don't like hotels.'

She dragged him through the crowds thronging Oranienburger Strasse. He said, 'Good God. What are all these people doing here at three in the morning?'

'Looking for what you've already found, darling.'

Entering the deserted alleys leading to her flat Kristina felt his muscles stiffen at a sharp hiss from a dark doorway. He turned to protect her but she pulled him along whispering, 'Take no notice. It's only a cocaine seller.'

In the next dim alley a man strolling in the opposite direction made the same hissing sound.

Stewartby said, 'What the hell *is* that?'

'I told you – cocaine sellers. Listen to the next one and you'll hear he's saying 'Tssigars' or 'Ttssigarettes'. It's a signal. If you want to buy cocaine you signal back with a loud sniff and he'll sell you as much as you want.'

'Christ – what a city.'

'Wonderful place,' said Kristina. 'You can find anything you want – cocaine, heroin, alcohol, boys, girls, a mixture of both; as many as you want in one night or one day or in one bed. You'll see. I'll show you.'

She hugged his arm; happy she'd worn low-heeled shoes – managing to be shorter than Stewartby by at least a centimetre, thank God.

At the house she led him on tiptoe past Madame's door and into the flat, throwing her fur coat aside as soon as she entered.

Kristina checked round. *Good. The maid's followed instructions.* With the small stove burning coal and lamps set low, the place looked warm and comfortable. Through the open door she saw plenty of towels, oils and perfumes laid out in the bathroom.

In a flash she stripped, sliding the pearl-grey down to fall round her feet. She stood naked in a pool of soft silk, laughing at Stewartby's expression of surprise and lust.

'I never wear knickers with that dress, darling,' she said, taking his hands and pulling him into the bedroom – dancing backwards on tiptoe; head tipped sideways, breasts jiggling – to start a frenzy of sex and debauchery that lasted two days.

That first night Kristina used all her knowledge and experience with fingers, lips, tongue and body to massage, tease and taunt him. Near dawn – slippery with sweat and oil and God knows what else – she collapsed across him; sighing, 'Darling. We must sleep.'

She woke at noon and slipped from the bed. Stewartby did not move so she crept to the bathroom and revived herself with a delicious sniff of cocaine. Not too much – just enough to give a pleasing tingle.

When the buzz subsided she splashed water over her face – checking her skin and eyes and adding a touch of makeup – then ran a bath and laid out shaving soap and razor before waking Stewartby with a kiss, whispering, 'Come on, my sweetheart. Time for a shave and a soak.'

He lay back in the water, soft as a puppy; eyes closed and said, 'Am I in heaven?'

She climbed in and knelt between his legs, soaping his chest and shoulders – 'I'll make you lovely and clean before you leave.'

His eyes opened. 'Leave? Why do I have to leave?'

'You must be gone by one o'clock. I need rest before going to work this evening.'

'Work? You're not going to work.'

He thrust to a sitting position in a surge of water, nearly tipping her over. Fearing his sudden anger she pulled back and perched on the bath edge; water and soap running in rivulets down the shining skin of her breasts and stomach. She snapped, 'I told you I do this for a living. Every client pays and is gone by one. Only a protector can stay.'

'A protector? What the hell is a protector?'

'A full time client – usually from out of town. He pays my rent, buys me clothes; takes me to restaurants and the theatre. In return I'm exclusive for the time he is in Berlin. At the end of his contract he gives me a gift and says goodbye until his next visit.'

His anger disappeared. 'That's simple. I'm here for a month. I'll be your protector.'

'Can you afford me?'

He ran a hand along her inner thigh – 'Of course. What do I get in return?'

She wriggled her hips against his slippery fingers. 'Whatever you want whenever you want it.'

'In that case – come back in here and show me how good you are in the bath.'

She swooshed down into the fragrant water, triumph shining in her violet eyes. *God how easy this is....*

During the afternoon while Stewartby slept, Kristina collected his clothes and wrapped in a robe padded barefoot down the corridor to scratch on Madame's door. 'Take these to the laundry. Have the shirt and collar starched, the suit sponged and pressed. I need them back before seven.'

Madame tipped her head to one side, crafty eyes peering – 'Will your friend be staying long?'

'On and off for a month.'

Madame raised an eyebrow.

'Don't worry. I'll see you get double rent.'

Kristina allowed Stewartby to sleep without interruption and dozed alongside him, allowing her mind to drift and dream. *A month. I have a month. I'll be a spider, spin a web and catch him in the middle ....*

At seven, quivering with excitement at her fully formed plan, she woke and bathed him again, laughing at his surprise on seeing his starched shirt, crisp clean underwear and smart pressed suit – 'I can't allow you out looking like a tramp.' – and brought half a dozen gowns from her wardrobe. Holding them up, one by one, she twirled round the room crying, 'Which shall I wear, darling? Tell me your favourite colour.'

'For God's sake keep still. You're making me dizzy. Where are we going?'

'To dinner. To dinner at Hiller's, the best restaurant in town. All the best people eat there – including your friend Harry Kessler.'

'Can we do that? Won't people know you?'

'Of course. But with you I'm a Countess not a courtesan. That's how it is in Berlin society. You'll see. Everyone in the same boat, darling. Not a wife in sight.'

Wearing an expensive plum-coloured gown and her best jewellery she led him into the restaurant, greeting elegant friends – both men and women – seated around the beautiful room.

Kristina whispered back, 'Give me a thousand marks.'

'Why?'

'You want a table, don't you?'

Settled at a corner table, Stewartby looked round and said, 'Well damn me. I know some of these fellows. I thought them honourable and decent. What are they doing here with these…courtesans? Do I speak to them?'

'Tonight yes. Tomorrow no. At least not about being here.'

'And I recognise one of the women. Isn't that your friend from last night?'

Kristina laughed. 'She's often here. Her clients like to be seen with a real Duchess'

'She's real?'

'Yes. She married a Romanov. The Bolsheviks shot her husband. She escaped to Austria. I met her through a friend of Kinskii's – an army officer in Vienna; a sort of helper to destitute refugees – especially beautiful *women* refugees. She passed through his hands a couple of months before me, so to speak. I met her by chance after arriving in Berlin. We laughed when we discovered we'd followed the same route.'

Stewartby frowned. 'And the Condesa? Is she real?'

Kristina chuckled. 'She *says* she's high born Spanish but I think she's a gypsy. The Duchess thinks she's Moroccan.'

'So why are they friends?'

'The Duchess…likes…women. They live together. They work together. You'll see when I invite them round one evening for a party. Just the four of us. I want to show you how things are in the *real* Berlin.'

She smiled into Stewartby's greedy eyes; ran teasing finger tips along his thigh and waved at the Duchess who acknowledged with a graceful dip of her handsome head.

For the next three weeks Kristina guided Stewartby through the sinks and sewers of Berlin's nightlife, showing him all variations of sex and vice available in that great city. He tried cocaine once but disliked the effect and loss of control – 'Bloody awful stuff.' – and refused more.

She worked hard; wrapping and bundling him in silky strands of sex and desire, weaving her complex web and trapping him in the centre.

Apart from cocaine he turned out to be a willing victim; accepting every deviation without complaint.

Some nights she took him to little nightclubs catering for every possible taste – the Oh La La for lesbians and prostitutes, the Mikado where he slow danced with a beautiful transvestite – 'Bloody hell, that was different' – and the Aleifa, a small club run by a family in their flat – mother, father and daughter – where a non-stop party ran all day and all night. 'This is a place for contact, darling,' Kristina told him. 'Men with men, women with women, women with men. If you like anyone, or any two or three, let me know and we'll take them home for our own party. We can have the mother and daughter if you wish.'

Other nights she dressed in jewels and finery and insisted on going to the theatre or fine restaurants – 'Just like a normal couple.'

'Christ, this is like being married,' he said one evening walking home arm in arm.

She laughed and said, 'Tomorrow we'll go shopping. I need new clothes.'

He paid without murmur from a wallet fat with Swiss Francs. 'What wonderful money, darling,' whispered Kristina. 'How lucky I am.'

Occasionally he disappeared for two or three days at a time, saying, 'Work. Some of 'em are still trying to hang on to their colonies.'

'What are you doing?' she asked.

'Helping transfer German African colonies to the Allies. It's frustrating that I must wait days between meetings. Still – I have no other duties so it allows us to be together.'

As a treat she surprised him by arranging a sophisticated evening of dinner and opera followed by a four-in-a-bed orgy, with the Duchess and the Condesa, amused by his fascination when they pushed him away and started their own lesbian games.

Laying to one side and watching, he whispered to Kristina, 'The Duchess is so bloody warm and stately – why the hell she prefers women I don't know.'

'Ask her,' said Kristina, so he did.

The Duchess laughed, raised her head from the Condesa and said, 'Oh no darling – I don't *prefer* women. I prefer *sensation*. The Condesa is so wonderful; so full of ideas. A most *inventive* partner.'

The Condesa glowered and said, 'Don't believe her. She prefers women. Why would she stay with a slut like me otherwise? Because of what I do to her. No man can match it. Watch.' She went to work and in no time reduced the Duchess to a quivering wreck, writhing and lost to abject pleasure.

When she finished the Condesa said, 'Come here man. I'll do the same for you,' but Stewartby shook his head and said, 'No. I've had enough for the night.'

Kristina sensed a weariness and jading of Stewartby's appetite. Next morning she woke Stewartby with a cuddle and said, 'I think we should relax for the next few days. You only have a week left in Berlin and we must make the most of it. We'll go shopping and for picnics and early to bed after dinner or the theatre. No more nightclubs. No more orgies. We'll spend time alone. Just the two of us.'

He snuggled against her and said, 'Good idea. Shopping, picnics and early to bed sounds wonderful.' He laughed. 'As I said before – like a married couple.'

Kristina tickled his ear with her lips, whispering, 'Yes, darling. Just like a married couple.'

She winked at her reflection in the long mirror.

Kristina worked hard to act the wife – a difficult part after so little practice. But concentrating on her new role she prepared picnics along the river, took him shopping and for walks in the park and went early to bed after demure dinners in quiet restaurants. She avoided cocaine – gritting her teeth when the need stretched her nerves – and drank only a little wine. She even prepared a couple of meals in the flat, surprised to find she could cook quite well.

It all seemed quite peaceful and friendly until, one night a simple joke swung his relaxed mood to murderous anger in seconds.

After a pleasant spring day on the river they ate dinner at a waterside restaurant and went early to bed where she cooperated in an especially active sex session. Playing to his vanity she cuddled against him afterwards and whispered, 'Darling Stewartby, where did you learn those things?'

He chuckled and said, 'From many years in different parts of Africa.

She gasped and said, 'African women? My God, Did they teach you those things?'

'That and more.'

She raised her head and giggled.

'What did Beatrice think of it?'

'I can't tell you that.'

She sat up and pulled at his fingers; playful and coy.

'Oh you can, you can. I'd love to know. She seemed such a prim little thing.'

A picture of Beatrice with her peaches and cream complexion and soft anxious eyes rose in Kristina's memory. 'I can't imagine she would do these things with you.'

In the yellow lamplight she saw his face darken and his eyes flash with fury. He pulled himself upright; shoulder muscles tensed; fists clenched.

For a moment she felt fear at this abrupt change – *My God, I've gone too far* – but through clenched teeth Stewartby said, 'She'd do them with any bloody man. Can you imagine that most of 'those things' were her idea? The insatiable bitch showed her refined little Englishwoman impression to the world but in bed she had the habits of an alley cat; a disgusting wriggling little whore – just like you. I hated her at the end when I knew that bastard Hocklyffe-Evans was getting it all and not me. I should have killed them both.'

Kristina gasped in delight – '*Did* you kill her?'

'No. Wish I had. But some bug got her when she went upcountry with that smarmy shit Hocklyffe-Evans. It saved me the trouble – and saved Hocklyffe-Evans. I'd have murdered them both and hanged for it but she died first.'

'Why didn't you kill him anyway?'

'No point after she died. If I couldn't do them both together I lost interest. I just hit him in the face a couple of times and left it at that.'

Kristina hugged herself in horror and glee. What a wonderful story. Overcome by the ferocity in his voice and his tense strong body, she held him tight, wrapped her legs around him and rubbed herself up and down his thigh.

'Am I really a disgusting wriggling little whore?' she asked. 'Tell me I am. Tell me again.'

Alight with lust she fell upon him, serving and ravishing him until they both collapsed in a sweaty heap, unable to move, sore and limp from the effort.

'Am I whore enough?' she whispered.

'Almost. Try harder next time.'

The next day she returned to her act as wife and insisted on lunch by the river. Walking arm-in-arm in the park afterwards he angered her by asking, 'What happened when you arrived in Hungary? I know you went there to find Kinskii's family.'

Her mind raced – *What did he hear before leaving Nairobi?*

Nervous and short of breath she gabbled, 'I found Kinskii's estate but the Bolsheviks took it over and his family lost everything. After my darling children died from that awful 'flu I managed to reach Vienna then Berlin where I found my family dead, our house destroyed by

Communists **and no sign** of my cousin Paul. I only intended to stay a short time in **Berlin but ran** out of money and became stuck.'

'Why did you come to Berlin? Why not go straight back to East Africa from **Budapest?**'

'Because of Kinskii. You must understand when he died I discovered I knew nothing about him. I followed his trail to Vienna and Berlin. Then I met Major Kreuz in the street. He knew all about why the Austrian Army sent Kinskii to Berlin. He knew what Kinskii did here and why he left in a hurry. Kreuz knew it all.'

'Kreuz? I've heard of him from the war in Africa. Clever bugger. Military intelligence. He *would* know everything. What did he say'

Kristina said, 'I can't tell you.'

'Oh yes you bloody well can.'

'It's difficult.'

'I'll make it more difficult if you don't tell me.'

'Someone may hear.'

'Don't talk nonsense. We're in the middle of a bloody great park. We'll sit on that bench. No one will come anywhere near us.'

'Are you sure?'

'Just bloody well sit down and get on with it.'

Kristina perched on the bench and paused; looking across the shining river feeling the warm sun on her face. She breathed in the crisp spring air and decided to tell the whole story.

'A couple of weeks after arriving in Berlin two years ago I went shopping on Kurfürstendamm and bumped into Kreuz and his son....'

Chapter Fifty-One

Mariska

Berlin: November 1920

Holding a tiny parasol against driving cold rain Kristina hurried along the Kurfürstendamm, cursing a splatter of mud that disfigured her new shiny shoes. A brightly lit shop – full of expensive underclothes – caught her attention. She ducked in, shaking droplets from her hat and parasol, smiling at a well dressed gentleman hunching his shoulders to slip through the closing door.

'The weather must be bad weather to force a man into a place like this,' she said.

He said, 'I saw you from across the street and ran to catch you.'

'Oh. So this is how handsome men pick up ladies in Berlin.'

He smiled and doffed his hat revealing a broad tanned forehead and thick brown hair. With a slight bow, said, 'Countess Kinskii, I believe?'

Kristina stepped back in surprise.

'How do you know me?'

He laughed. 'My name is Kreuz. We last met near Namanga in 1913.'

'Good God, I remember. A few months before the War. I translated at those political meetings between–'

'Please, Countess Kinskii. Say no more in public. Across the road is a café. Please join me for a quiet chat and coffee. I can recommend their pastries.'

In the café he asked for a table near the door – 'To see when my son arrives. He's at the hospital and I told him to meet me here.'

'At the hospital? I'm sorry. Has he been for treatment?'

'No. A physical examination. A formality to enter military academy. Ah – there he is.'

Kreuz stood and waved at a smart young boy of about nine or ten making his way towards them between the tables. Kreuz said, 'This is my son Heinrich.'

With his arm stiff at the elbow and a sharp formal bow, the boy shook hands, examining Kristina with disturbing self confidence. Such knowing eyes in so young a face – *God, he'll be dangerous when he's older....*

Kristina offered her most winning smile. 'Goodness. Did I hear your heels click?'

Kreuz said, 'Heinrich; this is Countess Kinskii. I knew her husband

366

some years ago.'

'My husband is now dead.'

'I know,' said Kreuz. 'My condolences.'

'Did he die in the African war?' asked the boy.

Startled at his thick Polish accent Kristina said, 'Where do you live? Not Berlin.'

Kreuz laughed and said, 'Heinrich lives on our family estate in East Prussia, near Stettin. Our servants and most of his friends are Polish. I'm hoping that military school in Berlin will get rid of that awful accent. Sometimes he's not sure if he's German or Polish – whether he's Heinrich Kreuz or Henryk Krzyz.'

The boy giggled and speaking with an exaggerated Berlin accent he said, 'Does *this* suit you better, father?' Then, to Kristina's relief, he settled down to eat three cream cakes and drink fizzy fruit soda like any other small boy.

Over coffee Kreuz said, 'How long have you been in Berlin?'

'About two weeks. I came to find my family but they seem to have died or disappeared. Our house is destroyed and the land taken as a commune by filthy Bolsheviks. They threw me off and I can find no authority here in Berlin to give me help. I don't know what to do.'

'You can do nothing. The collapse of this city is frightening. The centre seems normal but the suburbs are in dangerous chaos. I suggest you keep to the city centre and return to Africa as soon as possible.'

'I intend to. But first I must find my cousin Paul. I know he survived the war.'

Kreuz nodded and said, 'Yes. He survived.'

'Oh, thank God. Do you know where he is?'

'Away for a while.'

'Where?'

'I cannot say.'

'In the army?'

'We have no army.'

'But you know where Paul is.'

Kreuz leaned forward and whispered, 'Countess. Please. Do not speak of such matters in public. A few of us…loyal soldiers of Germany…keep contact and prepare.'

'Prepare for what?'

'Madame. He is away. Please do not speak of him again.' He managed to frown and look kind at the same time. After a moment he said, 'When do you return to Africa?'

'Soon. But I have another problem. I need to find out why my husband came to Berlin in nineteen hundred and three or four. I know he spent time here after leaving Hungary.'

Kreuz said, 'You came from Africa to discover this?'

Kristina said, 'No. I went first to Hungary to find my husband's estate and meet his mother....' She ran through her story, shortening the two year time scale to a few months; leaving out her adventures with Béla Kun and her involvements in Vienna, ending: '... What my husband did in Berlin I don't know and I'm anxious to find out about his time here.'

Kreuz sipped the last of his coffee and murmured, 'I may be able to help. Join me for dinner tonight. I'll bring a friend from my days with the army in Berlin. We both knew of your husband at that time.'

Kristina said, 'I realised at Namanga that something happened between you and Kinskii in earlier life but he never told me what.'

Kreuz took a card and scribbled a few words. 'Meet me here at eight. My friend had...official dealings with your husband. If he's free this evening I'm sure he'll help you over a private chat at this place.'

Restaurant Jäger: November 1920

Just before eight Kristina skipped across the pavement from cab to restaurant, shielding her hair against swirling wet sleet. A vigilant doorman hurried her through and she stopped; startled by the heat and noise of a room that seemed packed full of men – all smoking, drinking and turning to stare.

She shivered under the scrutiny – *Am I the only woman here?* – and peered through the heavy atmosphere, thick with mixed odours of cigar smoke, damp overcoats and male sweat, wondering why the hell Kreuz had suggested meeting in such a crowd.

Overcome with fright she stepped back towards the door but before she could leave a smart young waiter appeared murmuring, 'Countess Kinskii? Fo'low me please,' and ushered her through the throng to an alcove where Kreuz sat at a table with a short heavy man.

Kreuz stood and said, 'Countess Kinskii. Allow me to introduce *Herr* Staube of the Berlin police.'

Staube held out a hand but made no attempt to rise, speak or smile, his tiny black eyes completely without expression. Kristina shook hands, chilled by his dry touch and by intuition of great intelligence and great cruelty lurking behind this broad, bland face.

She sat opposite the two men, her back to the crowded restaurant and, to recover her nerve, glared at Kreuz and said, 'This seems a public place for a private chat.'

Staube shrugged and folded his hands across his stomach, just under a loop of watch chain.

Kreuz said, 'This has been our special corner for years. The noise outside masks our discussions – perfect for our needs.'

'Your needs?'

Kreuz said, 'Staube is head of police intelligence.'

'What does that have to do with me – or my husband?'

Staube took a deep breath and in a harsh whisper that penetrated the background noise with perfect clarity, said, 'In nineteen hundred and three your husband came to Berlin with evil intent. He came as a spy, a saboteur and a terrorist.'

Kristina's stomach clenched in shock at this strange man and his malevolent hiss but she managed to say, 'My husband was a soldier and a gentleman.'

Staube said, 'We know *exactly* what your husband was, Madam.'

'What do you mean by that? My husband came from a noble family. I went to his estate and met his mother....'

She gabbled on, repeating the story she told Kreuz earlier.

Not a flicker of movement showed in Staube's face. The damned man sat entirely still, his tiny black eyes holding Kristina in a vice. She felt the little beast stripping away the layers of lies until he reached her core of deceit. Fear gripped her heart at what he may already know – or what she might reveal.

Running out of story – and out of breath – she faltered into silence annoyed to see Staube's little fat fingers flutter on his stomach in obvious satisfaction. He said, 'Why do *you* think your husband came to Berlin?'

'I think he wanted to avoid family problems in Vienna.'

Staube took another deep breath and said, 'The Austrian secret service launched an intelligence operation against Germany using your husband as spearhead.'

'What nonsense. How do you know this?'

Staube ignored her and in that evil hiss continued, 'He came to Berlin and took cover in a previously arranged position as porter at the Hotel Continental.'

Kristina's fingers stole into her bag and stroked the photograph of Kinskii dressed as a servant, standing in a Berlin street with that...*woman.*

She said, 'Who arranged the position?

Staube hissed, 'Austrian intelligence. Such work gives easy contact with people of influence and allows smooth passage of secret information in the many messages a busy hotel porter gives and receives each day. But we knew his mission, his intentions, his targets, several weeks before he arrived in Berlin.'

Kristina caught her breath. 'You knew he was coming?'

She saw a brief shading of conceit pass through Staube's eyes but he stifled the stray emotion and said, 'Of course.'

Kreuz said, 'We also have spies.'

Staube said, 'We allowed him your husband rein but he made two serious mistakes and eventually gave us all we needed.'

'What mistakes did he make?'

'Firstly he kept the name Otto Kinskii and for disguise simply shaved off his moustache. Any self respecting spy will use false names and proper disguise when he travels. Your stupid husband did neither and his second serious mistake enmeshed him in our trap....'

Hotel Continental: September 1903

Otto stood by the concierge desk looking round the busy hotel entrance hall and stroking his naked upper lip, regretting the loss of his beautiful moustache.

Ebenstein's last instructions echoed in his head – 'Be patient. Settle and blend in. Our people will make contact with you after a few weeks.'

A few weeks? Almost three months. Three bloody months of running round this hotel, carrying bags, touting for tips – 'Make sure you act like a true porter,' Ebenstein said. 'Look and act humble – take off that damned great moustache, for instance and stop looking like a cavalryman. Remember you're playing a part....'

Playing a part? No problem for Otto. Like any good actor, his whole life is made up of parts – the young horseman, the brilliant circus performer, the brave soldier, the noble Count and now the humble porter; eyes down, palm extended, tingling for a tip. But what a dreary low grade part after all the major roles; the brilliant lies and perjuries. Oh God – how are the mighty fallen....

Pleased with the quote he smiled to himself and received an answering smile from a young maid scurrying past in her black dress and white mob cap.

He switched his face to a frown trying not to stare at the young woman weaving a dance through the packed lobby; so neat and interesting in that crisp little uniform: *Don't want her to think I'm making eyes – and in any case the mighty fell in battle, not in boredom....*

The young maid trotted on, peeking over her shoulder still smiling; head tilted in obvious invitation. Otto watched her tiny figure disappear into the shadows of a corridor; white cap and escaping strands of delicate blond hair bobbing in the gloom.

Her room's only a few metres from mine in the servant's quarters. I wonder...?

Restaurant Jäger: November 1920

Kristina said, 'Your trap? A serious second mistake? What are you talking about?'

Staube sucked in air and said, 'Stop interrupting. Listen. As a true born Prussian you will understand that our historic Germanic lands must include Austria but without those rag-ends of barbarian nationality that cling to our borders – the cunning bastard Czechs, the mad idiot Serbs, the damned Croats and Slovenes and all the other low thieving races that try to live off our German progress and culture – including those gypsy whore Hungarians with their airs and graces and their filthy horses and their wily ways.'

He spoke without emotion or expression in those tiny black eyes fixed so firmly on Kristina. She stared back, surprised by quiver of sexual arousal at this man's deep evil and infinite calm. *By God – this would be sleeping with the devil....*

Pressing her thighs together, she sighed at the sweet attraction of depravity and felt Staube's scalpel eyes probe deep into her inner being – *The damned man knows what he's doing to me. The beast. The vile beast....*

But unable to resist she squeezed herself in rhythms of sly pleasure and tried to concentrate on Satan's harsh whisper.

'To repel these *Untermenschen* we needed Austria as part of our Greater German fortress – an impregnable wall holding back the eastern tribes. Your fine *Hungarian* husband came to Berlin to spy on the architects of that wall and destroy their efforts. But his masters in Vienna left him without contact for too long and he became bored. This led to his second serious mistake....

Hotel Continental: October 1903

Otto strode along the hotel corridor, pausing under a lamp to check his scrap of paper, unsure of the problem in room two-seven-eight. 'Just get along there,' said the manager. 'You're needed to help.'

Otto turned his master key, tapped on the door of two-seven-eight and stepped in to find the room almost in darkness. He paused, his muscles tensing at a scent of danger.

A woman's voice whispered, 'Thanks for coming. I've been waiting to meet you.'

A second passed before Otto realised the woman spoke in Magyar. His eyes searched the gloom and he saw a tiny figure outlined against light seeping through a curtain. He said, 'I didn't realise you are Hungarian.'

She moved forward, taking off her white cap, fluffing delicate blond hair with flicking fingers. She said, 'Close the door and come in.'

Otto said, 'Who are you?'

'Your contact. We are on the same side.'

Restaurant Jäger: November 1920

Kristina's slipped the photograph from her bag and placed it on the table in front of Staube. He leaned forward and whispered, 'Ah. Mariska....'

Kreuz peered down at the picture and murmured, 'I remember....'

The young waiter pushed in carrying steaming bowls of food – 'I ordered goulash,' said Staube. 'It seemed appropriate.'

He slid a hand over the photograph until the waiter left then lifted the grey card towards the light for closer study.

'Please eat,' he said. 'Where did you find this picture?'

'Among my husband's things.'

'Did you find anything else of interest?'

'No. Only this. It is why I came to Berlin.'

'So he kept a copy.'

'Why shouldn't he?'

'Because it nearly killed him.'

Hotel Continental: March 1904

Laying alongside Mariska in the cool dawn, Otto lifted his head and stared at this wisp of a woman – this tiny frame filled with such passion and strength of purpose. *But Ebenstein is bloody clever. Who'd think this little thing would run a network of agents?*

Otto grinned at his own surprise that day in two-seven-eight. What had she said? – *'I'm your contact.'* He remembered sitting in the darkened room while she confirmed Ebenstein's feeling that her network had become jaded and said, 'So now you are in charge. You must make it all work again.'

He remembered how she handed over to him with relief – or so she said. 'I never wanted to be leader but Ebenstein insisted when things began to go wrong and von Beck disappeared.'

'What happened to him?'

'We don't know. He walked into the dark after one of our secret meetings and we never saw him again. Perhaps the Kaiser's secret police killed him or perhaps the Serbs or perhaps he became sick of the whole thing and gave up.'

Restaurant Jäger: November 1920

Staube said, 'So your husband took over and set about revitalising his network by sending some members back to Austria and isolating those who remained into cells – one agent per cell and no contact allowed except with your husband. A good idea we have since copied.'

'So he wasn't such a stupid spy.'

'In some ways no – certainly not the typical empty-headed cavalry officer we expected. He learned fast and built his network quickly with new trusted agents but still failed to detect and dispose of an agent we had previously inserted into the operation. At first we allowed your husband some success then through this agent began to direct him along the political route we wanted.'

'I don't believe you. My husband was not easily pushed one way or another.'

'We didn't push him. We showed him an attractive path and led him along it towards our Greater Germany. He turned out to be a great help.'

'How?'

'Our Kaiser knew that whiskered old fool Franz Josef and his stupid son stood in our way and considered shooting them both but we persuaded him not to. Assassination may be fast and effective but you can never predict the end result as we saw ten years later at Sarajevo. That affair had nothing to do with us by the way. Those stupid Serbs acted alone and wrecked our whole plan. If only they'd been patient we'd have given them everything they wanted.'

'You were working with the Serbs?'

'We worked with *everybody*. Serbs, Czechs, Austrians, Hungarians – even the damned Russians. To control strategy our Kaiser set up and financed a group of dissident Austrian politicians sheltering in Berlin from their Emperor's political police He instructed them to fund and run Austrian political factions in favour of union with Germany. Our Kaiser promised everybody what they wanted – security to the Austrians, Bosnia to the Serbs and independence to the Czechs and

Hungarians. A brilliant plan soon detected by the Austrian secret service so they set up a counter operation in both Berlin and Vienna.'

Kristina said, 'Not everyone wants to be German.'

Staube continued without break – 'The Austrians infiltrated our group in Berlin and began to intercept funds and neutralise our people in Vienna. But we soon knew of their attack and detected the traitors.'

'How?'

'By counter infiltration. We slipped an agent into their ranks. An agent so secret and difficult to spot that our counter attack worked perfectly until your husband came into the picture. For a while our agent had to lie low and co-operate with his reorganisation. But once your husband settled in, made his changes and thought his operation secure, we recommenced penetration with excellent results and by careful manipulation things began to go our way again.'

'And my husband never suspected?'

'Our agent was extremely cunning. Of course it helped us that during those months the Serbs assassinated their King and the Hungarians became restless for freedom from the Austrian Empire. Confusion and turmoil throughout the Balkans helped our cause. By the time our agent resurfaced your husband had established a good reputation with his masters in Vienna and both he and they swallowed all the wrong information we fed into his reports without question.'

'Surely my husband was not that stupid?'

'Not stupid – blinded and led astray. Our very clever agent suborned him for a while and almost convinced him to work for us but then made a mistake and your husband slipped free of our control with tragic results.'

Hotel Continental: May 1904

Otto sat in his small room finishing the letter to Ermine in Vienna. He paused, leaning back to flex stiff shoulders and run his memory over the past few months, wondering if this report should hint at his current worry.

Without doubt Mariska's recent actions and comments showed a pattern that gelled in his head last night when she held him close and whispered, 'You must remember why we are *really* here in Berlin – to save our country.'

Balanced on his elbows, he looked down at her tiny face – peeking out so small and vulnerable from a gathering of white sheet – and stroked her soft blond hair, spreading a graceful fan across the pillow.

He said, 'You mean our Empire.'

'No. Our *country*. Hungary. Freedom is almost in our grasp.'

In half-light squeezing through the thin curtains he saw her eyes shine with almost religious intensity.

'You've had too much wine,' he whispered. 'Go to sleep.'

She giggled and turned away, leaving him puzzled – not so much by her words as the brief ferocity in her eyes. While she slept he stayed awake, pondering the connection between Mariska and Ermine.

At dawn she left with barely a snatched kiss and he did not see her all morning and missed her usual practice of coming through the lobby to brush by and exchange a secret touch in passing.

Secret. The word rang in his head. He set down his pen and stood to pace the room, agitated by implications of... *No. It's not possible....*

He checked his watch and saw he had time to get down to the river and back for his evening shift at four o'clock.

Tucking the letter into his jacket, he wiped a damp cloth over the white braid at collar and cuffs; brushed lint from his peaked cap and checked in the mirror that he looked smart enough to be outside on the street wearing his Continental uniform.

He walked fast to the riverside then slowed to a stroll among young families and wandering lovers enjoying the late afternoon sun. A well-dressed elderly gentleman appeared, shuffling along the path with the aid of a thick walking stick.

Otto checked and saw no one out of place among this relaxed gathering so turned aside to sit on a bench and look out across the river Spree.

The elderly gentleman settled alongside Otto and placed his tall black hat on the bench brim up, sighing and closing his eyes in the obvious exhaustion of old age. Otto watched the strolling throng until sure only new faces flowed past then slipped the envelope from his pocket, dropped it into the old man's hat and stood to leave.

Opening his eyes, the old man grabbed Otto's arm and said, 'Excuse me, Sir. I wonder if you'd help me to my feet?'

'Of course,' said Otto, bending to lift.

The old man thrust his head close and whispered, 'A message from von Beck. Do not trust the Hungarian woman and beware of her friend Staube.'

'Von Beck? But–'

'Say nothing. Go.' The old man shuffled away with surprising speed – an elderly banker hurrying back to close his books for the day.

Otto waited for a moment, smiling at two pretty children skipping along the pathway. The words *'Freedom is almost in our grasp'* ran through his head. He took a last deep breath of fresh air and made his way back to the Continental deep in thought; trying to plan what he should do next.

Halfway through his evening shift the incoming flood of new guests eased and Otto found a moment to drink coffee in the kitchen with his friend the head waiter. Leaning against a counter discussing the new intake Otto said, 'Has Staube been in recently?'

The head waiter said, 'He's eating dinner here right now. Why do you ask?'

'His name came up in conversation and I wondered what he did.'

'He's one to keep away from. Secret police but not so secret we don't all know. Who spoke of him?'

'It doesn't matter. I've never heard the name before and wondered who he is.'

'Well now you know. He's a dangerous bastard so shut up and don't ask anyone else about him.'

'Did you ever hear of a man called von Beck?'

'Christ, Kinskii. Who *have* you been talking to?'

'Oh for God's sake, Hans. Idle conversation in a bar, that's all. The names came up and I wondered why.'

'Von Beck used to come here too. One of those damned renegade Austrian politicians always hanging round Berlin hoping for a handout. He disappeared a year ago and turned up in the river six months later. Someone had weighed the poor bastard down and chucked him in. He'd been underwater all that time, poor sod. What sort of friends do you have to talk about such dangerous things?'

'Why dangerous?'

'Politics, my friend. These days, politics are dangerous. Keep your nose out or you could end up in the river, too. No one would notice or care about a damned Hungarian. You wouldn't get one lousy line in the evening paper.'

That night Otto wrote a chatty letter to Ermine. *I met your uncle in the park this afternoon. He gave me some interesting news about an old school friend I thought left Berlin a year ago....* Using the agreed book code Otto spelled out von Beck, Staube and Mariska and in an apparently amusing letter on life and work in the Continental told Ebenstein that the Berlin network seemed penetrated and asked for instructions.

Using standard panic procedure he sent the letter through normal post to the address of an elegant villa in the Vienna suburbs and continued to work and act as normal whilst awaiting reply – even sleeping with Mariska most nights; even managing to act the tender lover and mask his suspicion and growing mistrust.

'How do you know this?' asked Kristina, turning the photograph with a fingertip and staring down at this damned tiny blond woman smiling across the years. *God, how I hate her....*

'Because *she* told me. Mariska. *She* was my special secret agent – and absolutely brilliant but erratic and difficult to control. Always full of new ideas and always chasing the men. A real minx. That was how she spied. It never failed. *Off with your trousers. Into bed. And tell me all your secrets, darling.*'

'So she was a whore.'

'That may be. But it certainly worked on your husband with the added bonus that he *really* fell in love – so much that he continued sleeping with her even after knowing she betrayed him.'

Kreuz said, 'Does that worry you?'

Kristina shrugged, trying her best to display indifference. 'My husband lived a life before I met him. This woman means nothing to me.'

She felt Staube's scalpel eyes dig into her brain and unmask her furious jealousy. She glared back, saying, 'If she was *really* brilliant she'd have kept her mouth shut, drunk or not.'

'True. If she'd stayed sober that night your husband would never have guessed she may be my spy. And I would have continued to control his network in Berlin. In the end, because of *her* stupid mistake I had to meet your husband and let him know our game and give him a chance to join the party, so to speak.'

Otto received and decoded a pretty postcard from his friend Ermine, apparently on holiday in the Tyrol mountains: *She's ours. Don't worry and act as normal. Say and do nothing until courier arrives with more information....*

Otto ripped the postcard into shreds. *What the bloody hell is Ebenstein up to? Didn't he trust me with his special agent?*

He sat in his room burning the strips of card one by one, poisonous suspicion seeping through his soul – *Damned Ebenstein. Damned Mariska. Oh God, why didn't I die fighting the Serbs...?*

Two weary days later he tried to refuse when Mariska suggested a lunchtime break – 'The weather is so lovely. We shall sit by the river and eat sandwiches.'

'I only have an hour. It's not worth it. I don't have time to change.'

'Oh darling. You look so smart in your Continental uniform and in any case I have a picnic in this basket.'

Otto looked down at her winsome blond-framed face. She lowered her eyes and pouted. '*Please,* darling.'

'Oh...very well.'

Unable to trust anything she said or did he sat with her by the river bank, eating sandwiches and drinking beer; concentrating on every syllable, trying to detect false notes in her flow of happy chatter.

Walking back to the hotel she linked her arm through his and continued to prattle. When a street photographer stepped forward, waving his camera – 'A picture of the handsome soldier and his lady.' – Otto shook his head and snapped, 'I'm a porter, not a soldier.'

Taking no notice the photographer planted his tripod and said, 'Stop just there and give me a smile.'

'Oh for God's sake,' snarled Otto but Mariska hung back, dragging at his arm.

'Oh *please* darling. You've been such a grumpy bear for the past three days. Please stop and smile for the man. I'd love a picture. I'll pay.'

Otto looked down and saw pleading in her eyes. She said, 'Just one picture darling. Please. For me. Take your hat off so your handsome face shows. Don't look so serious. Smile. Just for me. Smile....'

Oh, what the hell. Unable to resist grinning at her tenacity, he removed his hat and turned, head bent. She held his arm tight, fluttering her fingers across the back of his hand, whispering, 'Good boy,' and the flash tray went *Whoosh.*

Before Otto could move, the photographer thrust a card at Mariska, snatched his tripod together and disappeared into the crowd.

'My God, that was quick,' said Otto.

'Don't worry.' Mariska waved the card. 'I know him. I'll go to his studio tomorrow.'

Next evening Otto stood by the concierge desk watching the flow of incoming guests and diners. A short thickset man passing through the lobby stopped and stared. Otto lifted a finger and prepared to be called but the man stood without moving, tiny black eyes and broad bland face completely without expression

Otto shrugged and turned away, murmuring, 'We meet some odd people here.' The head porter grunted and whispered, 'And Staube's odder than most.'

'That's Staube?'

'Didn't you know? Watch out for the bastard – especially if he shows interest in you.'

In the kitchen a few minutes later the head waiter sidled up to Otto and said, 'Staube asked after you. What have you been up to?'

'Nothing. How does he know me?'

'He certainly knows what you look like. He described you and asked your name.'

'Did you tell him?'

'Of course.'

The picture. She gave him the picture....

'Should I worry?'

The head waiter shrugged. 'He seemed in a good mood. Perhaps he wants you to work for him. Some do in this hotel.'

'Who?'

'God only knows but it's common knowledge.'

'Do you?'

The head waiter laughed – 'Only when he asks.'

'How does he ask.'

'Calls you to a meeting.

'How?'

'You receive a message. Then you either go to the meeting or leave the country.'

Numbed by Mariska's treachery and Staube's cunning, Otto kept working to the end of his shift then hurried to Mariska's room and relieved tension by hammering at the door with a clenched fist, calling – 'Come here. I must speak with you.'

After a short delay she peeked out and whispered, 'I'll come across in five minutes, darling.'

Darling. How the hell can she call me darling....

In his room Otto paced the floor in growing agitation, his mind reeling as certain things fell into place: *For instance – why does she never let me into her room? She always comes across the corridor to mine. Why? Because she has too much to hide....*

Mariska slipped through the door and ran to embrace him, 'I know what's happened but don't be angry with me darling. What I'm doing is for us – and for Hungary. Listen to me. Please sit down and listen. There. That's better. Be comfortable for a few minutes while I explain. Look – I owe nothing to Austria. *Nothing.* You owe even less. Those bastards in Vienna have all screwed you into the ground – even your own father.'

Otto listened in disbelief while this little blond wisp of a woman spat hate against Austria and the Empire in a tumbling frenzy of words – 'How can we be free? Only by fighting. It's easy for a man but I'm just a weak woman so what can I do? I have no strength or weapons so I fight in my own way. I use trickery. Ebenstein thinks I work for *him*. Hah. I work for Hungary and use that horrible snake Staube as my weapon. Join me, darling. Join with me to free our country.'

'How did you get started on this?'

'Through Ebenstein. I came from Budapest to Vienna. Ebenstein keeps watchers at the station and picks up women then seduces them – sets them up in a lovely apartment with promises of wealth and security then tricks them into doing what he wants; to spy or to make money for him.'

'How?'

'In different ways. With me he used Staube's daughter. Ebenstein made sure we met and became friends when she studied in Vienna. I returned with her to Berlin for a holiday and stayed in her house and her father set me up in the Continental to spy for him not knowing I was Ebenstein's plant. But *Ebenstein* didn't know I'd come to Vienna to work for *Hungary*, so when his net caught me he didn't know he'd pulled in a shark – or better – an eel.' She laughed. 'As an eel I can slither through anything.'

'Did you get rid of von Beck?'

'I wanted him gone but hated it when the Kaiser's men killed him. Poor man was such a cuddly old dear. Still – if his death helps the Prussians break up the stupid Austrian Empire, poor old von Beck will have served his purpose.'

'So you want me to join your crusade?'

'Yes, darling. Please, darling. Staube wants to meet you.'

'And he asked you to arrange it.'

'Please, darling. It will help us both.'

'You arranged that photograph for Staube.'

'Darling. I had to. He forced me. He needed to see what you looked like.'

'Have you told him everything I told you about my family?'

'No darling. Of course not. I'd never let you down.'

Otto almost spat into her wide innocent eyes but – for Austria – held his temper and managed to keep control. Through gritted teeth he said, 'Very well. I'll speak with the man.'

'Oh thank you, darling. Thank you, thank you. I'll tell him. He'll send you a message and tell you where to meet. Thank you, darling. Thank you so much. You will help me so much. Can we go to bed now?'

'No. Leave me. I need to think. And do not speak of this to anyone until I meet Staube.'

'Very well, darling. Not a word.' She kissed him on the cheek and tiptoed out, peeking back with a shy smile.

God. What an actress. And why did I tell her so much about myself? Never again. I'll never open my mouth to a woman again....

Consumed with guilt and hate Otto prowled back and forth across his room until near dawn. After several attempts to calm down he felt steady enough to sit and draft a coded telegram to Ermine. He went by tram to send it from a small suburban post office, returning twenty-four hours later to collect a reply that said – *Meet courier on day seventeen at same time and place you met my uncle.*

Two days later Otto wandered again through pleasant spring air along the river bank, his eyes alert for some signal from the strolling crowd. He ambled along the riverside and approached the bench at exactly five minutes past the hour. A young woman sitting with two small children eating ice cream caught his eye and hurried away leaving the bench empty.

Otto leaned back and stretched his legs. A tall young man with thick well barbered hair and a beautiful moustache curving perfect arcs across his cheekbones walked from the crowd and said, 'Is this bench free?'

'Of course,' said Otto. 'Do sit down.'

Otto relaxed and watched the passing crowd for two minutes then murmured, 'Why are you here, Ebenstein?'

'I sent the woman Mariska to penetrate Staube's operation. She did it brilliantly and we learnt a lot about the Kaiser's secret police. Before von Beck disappeared I began to suspect she had turned and become a double, working for Staube. Von Beck certainly thought so, as you know.'

'How do I know? I never met or spoke with him.'

'Yes you did. A couple of weeks ago on this very bench.'

'The old man....'

'Exactly. *That* was von Beck.'

'But I thought he'd drowned.'

'So did we. Until after that body came out of the river and he sent me a cable saying, *'Now I'm dead I know I'm safe.'*

Ebenstein chuckled and smoothed his moustache; first with the back of his hand then with fingertips teasing a few stray wisps into place.

'The old goat's quite witty and clever. He's been a spy all his life. Now we have him tucked away deep in a government bank, helping finance the Kaiser's military build-up. He blends in as the perfect civil servant – even has an unbreakable Prussian accent. No one would ever think he's Austrian. He's sending us amazing economic intelligence.'

Fighting rising anger, Otto managed a friendly smile – two young men chatting in the park – and said, 'Why the hell didn't you tell me.'

'If you'd known you'd never have flushed the woman out. I had suspicion but no fact.'

'What suspicion? And why did von Beck run?'

'I told him to. I suspected she'd called the Serb to Berlin and guessed the target. But instead of coming to me von Beck disappeared. Until he surfaced – so to speak – I thought the Serb had got him.'

'The Serb?'

'Your girl friend's lover. A heartless butchering political assassin. You'd never think it to look at him – curly brown hair, happy smile, big brown eyes – the image of a carefree young student. We'll get him one day – or you will.'

'Me?'

'He's the hunter. You're the bait. Mariska's the lure. The Serb's still in Berlin and under her orders. Soon she'll set him on you same as she did von Beck. Then he'll be out in the open. That's when you kill him.'

'Why the hell should she set him on me?'

'All in the cause of Greater Serbia, my friend. Your work here is too good and affecting their operations. They both want you gone – Staube for his damned *Gross Deutschland* and the woman for her damned Greater Serbia.'

'Ebenstein. I can't believe any of this. It's too far fetched. You're making it up. And if von Beck didn't die, who did?'

'God knows. Some old buffer the same age as von Beck.'

'So who threw *him* in the river?'

'Probably von Beck.'

'Bloody hell, Ebenstein. This is ridiculous.'

'No. I told you – von Beck's a cunning old devil. He knows how to cover his tracks.'

Ebenstein smiled and tickled at his moustache – 'I promise you this all is based on a first class source.'

'Who?'

'Can't tell you.'

Otto jumped to his feet. 'In that case I *really* don't believe a word.'

Ebenstein laughed. 'Being a spy is not as simple and clear-cut as being a cavalry officer.' He patted the wooden seat. 'Sit down. There's more to say.'

Otto checked his watch. 'I only have ten minutes.'

'Listen. You'll soon be talking with Staube. Your orders are to work with him so you're in place when Mariska disappears. I don't want to lose my link into the Kaiser's secret police.'

'How the hell do you know I'm meeting Staube?'

'Never mind. Just follow orders and wait for the Serb.'

Otto turned to speak just as Ebenstein's eyes and concentration switched to a group of young girls walking by, their flimsy summer dresses fluttering in the sunlight. Otto waited until Ebenstein had seen enough then said, 'So I act the double agent and become a murderer.'

'That's exactly what you do.'

'Do I eliminate Mariska too?'

'No. When you've killed the Serb I'll kidnap her back to Vienna and squeeze her dry about Staube's operation and her friends in the Hungarian independence movement and what the hell those mad Serbs are planning next.'

'She knows all that?'

'She's probably the best agent in the world. A pity she always works for the other side. Keep her safe. I need her. I'm ordering you to protect her. Her life is more value to the Empire than yours.'

'Thanks.'

Restaurant Jäger: November 1920

Kristina said, 'How do you know all this?'

'Ebenstein told me a few hours after speaking with your husband.'

'You talked with *Ebenstein*?'

'Of course. Our interests coincided.'

'How?'

Kreuz leaned forward and said, 'As I think you already know, Ebenstein's main interests are money and women.'

'How on earth would I know that?'

Kreuz tipped his head to one side, eyebrows raised. 'We *are* intelligence officers,' he said. 'We know of your...*friendship*...with Ebenstein.'

Kristina pulled her lips together and looked down at a black line of goulash gravy trickling across the white tablecloth from Staube's plate.

Staube dragged in a deep breath – Kristina heard it scrape into his lungs – and said, 'Your husband followed Ebenstein's orders and waited for my contact. In the meantime, the woman Mariska disappeared. We all lost sight of her until your husband....

Hotel Continental: June 1904

When Otto returned from his meeting with Ebenstein, the duty manager hurried forward and said, 'Where's your girlfriend? She's gone.'

'Gone? Where?'

'I hoped you'd tell me. She didn't ask permission. Simply walked out this morning. Not a word to anyone. Have you any idea why?'

'No. Absolutely not.'

'Well as far as I'm concerned, she's sacked. You can tell her if you see her again.'

'Did you check in her room?'

'Of course. It's empty. Completely empty.'

'May I go and see for myself?'

'If you wish.'

Using his master key Otto entered Mariska's tiny room, pausing at the threshold to sniff at the air for some lingering scent of her presence.

Unsettled by a feeling of menace, he browsed through the empty drawers and wardrobe; checked the folded bedclothes; ran fingertips along floorboards and under the bed, seeking imperfections that may reveal a hiding place for...what?

He pulled out the chamber pot. Clean and fresh and showing no sign of use – just like everything else in this bare room. *For all I know she never slept here. Perhaps that's why she banned me from entering. Did she allow anyone else in? Doesn't look like it.*

Replacing the chamber pot he rose and caught a reflection in the dressing-table mirror and stiffened at the shocking sight of...a porter. A *porter*. A damned, stupid, servile, low class porter. A brainless beast without even enough common sense to see through the tricks and wiles of one cunning woman.

Good God. What have I become?

He stared in dismay at this stupid uniform and his stupid life so far. Otto the stable boy. Otto the circus show-off. Otto no-name until he blackmailed *Kinskii* out of the man who refused to call him *son*.

Kinskii.

As Otto-the-porter watched, the mirror-picture blurred and

384

reformed to increasingly clear images of Kinskii the soldier, Kinskii the hussar; Kinskii the Emperor's young lion. Substance and strength flooded through the mirror-picture and Otto-the-porter faded and died along with Otto no-name.

Kinskii. I'm Kinskii and to hell with anything else.

He turned and marched from the room, bumping into the hurrying head porter who said, 'Thank God I've found you. A young fellow brought this. Said it's important and to do with Mariska.' He thrust an envelope into Kinskii's hand. 'What does it say? What's happened to her?'

Kinskii broke the seal and scanned the note. 'It says she's well.'

'Thank heaven for that,' said the head porter. 'I thought she'd been abducted or something. Will she be back?'

'No. The young man. What did he look like?'

'A student. Cheerful type of chap – curly hair, happy smile, big brown eyes – probably foreign, from his accent.'

Kinskii said, 'I can't work tonight. Find someone else for my shift.'

'You're going to see Mariska?'

'Perhaps.'

In his room Kinskii changed into a pair of grey trousers, a soft shirt and a loose jacket with big pockets. Crouching to pull the bed aside he removed a section of floorboard and hooked out two pistols wrapped in heavy waterproof paper.

He wiped away excess oil and slipped the smaller short-barrel Smith & Wesson into his right-hand jacket pocket where it nestled with barely a bulge and drew without snagging in several practice snatches.

He repacked the Luger and – with reluctance at loss of heavy bullet knockdown power – tucked it back into its hiding place under the floor. *Never a hope in getting the damned thing out of my pocket in time.*

From another cubby-hole he unwrapped a box of .38 cartridges and loaded the revolver, sighing with pleasure as the sleek bullets slid into their shining chambers. *My God, it's good to be a soldier again.*

Leaving the hotel by a back route he walked along pavements thronged with shoppers; dawdled between market stalls; wandered through a busy department store and skipped at the last second on a passing tram. A young man with curly hair – possibly a student – jumped from the crowd and tried to scramble up but the tram jerked away and he slipped from the step. His ankle must have twisted because he staggered and dropped a square of paper, diving to retrieve it from between the rush of passing feet.

Following directions in Mariska's note Kinskii changed trams several times and near dusk arrived in the run-down eastern section of Berlin. He stepped out into a grimy street packed with home-going factory workers walking or thrusting past on bicycles.

He checked the landmarks given by Mariska and strolled three hundred metres back the way he had come, stopping to ask a workman for further directions – leaning forward to hear the man's reply over the rattle of an oncoming tram hauling into the stop he had just left.

Turning into an alley by a small café he looked back and through the mass of moving heads saw a young man hop off the tram and hurry down the road, curly brown hair waving in the evening breeze. Kinskii ducked into the alley and passed quickly through into the narrow rubbish-filled courtyard of a block of badly built workers' houses.

The area stank of boiling cabbage and urine. Groups of housewives dressed in worn aprons stood gossiping, ignoring gangs of ragged children running and shouting in complex games between piles of debris.

Kinskii stepped across the courtyard, trying to read house numbers through deepening dusk. His eye caught movement in a shadowed doorway – a tiny woman ducking back into the house; blond hair shimmering in the twilight.

Dodging between the gossiping groups Kinskii plunged into a dark hall and followed the clatter of heels up bare wooden stairs, through a swinging paint-peeled door into a small room bare of curtains or carpets. He paused, sniffing dust and decay; blinking to adjust his eyes to the uncertain light.

Mariska stood by a dirty window, peering into the courtyard.

She opened her arms. 'Oh darling Otto,' she cried. 'It *is* you. I wasn't sure. Come here and give me a kiss.'

He stepped forward and she giggled, hitching her large handbag out of the way before embracing him and whispering, 'Darling, you're so *clever* to follow my directions and find me.'

From below he heard an echo of footsteps in the hall.

Mariska clung to Kinskii, murmuring, 'This must be Staube. He's always on time. Give me one last kiss.'

Kinskii lifted and hugged Mariska, swinging her feet from the floor in a half turn towards the door and set her down, patting his right-hand jacket pocket. 'God, I need a cigarette,' he said. 'Do you have matches?'

She stepped back. 'Are you nervous, darling?'

'Of course. Give me a light.'

He closed his fingers round the pistol butt while she fished about in her handbag. The footsteps started up the stairs and increased speed.

Mariska said, 'Ah, here they are,' and Kinskii heard the click of matches in their box.

The door burst open and a young man leapt through swinging a heavy revolver. Kinskii swept the Smith & Wesson from his pocket in a smooth curve shooting twice before the young man had time to find a target. Hearing the rattle of a falling matchbox Kinskii turned to see Mariska bringing a little pistol to bear on his head and shot two bullets into her face and throat.

Both bodies collapsed, heads thumping the wooden floor and raising dust. Blood pumped from Mariska's throat and oozed from a small hole in her face. Kinskii stepped over her corpse and knelt to check the young man. Both bullets had passed plumb into his heart leaving no trace in his thick wool jersey. Kinskii heard the front door open. The young man's curly brown hair stirred in a slight breeze from the stairwell.

Kinskii ran hands through the young man's pockets, finding nothing but a few coins and the photograph of himself and Mariska. He slipped the picture into his own pocket and, prising the pistol from the young man's fingers placed it on the floor in line with his Smith & Wesson and Mariska's small gun.

Moving to the window he glanced out to see the courtyard deserted and smiled – *Nothing like a few gunshots to send everyone indoors.* He turned to face the door, hands in plain sight, listening to the slow footfall of heavy boots ascending the stairs.

Staube stepped through the door, his tiny black eyes flicking round the room – at the bodies, the guns and Kinskii's empty hands.

Kinskii stood in silence as Staube pulled a photograph from his pocket, checked it and took a deep breath. In a harsh whisper he said, 'A good likeness. I'd have known you anywhere.'

Kinskii said, '*Herr* Staube? I think you arranged this meeting.'

Staube grunted and said, 'No. *She* arranged this meeting. I think she wanted you eliminated before we could get together. I wonder why?'

He bent down and examined the young man. 'I see you got the Serb. Well done. But you got the woman as well. That makes *me* happy but your boss Ebenstein won't be pleased – you've smashed his big plan.'

Staube turned and studied Mariska and her shattered throat. 'Good shooting, ' he said. 'Two targets. Four shots. So fast and so accurate.'

He reached over and with his fingertips traced the Serb's two entry wounds. 'Amazing,' he said. 'These shots are within a centimetre of each other. Perhaps you should work for me. Or perhaps we should send you to Africa as a hunter.'

Staube looked at Kristina and said, 'So in the end that's what he did – went to Africa.'

'You let him go?'

'Not really. I took him in and arrested all his spies.'

'What happened to them?'

'Died during arrest and interrogation.'

'Why didn't you kill my husband?'

'I needed a reason for two dead bodies in an incident seen by fifty or so witnesses. I couldn't allow a court case – God knows what would have come out. So for the newspapers we classed the murders as a tragic lovers' quarrel and allowed your husband to 'escape' with his word of honour that he'd never return to Austria, Hungary or Germany and never talk of the matter.'

'Why couldn't he go home?'

'He faced trial and execution for treason – killing Ebenstein's valued agent and betraying the Austrian network to me.'

'But he *didn't* betray the network.'

'We let Ebenstein think he did and that was sufficient. We closed the case and heard no more of your husband until he turned up with the British in that meeting with Kreuz in Africa just before the war.'

Kristina whispered, 'You killed most of the others. My husband was lucky.'

Staube shrugged. 'He did me a favour by executing that woman and a favour for Ebenstein by executing the Serb. The Austrians used him as a scapegoat for the loss of their spy ring and co-operation between our two countries in certain political and national matters continued. So in the end, everyone gained.'

Kristina whispered, 'God, you're all so evil.'

Kreuz said, 'Staube will take that as a compliment.'

Staube dismissed both comments with a flick of his fingers and in the same gesture dismissed Kristina. She started to rise but Staube said, 'Wait. I've told you everything you wanted to know and now I need something in return. Meet me here at eight tomorrow night. We shall eat dinner again and I will explain a small but important task you must carry out for me. Don't be late.'

Kreuz ushered Kristina from the restaurant. On the pavement he shook hands but Kristina held on and said, 'What does he want of me?'

388

'Some small errand,' said Kreuz. 'Probably to do with his police work. Just for a few weeks. A month perhaps. Then he'll let you go.'

'Will you be there tomorrow night?'

'No. My own task here is finished. Tomorrow I return to my estate in the country.'

Kristina whispered, 'Your task? Your *task?* Was I your task? Have you been following me? Did you plan our 'chance' meeting this afternoon?'

'My dear Countess. When your friend Ebenstein...*selected*...you in Vienna he saw great possibilities for profit but you refused to stay with him so he....'

'Passed me on to you?'

'I suppose you could say that. Rather in the same way he passed on your husband.'

Kristina snatched her hand away. 'I will not come back here to see that evil man. I'd rather die.'

Kreuz said, 'If you don't come back Staube may arrange that you do.'

'Are you serious?'

Kreuz shrugged. 'I can discuss this no more. I'll call you a cab then I must find my son. He starts at Doctor Fischer's academy soon and needs time at home to prepare. Your sister plans a place for her son in the same school. I am writing to her tomorrow. Shall I tell her we met?'

'Only that we passed in the street and spoke for a moment and that I expect to be back in Africa within two months.'

'Very well. Good luck tomorrow night.'

'Will I need good luck?'

Kreuz smiled and stepped into the road to stop a passing cab, tipping his hat as Kristina climbed in.

Next evening – after a long tense day – Kristina returned to Restaurant Jäger with its masculine smells and arrogant stares. At first disturbed and fearful, she sat with Staube, listening to that hateful hiss, increasingly thrilled and excited at the prospect of unique and exquisite debauchery in his demands.

His black eyes bored into the cesspit of her soul and her resistance faded. She leaned forward and whispered, 'You want me to do *that?*'

'Only for a few months. Then you'll be free to go.'

389

Chapter Fifty-Two

Black Widow

Kristina finished her story with a sigh and a lowering of eyes. Stewartby frowned, his face tight and angry. Her heart lurched. *Oh God – have I overdone the drama?*

But Stewartby said, 'Let me guess. The little bastard turned you into a tart. You slept with his targets, wheedled secrets; played to their perversions and told him everything. That story's as old as men and power. He forced you to be a whore. I can tell.'

'You're right darling, you're right. He forced me. I had no choice.'

Kristina raised her head and tried to weep. Squeezing a tear from one eye she summoned a sob.

Hiding her face in a white handkerchief, she whispered, 'Once he'd broken me in with a couple of assignments, Staube introduced me to the Duchess. He made us work together and do disgusting things but we became friends and found -' she produced a heart-rending gulp – 'he'd bought us both from Ebenstein. *Bought* us. Like slaves. Like damned slaves. That's all we were. That's all those two men saw us as. Damned slaves.'

She lowered her handkerchief and peeked at Stewartby, sure he'd swallowed the story whole but he snapped, 'If the little bastard promised to let you go in a few months why the hell are you still here?'

'No money. I had no money.'

'The bloody man didn't pay you?'

'He promised but he died, leaving the Duchess and me with nothing, so we had no choice – continue working or starve.'

'Died? How did he die?'

'Somebody shot him. In an alley. Late one night.'

Kristina dipped her face back into the handkerchief, hiding the triumphant memory of Staube flopping into the mud and urine.

'Bloody hell. Who shot him?'

'One of his agents. He'd treated her badly and she took revenge.'

'A woman? A woman shot him?'

Kristina closed her eyes and relived that wonderful moment when Staube turned away and the bullet struck him behind an ear. He flung his hand to the wound and fell without a sound.

In a flowing movement the Duchess bent down – such a delicate and graceful woman – and ran her piano player's fingers through

Staube's pockets, plucking out money, papers and his police badge. She straightened and staggered, affected for the moment by an excess of heroin, then counted and split the cash with Kristina and threw everything else down a drain.

Now – sitting in the sunlit park with Stewartby – Kristina found it difficult not to laugh at the picture of two well dressed modern ladies hurrying from that alley and clipping along the brightly lit street in high heels, fur coats and fashionable hats, chatting and giggling; ignoring the midnight crowds of Berlin pleasure seekers.

Kristina said, 'Someone told me a woman killed him. The police never found the murderer.' – *And they never found the pistol. My clever friend the Duchess took it and tossed it into the river before we reached the Telephone Box and then insisted we keep the appointment Staube had made for us....*

Oh what a night that had been. Six elderly bankers – three each – and the first money earned and kept. After that the cash rolled in. A pity the Duchess spent it all on heroin and drifted away with the Condesa.

Kristina lowered the handkerchief and whispered, 'Oh I've had an awful time since then. Money loses value every day in this damned country so saving means nothing. I can go nowhere. Berlin's a prison. I'll never earn enough to return to Africa. When you've gone I'll have no choice but to stay here and work with the Duchess.'

Stewartby frowned and said, 'I've been thinking about that. I'm off to Geneva the day after tomorrow. Why not come with me and have a couple of weeks break.'

'To Geneva? For a couple of weeks? What then?'

'Well – we can see.'

'What does that mean?'

'It means – come to Geneva for a couple of weeks and we'll see.'

'See *what*?'

'See if you prefer returning to Berlin or…perhaps… coming to East Africa with me.'

Kristina dipped her head and said, 'My dear Sir. I do believe you're making a proposal.'

Stewartby laughed. 'What makes you think that?'

'Oh for God's sake – if you're proposing, get on with it. If you're not proposing tell me what you *are* doing?'

'I'll tell you tomorrow – at dinner. Our last dinner in Berlin.'

She slapped his shoulder. 'You are a *beast* keeping me in suspense.'

He grinned and said. 'Don't talk about it again – not until tomorrow night. I'll have decided by then. Come on, let's walk. It's such a lovely afternoon.'

Kristina took his hand and strolled along the river bank, concentrating on keeping his mood even and that night – with the end of her game in sight – she worked extra hard on giving him pleasure. Preparing supper in her flat and dressed only in a long necklace of brightly coloured stones she fed him like a child and hugged him close and allowed him to sleep while she lay in the scented dark, working out how to bring him finally and completely into her web and under control.

Next morning Stewartby rose early and left, saying, 'Must clear my office and say my goodbyes. I'll be back this evening at seven. Make sure you're ready for our special dinner.'

During the hours alone Kristina spent a restless day until he returned and took her by cab to Hiller's and one of the best tables in that beautiful restaurant.

Kristina wore the expensive plum-coloured gown and jewellery from Stewartby's first visit to Hiller's and knew she looked stunning. She entered the restaurant full of confidence, her arm linked with his to show her changed status.

She ordered an expensive dinner and gave Stewartby full attention but the damned man ignored her intense gaze. Instead he twisted and turned to study the crowded restaurant, saying, 'This is where I saw your friend the Duchess with some minister or other. Less than twenty four hours before, she'd been diddling with that young fellow Heydrich? What a woman. Did she see him again?'

Annoyed at this small talk, Kristina said, 'A couple of times. But why on earth do you ask? What interest is he to you?'

'He struck me as mad.'

'Not mad. Just young. The Duchess felt sorry for him. The night before leaving he got drunk and played Russian love songs on a violin. She said he reminded her of life in St Petersburg and made her cry but felt glad to see the back of him. Now he's disappeared into the navy we'll never hear of him again, thank God.'

'You never know. It's odd how people keep turning up in Berlin. Kreuz and Fischer from the war in Africa, for instance.'

'Who's Fischer?'

'The fellow Kreuz said had opened an academy. Unless I'm mistaken he's the doctor who saved Early's life after that battle at Bukoba. Not sure I trust the coincidence of these fellows all creeping around the same town at the same time. I wonder what they're up to?'

Kristina snatched his hand and held it tight. 'For God's sake Stewartby, who cares? You have something to tell me. Just bloody well get on with it. By the way. What's your first name?'

'Lionel.'

'Lionel? *Lionel?* What an awful name. I think I'll stick to Stewartby.'

He shrugged and looked down, playing with her fingers.

She removed her hand and tapped the table with a stiff forefinger. 'I'm waiting. Am I coming with you to Geneva or not?'

He pulled a long envelope from his pocket – 'Here's your train ticket.'

'So I'm coming with you.'

'If you wish.'

'Of course I wish. Now that's decided – what about the second question. Are you proposing?'

'Not yet.'

'What the hell does that mean?'

'I don't want to do anything in Berlin. I want to choose a better place. A place where you....'

'Didn't work as a prostitute?' snapped Kristina, clenching her fists.

'Where you are not...so well known. If I propose it will be in Geneva.'

Kristina's took a deep breath, disturbed at this twist in the game, her mind working fast on a new set of rules.

She sighed, took hold of his hand again and said, 'Very well. If that's what you want. Let's relax now and enjoy our evening.'

Sensing his relief, she contained her anger and in the cab home she whispered, 'Leave me tonight, darling. I need to rest and pack. Sleep at your hotel and we'll meet tomorrow morning at the station. No. Don't come and pick me up. I'll make my own way down. Don't worry. I'll be there in good time.'

Rushing into her flat Kristina sucked a huge snort of cocaine as reward for her cleverness. In a cloud of bliss she floated to the mirror and watched her image dance round the room – twirling and twisting and humming a song of no words – until it fell on the bed and she drifted to sleep and Kinskii came, creeping from the deepest dungeon of her mind.

Oh God, how handsome he looked.

'You never change,' she said.

'Nor will you if you join me. Come now. It's easy.'

Fighting the attraction of death and oblivion she hissed, 'Go back to hell, you lying cheating bastard. I'm going to Africa to piss on your grave.'

He faded away leaving an echo that could have been a chuckle and Kristina jumped awake, cursing and spitting; mumbling at the wall and the ceiling and visions of her two children so dreadfully dead.

She fought for control and brought herself back towards common sense – *Don't be stupid. They're not dead. They're safe with Anyuka...in Hungary...some day I'll go back and get them....*

She banished the twins and lay staring at darkness and going back over her evening with Stewartby. God, what an effort to remember it all. *But wait. Here's an important point....*

She'd said, 'What will you do in Africa? Go professional hunting or go back into business with Adam?'

He'd said, 'I've built a hotel in Nairobi. That little Greek Cretikos is looking after it for me. Doing quite well I understand. I'll have to watch that the bugger's not cheating me.'

Kristina giggled at the invisible ceiling. 'A hotel? A bloody *hotel?* The stupid man's going to be a hotel keeper.'

And what else did he say?

She'd asked for news of friends.

He'd said, 'That bastard Hocklyffe-Evans is a bloody Lord. His brothers all died in the war and his father followed soon after so the fellow inherited the title and all estates.'

Kristina hugged herself in glee. *H.E. a Lord? How wonderful....*

And Adam? What happened to Adam. She'd said, 'Last I heard was that he'd been charged with murder.'

Stewartby's face turned brick red and he snarled – 'The bastard got away with it. Guilty as hell but they let him off.'

He paused and glared with angry eyes – 'Why do you ask now? Why didn't you ask before? After all the damned man's your brother-in-law. You've not mentioned your family since we met. What's wrong with you? Don't you care about them?'

Taken aback, Kristina blurted out the truth – 'I knew Adam was in trouble over Christy's death. I wanted to hear the whole story from my sister but now I'm returning to Africa with you I thought it better to know what happened before leaving.'

'Who says you're returning to Africa with me? That's a damned assumption. You're coming to Geneva that's all. Then I'll decide'

In the dark bedroom, Kristina kicked her legs in the air, howling with laughter at the ceiling and yelling, 'Oh *is* it an assumption, my little man – my little *hotel* keeper. We'll see who decides. *And* we'll see who wins *this* little game.'

Along the corridor, Madame banged on the wall, her thin voice piping for quiet. Kristina stuffed a pillow-corner into her mouth and managed to subside. She considered more cocaine but fell asleep, waking just after dawn – plenty of time to beautify and pack and get to the station before Stewartby.

Dressed for travel – smart but sensible with hat and veil and a fresh flower in her buttonhole – Kristina carried her small valise through the crowds and stood by the train carriage shown on her ticket.

Kristina smiled at the look of wary pleasure on Stewartby's face when he approached ten minutes later and giggled when he said, 'So you came. I thought last night you'd dumped me. Is that all your luggage?'

'How much do I need?' she asked.

He laughed and turned away to supervise the stowage of his trunk. The last passengers climbed aboard and the platform emptied. Kristina waited, preparing herself for the next act. Stewartby came back and said, 'Come on. Let's hop aboard and settle.'

Kristina dropped her head and whispered, 'I can't come.'

'What?'

'If you can't marry me I can't come.'

She squeezed out the first of her tears.

'What the hell are you talking about. Get on the train.'

She shook her head and sobbed. He stepped forward and tried to kiss her through the veil. She pushed him away and – caught up with the moment – to her surprise began to cry properly.

'I can't,' she wailed. 'I can't'

'Please, darling. Please. Get on the train.'

'Propose to me.'

'No.'

'Then I can't come.'

'We'll see about it in Geneva.'

'Propose to me here.'

'No.'

'Then damn you. I won't come.'

Stewartby looked along the platform and said, 'For God's sake get on the train or it'll leave without us.'

The guard blew his whistle and shouted, 'Get on if you're going.'

Kristina picked up her small case and stepped back.

'Go without me,' she cried through almost genuine tears.

The guard blew his whistle and clambered aboard, shouting, ' Shut the door. We're leaving.'

Stewartby said, 'Come here and kiss me.'

'No. Not unless you propose.'

'Damn you,' he snarled and jumped up the steps, slamming the door a moment before the train started to move. He leaned out the window, face stricken; eyes pleading.

He shouted over the noise of departure and blew a kiss but Kristina stood absolutely still as the train steamed out. Reading his lips, she caught the word 'telegram' and – seeing the agony in his eyes – knew she'd won.

Chapter Fifty-Three

The Respectable Countess Kinskii

With her train approaching Geneva station, Kristina checked makeup and hair, tipped a sweet little hat forward over her forehead – taking care not to disturb her careful coiffure – and peeked from the window.

She saw Stewartby before he saw her and felt triumph at the way his anxious eyes raked the line of carriages. She allowed him a glimpse then drew back, ignoring his frantic wave and waited until most passengers disembarked before picking up her Kinsky valise and making regal progress down steep carriage steps to the platform.

Stewartby dived forward with an enormous hug and she pushed him away crying, 'Darling. Not so rough. Mind my hat.' She giggled and gave him a peck on the cheek. 'There. That'll do for now.'

'Bloody hell, I've missed you,' he said.

She laughed and said, 'How could you miss me? We were together only four days ago.'

'A lifetime,' he said. 'An absolute lifetime.'

'Darling Stewartby. How poetic.' She pecked his cheek again and said, 'I'm hungry. Shall we have lunch?'

'Where's your luggage?'

Kristina lifted her valise and waved back and forth, holding the handle between forefinger and thumb.

'Is that all?'

'How much do I need?'

'Oh God, not that again. Never mind. We'll go shopping today. We'll buy proper outfits for tomorrow.'

'What's happening tomorrow?'

'We're getting married.'

'Wait. You haven't proposed.'

'I'll propose now. Will you marry me?'

Kristina frowned and said, 'I can only consider it if you promise never to leave me, like Kinskii.'

'But Kinskii didn't leave you. He died.'

'Dying is only another way of leaving.'

'Very well. I promise never leave to you.'

Kristina curtsied and in a gesture of affection slipped her arm through his. 'Good,' she said. 'So now I'll consider it.'

'Wait,' he said, laughing. 'Now *I* have a condition.'

Kristina raised her eyebrows.

He said, 'I'll marry you if you promise to grow your hair long again.'

'You like my hair long?'

'It's how I always think of you – how you looked the first time I saw you.'

Tipping her head sideways she smiled into his eyes and said, 'Very well. I'll consider that, too. Now take me to lunch then take me shopping.'

She shopped until early evening – 'After *all*, darling, I need a *complete* new wardrobe.' Stewartby showed no surprise or reluctance to pay, dipping into his wallet without hesitation at each demand, indulging every whim and fancy with apparent pleasure.

In one shop he asked, 'Which dress is for the wedding?'

'Oh darling, I haven't decided yet. I'll think about that tomorrow.'

Just after six Kristina supervised her last purchase being wrapped and folded into a trunk then flopped on to a chair and said, 'Enough. My energy's gone. I need a bath and dinner then bed. Where am I staying?'

Stewartby ushered her into a taxi – 'Don't worry about the trunks. They'll follow.' – and instructed the driver to a large hotel in beautiful gardens overlooking the lake.

Kristina hugged his arm and whispered, 'How romantic. What wonderful colours – those roses and trees and the sun on the water. It's all so lovely.' She rolled her head on his shoulder, sighing and nuzzling his neck; thinking hard, unsure how to broach the next part of her plan.

To her surprise and delight Stewartby did it for her by responding with a hug and murmuring, 'I know you won't like this but I've booked us into separate rooms on different floors.' Unable to believe her luck Kristina gripped him as though in distress, and – managing to inject her voice with shock and disappointment – cried, 'Oh, darling. Why?'

'It's essential that we appear respectable to my friends here in Geneva. They're important people from the Embassy and League of Nations. To give hint of scandal tonight would be disastrous. So we eat dinner together then go to our separate rooms and sleep alone. I'm sorry. But that's how it must be. I'm the respectable diplomat and you're the respectable Countess Kinskii, Prussian widow of a Hungarian nobleman.'

'Very well. I'll be the respectable Countess Kinskii.'

In her room – a luxury suite – Kristina curtsied to her image in the mirror and said in as grave a voice as possible, 'Welcome to Geneva, the respectable Countess Kinskii,' then fell on the bed, kicking her legs in the air and squealing, 'The silly bugger's walked right into it. He's done it for me.'

She pulled herself together long enough to accept delivery of her three trunks then, bathed and perfumed and buzzing from a sharp sniff of cocaine, dressed in a fresh new – expensive – gown and prepared to lead Stewartby towards his final humiliation.

Making her way along the corridor and down the stairs, Kristina forced herself into a state of calm. By the time she met Stewartby in the dining room she looked and felt withdrawn and serious.

'Are you well, darling?' he asked.

'Yes, thank you.'

'Tired after your journey?'

'Probably.'

Stewartby ordered dinner and she picked at the food, eyes lowered. 'I have something to cheer you up,' he said, and ordered champagne.

The waiter poured two flutes. Stewartby plucked a shining diamond ring from his pocket and said, 'This is for you.' He lifted his glass – 'To us and to our wedding tomorrow.'

Kristina forced a tear and said, 'Darling. I can't get married tomorrow.'

'What?'

'I can't get married here in Geneva. It's not fair.'

'Not fair. What do you mean?'

'I can't get married without my family. Eva's the last of my family left. She'd never forgive me. I can only be married in Nairobi. I can only be married with Eva at my wedding.'

Anger flared in his eyes. 'But I've arranged it all with the Embassy. The ceremony *and* reception. I can't cancel now. What the hell will they think?'

'Oh darling. We can still have the reception. Your friends can still celebrate with us. You can explain. I know you can. They'll understand. Please, darling. Please.'

'What do I do with this damned ring.'

'I'll wear it. Give it to me now. There's no reason for me not to wear it.' She took the ring and slipped it on her third finger.

He said, 'What about our honeymoon?'

'What did you plan?'

'The voyage home. That's our honeymoon. I've booked a bridal suite. We sail from Marseilles in three days.'

Kristina clutched his hand. Dabbing her eyes she whispered, 'Oh darling. You're so good but the honeymoon will have to wait. As *you said* – we must be respectable. We *can't* sleep in the same cabin. A hint of scandal on the ship will be as bad as a hint of scandal in Geneva. The whole of Nairobi would know within a few hours of arriving. It's important that the respectable Countess Kinskii *remains* respectable until she walks up the aisle. You *must* see I'm right.'

His face turned red with rage. 'When the hell did you think of all this?'

'Oh darling. In my room. When I looked at my lovely new clothes and wondered which dress to wear tomorrow. I realised I couldn't go ahead. Not tomorrow. Not here. Not in Geneva. Not without Eva.'

'Oh for Christ's sake. What a bloody charade.'

For a moment she feared his anger may boil over then – to her relief – his resistance collapsed.

'Oh bloody hell. Oh bloody hell. Alright. I'll send messages round tonight. No wedding. Just the reception. Same time, same place. Oh bloody hell. I'll do it. But just for you. I hope you appreciate it.'

'I do,darling, I do. Thank you. Thank you.' She would have burst into tears again but worried it might be too much dabbed at her eyes a few more times then settled to being sweet and pliant for the rest of dinner.

Next morning Kristina slept late, ordered breakfast in her room and drifted through two happy hours bathing and preparing herself, with most time spent choosing her outfit. In the end she decided on the yellow dress, gathered at the waist to show her figure, teamed with a dark blue scarf knotted loose at the throat and trailing over her shoulder.

When Stewartby came he barely acknowledged her beyond saying, 'I've managed to make all the new arrangements and explained everything to everyone. So stick to the story and, for God's sake, remember these people respect me as a colleague. Don't let me down by saying anything stupid.'

'Of course not, darling,' she said, holding his arm to enter the private rooms hired for the occasion.

Stewartby introduced Kristina to thirty or so guests then left her with a group of plump wives who gave her a few moments polite conversation before turning away to exclude her and chat among themselves.

For ten minutes Kristina stood in a corner sipping her champagne, alone but unworried, until she caught the eye of an elegant young woman entering the room on the arm of a tall silver haired gentleman sporting a beautifully tended moustache.

Kristina felt instant kindred spirit and recognised signals of her recent profession in the woman's bold glance. Smiling, she raised an eyebrow in reply. The woman nodded and drifted through the crowd towards Kristina, exchanging a few words with each group as she came, flicking her head to laugh and smoothing her long light-brown hair after each flick.

'So you're the mysterious Hungarian countess,' she said in a cultured English accent. 'I'm late so missed the introductions. You're Kristina and I'm Louise. This lot are used to dealing with kings and emperors so a Hungarian countess is small stuff. Sorry they're ignoring you but glad to see you're ignoring them back. They deserve it.'

She laughed – an attractive gurgle that creased her long face in a most pleasing way.

Kristina laughed with her and said, 'Actually, I'm Prussian. I married a Hungarian.'

'But you're a real countess.'

'Oh yes. I'm a real countess.'

'And you were a countess before the little colonel found you in Berlin?'

'Of course.'

'How wonderful That makes you one up. When my old faggot found me in Paris I was lowly Lou-Lou – wellborn but reduced to entertaining the nobility as best I could in various establishments. The poor fool saw me dancing one night and insisted on marrying me so now I'm Lady Louise with a proper title and a shady past.'

'You were a dancer?'

'That's what we tell people who *ask*, darling.'

'You came in with your husband?'

'That's him. His name's Marcus. He's old but he's a handsome bugger, don't you think?'

'Very striking. And such a lovely moustache.'

'His pride and joy. I comb it for him every morning and every evening. Nearest we get to sex. Lovely dress, by the way. Did the little colonel buy it for you?'

'Yesterday. Here in Geneva.'

'Did you get anything else out of him?'

'A full wardrobe – three trunks full.'

'Well done, darling. Screw all you can out of the bugger while he's still willing.'

From across the room Kristina saw Stewartby beckon and point to the private dining room, his lips forming the words, 'Time for lunch.'

Kristina said, 'I must go to take his arm and lead you all in. Sorry we can't have a longer chat.'

'Never mind darling. Next time round.'

Kristina turned away but Louise gripped her hand and whispered, 'I hope you're not going to actually *marry* the little prat.'

Kristina turned back and drooped her eye in a slow wink.

'Thank God for that,' said Louise and Kristina made her way through the crowd to Stewartby with the hot trail of Louise's fingertips tingling across her palm.

Before boarding ship at Marseilles, Kristina insisted on holding her own ticket.

'Why?' asked Stewartby.

'I *told* you. No hint of scandal. We can't board together. We can't look as though we're travelling together.'

He said, 'Oh bloody hell, what are you up to now?' and handed over her ticket. For the first time Kristina detected a hint of suspicion in his eyes.

She hurried away to supervise her own luggage aboard and, removing her engagement ring went straight to the purser's office. Speaking French, Kristina said, 'I want to change my cabin. I see I'm next to a man who has been pestering me on the train. Move me to a different deck.'

The purser passed his sad eyes over her ticket and said, 'Countess Kinskii.' He ruffled through the pile of papers on his desk and sighed, 'Ah yes, Madame. Would the man pestering you be a Colonel Stewartby?'

'I believe so.'

The purser peered at his papers and sighed again. 'The same Colonel Stewartby who booked a bridal suite then changed it for two single cabins?'

'Possibly.'

The purser's mournful face puckered in sympathy. He ruffled again through his papers and said, 'I can move you up two decks but the fare....' He shrugged.

'I don't care how much it costs,' said Kristina reaching into her bag and pulling out the dollars, francs and sterling earned and saved in

Berlin. 'And make sure I'm sitting nowhere near him in the dining room.'

Ten minutes later she settled into a luxury cabin looking out over the afterdeck, thanking God that a true Frenchman will always understand affairs of the heart and come to the aid of a lady in distress – especially if he earns a large tip for helping.

Kristina enjoyed the voyage, keeping herself mostly to herself during four restful shipboard weeks, avoiding other passengers bound for Mombasa.

She ate breakfast in her cabin and in the dining room sat with her back to Stewartby, avoiding his angry eyes. When on deck she sat always with a group of French and English wives travelling to join husbands in Madagascar and Cape Town, making a defence Stewartby could not breach.

The first night on board he came late and rapped on her cabin door.

'Who is it?' called Kristina.

'You know bloody well who it is. Let me in,'

'A gentleman should not disturb a lady in her cabin,' she said. 'Go away. You know the arrangement.'

Beyond baleful looks he made no further attempt to communicate with her the entire voyage.

Before sailing Kristina sent a telegram to Eva at Mzito, giving detail of her arrival in Mombasa. So when the ship rolled in sparkling morning sunlight over blue breakers and swung through the harbour entrance towards Kilindini, she felt no surprise at seeing Eva standing on the crowded dockside with Adam and a small blond haired boy.

In a surge of excitement Kristina leaned out, waving and calling, her words whipped away by a brisk breeze. Unable to catch Eva's attention, she snatched off her hat and fluttered it in the wind. A large fat man standing behind Adam lifted binoculars in Kristina's direction and tapped Eva's shoulder, pointing.

Kristina waved her hat high and saw Eva lift both arms in welcome, her face breaking into a huge smile. Overcome by unexpected emotion, Kristina gulped back tears – *My God. I'm home.*

From behind her Stewartby's voice snarled, 'Bloody Hocklyffe-Evans. What's he doing here?'

'Why shouldn't he be?' she asked, recognising the fat man with a jolt of surprise.

'You told them you'd be on this ship?'

'Of course.'

'So you made sure that bloody Early would be here, too.'

'Of course I did.'

'Then we can't get off the ship together. I want nothing to do with those two buggers. I'll have to go up on the train alone.'

'Never mind, darling. I'll see you in Nairobi. In a few days. At your hotel. What is it called?'

'The Beatrice.'

'Oh darling – what a lovely name.'

'It's down by the post office. Don't be too bloody long in Mombasa. We'll tell people we met on the ship and decided to get married.'

'Of course darling. But keep it secret until I arrive.'

Chapter Fifty-Four

Love Unlocked

The ship edged across the harbour and Kristina leaned out the better to see her sister. *She's changed. She looks happy. When I left she hated Adam. Now...she's hanging on to him like a young schoolgirl. What's happened?*

And H.E.? *So big and heavy – but even more dignified and still with that lovely long hair. Oh, he makes a perfect Lord.*

And Adam? *Difficult to see many changes. Older and more serious. Perhaps I'll try to cheer him up.*

And the small boy holding Adam's hand? ***That's Jonathan. How he's grown and my God he looks just like Christy. How wonderful. Everyone must know the truth....***

Skipping ashore, Kristina fell into Eva's arms.

'I'm so happy to see you all,' she wept, hoping Stewartby could slink away while she had them engrossed.

'What the hell have you been up to in Europe?' boomed H.E., grabbing her into a hug.

Kristina wrapped herself around his huge bulk and tickled his ear with her tongue, whispering, 'Oh darling – twenty years ago I fell in love with you on this same dock. Now it's happened again.'

She turned to embrace Adam, squeezing the length of her body against his. 'Oh Adam. How long since I saw you? You look so handsome now you're older.'

From the corner of her eye she saw Stewartby hurry along the dockside and disappear into the customs shed.

She released Adam and turned to the boy, crying, 'Oh Jonathan, how you've grown. And aren't you *handsome*. The *image* of your father with that lovely blond hair. Come and give me a kiss.'

But Jonathan stepped back half a pace and shook his head. Eva pulled him close and glared.

With a bright smile, Kristina said, 'Oh Eva, darling. We've so much to talk about,' – she thrust her luggage tags at H.E. – 'Why don't you men go and get my trunks. Tell the customs officer I've brought nothing but clothes. He'll believe you.'

She shooed them away and turned back to Eva whispering, 'Sorry, darling. I had no idea that Jonathan looked so much like...Well...you know...I'm so sorry....'

Eva shrugged and said, 'Try not to say such stupid things. You're speaking of the past. We live in the present and we're all happy.'

'It's obvious you've come to some arrangement. You and Adam are like young lovers. How did you do it?'

'Something happened that brought us together.'

'Oh do tell me.'

'No. It's none of your business. Let's get out of this hot sun and sit down. I want to hear what you've been up to in Europe during the last four years.'

'Surviving, darling, surviving.'

'What happened to the twins?'

Kristina frowned, her mind blank – *Twins? What twins?* Seeing Eva's raised eyebrows she blinked and remembered – *Oh God. Such a long time since I thought of them....*

She said, 'Are we staying at the Creek House? I need to rest.'

'Yes. For as long as you want.'

'In that case I'll tell you all about Europe – and the twins – in a few days. When I feel better.'

Adam looked across the customs shed and said, 'Is that Stewartby? Look. Over there. He must have been on the same ship.'

H.E. grunted. 'Yes. I saw him with my trusty binoculars – standing next to Kristina on the deck and giving her an earful. Now why should the little bastard be doing that? *And* I reckon he slipped away when he saw us.'

'You think they travelled together?'

'Certainly on the same ship. But together...? Not sure, old chap. One is *never* sure with the crafty Kristina. It may be coincidence they're on the same liner. But...'

Watching Stewartby claim half a dozen trunks and follow his porters out into the sunlight Adam said, 'I think you're right. The damned man must have seen us and kept out of our way.'

'Not surprised,' said H.E.. Probably worried at seeing you again after he tried to get you hanged.'

'The past is over,' said Adam. 'I don't want the past to spoil anything now.'

H.E. grinned. 'I can see that. Look at how you're snuggled back with your darling wife after all the grief she gave you. Such a happy family now. What brought that about?'

'Something happened.'

'Must have been a big something.'

Adam shrugged and said, 'We never talk about it.'

'So you're not going to tell me.'

'Nothing to tell,' said Adam. For a moment the cold shock of that awful moment a year ago caught at his throat.

'Are you alright, old chap,' asked H.E.. 'You've gone quite white.'

'I'll go outside for some air,' said Adam. 'You stay here and sort out Kristina's trunks.'

Wiping sweat from his brow Adam stood in the shade of a palm tree. Across the creek heavy blue-green waves rolled in from the ocean to thump against low coral cliffs bordering the harbour entrance. Oh it looked so beautiful in this shining sunlight but he shivered in fear and remembrance of that day last year when Eva – after the usual argument – finally agreed to crew for him in the new boat...

'I hate sailing,' she said. 'And I hate being here in Mombasa with you. I hate pretending to be the happy wife and entertaining your friends. I'll never do it again.'

'So you'll never come to the Creek House again?'

'Of course I will. But alone. I'll come alone. I love the Creek House but not when you're here. I'll never come again with you. At Mzito I don't have to see you or be with you for more than a few minutes. Here we're forced together all day and I hate it.'

Adam gritted his teeth and said, 'If you can't bloody-well do as I ask this once I'll divorce you. Then what'll happen? You'll have to go back to bloody Germany and look after yourself. These people are not my friends. They're business and I need your support. Just this once. I need you to crew. If you refuse I'll book passage tomorrow and you can bugger off back to Berlin and starve.'

He saw surrender in her eyes. She pouted and said, 'Just this once. And only if you promise never to make me come here with you again.'

'It's the last thing I want,' he said, and went off to rig the boat and prepare to sail across the creek to the yacht club.

Adam pushed off from the jetty and set curving course across the creek, heading towards the harbour entrance looking to catch a lift on the incoming waves.

Halfway across he sniffed at the breeze and looked over his shoulder, shading his eyes to peer at a heavy black cloud rolling in from the ocean.

Eva must have seen him checking because she said, 'Will we be safe? You know I've only done this a couple of times and can't swim properly.'

'We'll be fine. That cloud's going ashore several miles up the coast. We'll feel no more than a few stray gusts. Nothing to worry about. Sit in the middle of the boat and do exactly as I say. For a start, pick up that rope beside you and pull on it or release it when I say. We'll be across the creek in about twenty minutes. Racing doesn't start for an hour so we've plenty of time.'

'Who are these people you're entertaining?'

'Buyers from a big company in Switzerland looking for pencil slats. I'm helping Anwar sell them the wood. They sail the lakes at home so I invited them to join in the club regatta. Next week we take them up-country to the sawmill. Now just sit there, hold that rope and enjoy the journey.'

Eva settled down halfway along the boat, keeping a light grip on the jib sheet and lifting her face to the warm breeze, eyes closed, light and shade dancing through her hair.

Adam watched her slender body swaying in time with the boat and – for a moment – felt kinship with her and with the lovely morning. He almost spoke but gagged by the harsh indifference she always showed him, turned away to check a shift in the wind.

He eased the mainsail to a sharp gust and over his shoulder saw the storm cloud racing south, straddling the creek with an impenetrable sheet of black rain.

He said, 'Christ – that weather's changed course. Be ready to hang on. We may be in for a rocky ride.'

'What shall I do?'

'Nothing. I'll run ahead of the cloud and turn by the harbour entrance. That'll take us straight across to the Old Town. We'll wait there until it blows over.'

'Will we be safe?'

'Of course. I've done this a dozen times.'

But another glance over the stern showed a creek-wide tidal wave rushing forward under the cloud, pushed by a swirling wind that whipped the normally calm water into a churning mess of white waves and snatched at Adam's sail. He let the mainsheet slip further and hauled on the tiller to try and hold course.

A moment later the black cloud overtook, blocking the sun. Within seconds daylight almost disappeared and a gale force wind struck, lifting the dinghy into a frightening high-speed plane on the front of the tidal wave.

Adam lost all feel of steering as the boat hurtled forward. He crouched amidships, trying to balance and direct the boat with his weight, shouting 'Hold tight Eva – I'll go for shelter behind those rocks at the harbour entrance.'

As he spoke the rain arrived – a freezing dense downpour that crashed from the sky obscuring all sight of shore.

For the first time, Adam felt fear. His last landmark – a pillar of rocks – must be almost dead ahead. At this speed only seconds remained to save the boat from smashing into the coral.

To release the tidal-wave grip he threw his weight left, swinging the planing bow to starboard. The boat staggered and broached as the wave swept underneath, rushing on, to disappear in the murk. The stern slapped backwards into a ferocious cauldron of spit and spray whipped by a whirling wind that gave no respite or help in steering.

With the sail empty and flapping, Adam dragged at the tiller with both hands, trying to regain control but the dinghy lost way, wallowing in broken water, thrown from side to side by the twisting gale. The hull heaved to an ocean swell and Adam realised – *Christ. We're sliding out to sea.*

A wind-squall pushed the rain aside to reveal a huge wave crowned by gale-blown spray thrusting in from the ocean and bearing down on the boat. With a shriek Eva jumped up, pointing.

Adam shouted, 'Sit down,' and half stood, leaning forward to grab at her. The wave struck with unimaginable force, dumping tonnes of water on the boat, swinging the stern windward.

From the corner of his eye Adam saw the sail fill with a loud crack and whip across in a fierce gybe. He tried to duck but the heavy boom smashed full force against his head and thumped into Eva's back. somersaulting her overboard.

Adam collapsed across the centre thwart as the dinghy capsized, tipping him deep underwater. Entangled in a skein of loose ropes he fought upwards in a flurry of bubbles, managing in a surge of strength, to grasp the hull and hang on, coughing and blowing out seawater.

Kicking and fighting at the ropes he struggled free, pulling himself up to lay spread-eagled confused and dazed across the upturned hull.

Shaking a mixture of blood and water from his eyes he saw Eva throw up her arms and sink in choppy water, twenty yards away near a cruel pile of sharp rock.

Although half stunned, his brain filled with vivid pictures of Eva and Christy at the height of their love affair and triumphant hate swelled.

'Drown, damn you' he shouted, peering at her through his gun-sight on that hillside near Namanga all those years ago.

At that moment Eva surfaced, head tipped at an awkward angle, her face contorted in fear and shock, stricken eyes wide open, sea foam and spittle bubbling from her lips. Unable to make herself heard through the howling storm, she mouthed 'Adam …help me…,' and he saw Christy at Bukoba, dying in just the same way, dribbling and pleading.

A swirl of wind flicked at the wave-tops, whisking at Eva's wet hair and Adam watched her hat lifting and flying away at Namanga, saving her life as she ducked and followed it down the slope, laughing.

No friendly breeze to save her this time – instead a final thrust of the passing storm rolled a huge plunging slope of water through the rain-mist – a mighty breaker that curled and broke, dropping with weight and power on to Eva, throwing her tumbling towards the rocks in a maelstrom of white foam.

The same wave crashed across the dinghy almost ripping Adam free but with frantic fingers scrabbling at the coaming he managed to cling on.

Close to exhaustion he scrambled to his knees, balancing on the side of the hull and in sudden desperation, searched for Eva. A flash of bright material caught his eye and he saw his wife spinning in a whirlpool alongside the sharp coral rocks.

Seeing her helpless in the water swept all hate away in a blinding surge of love for the lovely young girl he had married. 'I'm coming,' he screamed over the howl of wind and water. She must had heard because a hand flapped in reply and in panic he saw that – unable to swim – only air trapped in her clothes kept her afloat.

Coiling a free rope round an arm he flopped into the water and thrashed awkwardly towards her, dragging the rope behind.

As he arrived she sank. Sweeping past in the rushing current he made a desperate lunge, managing to reach down and twist his fingers into a hank of hair and pull her back up, hanging on with all his strength; her weight nearly breaking his grip on the rope.

The capsized dinghy, acting as sea anchor, swung them clear of the whirlpool, almost dislocating his shoulder. Ignoring the pain he fought to uncoil the rope and lash a loose knot around her body, shouting, 'Lay on your back and I'll pull you to the boat.'

She did not respond and floated with her head rolling, mouth open, eyes closed, arms and legs splayed. Kicking at the water he pulled her through the waves, taking what seemed like hours to reach the dinghy and with the last of his strength shoved her up to lay on her stomach across the hull.

To his relief she coughed and groaned and gulped in air before spewing a great gout of water out over the coaming. With his good arm Adam held her firm against the hull, whispering, 'Thank God I reached you. And thank God the storm's easing.'

He heard a shout and turned to see a steam launch ploughing through the green water towards him. He waved, cursing the pain in his shoulder. 'What took you so long?' he shouted as it pulled alongside.

A cultured voice shouted back, 'We meet again, Mr Early.'

Adam looked at the long nosed face grinning down from the steam launch and called, 'Bloody hell, Mayne. Never thought I'd be glad to see you.'

Two African crewmen jumped into the water and half-lifted Eva towards helping hands that drew her aboard the launch. Adam followed, scrambling up and toppling over the rail to fall flat on the deck, wrenching his shoulder.

Mayne helped him up, laughing and said, 'We last met on board ship after the Hun surrendered and the damned war ended. Remember?'

'Only too well,' said Adam. 'Thanks for coming to get us.'

'Not at all. Lucky we saw you sailing into trouble.'

'Where's Eva?'

'In the cabin wrapped up. Go and join her. We'll get a line on your boat and tow you in. Where to? House or yacht club?'

'Creek House if you don't mind I'll stay and help'

'No. Better go and look after your wife. We'll chat later.'

Adam ducked into a small cabin where Eva sat hunched in a huge blanket. She opened her eyes and said 'Oh darling you've cut your head. Does it hurt?'

'No. Thank God you're alive. Are you cold?'

'Freezing.' She opened her arms, making a tent of the blanket. 'Come in here and keep me warm.'

She lay against him, shivering and whispered. 'You didn't let me drown. You could have, but you didn't.'

He held her close, still consumed by intense love and surprised when she reached up and kissed his cheek, her lips soft and cold. *Christ! Has the same thing happened to her?*

The storm departed as fast as it came, racing south with its wind and rain, leaving the harbour calm and warm again in the afternoon sun.

At the Creek House Adam had a few words with Mayne, called his boatman to secure the dinghy then helped Eva ashore. Walking through the palm trees she held him tight, her head on his shoulder. At the door to her room she took his hand and drew him in whispering, 'I need company. I need my husband. I need you to be with me.'

Adam stepped into the fragrant shadows of his wife's living quarters. White muslin curtains rippled in a cool breeze, diffusing the sunrays through half open shutters into a calming dapple of light and shade. Tears started in his eyes and he said, 'Are you sure?'

She buried her head in his chest, 'Please stay, I need you.'

'I almost let you drown. I wanted you to drown.'

'I know. I saw it. And I saw the change. After that big wave. Before I went under for the last time I saw you change. I knew you'd come. I knew you'd save me. Why did you change?'

He said, 'I don't know. I can't say. At first my mind seemed full of you and...*him*. Then I just...couldn't let you die. The past disappeared and I....Bloody hell...I just realised....'

She said, 'Don't say any more. I know what you mean. It happened to me too. I suddenly knew that...,' she began to sob.

He said, 'You can't explain it either.'

'No. Oh darling, no. But it's happened. We're lovers again. Let's leave it like that. Let's not explain it. Let's just be lovers again. Like before. Please stay with me.'

She sat on the bed, covered her face with her hands and wept.

He sat beside her and said, 'Stop crying. I'll stay with you. I will.'

'For ever?'

'For ever.'

He hugged her hard and winced at a pain in his shoulder.

Eva cried, 'Oh darling. You're hurt. And your head. Let me clean it up.'

She pulled away. 'You lay down. I'll run a bath. Take your clothes off and wait here till I call.'

When he entered the bathroom he saw her eyes widen at sight of the terrible scars on his thigh and stomach. But she said nothing until they lay in the warm dusk, exhausted from several hours love-making.

In the last light of day she sat up and touched his scars, running her hand round the twisted yellow crater on his thigh and dipping a finger in the puckered hole that disfigured his stomach muscles.

She whispered, 'This happened at...Bukoba...when....'

He said, 'When Christy died? Yes.'

'You were near when he died?'

'Yes.'

'Did you kill him?'

'No.'

'Thank God.'

She turned her face away. 'Did he die bravely?'

Adam felt anger rise at the tears in her voice. 'He died in the face of the enemy. That's the best a soldier can hope for.'

'But did he die *bravely*?'

'He died in battle.'

'So he died bravely.'

She sobbed – a shuddering gulp – and said, 'Now we've spoken of it I'll never mention him again. For the rest of my life I'll never speak of him. But I'll not be able to stop thinking of him. You'll allow me that?'

Adam said, 'Provided he never comes between us.'

'Never,' she said. 'Never ever again.'

H.E. marched from the customs shed, followed by six Africans lugging three heavy trunks and Adam pushed the memory of that day aside with relief.

'All done,' said H.E.. 'Let's go home.'

'Where are you staying?' asked Adam.

'With you I hope. Taken a few days off to greet the lovely Kristina properly. So let's collect the ladies and get across to the Creek House.'

Eva clapped in joy at the suggestion and said. 'Stay as long as you like.'

Kristina kissed H.E. on the cheek and said, 'What bliss to spend a few days together. I thought of you so often.'

H.E. raised an eyebrow and looked down, his blue eyes wary.

Taking Eva's hand Adam said, 'Our launch is just along the jetty. We'll just about be able to take those trunks. Come on.'

Kristina linked arms with H.E. and pulled him along behind, saying, 'Is it true you're a proper Lord now?'

'Afraid so, said H.E..

'How wonderful,' said Kristina. 'So if I married you I'd be a proper Lady.'

H.E. laughed and said, 'I'm not sure you'd ever manage that.'

'Manage to marry you?'

'No. Manage to be a proper lady. By the way – did Stewartby travel on the same ship?'

Kristina said, 'I believe he did. But I didn't speak to him. Why should I have anything to do with such a horrible little man.?'

Chapter Fifty-Five

The Whirligig Of Time

Kristina stepped from her rickshaw in front of Hotel Beatrice and paused to straighten her hat and smooth her dress. After all – no point in wearing the latest fashion from Europe and letting standards slide at a time like this.

She turned to pay the rickshaw driver, twisting her body in the sparkling sunlight to show off her clothes and figure. Stewartby may be peeking out of a window and she wanted to look her best for him. Her telegram told him, *I'll see you prompt at noon in the restaurant.*

Dipping into her handbag she peeked at the big pocket watch borrowed from Adam. Two minutes to twelve. Perfect. Just enough time to make her entry and settle at a table, ready to greet him as the gracious Lady.

She moved off the dusty street and up the veranda steps, her modern high heels clicking on hardwood planks – a most satisfying sound. Several women turned from lunchtime drinks to stare.

In the reception hall Kristina, blinded by the change from bright sun to deep shade, paused and squinted. Before her eyes could adjust a small shadow stepped forward and in a quiet musical voice she thought familiar said, 'Madame Kinskii, my head porter will take you through to the restaurant. I'll tell Colonel Stewartby you are here.'

The small shadow snapped his fingers and a porter led Kristina into a tall wood-panelled room with large windows giving view along First Avenue. She looked round, appraising the place. Quality furniture. Crisp white tablecloths. Plenty of waiters – and a few early lunch customers turning their heads to look at this woman making her entrance in such beautiful clothes. Good.

Kristina smiled and nodded as she passed between the tables, a picture of grace and modern fashion. She ignored the porter's directions and chose a quiet window seat away from the other lunch guests. From here she could see rickshaws dropping customers at the hotel entrance.

She could also see across to the restaurant door and Stewartby bounding through, waving and smiling. My God, he looked smart in a sort of business suit cut from white drill. She smiled and waved back, considering again that he really *is* a handsome little bugger.

Naturally, everyone in the room followed his progress towards this beautiful, well-dressed woman. Kristina felt sure that no one could fail to see his delight and eagerness. Nor could they fail to see his puzzlement at her offer of a formal cheek to his enthusiastic embrace and attempt to kiss – made awkward by the fact she swayed away, forcing him to bend in a half stumble and half hug.

The room fell silent.

Kristina said, 'How nice to see you again.'

Stewartby straightened and recovered his poise. 'So. At last you've arrived. I missed you. Why stay so long in Mombasa? Why couldn't I meet you at the station? When did you get in?'

'Yesterday. I needed to go to Mzito first to freshen up. You know what it's like on that awful train, all dust and perspiration. I wanted to be at my best to see you again.'

'My dear. Don't worry. You look wonderful. As soon as your telegram arrived I made arrangements for our wedding.'

She reached up and held his hand. 'When is it to be?' she asked, glancing past him to the door.

'A week on Saturday.'

She frowned and looked deep into his eyes.

'A week on Saturday? I'm not sure I'll be available that day.'

'Not available?'

'I think not. I'll have to ask my husband.'

'Your husband?'

His hand clenched at her fingers in a twitch of shock. Kristina almost squeaked with delight, her violet eyes glowing with malice.

'Yes. He'll be here in a minute. I just saw his rickshaw arrive. We can ask him.'

Stewartby snatched his hand away and stepped back. 'Don't joke with me in front of all these people. And keep your voice down or they'll hear.'

'Oh, I'm not joking. Here he is now.'

She pointed and waved, calling, 'Over here, darling. We're over here.'

Every head in the room swivelled to watch H.E. easing his huge body between the tables.

'You've married *him*?' hissed Stewartby. 'I'll kill you if you're serious. You promised to marry *me*.'

'Oh no, darling. I promised to *consider* marrying you. So I considered and decided...no thank you. I couldn't marry a *hotel* keeper. My standards are too high.'

'I'm not a hotel *keeper.* I'm a hotel *owner.*'

'But darling – you don't have a title. I'm used to titles and now I

415

have two. I'm Countess Kinskii and I'm Lady Taunton. But *you* can call me Kristina. Or just Countess. Whichever you prefer.'

She offered a gracious smile. Stewartby stood rigid with shock, gripping the back of a chair.

'Thanks, old boy,' said H.E.. 'Just pull it back a little so I can sit down. And be a good chap – run off and fetch us a couple of menus.'

Stewartby flinched and said, 'You've married this woman?'

'Yes. In Mombasa last week. Are you going to congratulate us?'

Stewartby said, 'You've married a whore.'

H.E. laughed. 'It's a feature that attracts me no end.'

'She was a whore in Berlin. She was *my* whore in Berlin. She's a degenerate slut. She slept with men for money.'

'I know, old chap. She told me everything about Berlin. One must do what one must to survive in difficult circumstances. But it's a matter best kept between the three of us. Private business, you understand. So keep your trap shut like a good fellow.'

'Damned if I will. I'll tell everyone. You'll be ruined.'

H.E. chuckled and said, 'I have plenty of your dark secrets on file in my office. Say a word and I'll let 'em all out. So be sensible, old chap. Face facts. This lady has been my fiancée for years. Now we're married. Sorry if you feel let down, but....'

Rolling his huge shoulders in a theatrical shrug he dismissed Stewartby's hopes with upturned hands and raised eyebrows. Kristina threw a hand over her mouth, choking back a laugh.

Stewartby glared down at her in fury, gripping the chair back so hard his knuckles cracked.

'You've humiliated me,' he said. 'You planned this from the moment we met in Berlin. You planned it quite deliberately.'

'Not *all* of it, darling. I didn't expect you to give me such lovely clothes.'

She tipped her head sideways and smiled her thanks while H.E. snorted his amusement.

Stewartby turned to H.E. and hissed, 'Damn you Hocklyffe-Evans. This is the second time you've ruined my life. First with Beatrice and now with this woman. You may think you've won – but I'll....'

Kristina said, 'This has nothing to do with H.E.. This is between you and me and the way you treated me in prison. *I* know all about humiliation and now *you* know how it feels.'

Stewartby said, 'I'll see you both damned. Get out of my hotel. Leave now and don't come back. You're barred for ever.'

'I think not, old chap,' said H.E.. 'My department approves and

416

withdraws public building licenses. Kick us out and I'll close you down. Nothing you can do about us being here, so be a good fellow and send over the menus. We fancy a spot of lunch, don't we darling?'

Kristina nodded and watched with glee as Stewartby stalked from the room. 'Oh darling H.E.,' she whispered. 'I've waited so long to see that little bastard brought down.'

Patting her hand, H.E. said, 'It's the whirligig of time, my dear. In the end it brings revenge.

As soon as Stewartby disappeared a small olive-skinned man with bright black-button eyes and a friendly smile skipped forward bearing two menus.

'You are welcome, Lord and Lady,' he lisped in a quiet sweet voice. 'I recommend the fish. It came direct from Lake Naivasha this morning. Very fresh. Very fresh indeed.'

'Ah, Cretikos,' said H.E.. 'I think you know my wife.'

Kristina said, 'You met me at reception when I came in.'

Cretikos bowed and said, 'Yes, Madame. But we have met before.'

'Of course. I remember. You worked for my husband. Do you work here now?'

'I own the place, Madame. Or at least, part of it. I am the Colonel's partner.'

'Good luck to you,' said Kristina. 'I'll have the fish.'

Over lunch Kristina giggled and said, 'You saw the little bastard off by pretending you knew about Berlin.'

Head down, concentrating on cutting a piece of fish with his fork, H.E. said, 'I didn't pretend. I know about your antics in the Telephone Box in Berlin – *and* most of what you were up to in Budapest and your naughtiness in Vienna.'

Kristina narrowed her eyes and stared at the top of H.E.'s head. She snapped, 'What nonsense. What the hell is the Telephone Box? I've told you nothing about Berlin and never mentioned Budapest or Vienna. What have you heard? And who from?'

Raising his head, H.E. chewed at his fish and winked. 'Diplomatic intelligence, my dear girl. Diplomatic intelligence....'

'Damn you, You had me watched and followed.'

'Good Lord, no. My old chum Sir Marcus Ledburn cottoned on to you in Budapest. He was in charge of embassy intelligence when an agent brought news of a mysterious Prussian woman sleeping with that Bolshevik bugger Bella-something.'

'Béla Kun.'

'That's the cove. When I sent money to the embassy for you, a damned Hungarian doctor turned up with the keyword to collect the cash and spilled the beans about your cosy arrangement with the Bolshevik boss. Dear old Marcus checked with me by telegram. Of course I realised you were the Prussian woman. Marcus gave your doctor the cash then saw him grabbed by Bolshevik gorillas in the street and whisked away. What happened to him, by the way?'

Kristina said, 'They shot the poor man.'

'Not surprised. Very efficient people. Did you ever get the money?'

'No.'

'So it probably ended up in some Bolshevik's pocket.'

'Did you worry about me?'

'Not really. I reckoned you'd take care of yourself.'

'What did you hear about Vienna?'

'Nothing except that the mysterious Countess arrived on the Bolshevik escape train and disappeared. We later heard she'd taken up with a fancy-man army officer, all epaulettes and gold braid who'd set her up in business. Damned Austrian Hussars get all the best girls. Must be those fancy uniforms. I guessed you'd found a safe billet and would turn up at some time when you'd wrung the poor bugger dry.'

'And Berlin?' Kristina asked with lowered eyelashes and a sweet smile.

'Knew nothing at all until you met Marcus's wife, the lovely Louise. Bit of a character isn't she?'

'Louise in Geneva?'

'The very same. Luscious Lou-Lou. Dancer extraordinaire. Well known in London and Paris for all the wrong reasons. What a goer. Poor old Marcus ruined his career over the depraved little baggage and ended up with that backwater job in Geneva. But she's brightened his declining years no end so he thinks it's worth it.'

'How did Louise know about The Telephone Box?'

'She didn't but Marcus checked with the Berlin embassy and found out what Stewartby had been up to in his spare time. So we decided between us that the lovely Countess he intended to marry in Geneva and the racy woman in Berlin and the Bolshevik's comforter in Budapest – not to mention the Austrian Hussars' favourite ride – were one and the same. I think we were right. Right?'

She dipped her head and blew a little kiss.

H.E. chuckled and said, 'What a woman. What a wonderful time you must have had. And what wonderful service you must have given.'

'Do you mind?'

'Of course not. You had to survive. I'd have done the same. Although without your figure and looks I may have found it more difficult.'

'So you don't mind being married to a whore?'

'Why should I? As I said – it's a feature that attracts me no end.'

'Oh darling. You *are* wonderful.'

'Not really. I reckon we're a couple of wrecks heading for disaster so if we lash up together we may stay afloat longer.'

Kristina laughed and kissed his hand. 'You may be right,' she said. 'By the way. Those words you used. The ones about time and revenge. Say them again.'

'I quoted Shakespeare: *And thus the whirligig of time brings in his revenges*'.

'What does it mean?'

'Wait long enough and you'll get your own back.'

Kristina put down her knife and fork and dropped her head in deep thought, her lips moving over Shakespeare's line.

After a moment, she said, 'I like those words. They remind me that I must go up the mountain to Kinskii's grave. I need to speak with him.'

'But the poor bugger's dead.'

'Not to me.'

Chapter Fifty Six

Kinskii's Presence

In deliberate repeat of that awful night Kinskii died, Kristina struggled up the mountain, through darkening forest.

A tracker led, the flame of his oil lamp swinging and flaring as he forced a way through clinging bush and bramble. Banshee shadows flew among the trees, their imagined screams howling in her brain. Kristina flinched away, lowering her eyes to the rough path; frightened that one of the fluttering black phantoms might be Kinskii's ghost.

Cursing her stupidity at such childish fear, she pushed upward through dank, damp brushwood, the smell of her own sweat mingling with greasy smoke from the oil lamp and the reek of the half dozen porters stumbling with her in the black night. Unseen thorns whipped and scratched at her face, picking and dragging at her clothes and hair but she overcame the pain and kept going, hauling herself up through thick mountain forest.

Finally the ground flattened. Acrid wood-smoke seeped among the leaves and Kristina remembered her wild hope of eight years ago that all is well and Kinskii safe.

She stumbled into the clearing through a final barrier of bush and stopped, staring in shocked silence, gasping back tears, fighting for control, unsure whether she wept in exhaustion or in remembrance. Except for the blanket-bundled body of her husband everything seemed exactly as that night she arrived to see Kinskii dead.

Four fires burned and crackled, wood heaped high, sparks flying off into the black canopy of leaves, thick smoke trapped and eddying in the cold still air. Wavering firelight showed Sakayo and his tracker sitting blanket-wrapped and still beside a tall cairn of heavy stones, their eye whites gleaming red-yellow in the flames.

Sakayo said, 'This is what you wanted, Memsahib?'

Kristina stepped into the square of fires, looking with curiosity at the cairn, surprised that so few weeds grew between the rocks. 'Yes. This is what I wanted.'

She wandered past Sakayo to a buffalo skeleton – bones all in place except for the missing head, huge chest ribs still attached and curving from the spine; massive shoulder slabs reflecting the orange fire glow.

Kristina turned to Sakayo.

'My husband and this buffalo – they've been together all these years?'

'Yes Memsahib.'

'No animals have disturbed them?'

'No animals enter here, Memsahib. This is a special place.'

She strolled back through the leaping firelight and looked thoughtfully at the cairn. All stones in place and unmoved. No evidence of scavengers. Perhaps the buffalo guarded Kinskii. Perhaps they guarded each other.

Sakayo stood and led her to the chair he had carried up the mountain and draped blankets round her shoulders and legs.

Kristina said, 'Thank you Sakayo. You've done everything I asked. Now please leave. Take all the men with you. Come back in the morning.'

'Memsahib. I cannot leave you here alone.'

'Why?'

'I cannot. If I return to camp without you, Musa will kill me.'

'I want to be alone. Go away. Do not come back before dawn.'

Sakayo said, 'I will take the men down the mountain a few hundred paces. You will be alone but I can hear if you call.'

Kristina pursed her lips at this disobedience but after a moment of thought said, 'Very well.'

Kristina settled back and cuddled her blanket, allowing a dark peace to settle on her soul.

She stayed for an hour or two without moving until some time after midnight when a log fell. Fire flared, throwing fingers of light across the clearing to catch a glimmer of metal from a dark corner. Her heart jumped in fright. 'Kinskii,' she hissed. 'Is that you?'

Certain she would see him dressed in full uniform Kristina jumped up, patting and primping at her hair, concerned that he would not like her untidy at this reunion.

She stepped forward and with a giggle of relief saw the firelight shimmering on a square of copper pinned to a tree trunk. *Of course – Adam's plaque. He came back and set it up as a gravestone....*

Holding up a burning twig from the fire she read...

This is the grave of Colonel Count Kinskii
Brave soldier and gentleman of the Austrian Empire
Son of a noble family
Killed here by buffalo January 1914 while saving the life of a
companion
RIP

Unable to contain her anger Kristina snarled and spat three times at the plaque, covering it with a fine spray that collected and trickled down between the letters in satisfying rivulets.

Returning to her chair and wrapped back in the blanket she fought the unease of her fury. After all, she couldn't blame Adam for the words. *None of us knew the truth at the time Kinskii died – except perhaps H.E. and he never said a word, then or now.*

She hugged herself against the increasing cold and cursed Kinskii, cursed Kinskii's father and mother, cursed Ebenstein and cursed the Austrian Empire.

Feeling better Kristina moved her chair nearer one of the fires – and nearer Kinskii's tomb. Relaxing in the warmth she closed her eyes, drifting half asleep and half awake without sense of time until – in the dark hours before dawn – she felt Kinskii's presence materialize. She whispered, 'Are you there?'

'Of course,' he replied from the depths of her soul.

Fighting the lethargy of sleep she half opened her eyes. The fires – now collapsed to four piles of glowing embers – threw soft light across the clearing and shone red on the buffalo bones. She felt Kinskii's presence become stronger, filling the place and overwhelming her senses. She groaned and closed her eyes, the better to see him.

He came from the dark outer limits of her mind and oh, how handsome with his sad smile and lovely moustache as elegant as always. In a surge of love for this poor dead man, Kristina whispered, 'Why did you leave me?'

'What choice did I have? Life led me to this place then abandoned me. You have a choice. Join me. It's so easy.'

'You're a liar and a cheat and I hate you. Look what you made me become.'

'You were already what you became when we met. Join me now and you'll always be at peace.'

In that moment of temptation Kristina realised the attraction of death lurked within her and always had. And Kinskii knew, the clever bastard. He knew that in her secret heart she wanted to join him in this tranquil place. *Is that why I'm here? Is that why you keep returning? To take me with you?*

Kinskii smiled his sad smile and oh, she nearly believed him. She nearly believed that serenity came with death and that life continued in another place.

But.... *Kinskii's presence is another of his lies....*

She shouted, 'You're not here. You're dead. You're gone. You're lying again. I'm here to piss on your grave, you bastard. To show what

I think of you. Bugger off. Leave me alone. Never come back.'

Leaping up Kristina opened her eyes and Kinskii disappeared. She threw off the blanket and ran to the stone cairn, clambering to the top. Crouching and lifting her skirt she started to pull down her drawers but heard the sound of voices and footsteps hurrying up the mountain.

In panic she dragged her drawers back up and scrambled from the cairn, falling to her knees at the bottom, arms spread across the rocks; head resting on a cool stone, just as Sakayo and a couple of porters burst into the clearing, waving sticks and a rifle.

Sakayo raised a hand, halting the porters. They bowed their heads and Sakayo said, 'Sorry, Memsahib. We thought you called for help. I now see....'

Kristina knelt by the cairn fighting back a giggle – *The poor buggers think I'm praying. They think I howled in grief.*

Sakayo shuffled backwards, ushering the porters away but Kristina stood and said, 'Don't go. I'm finished. Stay here with me. Find more wood for the fire and stay in the warm.'

Brushing dirt from her skirt and checking a small cut on her arm she walked to the chair and allowed Sakayo to fold her again in blankets. He crouched, African style beside her and together they sat, wide-awake until dawn, just as the night Kinskii died. The porters slept on bare earth, waking from time to time to add wood to the fire.

When early daylight drifted through the trees Sakayo stood and said, 'Shall we go down Memsahib?'

Kristina said, 'Yes. Clear up and we'll go. But first....'

With the corner of a blanket she cleaned and polished Kinskii's plaque, using a fingernail to dig green mould from between the letters. By the time she finished, the plaque shone bright and clean in the clear morning sunlight and she felt happy at leaving this place.

Fifty-Seven

Sundowners At Sunrise

After a tiring day riding throughout Mzito estate, Adam pulled his horse to a halt in front of the house and saw H.E. lazing on the veranda, sipping at a glass of beer.

Adam hitched a heavy hunting rifle from the saddle holster and jumped down. Waving his glass in welcome, H.E. called, 'Why the artillery?'

'Lion,' said Adam trotting up the steps. 'Abdi brought news of lion roaming near our northern boundary and thought they might be after cattle. We've been out looking all day.'

'Did you find 'em?'

'Not really. Just the tracks of one big bugger about an hour ago. He'd been making for the cattle pens but something must have frightened him off. He turned back towards Rowbas village so I sent Abdi and his men to warn them.'

'You look tired. Come and have a beer. Sit with me and watch the sun go down.'

'I will. What are you doing here?'

'Stopped for dinner and a rest on our way to Chania. We'll probably stay the night.'

Adam looked round. 'Is Kristina with you?'

'She's off with Eva looking for Jonathan. He's playing somewhere in the bush with Kristofa. Every time I come here Jonathan's in the bloody bush with Kristofa. What do they get up to out there?'

'Sakayo's teaching them how to track and live off the land. It's a good idea but Eva's worried Jonathan will become more African than European. She'll be happy to see him away to school in Germany next month.'

'Quite right,' said H.E.. 'It's unhealthy here for Jonathan – no European boys nearby.'

Adam said, 'He and Kristofa are great friends. They get on well together.'

'I suppose they would, under the circumstances.'

Adam frowned but ignored the remark. He took a beer from the cold box and asked, 'Are the women alone? Did they say where they were going?'

'Down to the village.'

Adam jumped up, grabbing the gun. 'Christ. I'd better follow. God

424

knows what'll happen if they meet the lion.' He ran down the steps, calling for his horse but H.E. shouted, 'Don't worry. Here they come.'

Hopping back onto the veranda Adam saw Eva and Kristina about half a mile away, strolling up the slope towards the cattle pens. Jonathan and Kristofa followed a few yards behind – two dark figures flitting through the bush, almost invisible in the long shadows of sunset.

'Bloody hell,' said H.E.. 'I see why Eva's worried. Jonathan looks just like an African. What the hell has he done.'

Adam laughed. 'Covered himself in mud from the river to camouflage his skin and hair. He's always doing that. It drives Eva wild.'

'Do *you* mind?'

'Not at all. Look how difficult he is to see. He's becoming an expert tracker. Think how useful that'll be when he's older.'

'In Germany or here?'

'Who knows. But any skill is better than none.'

'For God's sake, sit down and drink your beer.'

'No. I'll shower first. Then I'll join you and the ladies for a proper sundowner.'

Thirty minutes later Adam sat with Eva, Kristina and H.E., watching the last sunrays of day tint the distant Mount Kenya snow cap subtle shades of pink.

Sighing, he sniffed the pure evening air and said, 'By God, this is a place to really fall in love with.'

'My dear fellow,' said H.E.. 'You sound like a damned poet. Are you ill?'

Adam laughed. 'No. Just struck by how lucky we are to be here.'

H.E. took a swig of beer and said, 'You're right. How lucky we are to be here at sunrise.'

Eva said, 'You mean sunset.'

'No. Sunrise. For we British it's sunrise. In this country *our* sun is rising. I told you years ago we'd take it over lock, stock and barrel and now we have. It's our country – our colony. We named it after the mountain. Kenya. Wonderful name. Wonderful place. And it's all ours.'

Adam said, 'Oh bloody hell, H.E.. You're not going to go through all that again.'

'My dear fellow. You *know* I'm right. And winning the War gives us the old German territory, too – Tanganyika. That's another good name. So now we have Kenya, Uganda *and* Tanganyika. Next plan is to link them as a big strong country rivalling South Africa and Rhodesia. A few more years and Britain will own everything from Cairo to the Cape.'

Kristina said, 'Oh do shut up. It's all you've talked about for months.'

H.E. laughed and said, 'But it's important. Don't tell me it isn't. You have to agree – the sun is rising from the west. A lot more Europeans are on the way to join us. Good British stock. Army officers looking for something to do now the War's over. Soon we'll have the whole area booming with farms and industry and towns. You'll see.'

'You're probably right,' said Adam. 'But can we talk about something else? I'm sick of politics. It's all I ever hear at the Club. I don't want it at home too.'

'Very well, said H.E.. 'Here's something different. I'm finally leaving government service to run my farm at Chania. There's more money to be made in farming than in government.'

'Do you think so?' said Adam, from the corner of his eye seeing Kristina shrug and make a face at Eva.

H.E. laughed and said, 'I hope so. And we've decided to call the place High Valley Estate – after all, it's high and in a valley.'

'As good a name as any,' said Adam, stretching his legs.

Eva said, 'I think it's a lovely name. You'll be happy there.'

Kristina jumped to her feet and said, 'We'd bloody-well better be. Come on Eva. Let's go and dress for dinner. Leave these men to talk politics and farms and other rubbish. We'll go and make ourselves beautiful.'

Adam waited until the two women disappeared, then said, 'Kristina seems better after her trip to Kinskii's grave.'

'Much better,' said H.E.. 'She seems to have cast one of her devils out. If Kinskii *was* a devil.'

'How many devils does she have?'

'Plenty. And I suspect she found a new batch in Europe. Does she tell you or Eva anything?'

'Not a word. And we don't ask. I wonder if we'll ever know what she found in Hungary.'

'Probably not,' said H.E.. 'But it must have been something of a shock. Remember how she mentioned Kinskii's mother? It's the only thing she's said about his family and did you notice – when she spoke of his mother she almost shuddered. I wonder what the hell she meant.'

Adam nodded and said, 'Strange how she wouldn't allow us to go up the mountain with her. Remember when she told us? A couple of months ago. Right here on this veranda....'

In the moment of silence after Kristina had spoken, Adam looked at H.E. and asked, 'Will you go, too?'

'Not a hope, old boy. She won't allow me.'

Eva said, 'Darling Kristina. Adam will come with you.'

Kristina shook her head. 'No. I'll go alone. I've planned it for a long time. Ever since I met Kinskii's mother.'

She lowered her eyes and Adam noticed that, for a moment, she seemed overcome with...what? Grief? Anger? He saw her hands grip together, fingers clenched tight.

Eva said, 'But darling. You *can't* go alone. How will you find the way?'

Kristina said, 'Eva, don't fuss. I'll take that same tracker. What was his name?'

'Sakayo,' said Adam. 'He's still here with us.'

'Will he think I'm mad?' Kristina asked.

'Not a bit,' said Adam. 'He'll understand exactly why you want to go back.'

'Oh will he,' said Kristina, her fingers twisting until the knuckles cracked.

Now, in the cool evening, Adam stared at H.E. and said, 'She certainly seemed distressed. Is there anything *you* know that you're not telling us?'

'Not really, old chap. One hears odd bits of gossip through the diplomatic grapevine, but nothing of substance – and certainly nothing one would repeat or pass on. So don't ask. Let's change the subject. I hear that your old friend and erstwhile enemy Kreuz is helping place Jonathan at school in Berlin. Is this wise? Is this your past returning in a way you might not like?'

'I'm not sure,' said Adam, closing his eyes and leaning back, turning his ear to the sound of Eva and Kristina chatting and giggling in a bedroom along the veranda.

'What are they saying?' asked H.E..

'Don't know. They're using some Prussian dialect I can't understand. Used to do the same when I first knew them. It's a way of keeping their little secrets.'

'Regressing,' said H.E.. 'We're all bloody-well regressing. Have you noticed how events and people go in a circle? We're almost back to where we started, like ghosts returning to haunt each other.'

'What do you mean?'

H.E. laughed and said, 'Doesn't this remind you of Mombasa all those years ago when Kristina came for your wedding? The four of us young ones in the same house with the same noises – you and I chatting and the two women giggling somewhere down the hall? Look at how much has happened since then. And look at how we're all coming back together again.'

Adam said, 'Odd you should say that. Because the school Kreuz suggested for Jonathan is run by the German doctor who saved my life in Tabora. And in his last letter Kreuz mentioned both Paul and Weiss, the other two I found in the bush, along with Eva.'

'I thought Weiss died in the war.'

'We all thought the same. But Kreuz says Weiss turned up in Berlin a month or so ago – not making clear where he's been all these years but no one questions him since no one cares.'

'What about Paul?'

'Kreuz hinted he's doing something for the new government – or at least for some organisation involved with trying to save Germany from disaster.'

'Plenty of those,' said H.E.. 'Mainly ruffian bands beating hell out of each other in the streets.'

'No. I think from the way Kreuz wrote that Paul is up to something official and secret.'

'In that case, don't tell me any more. But talking of ghosts – look along the veranda.'

Adam turned, and his heart lurched. In the shadows near Eva's room stood an apparition of Christy; white-blond hair and golden skin glowing in a shaft of yellow lamplight; bright blue eyes merry and light.

My God. The bastard's come back for Eva.

Adam jumped to his feet about to rush at Christy's ghost and make it disappear when Eva stepped from her room and said, 'Jonathan, darling. Hurry and say goodnight to Daddy.'

The apparition skipped along the veranda with a slip-slapping of bare feet on wood. Adam blinked to clear his vision and looked in agony at Eva: *Does she see Christy like this every day?*

The boy jumped into his arms and Adam clasped him in a hug. Eva smiled and said, 'Put him down Adam. Come on Jonathan. Bed.'

Jonathan kissed Adam on the cheek and wriggled free, trotting away to his room, followed by Eva.

As Adam watched the boy go, H.E. whispered, 'Spitting image of his father, don't you think?'

Or did he? Or did the whisper come from one of Adam's own devils, deep inside?

Adam turned to confront H.E.'s raised eyebrow and lazy smile. 'What did you say?' he snapped.

'Not a word, old boy.'

At that moment – to Adam's relief – Eva and Kristina stepped from the bedroom with a clatter of high heels and a waft of perfume; two handsome women, vital and interesting, dressed in their best, ready to entertain their men. A surge of love for Eva banished Christy from Adam's mind and he stepped forward, wanting to be near his wife.

Eva smiled and took his hand. 'Darling. You look so serious. What on earth are you talking about?'

'Nothing much,' said H.E.. 'You know what men are like when they've had a few drinks.'

'Only too well,' said Kristina.

At that moment Musa padded barefoot from the kitchen, carrying a soup tureen.

'We're ready, Musa, we're ready,' called Eva. She linked arms with Adam and drew him along the veranda towards the dining room. 'No serious talk at dinner. Keep it light. We girls want to be entertained.'

'Shall I tell you again about sunrise and our wonderful future?' said H.E..

'Oh, God no,' said Eva.

'Absolutely not,' said Kristina.

'Just bloody-well shut up H.E.,' said Adam, trailing his fingers across the back of Eva's hand in a gesture of love.